Praise for Victoria Christopher Murray

"Murray has always impressed me with her ability to live the life of her characters and make them come alive with each turning page."

—*Indianapolis Recorder*

"Victoria is an exceptional writer who knows how to deliver a story."

—Kimberla Lawson Roby, author of *Changing Faces*

Praise for *Too Little, Too Late*

"An excellent entry in the Jasmine Larson Bush Christian Lit saga; perhaps the best so far . . . Fans will appreciate this fine tale. . . . A well-written intense drama."

—*Midwest Book Review*

"One would think it isn't possible, but like fine wine, Victoria's writing has improved with her newest novel."

—RomanceInColor.com

"[In this book] there are so many hidden messages about love, life, faith, and forgiveness. Murray's vividness of faith is inspirational."

—*The Clarion-Ledger* (Jackson, Mississippi)

"Juicy Jasmine Larson Bush returns . . . Murray efficiently illustrates the importance of honesty and trust in marriage, and manages to contain Jasmine's outrageousness within the context of Christian faith."

—*Publishers Weekly*

Praise for *The Ex Files*

"*The Ex Files* is a moving-on song in four-part harmony."

—Donna Grant and Virginia DeBerry, authors of *Tryin' to Sleep in the Bed You Made* and *Gotta Keep On Tryin'*

"My girl, Victoria Christopher Murray, has done it again! I love her work and this book will bless you, so read it."

—Michele Andrea Bowen, author of *Church Folk, Second Sunday,* and *Holy Ghost Corner*

"The lessons of growth, love, and faith are what Victoria does best. . . . [An] excellent read."

—Naleighna Kai, *Essence* best-selling author of *Every Woman Needs a Wife*

"The engrossing transitions the women go through make compelling reading. . . . Murray's vivid portrait of how faith can move mountains and heal relationships should inspire."

—*Publishers Weekly*

"This is a book everyone can enjoy . . . and more important, this is a book that can reach out to the brokenhearted no matter who they are and where they are."

—Book Bit (WTBF-AM)

"Reminds you of things that women will do if their hearts are broken . . . Once you pick this book up, you will not put it down."

—UrbanReviews.com

"Murray does it again and definitely delivers a great story. This one will grip your heart."

—APOOO Book Club

"Victoria Christopher Murray continues to confront real-life issues in her latest novel. . . . A heartfelt read."

—AOL Black Voices

Praise for *A Sin and a Shame*

"As with Murray's previous novels, *A Sin and a Shame* is intriguing and well written. If you loved and hated Jasmine in *Temptation,* you'll love and hate her again."

—*Indianapolis Recorder*

"*A Sin and a Shame* is Victoria Christopher Murray at her best. . . . A page-turner that I couldn't put down as I was too eager to see what scandalous thing Jasmine would do next. And to watch Jasmine's spiritual growth was a testament to Victoria's talents. An engrossing tale of how God's grace covers us all. I absolutely loved this book!"

—ReShonda Tate Billingsley, *Essence* bestselling author of *I Know I've Been Changed*

"Riveting, emotionally charged and spiritually deep . . . What is admirable is the author's ability to hold the reader in suspense until the very last paragraph of the novel! *A Sin and a Shame* is a must read . . . Truly a story to be enjoyed and pondered upon!"

—RomanceInColor.com

Also by Victoria Christopher Murray

Too Little, Too Late
The Ex Files
A Sin and a Shame
Grown Folks Business
Truth Be Told
Temptation
Joy
Blessed Assurance (contributor)

Lady Jasmine

Victoria Christopher Murray

A Touchstone Book
Published by Simon & Schuster
New York London Toronto Sydney

Touchstone
A Division of Simon & Schuster, Inc.
1230 Avenue of the Americas
New York, NY 10020

First Touchstone trade paperback edition June 2009

TOUCHSTONE and colophon are registered trademarks of Simon & Schuster, Inc.

For information about special discounts for bulk purchases, please contact Simon & Schuster Special Sales at 1-866-506-1949 or business@simonandschuster.com.

The Simon & Schuster Speakers Bureau can bring authors to your live event. For more information or to book an event contact the Simon & Schuster Speakers Bureau at 1-866-248-3049 or visit our website at www.simonspeakers.com.

Manufactured in the United States of America

10 9 8 7 6 5 4 3 2 1

Library of Congress Cataloging-in-Publication Data
Murray, Victoria Christopher.
Lady Jasmine : a novel / by Victoria Christopher Murray.
p. cm.
"A Touchstone Book."
1. Bush, Jasmine Larson (Fictitious character)—Fiction. 2. African American women—Fiction. 3. Christian women—Fiction. 4. New York (N.Y.)—Fiction. I. Title.
PS3563.U795L33 2009
813'.54—dc22 2008043781

ISBN 978–1–4165–8917–4

To my literary goddaughters: Courtney Parker, Sherri Lewis, Tia McCollors, Rhonda McKnight, Mikasenoja, and DiShan Washington. I am so proud of each of you, walking in the path God has set for you. Continue to do His work and He will make your way great.

MARCH 2007

PROLOGUE

DEATH WAS ON HER MIND, but Jasmine wasn't thinking of her own demise. Her hands still trembled as she looked down at the letter she held.

Would the charge be first degree murder or would it be more like manslaughter? Either way, she would go to jail for both before she allowed anyone to reveal this secret.

Jasmine read the words that she'd already memorized: *Get your husband to step down from the pulpit or else everyone will know what you did in the summer of 1983.*

Hours had passed since she'd first read the letter last night, and she still trembled. Until a few weeks ago, those days had been totally forgotten; expunged from her mind many years before. The summer of '83 was just a small blip on her life's radar. A mistake. A secret.

But it was a big secret that she'd kept from everyone—including her husband, Pastor Hosea Bush.

Jasmine closed her eyes and remembered the question Hosea had asked her just five months before when they were in Los Angeles.

"Are there any other secrets, Jasmine? Any other lies?"

She'd told him then every truth she could remember, revealed every lie that she'd ever told—how she was forty-three and not thirty-eight. How she'd been married before. She'd even told him how much weight she'd really gained since she'd had her baby. She'd told her husband everything she could think of.

But she hadn't told him this.

"I have to talk to Hosea," she whispered, remembering the commitment they'd both made never again to keep secrets.

She could tell him—convince him—that this was something she'd simply forgotten. But even as she had that thought, she knew that would never happen. There was nothing that would ever make her tell *this* truth. If Hosea found out about this, she'd lose more than her husband: Hosea might even try to take their daughter, Jacqueline, away from her. This was an unforgiveable sin; at least it would be in Hosea's eyes.

No, she would commit murder before she allowed this to come out. No one could ever know that she'd spent the summer of '83 hanging high and swinging low from a pole.

No one could ever know that Jasmine Cox Larson Bush, the first lady of New York's City of Lights at Riverside Church, used to be a stripper!

A FEW WEEKS BEFORE

ONE

THE SHOCKING SHRILL PIERCED THE black quiet of midnight, but Jasmine had no intention of answering the telephone.

"Don't stop, baby," Jasmine panted when Hosea lifted his head from beneath the sheet.

"Gotta get that," he gasped. "Might be important."

Jasmine glanced at the clock: 12:17. She rolled over, closed her eyes, and, in her mind, returned to the place where she and Hosea were before the telephone rang.

Hosea still knew how to take her straight to heaven. And it was even better now, since he'd stopped thinking about their having a baby. Once conception was taken out of the equation, only pure pleasure remained.

Like tonight. He'd had her singing praises in seventeen languages. And she still had a few native tongues she wanted to test, so whoever was calling, whatever the reason, it had better be worth interrupting some of the best—

"What!" Hosea shouted and clicked on the lamp. "I'm on my way!"

Jasmine sat up straight. "What's wrong?"

"Pops! He's been shot!"

Tossing aside the satin duvet, Jasmine ignored the shock of the cool air as it wrapped around her nakedness. "Shot?" She stood stiff as Hosea leapt from the bed and dashed into his closet.

"That's all Brother Hill said," Hosea yelled back. "He's at Harlem Hospital with Pops now."

The shock finally released her, and Jasmine ran into her own closet. Her mind swirled with questions as she stuffed herself into a pair of jeans, then grabbed a sweatshirt. Shot? By whom? Where? When? By the time Hosea stepped from his closet, Jasmine was ready.

He said, "You don't have to go. I'll call you."

"I'm going with you." Her tone said there would be no further discussion. "I'll check on Jacquie and wake up Mrs. Sloss." She took two steps, then turned back and held Hosea in her arms. "He's going to be okay," she whispered.

His eyes shined with fright, but he nodded like he agreed.

Taking charge, she said, "Instead of driving, let's take a cab. I'll meet you downstairs." She dashed from their bedroom across to the other side of the apartment and tiptoed into their daughter's room.

For her second birthday last month, Jasmine had transformed Jacqueline's bedroom into a princess's pink haven. She peeked into the four-poster toddler cot and straightened the comforter that was bunched around Jacqueline's feet. She kissed her cheek, then knocked on the adjacent door.

"Ms. Jasmine," Mrs. Sloss, their live-in nanny, began the moment she opened the door, "something wrong with Jacquie?" Her voice was filled with sleep, but her eyes were wide.

"No." Jasmine was already rushing toward the living room. "Hosea's godfather just called. Someone shot Reverend Bush."

"Oh, no!" The nanny followed behind her. "Is there anything I can do?"

"Just take care of my baby."

As she waited for the elevator, Jasmine paced and tried to think. But even by the time she ascended to the lobby, she couldn't make sense out of this news.

"Mr. Bush is waiting for you," the doorman said, as he held the door for her. Jasmine stepped outside and paused to say a quick prayer. Then she jumped into the waiting cab and they sped off into the midnight quiet of the February night.

Their steps echoed like rapid fire through the hospital's hallway. Jasmine squeezed Hosea's hand right before they stepped to the nurses' station.

"I'm here to see—"

"Hosea!"

When Brother Hill ran up behind them, Jasmine's eyebrows raised a little at the sight of the man in a jogging suit. She'd never seen the church deacon without a tie.

"Where's Pops?" Hosea asked right after he embraced his godfather.

"He's in the Trauma Unit." With his hand on his shoulder, Brother Hill led Hosea toward a room as if his godson had come alone.

Jasmine took a deep breath and followed the two men. It took everything within her not to be upset with the way Brother Hill ignored her. She had to remember that this wasn't about her—this was about Reverend Bush, a man she'd grown to love.

But the truth: it was hard not to go off. Taking insults from Brother Hill and his band of bandits—the decades-long friends of Reverend Bush who didn't think she was good enough to be Hosea's wife—had become part of her life. These old-timers who'd known Hosea since his childhood were still holding on to her past; they'd never forgotten how Hosea had fallen in love with her while she was secretly sleeping with (and becoming pregnant by) another man. And they certainly hadn't forgiven her for tricking Hosea into believing he was the father of her unborn child.

What was their problem? If God had forgiven her, and Hosea had forgiven her, and Reverend Bush had forgiven her, who were these people to treat her as if she was some kind of sinner?

The sound of her husband's voice brought Jasmine back. "So tell me, what happened?"

Brother Hill started shaking his head before he even began to speak. "We walked out to the parking lot—we'd been at the church late reviewing the fiscal report and he was still working on his sermon for tomorrow. But when I got to my car, I realized I'd left my keys. I went back inside, and that's when I heard the gunshots. By the time I got back to Samuel—" He stopped. "The doctors gave us this room so that we could have privacy."

When they stepped inside, Mrs. Whittingham, Reverend Bush's assistant and one of Brother Hill's bandits, stood and hugged Hosea. The woman hesitated, then gave Jasmine a loose embrace. Turning back to Hosea, Mrs. Whittingham asked, "How you holding up, baby?"

Hosea's eyes blinked rapidly. "This doesn't make any sense. Why would anyone shoot Pops?"

Mrs. Whittingham said, "Detective Foxx was one of the first policemen there," she said, referring to one of the City of Lights members. "He thinks Samuel got caught in the middle of some gang fire."

"How bad is he?" Jasmine asked.

Brother Hill shrugged. "The doctors haven't told us anything. We've been waiting for— here's one of the doctors now."

Jasmine's eyebrows rose slightly as the African American woman clothed in surgical scrubs approached.

Brother Hill made the introductions. "Doctor McCollors, this is Reverend Bush's son, Hosea."

Shaking hands, Hosea asked the doctor, "How's my father?"

"Well, he was shot twice—once in his shoulder. But it's the shot that he took to his head that's the serious problem."

"Oh, my God!" Jasmine whispered the words that were spoken by all of them.

The doctor continued, "It's caused a lot of swelling and bleeding. We're going in to remove some of the pressure."

"I want to see him," Hosea demanded.

"We're taking him into surgery now. It'll be a couple of hours."

"Doctor McCollors?" A policeman, standing outside the room, motioned to the doctor.

"Excuse me," she said, before leaving the foursome standing in stunned silence.

Seconds later, the quiet was broken by, "Hosea!"

The high-pitched woman's voice made Jasmine frown before she swiveled around. She watched Pastor Wyatt, the associate pastor at City of Lights enter the room with a slight woman. The mousy-looking female, whose hair was upturned in a sixties-style flip, handed the tray of drinks she held to the pastor before she rushed to Hosea and wrapped her arms around his waist.

"I'm so sorry," the woman squeaked over and over.

"Ivy!" Hosea pulled back and, for the first time since they'd received the call, he smiled a little. "What're you doing here?"

"I'm visiting Sarai," she said, turning to Mrs. Whittingham. "I hadn't been home in a while and decided to take a sabbatical this semester. I'm so sorry about your dad, but I'm glad that I'm here so that I can help take care of you."

Jasmine cleared her throat and crossed her arms.

"Oh, Ivy, you haven't had a chance to meet my wife. This is Jasmine."

The woman smiled, revealing teeth that were far too big for her mouth.

"Jasmine, this is Ivy, Mrs. Whittingham's sister. Ivy and I grew up together."

"It's so nice to meet you finally," Ivy said, reaching for Jasmine's hand. "Sarai told me all about you."

With a quick glance over her shoulder, Jasmine looked at Mrs. Whittingham. If she'd been talking about her, surely nothing good had been said.

Turning back to Ivy, Jasmine said, "I didn't know Mrs. Whittingham had any family." She kept to herself the thoughts being hatched about the woman. "You're her . . . *sister*?" That was hard to believe—Mrs. Whittingham looked like she was twenty, maybe even thirty years older than Ivy.

Ivy gave a light chuckle. "People always say that, but she *is* my sister." Then she faced Hosea. "Any news about your dad?"

Pastor Wyatt tapped Jasmine's shoulder. "Would you like one of these?" he whispered, holding the coffee tray in the air.

"No, thank you."

She tried to turn back to Hosea, but Pastor Wyatt held her arm. "You sure?" His voice was still low, like he didn't want anyone else to hear. "It's going to be a long night."

Jasmine looked down to where he gripped her arm, then slowly inched her glance back to his face. "I said"—she wiggled away from him—"no, thank you."

He chuckled as he strutted away, taking the tray to Mrs. Whittingham and Brother Hill.

Jasmine frowned, wondering again about the pastor. It was never what Pastor Wyatt said, it was his flirtatious tone—he talked as if neither he nor she were married.

"So are you sure you don't want to share some of this java with me?" The pastor was back; he raised the coffee cup to his mouth and grazed the edge of it with his tongue.

Jasmine hated herself when she sighed, but how was she

supposed to help it? The man was six feet four inches of pure sex, dangerously tempting with his Terrence Howard looks, his Barry White voice, and his legs that she could imagine . . .

She snapped out of it, hissed, "How many times do I have to tell you I don't want any of *your* coffee?"

He squinted and shrugged as if he had no idea what had brought on her attitude.

"Darlin'," Hosea called to her, "do you want to sit down?"

Jasmine took her husband's hand, then sat next to him. On the other side, Ivy planted herself in the chair and chatted away as if Hosea was interested in all the details of her life.

Across from them, Mrs. Whittingham and Brother Hill were in a whispered conversation. And there was Pastor Wyatt—right across from her. When he grinned, the deep dimple in his left cheek winked at her.

Twisting so that he was not in her direct view, Jasmine leaned her head on Hosea's shoulder and closed her eyes.

Like Pastor Wyatt had said, this was going to be a long night.

TWO

THE DAY'S FIRST LIGHT CAST its morning shadows through the frosted windows. Jasmine pushed her legs forward and stretched, not sure how much longer she could sit.

"I should've sent you with Pastor Wyatt," Hosea said.

She shook her head. "I'm staying with you." There was no way she would have gone anywhere with that man anyway.

Pastor Wyatt had stood up at about three and announced that he was leaving so that he would be fresh for church in five hours. She was glad when he left and took his lecherous glances with him.

The door to the room where they'd waited all night opened and then a woman asked, "Samuel Bush's family?"

"Yes," they said together and all jumped from their seats.

Even though it was barely six in the morning, the tall, thin woman stood in front of them, dressed in a crisp navy pinstripe suit.

"I'm Mrs. Corbin, one of the hospital administrators. I have Mr. Bush's property here." She held a plastic bag stuffed with clothes in one hand and a large envelope in the other.

"I'll take—" Before Mrs. Whittingham could finish, Jasmine grabbed the items. Mrs. Whittingham rolled her eyes, and for the first time in almost seven hours Jasmine felt a little bit of cheer.

"Do you know anything about my father?"

The woman shook her head.

"You can't tell us anything?" Jasmine exclaimed, as if the woman was incompetent.

Mrs. Corbin's eyebrows rose just a bit. "The doctor will get to you as soon as she can," she said, returning Jasmine's attitude. Then, glancing around at them, she took in the evidence of their all-night stay in their reddened eyes and crumpled clothes. In a tone now that was full of grace, she said, "I know this may be hard, but you should go home." She held up her hand before anyone could protest. "At least some of you. Trust me, it's better for the family to do this in shifts. If a few of you go and refresh, you'll be able to come back and relieve the others."

Hosea nodded. "That's a good idea." When Mrs. Corbin left them alone, he said, "Why don't you guys go?"

Mrs. Whittingham began, "But, I want to—"

"I'll let you know as soon as I hear anything. But please, I'll feel better," Hosea said, looking at Brother Hill and Ivy, "if somebody got some rest." When he added, "Plus, it's going to be important for you to be at church when Pastor Wyatt makes the announcement," they all agreed to leave.

Mrs. Whittingham said, "Do you want me to take that?" She pointed to the bag Jasmine still held.

She handed Mrs. Whittingham the bag of clothes. "Let me look through this," she said, raising the envelope. "Make sure there's nothing important inside."

The way Mrs. Whittingham pursed her lips made Jasmine move even slower. She shifted through the contents—Reverend Bush's cell phone, his keys, wallet, a Mont Blanc pen. There were some loose papers and an opened FedEx package. The return address on the envelope made her curious, and she peeked inside at the thick mound of papers.

But before she could pull anything out, she heard, "Mr. Bush?"

When Mrs. Corbin marched back into the room, Jasmine rose from the chair.

Mrs. Corbin said, "I don't know anything specific, but Doctor McCollors asked me to take you to her office."

It took a moment for Hosea to say, "Is my father—"

"He's alive," Mrs. Corbin said, as if she knew that's what they needed to hear. "But I don't know anything else. If you'll come with me. Just you."

"And my wife," Hosea said.

The woman nodded.

He turned to the others. "I'll call as soon as we talk to the doctor."

Jasmine handed the envelope to Mrs. Whittingham and then took Hosea's hand. It had been an exhausting night, but now Jasmine was totally alert.

It was her pounding heart that had her wide awake.

THREE

Jasmine stood at the entry to the kitchen and watched Jacqueline lift the spoon to her nose, take a sniff, then dump the cereal back into the bowl.

"I don't want it!" she declared to Mrs. Sloss.

"Jacquie, you have to eat before we can go to the park."

"Don't want it!" she insisted.

Jasmine smiled. "Hey, baby."

Her daughter looked up, then wiggled from the chair. "Mama!" she shrieked, toddling toward her. She grabbed her mother's legs.

Mrs. Sloss turned away from the sink, her face etched with lines of worry. "How's Reverend Bush?"

Jasmine put her index finger to her lips and shook her head.

Jacqueline said, "Sing song, Mama. Sing song!"

Jasmine lifted her daughter and laughed. "You always want to sing song."

The girl giggled and nodded.

"Okay, I'll sing, but only if you sing with me."

"Okay," and then before Jasmine could begin, Jacqueline started in a musical key known only to a two-year-old, "He got . . . whole world . . ."

Jasmine joined in, "In His hands."

Together they sang, and then at her favorite part, Jacqueline raised one arm in the air, as if she was testifying, and screeched, "He got Mama, Daddy, and Jacquie in His hands . . ."

Jasmine laughed at her daughter mimicking what she'd seen adults do in church.

After they sang the song three times, Jasmine lowered Jacqueline back into her chair. "Okay, time to eat your cereal."

A moment ago, she'd been singing, but now, with her lips pinched together, Jacqueline whipped her head from side to side. "Don't want it!"

"Really? That's too bad, because I was thinking, if you ate your cereal, then we could watch your favorite movie tonight."

Jacqueline smiled again, clapped her hands.

Jasmine shook her head. "But we're not going to because you won't eat your cereal . . ."

Now the glee was gone from her face as images of the Prince of Egypt faded away. Jacqueline stared at the bowl of soggy flakes, looked up at her mother with the saddest eyes, and then with a sigh and much effort, she said, "I eat it."

Drama Queen! Jasmine chuckled as she kissed the top of her head.

"Mrs. Sloss, I'm going to take a shower."

The look in the nanny's eyes said that she wanted some news. But Jasmine wasn't going to discuss anything in front of her daughter.

Inside her bedroom, Jasmine stood at the door, hoping to gather some of the peace that she always felt when she stepped into this space.

When she and Hosea had returned from Los Angeles, she'd trashed their bedroom set (even though it was just a bit over a year old) and purchased all new furniture—all white. Stark white. From the bed to the dresser. From the ceiling fan to the chaise. The one-thousand-thread-count duvet that covered them with the gentleness of a cloud and the plush carpet that felt like velvet beneath her feet. She'd created an oasis that symbolized their love. Pure, untouched.

Their heaven.

But the serenity that always enveloped her when she entered this room was not here now. There was no tranquillity—only the burden of exhaustion. Her body ached, but what disturbed her most was the pain inside her head.

That throbbing had been there for the last hour, from the moment Dr. McCollors had introduced her and Hosea to the intensivist, Dr. Lewis, the doctor who specialized in intensive care and was assigned to Reverend Bush's case.

But all Dr. Lewis had said was, "We're not sure; the next few days will be critical to your father's survival."

Jasmine closed her eyes, but behind her lids, the image was there—of Reverend Bush when she and Hosea had walked into the ICU. The man in the bed looked nothing like her father-in-law.

He lay still, on his back, his eyes closed. He looked like he was sleeping—or at least that's what Jasmine had told herself. He really looked like he was dead.

It wasn't because his head had been shaved that made her think that way. Nor was it because three-quarters of his head had been draped with heavy gauze and bandages. It was in his face where she saw death—his eyes were puffed; his cheeks were swollen, as if his mouth had been stuffed with cotton balls; his lips were distended. He didn't look anything like the man she called Dad.

She had stood next to Hosea, staring down at Reverend Bush, watching the very slight rise and fall of the cotton sheet that covered him. A whoosh of air traveled from the machine behind them through the thick tube that was thrust deep into his mouth. And she knew it was only because of that tube and the other equipment surrounding them—with their squiggly green lines and numbers that made no sense, that her father-in-law was even alive.

Jasmine had to swallow the feeling of nausea she felt rising with those memories. She took deep breaths until the queasiness passed. Then she grabbed the telephone; she really needed to talk.

Two rings and then, "Jasmine Larson, what took you so long to call me today?" Mae Frances huffed. "It's after noon. I thought you were going to call before you left for church."

Jasmine settled back and rested in the familiarity of her best friend's discontent. She wasn't bothered one bit by Mae Frances's tone—this is just how she was.

Mae Frances asked, her tone sad, "Have you forgotten all about me down here?"

"No, Nama," she responded, calling Mae Frances by the name that Jacqueline had given her from the moment she started talking. "How's it going in La Marque?"

Mae Frances sighed. "How do you think? Today is just like yesterday. All my mother wants to do . . ."

The rant was the same—every day since Mae Frances had left New York for La Marque, Texas, on New Year's Day to take care of her mother.

"I'm telling you, if Billie Jean wasn't dying," Mae Frances said, "I wouldn't be here at all. Hmph, it wasn't like she cared about me when I was growing up. I don't know why I'm caring about her now."

"She needs you, Mae Frances. You're doing a good thing," Jasmine encouraged, just as she did each time they spoke.

"A good thing? Shoot, I'm darn near a saint. There's a special place in heaven for me—right next to Jesus. And when I get there and sit down with Him, there're a few things I'm gonna say."

It wasn't hard to imagine Mae Frances telling Jesus how He needed to run things. What was amazing, though, was that Mae

Frances even talked about Jesus. Just four years ago, when she and Jasmine first met, the cantankerous sixty-something-year-old woman had cared nothing about God, family, or friends. She'd been a bitter woman who'd spent three decades hating her ex-husband for divorcing her after *she'd* had an affair. But a little affection from the Bushes had brought love—and forgiveness—into her life.

"What took you so long to call?" Mae Frances asked again. "You know I need to hear from you so that I know what's going on in New York or I'll absolutely lose my mind. And what are you doing home from church already? I know Reverend Bush must've preached up a storm."

Those words reminded Jasmine that there was little room for joy in her life right now.

"I have something to tell you," Jasmine began.

"Oh, Lawd, sounds like bad news. What did you do now, Jasmine Larson?"

"I didn't do anything—"

Mae Frances continued anyway, "Oh, I know. You slept with somebody and Preacher Man found out. Oh, Lawd."

Jasmine sat up straight on the bed. "No!"

But her protest didn't stop Mae Frances from rolling with the story. "Don't worry, Preacher Man always forgives you. How many times have you lied to him—"

"Mae Frances!"

"He always comes back. That man is a boomerang. You toss him out; he flies around for a little while, but he always comes back. And he should. He's from good stock. Just like his daddy. So who did you sex up this time?"

"I didn't sleep with anyone," Jasmine said, not hiding her attitude. "I'm not like that anymore."

"Oh, I forgot. So what is it then?"

Jasmine took a long breath. This wasn't going to be easy news to share. Mae Frances was a de facto member of the Bush clan.

She was like a mother to Jasmine, a grandmother to Jacqueline, and to Reverend Bush . . . well, it was clear that Mae Frances held a special place in her heart for that man of God. Jasmine was sure that if Mae Frances had been a decade younger, her claws would have already been hooked in him.

She pushed the words out, "Reverend Bush was shot last night."

"What?"

"Last night, coming out of the church. Someone shot him."

"Is he—"

"No," Jasmine rushed to say before Mae Frances could ask. "But it's serious. He was in surgery all night, and then this morning, the doctor met with Hosea and me—"

"What did they say?" Mae Frances wailed.

"Well, there's some good news." Jasmine decided to start there. "The doctor said he's lucky the bullet didn't get lodged in his brain. They were able to get it."

"Thank God!"

Jasmine imagined Mae Frances with her hands in the air, getting ready to do a holy dance. "But . . . there was a lot of bleeding," she continued. "Blood that gathered and pushed against his brain."

"Well, they just need to get in there and get it out!"

"They did. When they opened his skull—"

"Lord Jesus!"

"They drained the blood, but—" This was where she had to stop. This was the part at which, when the doctor had spoken, Hosea had gasped and she'd started to cry. She could feel the tears rushing to her eyes now. "There might be a lot of damage from the swelling and pressure inside his skull," Jasmine sniffed. "They just don't know. Said it was too early to tell."

There was a long silence before Mae Frances said, "I'm coming home."

"You can't do that," Jasmine said, although she wished that her friend was with her right now. Since they'd met, Mae Frances had been by her side through her toughest times, and she really needed her. But so did Mae Frances's mother. "You have to stay in Texas."

"Billie Jean can take care of herself."

"How's she supposed to do that?" Jasmine asked.

Mae Frances's eighty-three-year-old mother, after a drunken night of holiday celebrating, had fallen and broken her hip. She'd had surgery and was confined to bed for weeks.

"Stay in Texas," Jasmine encouraged. "That's what Hosea would want. I'll keep you posted every day."

"Call me three times a day."

"I will."

"And make sure you take care of Preacher Man and my grandbaby."

"I will."

With a softer voice, she said, "Make sure you take care of the good reverend, too." A beat. "I'll be praying."

Jasmine hung up, and with a sigh she pushed herself off the bed. Even though all she wanted to do was ease underneath the covers and then dream that last night never happened, she had to go back to the hospital. There wasn't much she could do for her father-in-law, but her husband was waiting.

And she would do whatever she could to take care of him.

FOUR

Jasmine tiptoed into the room and stood behind Hosea, still in the same place where she'd left him late last night. Hosea's chair was pulled close to the edge of the hospital bed, his hands perched under his chin as if he were saying a perpetual prayer.

She'd wondered if he'd moved at all through the night. He probably hadn't had a moment of sleep—just like her. It had been hard to close her eyes as she'd lain in their bed worried about her husband and his father. She would have never left the hospital if Hosea hadn't insisted that one of them needed to be home with Jacqueline.

Gently, she put her hand on his shoulder, and he opened his eyes.

"I didn't hear you come in," he said.

She whispered, "How is he?"

"The same." His tone was filled with more hope than his words.

Jasmine dropped her bag to the floor, stepped between two monitors, and then kissed her father-in-law's forehead. Staring down at Reverend Bush, she said, "He looks good," because she couldn't think of anything else to say.

But the way Hosea's eyes moved up, then back down, told her that he knew she was lying.

"I brought you some things." She pointed to the bag. "Your toothbrush, a fresh shirt, some other stuff."

He nodded.

"But I wish you'd go home, Hosea. Just for a little while."

He was already shaking his head.

She continued anyway, "You've been here almost two days. I'll stay until you come back."

"I can't leave him," he said, his tone full of tears.

She wanted to cry, too, but she was working hard to stay strong. "You're not helping him, though. Not—"

A knock on the door stopped the rest of her words.

"Can I come in?" Brother Hill asked.

Hosea nodded, and as his godfather moved toward the bed, Jasmine edged back against the wall. She watched as the men stood side by side and whispered together.

Brother Hill took one of Reverend Bush's hands into his. Hosea bowed his head, and after a minute of silent prayer, Brother Hill said, "Let's go outside. We need to talk." In the hallway, he faced Hosea and Jasmine. "I hate to bother you with this, but Pastor Wyatt has called an emergency executive board meeting for tonight."

"For what?" Jasmine and Hosea said at the same time.

"He wants to replace your father."

"What?" Again the couple spoke together.

"Wyatt feels the church would be vulnerable to confusion without leadership."

"What is he talking about? It hasn't even been two days. My father could wake up in the next minute, the next hour, tomorrow." He paused. "Whenever . . . Pops will wake up soon."

Brother Hill hesitated before he said, "I know, but even when he does, he's not going to be able to step right back into his duties."

Hosea shook his head as if that was too much to hear. "Still . . . what's the rush? Why is Wyatt pushing this?"

"Well, you know the talk on him—he's ambitious. And so is his wife."

Jasmine folded her arms. "So he's trying to steal my father-in-law's church?" She fought to hold back her rage; she couldn't believe that man would take advantage of this situation that way.

Hosea said, "I can't even think about this right now. Let Wyatt do what he has to do. I'll take care of my father." He turned back toward the hospital room.

"Hosea, wait." Brother Hill pulled an envelope from his jacket. "This is a notarized letter from your father, and you can read it later, but basically it says that if anything ever happened, he wanted you to take his place. He wanted you to be the senior pastor."

"What?" Jasmine said. But the way her husband stood let her know that he wasn't as surprised as she was.

Hosea said, "Pops talked about this, but I didn't think he was serious."

"Why not?" Brother Hill asked. "It makes sense that your father would want you standing at the pulpit."

Hosea stared at the sealed envelope.

Brother Hill said, "Look, I agree that this doesn't have to be done now, but the fact is, Wyatt called this meeting, and as the associate pastor, he can do that. However, if there's going to be an interim pastor at City of Lights"—he put his hand on Hosea's shoulder—"it has to be you."

"Who else knows about this?" Hosea asked, holding up the envelope.

Brother Hill said, "I believe I'm the only one."

With a deep breath, Hosea said, "I need some time."

"You don't have that."

"I need to think about this, need time to talk to Jasmine . . ."

Brother Hill frowned. "Talk to Jasmine?"

Jasmine's eyebrows shot up. But before she could protest, Hosea said, "Yes, I'm going to talk this over with my wife." He looked Brother Hill straight in his eyes.

"I don't think—"

"You don't need to think, Daniel." His tone was sharp, like his stare.

It was the first time Jasmine had ever heard Hosea call his godfather by his first name.

When Brother Hill leaned back a bit, Hosea softened. "I'm sorry; it's just that—"

"I understand."

"Look, no matter what I decide, I'll be at the board meeting."

Brother Hill nodded. "He called it for six." A pause. "Just remember, this is what your father wants." With a nod to Jasmine, he left them alone.

They watched him amble down the hall, the weight of this tragedy as heavy on him as it was on them.

FIVE

Jasmine stared out the window, taking in the Schomburg Center across Lenox Avenue. Even through the thick-paned windows, four floors up, she could hear the harmony that was Harlem below: horns honking, sirens blaring, the melodies of calypso, reggae, hip-hop, and old-school tunes blending together.

She hadn't done much more than stand at this window since Brother Hill had left an hour ago. Over and over she'd read Reverend Bush's instructions: if he was ever incapacitated . . . or worse . . . his wish was for his son to stand in his stead.

Jasmine sighed deeply. That letter meant one thing: she would be the first lady of City of Lights at Riverside Church!

She trembled with excitement.

"Darlin'?"

She was so far away in her new world that she hadn't heard Hosea return. "I thought you were going for a walk."

He was looking at his father when he said, "I didn't want to stay away too long."

"Wanna talk?"

She followed him into the hallway, where they sat in two chairs across from the nurses' station.

"So what are you thinking?" Jasmine asked, trying not to seem anxious.

"I don't know." He shook his head. "It's not like I've ever led a church before."

"What are you talking about? What about Crystal Lake Cathedral?"

"I was on staff there and led a couple of ministries, but I never led the church. And even though Crystal was one of the largest churches in Chicago, it's still only half the size of City of Lights. There're eight thousand members here."

Eight thousand? She knew City of Lights was huge, but she never thought about the size of the congregation. She had to press her knees together to stop the shaking. She was going to be the first lady of an eight-thousand-member church!

Hosea sighed. "I want to honor Pops's request, but . . ."

"What?"

"I can't imagine it." He faced her and smiled a little. "And it's not like I can really see *you* being a first lady."

He chuckled, but she didn't.

He said, "I mean, are you really going to spend your time visiting the sick and shut-in? Or praying with a grieving widow?"

She didn't know why he was smiling; she didn't see anything funny. How could he not imagine her doing those things? The way she saw it, she was stepping into her destiny.

But all she said was, "Your father would never have written that letter if he didn't want it this way."

"I know." He leaned forward, resting his arms on his legs. Staring at the door that led to his father's room, he said, "Five seven."

Jasmine looked up. Saw the numbers on the wall.

Hosea said, "God's numbers. His grace and the number of completion." Sad seconds of silence sat between them. Until Hosea said, "I'm not ready to let my father go."

"Oh, babe," she said, putting her arms around his shoulders. "That's not what you're doing. You're keeping things in order until he gets better."

Slowly, he nodded, like he agreed. But when he faced her, she could see that he didn't. In his eyes, she saw her opportunity of being the first lady slipping away.

"This is what your father wants," she pushed gently.

There was more conviction in his nod this time. "You're right."

She hugged him, whispered in his ear, "You're doing the right thing." When she pulled back, she glanced at her watch. "It's almost three. We've got to get going."

"The meeting isn't until six."

"Yeah, but we've got to go home and get ready."

When he frowned, she added quickly, "I mean, don't you want to take a shower? Maybe even rest a little."

"I'm not leaving Pops until I have to."

"It'll give you a little time to see Jacquie, and you don't have to worry about your dad. There's an entire staff watching out. Nothing's going to happen."

He shook his head. "I can't—"

"Hey, Hosea." Jasmine heard the squeaky voice before she saw Ivy. The woman leaned over to hug him. "How's your father?"

As Hosea filled Ivy in, Jasmine frowned. Ivy hadn't said a single hello to her. Looked like she'd been initiated into the band of bandits. *That's okay,* Jasmine thought. By tonight, she would be the first lady, and everyone was going to have to step to her with some serious respect from now on.

"So you haven't been home?" Ivy's eyebrows rose almost to the top of her forehead.

Before Hosea could answer, Jasmine said, "But we were getting ready to leave."

"Oh, Jasmine," Ivy said, just noticing her. "I'm so rude." She giggled.

Now Jasmine ignored her; she spoke to Hosea. "You've got to go home and at least take a nap before we go to the church."

Ivy said to Hosea, "Go. I'll stay with your father."

"Are you sure? I don't know how late it'll be when I get back."

When Ivy caressed Hosea's hand, Jasmine's squeezed her fingers into fists.

Ivy said, "It doesn't matter. No matter how late, I'll be here waiting for you."

Jasmine hadn't been sure if she liked Ivy before, but she definitely didn't like her now. Not that this woman could ever be any kind of competition. After all she'd been through over the last months with Hosea's ex-fiancée, Natasia, Jasmine could handle someone as simple as Ivy. She'd beat her down, then toss her over the side of a cliff if she even thought about pushing up on Hosea.

"Thanks, Ivy." Jasmine snatched her husband's hand from Ivy's grasp.

"Let me check on Pops before we go."

The moment he was gone, Jasmine turned to Ivy. "Thanks again," she said, although there was little gratitude inside her tone.

"No problem." Ivy gave her a big-tooth grin. "I'd do anything for Hosea."

"You don't have to do *anything* for him. I've got *that* covered."

Ivy's eyes widened. "I just meant—"

"I don't care what you meant," Jasmine said, looking down at the five-foot-tall woman and speaking in the same tone she reserved for scolding Jacqueline. "You don't have to do a thing for my husband unless I ask you to." She spun around and left Hosea's old friend standing in the hallway of Harlem hospital with her eyes the size of half dollars and her mouth opened just as wide.

It had taken a lot, but Jasmine had talked Hosea into wearing a suit.

"There's no reason for me to get dressed up," he'd protested at first. "I'm going to run in there, tell everyone about Pops's letter, and then I'm heading straight back to the hospital."

"But babe, you still have to look the part."

"What part?" Then, as if he was just noticing her, he frowned as he took in her leopard-collared suit and pearls he'd given her last Mother's Day. "Jasmine, this isn't an audition."

But she had relentlessly laid her case, convincing Hosea that if he walked into the church looking like a pastor, there would be less drama. She suspected it was more fatigue than agreement that made Hosea finally give in. But whatever, she'd won, and now they were on their way to taking their rightful place at City of Lights.

As their SUV snaked uptown on Central Park West, Jasmine smoothed the front of her raw silk skirt, leaned back, and pressed Play on the movie in her mind.

Her life was already filled with wonder, with Hosea being the executive producer and host of *Bring It On,* a top-rated, award-winning Christian talk show. From their apartment on Central Park South to the celebrity-studded events that filled their calendar, she was living the kind of life she'd always craved. But being the first lady of a church as large and influential as City of Lights came with a whole 'nother level of benefits. First, there was the income. She wasn't sure what her father-in-law earned, but with a church so large, it could be well into the six, maybe even seven figures. Some of those TV pastors earned millions, not even counting all the extras—like the hundreds of thousands that came from speaking engagements and writing books. Maybe she and Hosea would write a book together!

The calculator was clicking in her mind as she thought about what she was going to do with the millions that would come her way. They'd keep their apartment because it didn't get much better than Central Park South real estate. But they would definitely get a summer place in the Hamptons. And they would get rid of this SUV. Hosea needed a driver. And she needed one, too, as the first lady because surely she'd be in demand now. She could see herself flitting around the city, speaking at this fundraiser or hosting that benefit.

The smile that had been in her mind made its way to her lips.

"Jasmine?"

Her eyes popped open. "Huh?"

"What're you thinking about? You look like you're in another world."

She wiped her smile away. "I was saying a prayer . . . for your dad and thinking about how proud he's going to be when he wakes up."

Hosea reached across the console and squeezed her hand. "I know you can't be all that excited about this."

She forced a sigh. "It's okay," she said, as if she wasn't thrilled.

"I love that you're in my corner."

"I love you, Hosea. I'll always be here for you. And for your father, too."

That was the truth. She still couldn't believe what had happened to Reverend Bush. Her plan was to send up as many prayers as she could for him to recover quickly.

But there was no need for Reverend Bush to rush it. When he came out of the coma, he would need care and time to heal.

She and Hosea would be there for him. Definitely. But he could take his time getting well.

And maybe Reverend Bush would be so proud of Hosea that he would retire and let his son take over permanently.

Oh, yes, he would be proud of both of them because she was going to rock her position as the new first lady.

She couldn't wait to get started.

SIX

HOSEA EASED THE CAR INTO the parking lot, then hesitated before he squeezed into the space next to the one reserved for the senior pastor.

After he helped Jasmine from the car, they moved slowly across the graveled lot, for the first time walking in the path where Reverend Bush almost died. She kept her eyes toward the church, not wanting to look down, not wanting to see any remnant of what had happened here on Saturday night.

But her imagination churned, and she could envision the police cars arriving, their flashing red lights breaking through the dark. She could hear the sirens of the emergency units speeding to the rescue. She could picture Brother Hill kneeling beside Reverend Bush, trembling with panic and dread and fear.

She glanced sideways and could tell that Hosea shared her thoughts. Her heart ached for him, and she squeezed his hand. But even though she knew that her husband hurt, she knew just as well that this was where they were supposed to be—following in the same steps that Reverend Bush had walked almost every day of the thirty years he'd led City of Lights. They were on their way to securing his legacy, fulfilling his will.

It was a deep breath that she released when they finally

stepped into the church, and as they approached the conference room, the melancholy that had overtaken her was nudged aside by her rising joy. But she pressed down her delight; she couldn't very well walk into the executive board meeting with a smile while her father-in-law was fighting to stay alive.

The board members were sitting around the conference table, their voices low, their faces grave.

"Good evening," Hosea said the moment they stepped inside.

Jasmine was glad that she was still holding on to her husband—or else the cold stares would have knocked her over.

Only her godbrother Malik smiled, stood, and gave her a hug.

"Uh, Hosea." Brother Hill pushed himself from his chair. His eyes moved between Hosea and Jasmine.

But before he could say anything more, Pastor Wyatt piped in, "Hosea, this is a closed meeting."

Hosea raised his eyebrows. "And?"

"That means," Pastor Wyatt spoke slowly, as if Hosea had a comprehension problem, "only board members are invited. You're a member," his eyes shifted to Jasmine, "but your wife isn't."

"And your wife isn't." Hosea gave a nod and a smile to Enid Wyatt, who was sitting against the wall behind her husband.

"But my wife . . . this is a special occasion," Pastor Wyatt explained.

As Hosea held out a chair for Jasmine, he said, "Then you can understand *my* wife being here with me."

Pastor Wyatt looked around at the others, and Jasmine followed his glance to the side of the table where Brother Hill, Sister Whittingham, and Jerome Viceroy, a Harlem city councilman who was responsible for community outreach for City of Lights, sat together. On the other side, Pastor Wyatt was in between Malik, Brother Stevens, and Sister Clinton, the presidents of the Men's and Women's Auxiliary, and Sister Pearline, the head of the Silver Saints.

Malik and Sister Pearline wore welcoming smiles; the rest glared at her as if there was no way she should be sitting in the midst of such holiness.

Jasmine was pissed—especially at Sister Clinton. She expected Brother Hill and his bandits to behave as if they had no grace, but Sister Clinton? Every Sunday the woman had smiled in her face, told Jasmine how wonderful she looked, how well-behaved Jacqueline was. And now she didn't support her sitting in on this little meeting? She had lost her mind—along with the rest of them. They needed to recognize that a change was about to come up in this place.

Jasmine took a hard breath. Calmed down. In ten minutes, Hosea would be appointed, and she would wear her crown.

When Hosea sat down and stared at him, Pastor Wyatt said, "Well, I guess it's fine." He turned to Jasmine and gave her one of his smiles that always made her twist. But his words were not as inviting. "I hope you understand that you won't be able to vote."

Before she could part her lips, Hosea answered, "Of course she wouldn't vote, *if* there was going to be one."

Pastor Wyatt gave a little chuckle. "I thought Brother Hill told you. We're here to make a decision about your father—" He stopped. "You know what?" Pastor Wyatt reached his hands forward. "We need to pray, right now, for your father. Let's take a silent moment."

They all bowed their heads and began to send up private prayers. But not even three seconds passed before Pastor Wyatt said, "Amen," startling everyone. "Okay, now let's get started." The man didn't even try to contain his excitement.

Sister Pearline spoke first, "How's your father, Hosea?"

"I spoke to the doctor before we came, and there's no change."

"Detective Foxx told me today that the investigation is going to stay open," Brother Stevens said.

Hosea nodded. "That's good, but I'm more concerned about Pops. The doctors said that he could wake up at any moment."

"That's my prayer," Sister Clinton said.

"But the truth is," Pastor Wyatt interjected, "we don't know how long he'll be this way, do we?"

Hosea looked straight into that man's eyes. "No, we don't. But God knows."

Pastor Wyatt nodded. "Of course, of course. And as we all stand with you, we still have to keep this church running. City of Lights is an important institution in this city. There'll be lots of things that need to be handled, including the media . . ."

"What media?" Hosea asked.

"You've been at the hospital, but we've all been contacted by the major networks—to get our views on what happened to Reverend Bush. I'm sure the radio stations and newspapers will follow. We're going to have to put out a statement; we may even need to hire a press agent."

Jasmine shifted. She'd always been aware that Reverend Bush was one of the premiere pastors in the city; he was often on television, responding to some reporter's questions on his views about what was happening in New York. But she'd had no idea that his shooting had attracted this much attention.

She'd speak to Hosea—she'd take over the media. She could already see her face in front of the camera, or her words in the *New York Times*! She needed to add a whole new wardrobe to her list of things to acquire.

Hosea said, "We don't need a press agent, Pastor."

Jasmine wasn't going to disagree with her husband in public—that's not what a first lady should do. But she'd change his mind later. She *was* going to need someone to help her with all the press.

Jerome Viceroy glanced at Jasmine, licked his lips, then said to Hosea, "You don't realize the power of this church."

"Yes, I do," Hosea said. "And Holy Ghost power doesn't need any kind of agent." Before anyone had a comeback, Hosea added, "Look, I expect my father to make a full recovery very soon. There's no need for any big changes. We just need—"

"A new pastor," Pastor Wyatt finished for him.

Hosea kept his stare steady. "An *interim* pastor."

Pastor Wyatt gave Hosea a half smile. "I stand corrected." The pastor laid his hands flat on the table and looked from one member to the next. "Of course, no one could really step into Reverend Samuel Bush's shoes, but I am fully prepared to take on the position of senior pastor of City of Lights at Riverside Church," he declared.

The way his wife grinned behind him, Jasmine wondered if the woman was going to stand up and applaud.

Brother Hill said, "Pastor Wyatt, there's something—"

Hosea held up his hand, stopping his godfather. "I really don't understand why you called this meeting," he said to Pastor Wyatt. "It hasn't even been forty-eight hours since . . ." He slipped the envelope from his pocket. "My father could wake up tonight, and this would all be for nothing."

Sister Whittingham spoke softly, "I understand how you feel, Hosea, but Pastor Wyatt is right. Your father would want someone to step in for him."

Hosea nodded as he unfolded the letter. "This is from my father. As the founder and senior pastor of City of Lights, he's requested that I step in. And I'm going to follow my father's instructions."

The hush that followed made Jasmine want to stand up and do her own cheer.

Then, "That's not going to happen," Pastor Wyatt exclaimed. "I'm second in line; I'm the leader of this church."

"Obviously, you didn't hear what my husband said," Jasmine piped in.

Every face in the room turned to her. Every eye told her to be quiet. But Jasmine stared right back at all of them—even Malik and Hosea.

Pastor Wyatt continued, "As I was saying, that doesn't make sense; we already have a church hierarchy."

"This is what my father wants."

Pastor Wyatt was frowning when his wife leaned forward and whispered in his ear. Then his eyes brightened. And when Enid Wyatt returned to her seat, her chin was raised high in the air in triumph.

Jasmine glared at her; she hadn't liked this woman (and the woman hadn't liked her) from the day they met over a year ago at the reception Reverend Bush held for the new associate pastor and his wife.

The rivalry started when Reverend Bush introduced the two.

"Jasmine, this is Enid Wyatt," he'd said.

"Oh, Mrs. Wyatt. Nice to meet you. You must be really proud of your son."

Hosea had jumped in and tried to save his wife. "Uh, darlin', this is Pastor Wyatt's *wife*."

It had taken Jasmine a moment to close her wide-open mouth and apologize. She'd later learned that Enid Wyatt was three years younger than her husband, but how was she supposed to know that? The woman's weathered skin had more wrinkles than an elephant. And she had so much gray in that old-fashioned beehive hairdo she wore atop her head that *she* could've been the leader of the Silver Saints.

Jasmine had shaken her head then, just like she did now. And she had the same thoughts: Why was someone as fine as Pastor Wyatt with someone who was one step below plain?

With his eyes shining like he was on the verge of victory,

Pastor Wyatt said, "I have a question." He glanced back at his wife. "When was that letter written?"

Everyone turned to Hosea, but he didn't even look down. "January first."

Both of the Wyatts chuckled before the pastor said, "Obviously, this was an oversight. Your father put this in writing *before* I joined the staff. Remember, I joined last February." He waved his hands in the air. "He probably forgot he had this little letter—"

"That's January first of *this* year. Five weeks ago. Eleven months *after* you joined the staff, Pastor Wyatt." Hosea let that news settle. "There must've been a reason why my father wrote this and then had it notarized—even if there is a *hierarchy* in place." Hosea slid the letter in front of the pastor.

The long quiet was broken by Sister Clinton. "But Hosea, you've had no experience."

"And," Brother Stevens asked, "how're you going to pastor with your television show?"

"I haven't had time to think about all of that, but when my father wrote this, he knew what I had on my plate. He knew I'd figure it out."

"Well, I have another concern." Sister Clinton's eyes went straight to Jasmine.

Jasmine's eyebrows rose.

The woman continued, "What will people say when they find out that the new pastor is married to a woman who works in a nightclub?"

"What does that have to do with anything?" Malik jumped in, before Jasmine could rise up from her seat. "I own that club."

"Yes, but you're only on the board. The pastor and his wife will be under more scrutiny," Brother Stevens said. "I agree with Sister Clinton. This could be a problem."

"And your wife has other problems," Pastor Wyatt added.

"If the media finds out that you're not even the father of that child . . ."

Ouch, that hurt! That was Jasmine's first thought. But then the warrior rose up inside of her. She was ready to hike up her skirt and climb over the table to beat that man down. Who was he—or any of them—to judge her like this?

It was only Hosea's gentle grasp of her arm—as if he knew the war she was about to wage—that made her stay in place.

"Pastor Wyatt," Hosea began, in such a calm tone that Jasmine wondered if he'd even heard what the man had said. "I'm going to accept your apology, and then we're going to end this right here."

The men glared at each other, their own battle brewing.

"I was only speaking the truth," the pastor said. "Your wife could be a liability to this church. We have no idea what else could be lurking in her past!"

That's it! Jasmine jumped from her chair and pointed her finger at Pastor Wyatt. "You don't know me. You don't know what you're talking about."

And then, a flash of her past.

Sudden.

A shiny silver pole.

Jasmine, crouched down and swinging around the rod.

Hair, courtesy of a wig, flowing down to her waist.

A man, grinning, his fists full of dollar bills.

She gasped, fell back in her chair.

"Jasmine?"

It was her husband's voice that snatched her away from that memory. Brought her back from a scene she hadn't thought of in years.

"Jasmine, are you all right?"

She swallowed, nodded, glared at Pastor Wyatt. "I'm fine, it's just that . . ." She couldn't say any more.

With his hand over hers, Hosea said, "You owe my wife an

apology." His voice was calm, though stern, his anger evident.

Pastor Wyatt waved his hand in the air. "Fine. I'm sorry," he said, backing down. "But as one of the largest churches in the city, we have to be careful with our image."

Hosea turned from Pastor Wyatt to the other board members. "I understand all of your concerns," he said, leaving out the associate pastor. "But everything that you've raised, my father already knew. However, if it'll help, I'll answer your questions." Facing Brother Stevens, he said, "My show is on hiatus and won't be back in production until May. Pops should be back by then."

"But what if he's not?" Sister Clinton asked. "How're you going to handle all of this? Not only your show and the church, but taking care of your father?"

It took a moment for Hosea to say, "I don't know." He looked around the table. "But let me tell you what I do know. I know that I love the Lord and that, whatever I need, He will give to me—including time and wisdom. I know that I love my father. This is not my wish, but his. And as the founder of this church, he's always done what's best for his congregation.

"I know that I love my wife. We may not be perfect, but that's why I'm so glad to have each of you in our lives." He let his eyes move among the members of the board. "Because by the examples of the wonderful marriages and homes that you have, Jasmine and I have something to strive toward; one day, we may get this as right as you."

Brother Stevens's cough slashed through the quiet. Sister Clinton twisted in her seat. Even Brother Hill, Mrs. Whittingham, and Sister Pearline looked away.

Only Pastor Wyatt, his wife, Jerome Viceroy, and Malik looked Hosea dead in his eyes.

Dang! Jasmine thought, already pushing down the quick memory of her past. She wondered about the stories behind Hosea's words; the way half the room had shifted, there had to be some mess. These saints acted more like sinners who'd been caught.

Pastor Wyatt said, "I still think we should vote."

Hosea shrugged. "We can vote if you want, but I already know the outcome because no one on this board is divisive. No one wants to see this board or this church and its members split."

Pastor Wyatt's eyes darted from one to another, in search of an ally. But no one stood up for him.

"Then I guess you all agree," Hosea said.

Brother Hill asked, "Does anyone here think we need to take a vote now?" His glance wandered from person to person.

They shook their heads—all except Pastor Wyatt. And behind him, his wife sat still as stone.

Brother Hill said, "Then Hosea Samuel Bush is the senior pastor of City of Lights at Riverside Church until further notice."

Again, Enid bent forward and whispered to her husband.

Jasmine frowned again. Could it have been any clearer who was running this show?

When his wife returned to her seat, Pastor Wyatt jumped up. "I'd like to revisit this at the next board meeting." He held up his hands when he looked at Hosea. "I'm not challenging you; we need to make sure things are running smoothly and—"

"That's fair," Hosea said, a truce in his tone. He shook Pastor Wyatt's hand. "I'm looking forward to working with you."

"We're a team," Pastor Wyatt said. "I've got your back."

Jasmine smirked. She didn't want that man—or his wife—anywhere near her husband's back. Not unless the two were frisked first.

When they all stood, Jasmine wanted to stop them and ask about the money. She needed to know exactly what her husband would be earning so that she could do their new household budget. But with all the chatter, she decided to ask Hosea later.

Minutes passed as all the board members came over to offer more condolences to Hosea.

No one said a word to her until Malik pulled her aside. "You okay?" he whispered.

"Yeah, why wouldn't I be?"

"Some of the things they said"—he motioned with his head toward the group—"were out of line."

She waved her hand like their words meant nothing. "That kind of stuff doesn't bother me."

"So you're going to be able to handle this?"

"Hosea being the pastor? Definitely. I'm looking forward to it."

He leaned back, as if that was not the answer he expected. "I thought since you and Hosea were all Hollywood now, you wouldn't want anything to do with the church." He nodded. "Good for you." He glanced at his watch. "I've got a stop to make, but I'll come by the hospital a little later." He hugged her before he bumped knuckles with Hosea.

"You ready?" Hosea asked her.

She nodded, and without saying a word to anyone else, she took Hosea's hand. As they stepped out of the room, Jasmine heard the voices rise behind them.

And then, Mrs. Whittingham screeched, "Oh, Lawd, that woman is going to be our first lady!"

Jasmine glanced at Hosea, but his eyes were straight ahead, his thoughts already beyond the church and with his father.

On another day, Jasmine would have stomped back into the room and jumped in that woman's face. But that wasn't the appropriate behavior for a pastor's wife. Anyway, Mrs. Whittingham had only spoken the truth—she was the first lady.

And every single one of those clowns in there were going to have to deal with that.

SEVEN

"Pops, I did it," Hosea whispered, leaning over the side of the hospital bed. "I'm going to lead the church the way you wanted me to."

Jasmine stood at her husband's side as he uttered the same words that he'd said last night when they'd rushed to the hospital after the board meeting. And like last night, Reverend Bush was still as unmoving as a statue, still living only because of the constant beep . . . beep . . . beep—the only sign that he was alive.

"Pops," Hosea called again, his lips touching his father's ear. "Can you hear me?"

Whoosh! was the only response—the air from the breathing tube that was performing that life function for him.

"Pops?"

Hosea's voice cracked, and Jasmine's heart did the same. She wanted to take her husband's hand and yank him away from this den of death. It had been only three days, but this room smelled and sounded like the end. And Hosea was sleeping in the middle of this every night. No wonder he was beginning to break down.

"Hello."

The voice startled them both as they turned.

Dr. Lewis said, "I was hoping I'd get a chance to talk to you." She gave Reverend Bush a quick glance before she looked down at his chart, which hung on a chain at the lower part of the bed.

As the doctor read, Jasmine searched her face. But it was as if the doctor wore a mask—there was no "good news" or "bad news" in her expression. The doctor scanned the notes as if she were reading a newspaper.

When she looked up at them, though, she was smiling. And that gave Jasmine hope.

Dr. Lewis said, "Can you join me outside?"

Hosea tucked the Bible he held under his father's arm, then the two followed the doctor into the hallway. She led them to the side of the nurses' station, but when she faced them, her smile was gone.

"As you can see," the doctor began, "your father's unresponsive . . ."

Tell us something we don't know.

"But the good news is, he's more stable than he's been."

"*Is* that good news?" Jasmine asked. "He's stable, but he's not moving. How long is he going to be this way?"

"We don't know," the doctor said, shaking her head. "And that's one of the problems. We don't know why he hasn't awakened or why he isn't breathing on his own. But . . . we did have some good signs today. The swelling in his brain has gone down considerably, which lessens the chance of brain damage."

"Okay," Hosea breathed. "That's good." He grabbed Jasmine's hand as if he needed something to hold on to.

"And then," the doctor continued, "the neurologist's tests came back—your father does have brain activity."

"What does that mean?" Jasmine asked.

Hosea answered before the doctor could, "You're saying he's not a vegetable."

The doctor nodded. "Those aren't the words I would use, but yes. His brain is active. That means we're going to move forward, keep doing everything to keep your father alive."

Jasmine wrapped her arms around Hosea's neck. "You hear that, babe. He's going to be fine!"

The doctor held up her hands. "Now, I do want to caution you," she spoke slowly, as if her next words were most important. "There are many questions we have about your father, and we won't be able to assess much until he wakes up." And then, as if she hadn't taken away enough of their joy, she added, "*If* he wakes up. It's too soon to know."

"That's okay, Doctor," Hosea said, waving away her last words. "This is still good news for us. Thank you."

The doctor stuffed her hands into the pockets of her lab coat. "If you have any questions, I'll be in my office. And you can always call me."

They nodded their good-byes and waited until the doctor was steps away before they held each other again.

"He's gonna make it, babe," Jasmine whispered in his ear.

Hosea nodded. "Yeah, he is." Leaning back, he said, "Okay, now let's go do our part; let's get in there and pray."

EIGHT

Jasmine massaged her eyes, but she couldn't wipe the sleep away. She glanced at the clock; only five minutes had passed. At eight o'clock, it was far too early to be falling asleep.

"What're you reading?"

Hosea's voice made her smile. Jasmine pushed aside the book, the reason for her weariness. "Is Jacquie sleeping?"

Hosea nodded. "I stayed until she closed both eyes, but she was fighting it. She tried to sing her song at least one hundred times."

"You know, your father"—and then her voice became softer—"taught her that song." After a moment of quiet, Jasmine added, "She missed you a lot."

He nodded. "I missed her, too. And I missed this." He pointed to the bed.

"I'm so glad you came home tonight."

"Well, Doctor Lewis kept insisting that I'd do Pops a lot more good if I got some rest, if I got back to some semblance of my life."

"She's right; your father wouldn't want you sitting in the hospital day and night."

Exhaustion was in his sigh. It had been a week since Reverend Bush had been shot, and although she'd come home every day, Hosea left his father only long enough for a quick shower and change. He'd spent his days reading the Bible to him and his nights praying for him.

But tonight, after they'd shared a dinner she'd ordered from Sylvia's, he'd stood when she'd kissed him good-bye.

"I'm going home with you," was all he said before he moved to the side of his father's bed. Holding her hand, suddenly, he'd knelt down and lowered his head. Not more than a nanosecond later, Jasmine did the same. She bowed her head and together, silently, on their knees, the two sent their requests to God.

Now, two hours later, here at home, Jasmine had never been so glad to have her family together.

"I called Pastor Wyatt." Hosea walked over to where she sat. "I asked him to preach tomorrow." He shook his head. "I'm not ready."

Looking up, she lied straight to his face, "I'm glad you did that." She hid the hope she'd had that tomorrow would be her debut, the first Sunday since Hosea was named pastor. She'd already purchased her outfit. "You'll be ready next week."

"Yeah," he said flatly. He tilted his head to glance at the book she'd pushed aside. "What're you reading?" Before she could respond, Hosea picked it up. "The Bible?" as if that was the last thing he'd expected.

"I've been trying to get some reading done."

"Wow."

"Well, you've been telling me that I needed to read the Word more."

"Yeah, and how long have I been saying that? But you've always complained that there were too many begats this and begats that for you to handle." He sat down on the bed.

"It's a different game now."

He frowned, unbuttoning his shirt. "Why?"

"Because you're the senior pastor." She pushed herself from

the chaise and walked over to the bed. Climbing behind him, she pressed the tips of her fingers against his shoulders and massaged. "And I'm the pastor's wife. It's important for me to be up on everything in the Bible."

He chuckled, a little. It was the first time she'd heard any kind of joy from him in over a week, though it didn't make her happy that he was laughing at her.

She slapped his back gently. "Don't make fun. I *am* the first lady."

"Only an interim one."

"For as long as it lasts, I'm going to be a proper one."

Pulling her into his arms, he said, "You don't have to change a thing, Jasmine. I love you the way you are."

"You might but the people at church don't."

"Who said that?"

"Oh, please. Don't tell me you never noticed how they treat me. And the board meeting was ridiculous. Some of those things they said . . . so much for their being Christian."

"Judge their words, not their hearts. They're not perfect."

"Seems that they're not. You ruffled more than a few feathers when you said that we wanted to be like them. What's the story behind that?" she asked, eager to know.

"No story." Hosea shook his head. "I just needed to remind everyone that there was only one who walked this earth perfectly. And anyway, all those things they said, I think, were good. Everything that anyone had on us is on the table; there's nothing left to throw in our faces."

Jasmine took a second before she said, "Babe, I've been thinking . . . maybe I should take a leave of absence. Malik can handle things at Rio for a little while, and this way none of those—"

"Be careful!" he warned playfully.

"—Saints . . . on the board will be able to say anything about where I work."

"You don't have to do that."

"I know I don't have to, but it takes away every piece of ammunition from those holy rollers, and the best thing is that I'd be there for you whenever you needed me. You're going to have your hands full."

He nodded slowly, as if giving thought to her words. "But you just got back from a leave. If you keep doing that, Malik is going to have to replace you."

"So what?" And then she spoke the words that she'd been thinking ever since she learned that she would be the first lady. "Maybe it's time for me to leave the club for good."

"To do what?"

"To stand by your side. To really be your helpmate."

"Helpmate?" He chuckled. "You *have* been reading the Bible."

"I should be at your side; that's what a wife's supposed to do. And it's not like we need the money."

"Whoa. I never thought I'd ever hear you say *that.* So you're willing to give up your six figures so that you can stand next to me?"

"Yup." She snuggled closer to him. "And like I said, it's not like we need my income. With your show and what you'll be getting from the church . . ."

"I'm not taking a salary."

It took a moment for her to make sense out of his words. "What?" She pushed herself away from him.

"I'm not taking any money," he said, as if he needed to repeat it a different way. "First of all, my prayer is that I won't be doing this for more than a few weeks."

"But you don't know that. Doctor Lewis said—"

"You know my faith is not in the doctors," he interrupted her. "I trust that they'll take care of my father, but my faith is with—"

"I know, I know." Jasmine waved her hands like what he was

about to say about God wasn't important. "But not even God can tell us when your father will wake up." She didn't add the one word that Dr. Lewis had used—*if*—the word that changed this whole equation.

"It doesn't matter," he said. "The point is, for however long Pops is down, it's temporary."

She shook her head, wishing he'd stopped talking about interim and temporary. No one knew if Reverend Bush would ever return to his position. And whether he did or not, they needed to be compensated for their work now.

"So how are we supposed to live?" she asked. *And what about my summer place in the Hamptons?*

"There's nothing wrong with the way we're living, Jasmine. So if you want to leave Rio, that's fine."

"But then, we'll just have your income from *Bring It On.*" *And how are we going to get two chauffeurs on that?*

He said, "My check is more than sufficient. And we have plenty saved. We might have to ease up on a few things, 'cause I know you're not thinking about moving away from here . . ."

You got that right!

He said, "But we'll be all right. So give Malik your notice, if that's what you want."

And how will I get a new wardrobe if I do that? "I'll think about it," she said, not planning to think about it at all. She was going to leave Rio, and he was going to get paid.

He rubbed his eyes, suddenly weary. "I need to check on Pops." He reached for the phone and looked up as she paced. "Whatever you decide, I'm fine," he assured her again.

She nodded, but her thoughts were on how she was going to get a check for Hosea into their bank account. She picked up her Bible and flipped it open, not really caring where the pages fell.

"Still no change?" she heard Hosea say.

There may have been no change with his father, but she

already had an idea about how she was going to change Hosea's mind.

Hosea hung up the phone with a sigh. "Pops's the same," he whispered as he stood up and embraced her. Inside his arms, she felt his emotions—his fear, his exhaustion, his hope. She held on to him, letting him know that she would always be there.

I'm not going to say anything else, she thought, as he led her to their bed. At least not tonight. But she was going to handle this. When she finished, not only would Hosea have a salary, but there might be a little something in it for her, too.

After all, she was the first lady.

NINE

"I KNOW IT'S A LOT to ask, Malik, but you know the pressure I'm under."

Jasmine had been waiting for a day to speak to her godbrother. She didn't want to call him from home yesterday and take the chance that Hosea might overhear. So she'd waited until this morning and then cornered him the moment he walked into the office.

Now he sat behind his desk and nodded as he listened to her plea. "How much time off do you want?"

She shrugged. "You saw Reverend Bush. And the doctors can't tell us anything."

Malik shook his head. "This is so deep."

"So between taking care of his father and the church and his show—how is Hosea supposed to handle everything? He needs me."

A pause and then, "I agree."

She exhaled, relieved. "Thanks."

But then he leaned forward. "Now you know I love you, right?"

"Yeah," she spoke slowly, wondering what was coming.

"And you know business is business."

"Definitely."

"Well, you just came back, and now—not knowing how long you'll be away this time—I may have to find someone else."

Not a second passed before she said, "You should."

"Really?" His face stretched with surprise. "I thought you'd be upset and fighting to hold on to the benjamins."

"Well, with Hosea's income, we don't really need mine."

He grinned. "Hello? Is this Jasmine Cox Larson Bush talking? You two have been living pretty high up there on Central Park South."

"And we'll stay that way. Especially after you take a recommendation to the board that Hosea should be paid."

"Brother Hill said that Hosea wasn't taking a salary."

Jasmine waved his words away. "That doesn't make any sense."

"It didn't make sense to me," Malik agreed. "But if that's what Hosea wants—"

"Hosea doesn't know what he wants. He's tired, confused, stressed. It's hard for him to think."

Malik chuckled. "So you're going to help him."

"Exactly, and you're going to help me."

Her words took his smile away. He leaned back, folded his arms. "I'm not getting involved in one of your schemes."

"Did I say anything about—"

"You didn't have to," he interrupted. "I've been pulled into enough of them to know . . ."

Jasmine sighed, tired of this old song. "When are you going to forgive me for that?"

"For which one? For when you tried to get me to hook you up with Reverend Bush? Or when you got me to lie to Hosea about your being married before? Or when I helped you lie about Jacqueline's paternity?"

"Dang! You kept a list?"

"No, 'cause if I did, there would be a dozen more times when I suspended judgment for you."

"But that's what you were supposed to do. Because you promised my dad that you'd take care of me."

"I'm sure when I meet up with him in heaven, he'll apologize for putting that on me. 'Cause taking care of you is no joke. Now, Serena . . ."

Jasmine rolled her eyes, knowing he was going to say that her sister was easy. Of course she was. She was a boring thirty-eight-year-old living a mind-numbing life in Florida. "If you would listen to me for a moment, you'll see that I'm not talking about doing anything underhanded. Just take a request to the board. Make sure Hosea gets paid. That's all."

He nodded, although his eyes were still filled with doubt.

She added, "You know if Pastor Wyatt had been appointed, he would have demanded more money."

That was all she needed to say; she knew her godbrother couldn't stand the associate pastor.

Malik nodded. "Okay, I'll call Brother Hill." She grinned, but he didn't stop there. "Just know that this is all I'm going to do. Because now that Hosea's the senior pastor, everything has to be on the up and up. It could get real messy if anything else came out."

"You don't have anything to worry about; I don't have a single secret left." She paused, thought about the flashbacks she'd had last week. But that was so long ago those days didn't count.

"If that's the case, then we're cool." He stood and hugged her. "I'll check on that salary thing, and you keep me posted on how long you'll be away."

"I will," she said, deciding not to tell him that if he got Hosea the right amount, she'd never come back. She had loved working at Rio—after four years, it was still one of the most happenin' spots in lower Manhattan, often cited in Page Six, the

New York Post's get-your-name-in-at-any-cost gossip column for the famous and fabulous.

But as wonderful as this life had been, there was a new day awaiting.

She marched down the hall, past cubicles filled with assistants chatting on phones, offering incentives to get celebrities to come and party at Rio.

Behind her closed door, she went to work on the next phase of her plan. When the board told Hosea that he would be paid, she had to make sure he accepted it.

Reaching for the telephone, she knew just how she'd get her way.

TEN

Jasmine had learned a long time ago that a little food and a lotta love in the afternoon was her key. Even though she'd brought a light lunch, she had no doubt that within an hour or two she'd have Hosea screaming, "Yes! Yes! Yes!" to all her demands.

As the cab slowed in front of City of Lights, she straightened the red bow on the picnic basket. It had been tough trying to buy this today; how in the world had she forgotten Valentine's Day? It must've been all that was going on with Reverend Bush that had her off her game.

Hosea hadn't mentioned anything about Valentine's Day either. Any other year, that would have been a major violation. But she had to give him a free pass—and it worked in her favor anyway. Hosea probably hadn't shopped for a gift, and she knew exactly what she wanted.

As she stepped across the parking lot, the thought of Reverend Bush's shooting filled her mind again. She was sure that every time Hosea took these steps, he had those thoughts. And though it had to be hard, she was still glad that he'd decided to come to the church—at least every morning. He had agreed to give up his day watch at the hospital only once they had come up with a schedule for someone to be with his father during the day.

Today, Mrs. Whittingham had agreed to sit with Reverend Bush—which was all the better. Jasmine didn't feel like having to deal with the old windbag right now.

As she trotted up the steps, she was pleased that she'd come up with this plan to surprise Hosea. She could imagine him sitting in his father's office with his head bowed, heavy with memories and thoughts of his father's fate. At least she'd bring a smile to his face, even if only for a little while.

Then laughter met her at the door. It wasn't your lean-your-head-back-and-let-it-rip kind of guffaw. It was light, but still it was laughter. And it was definitely Hosea, but who was with him?

She tiptoed past Mrs. Whittingham's desk and moved toward the glee. In front of Hosea's father's office, she stood, watching Hosea, his shoulders shaking with his chortle. And in front of him sat Ivy, giggling like a schoolgirl.

Neither one of them noticed as Jasmine took in the scene—the desk covered with aluminum pans and paper plates, filled with fried chicken, macaroni and cheese, collard greens, and biscuits.

Jasmine glanced down at the basket she held with red potatoes with caviar and cheese, baked lobster, and a single chocolate covered banana that was meant to be shared.

She stepped back and away. For some reason, she didn't want to be seen, just wanted to listen.

Hosea was still chuckling when he said, "I'd forgotten that."

"We did have some good times, didn't we?"

"Yeah." He nodded as he chewed a piece of meat off a chicken leg. "Those were the days. When life was easy."

"Hosea," Ivy said, putting down the chicken wing she held, "you know you can count on me. I'll always be here for you."

"That's a nice thing to say."

"I mean it. I was supposed to be going to Europe in a few weeks, but I'm staying until we know more about your dad."

Peeking around the corner, Jasmine saw Ivy cover Hosea's hand with hers.

Ivy said, "I couldn't leave knowing that you needed me."

Jasmine wanted to stomp into the room and tell Ivy to keep her pigeon fingers off her husband. But she stayed in place, shocked that Hosea was so engrossed he hadn't even noticed her.

"I'd feel terrible," Ivy continued, "if I was away and something happened to Reverend Bush." It must have been the way his eyes darkened that made Ivy add, "I didn't mean that anything *was* going to happen. I was just sayin'—"

He held up his hand. "I know what you mean." Hosea took a deep breath. "I haven't admitted this to anyone, but I'm really scared."

Jasmine's mouth opened wide. First, she'd found him laughing, and now he was telling this pip-squeak of a woman his fears.

"You do know that he's going to be all right. Your father is physically strong and his faith is stronger."

"That's what I'm counting on."

Her husband sounded so sad that she wanted to rush in and hold him. But still, Jasmine held her place, eavesdropping some more.

Ivy said, "Why are we sitting here being all dopey?"

Did she say "dopey"?

"Your father's going to be fine, and in a couple of weeks, we'll all be hanging around together laughing and remembering nothing but the good times."

"Pops will be glad to see you when he wakes up."

Ivy shook her head. "I don't know about that. Sometimes I find it hard to look your dad straight in his eyes."

"Why?"

"Because, remember? Our kiss!"

A kiss!

Flashback!

Of another kiss. With Hosea and his ex-fiancée, Natasia. Jasmine had walked in on the two of them just six months before. It was that flashback that made Jasmine stomp into the office and slam the basket onto the desk.

"Darlin'." Hosea stood up. "I didn't hear you come in."

"Obviously." Jasmine folded her arms. Stared at the food. Glared at Ivy. "So what's going on?"

"Nothing," Hosea said, wiping his hands on a napkin. "Ivy was nice enough to bring me lunch."

Jasmine kept her cold stare. "And bring you memories of a kiss." She turned to her husband with eyebrows raised. "You want to tell me about that, Hosea."

"Tell you about our kiss?" The tips of his lips twitched, like he was fighting back a smile.

He thought this was funny? Was he blind? Couldn't he see the steam rising out of her?

"Yes, I want to know all about it." Her stare traveled from Hosea to Ivy (who sat stiffly still) and back to her husband.

"Well, let's see." Hosea relaxed in his chair. "I think it was . . . thirty-three years ago."

Jasmine blinked. "Thirty-three years?" The question came out softly.

"Uh-huh." He nodded, his face still covered with his amusement. "We were five years old, sitting in Sunday School, and Stanley White dared me to kiss a girl. I didn't want to, but I couldn't go out like a punk. So since I knew Ivy, I kissed her. And Pops walked in."

Hosea laughed and Ivy (now relieved) joined him. The two shared that memory again, and Jasmine stood there, looking silly, feeling stupid.

"I guess I should be going," Ivy said, although she didn't make a move.

"Yes, you should," Jasmine said. "And you don't have to worry about cleaning any of this up." She shoved Ivy's purse—as politely as she could—into her hands. "I'll take care of *everything*"—she glanced at Hosea—"here."

"Uh, Ivy," Hosea said, "thanks for coming by."

"Okay?" she said, as if it were a question. As if she couldn't figure out how one minute she'd been giggling with an old friend, and the next she was being kicked out. She scurried toward the door, her small feet taking short steps.

Turning to Hosea, Jasmine said, "I brought you a surprise." She held up the basket, then dropped it back onto the desk. "But it seems like you've already eaten."

"Jasmine," he said, his tone carrying patience, "Ivy came by to see how I was doing. Mrs. Whittingham told her I'd be here, and she didn't want me to be alone."

"She should've called me."

"Jasmine—"

"I'm sorry," she said, putting her arms around him. "But can you blame me? I don't want anyone taking care of you except for me."

He embraced her and looked into her eyes. "Are you sure that's all there is to this?"

She was silent, though she knew the thought behind his question.

He asked, "This isn't about Natasia, is it?"

Jasmine pursed her lips, ground her teeth, squeezed her hands. She could hardly stand to hear the name—Natasia Redding.

Natasia was Hosea's ex-fiancée. Eight months ago, she had stalked into their lives, a predator intent on snaring her prey.

"I never think about Natasia," she lied, knowing that she had flashbacks about that dragon all the time.

She and Hosea were still in recovery, recuperating from the greatest threat ever to their marriage—a man-stealing woman who'd been determined to make Hosea her prize.

Natasia had joined the staff of Hosea's television show during their remote taping in Los Angeles, and from the moment they'd met, Jasmine knew the woman's game. Natasia had set a web of tricks and traps and had wreaked all kinds of havoc in their marriage.

He said, "You know all of that is behind us, right?"

She nodded.

"We'll have our troubles, but we can get through anything."

She relaxed her jaw, eased open her fingers. "I know. We were meant to be."

But even though Jasmine believed what she'd said, there was no way she'd ever again go through anything like those months with Natasia. Especially not after what Hosea had told her . . .

It was the night Hosea had come back home after they'd been separated for weeks. Together, they'd sat in the living room, their shoulders pressed together, holding hands, and Hosea had told her the truth.

"I never slept with Natasia," he said as he looked down at their hands, their fingers entwined. "But . . ."

When he stopped, her heart pounded so hard she wondered if her chest could contain it.

He finished, "But I wanted to."

A sob escaped from deep inside of her. And when she tried to pull away, he held her tighter.

"I want you to know the complete truth, Jasmine." And after a pause, he said, "I did some things I'm not proud of."

Even though she didn't want to know, she asked, "What?"

It took him a moment to say, "I'm only telling you because the most important things we need besides love are truth and trust. I want to tell you the truth so that you'll trust me again." He stopped. He swallowed. "We kissed. We did . . . more."

It was the "more" that brought all kinds of pictures to her mind and reminded her of the day she'd barged into Natasia's hotel room, finding her husband with his pants down and Natasia barely clothed. It was the "more" that made her snatch her hand away and rush into the bathroom.

Hosea followed and stood behind her as she bowed over the toilet and released her emotions into the bottom of the bowl. Then he helped her stand up straight, and even before she had the chance to clean up, he held her and comforted her.

"I love you, Jasmine," he had whispered as she cried in his arms. "With everything inside of me. Nothing like this will ever happen again."

The last words were the ones that she'd held on to, the ones that had helped her through. Hosea was right—nothing like that would happen again, because the next time any woman even had a thought about Hosea, she would stop the drama before it began. She would bury her—and she didn't really care if she was dead or alive.

That included Ivy. Sure, that girl wasn't any kind of threat, wasn't anything like Natasia. Without looks or sophistication, Ivy didn't have anything in her arsenal to attract a man like Hosea, or any man really.

But it didn't matter. She'd warn Ivy one more time, and if she didn't step far back, Ivy would be her first casualty.

"So," Hosea interrupted her thoughts of annihilation, "are you sure you've forgiven me?"

"Of course, babe," she said. "How could I not, after all the times you've forgiven me?"

His eyes told her he didn't really believe her, but he understood. "You know I love you, right?"

"This, I know. And I love you, too. That's why I came by. So that I could celebrate Valentine's Day with the man I love."

"Valentine's Day?" He frowned.

"Uh-huh. Today. And I thought"—she paused and kissed

him—"we could have"—another kiss—"a little love in the afternoon."

This time, he brought his lips to hers. "Is that what you thought?" he asked when he finally pulled back. "Well, maybe we can take a little Valentine's break." He glanced at his watch. "Maybe for an hour or so."

She grinned. She hadn't been able to take her husband's mind too far away from his father, but this was what they both needed.

With one swoop of her hand, she wiped the plates, one container still filled with chicken, and several books off the desk.

"Jasmine!" His eyes were wide. "Not here."

"Why not? We're married."

He shook his head as if he couldn't believe his wife. Grabbing her purse from the floor, he took her hand and led her toward the door.

"What about all of this?" she asked, looking over her shoulder at the mess they were leaving.

He didn't respond. Didn't say a word, didn't stop moving until they were inside their SUV. Even before he switched the key in the ignition, Jasmine knew where they were going.

"The Arlington," she said.

He nodded and passed her the widest grin she'd seen on his face in almost two weeks.

She said, "One of my favorite places."

"I remember."

Jasmine smiled as she remembered, too. Their last afternoon tryst, three weeks ago, had started with a simple text message: *The Arlington at one.*

Hosea had given her thirty minutes notice, but she'd walked right out of a Rio budget meeting, and dashed uptown, arriving on time. When she entered the lobby, he was waiting, but didn't acknowledge her. She'd followed him into the elevator, where they stood shoulder to shoulder, two strangers. On the eighth floor, she'd followed him to a room where they introduced themselves, and minutes later they were inside Suite 807 sweating up the sheets.

As their car sped down Fifth Avenue, Jasmine had no idea what role she'd play today. Maybe she'd just be who she was—the woman totally in love with Pastor Hosea Bush.

The February wind blew hard against the hotel window; still Jasmine kicked away the sheets. Her body glistened with sweat. Hosea had finished what he started eleven days ago, before the call came about his father. It had been worth every bit of the wait.

She exhaled a long breath and rested her head on Hosea's chest. "I love you so much."

"Spoken like a wife," he said.

"Spoken like a wife who's been very well taken care of."

He chuckled and then the way his arms drew her closer, she could tell that his smile was gone. His thoughts had already left Midtown Manhattan and were up in Harlem.

But he said, "I needed this."

She snuggled closer, tried to hold him tighter. "Your father's going to recover." She answered the question that he hadn't even asked.

She could feel him nod. "I thought he'd be awake by now."

"He'll wake up. People have been in comas for many, many years and come out fine. No matter how long, your father's going to be one of those survivors."

"That's my prayer." He paused. "Thank you for being with me through this."

She lifted her head. "Where else would I be? I'll always be by your side."

"I'm glad you said that, because I've been thinking about how I want to lead at City of Lights. I want you with me, Jasmine. Whenever you can be. I want you in as many meetings as possible so that you'll know what's going on."

"Really?" She lifted herself up on her elbows.

He nodded. "That's how Pops did it with my mother. He always said it was better for them to stand together than for him to sit alone. That's the way I want it to be with us. For however long we're there."

She leaned over and gently pressed her lips against his. "Thank you."

"This way, in case I can't be there one Sunday, I'll know everything will run smoothly."

She frowned. "You're not talking about me giving a sermon, are you?" She shook her head, not even able to imagine herself standing at the podium, her Bible in her hand, and light shining through the image of Jesus Christ from the stained-glass window behind her.

And then a flash—of her past.

Dollar bills falling from the sky.

A voice from the past screamed, "Let's make it rain, baby!"

There was laughter. Hoots and hollers as men tossed money.

At her.

As she stood as close to naked as she could get.

She gasped.

"Jasmine?"

She shook her head, to rid that scene from her memory.

"Jasmine?"

Those days—well over twenty years ago—had been far from her consciousness. But for almost a week now, these little images kept creeping up.

Why now? There was no reason to think about that long ago time. She was far away from those days.

"Are you listening to me?"

It took a moment for her husband's face to come back into focus. "Huh?"

"Where did you go?"

Pulling the sheet to her bare chest, she blinked, making sure the memory was gone. "I was thinking about what you said."

"I wasn't talking about you preaching. I want you to know everything that's going on so that you could have my back if I'm not there." He took her hand. "I really need you."

She tucked away all thoughts of her past. "I got you, babe. Always." It was time to go after her Valentine's Day gift. "Now, I have some news. Malik . . . he wants me to take a leave of absence," she lied.

"Why?"

"He thinks I'm going to be distracted. Especially after what he saw in that meeting the other day. He said I should keep my focus on you and Dad."

Slowly, Hosea nodded. "Your godbrother is a good man."

"He is, but Hosea, this time I don't feel good about taking my salary. He paid me the whole time we were in Los Angeles, and now . . . well, I don't want to take advantage that way. But—" She stopped, knowing that was enough.

He said, "I don't want you to take advantage of him, either." He paused, inhaled a deep breath. "Okay, I'll tell the board that I need to draw a salary."

"Thank you, babe." She hugged him; she'd forgotten to tell Malik how much she wanted, but she knew her godbrother would hook it up.

Finally! She was on her way to being the fabulous first lady of City of Lights at Riverside Church.

She couldn't wait until Sunday.

ELEVEN

Jasmine pushed the door open, but her smile turned upside down when she stepped into the hospital room.

"What are you doing here?" she asked, her tone without a tinge of warmth.

"That's no way to greet a friend." Pastor Wyatt held his arms wide, as if to welcome her.

Jasmine crossed her arms. "Where's my husband?"

The associate pastor shrugged. "I just got here, and the room was empty, except for"—he turned and looked at Reverend Bush—"our good reverend here."

Jasmine frowned, not liking the way he said that. With her eyes still on Wyatt, she stepped to the bed, checked every single machine and all the tubes that were keeping Reverend Bush alive. Satisfied that the man hadn't killed her father-in-law, she turned toward the door.

"Wait," Pastor Wyatt called her, but she kept moving, ignoring him. "Jasmine, come on. Don't make me chase you."

Those words made her whip around. For a moment, she had to hold her breath as he swaggered toward her. Pastor Wyatt was truly a fine specimen of a man. That had been her thought the first time she had seen him.

Jasmine had been holding Hosea's hand when she met Pastor Wyatt at last year's reception, but when the man parted his lips and smiled with that deep dimple, she'd had to remind herself that he was married, she was married and she didn't do that cheating thing anymore. But if she did, he would be the one.

In the year that had passed, he still made her wonder what it would be like to feel his lips on her. To feel his hands all over her. To feel the weight of him on top of her. Even though there wasn't a single thing—outside of his movie-star looks—that she liked about him, she couldn't deny the electricity that surged between them whenever they shared the same space.

"Thanks for stopping," he said. "I didn't feel like chasing you down the hall. Although"—he took a step closer to her—"I would have if you made me."

Jasmine took a step back, crossed her arms. "What is it that you want, Pastor Wyatt?"

"Why don't you call me Eugene?"

"I'm fine with Pastor Wyatt."

His lips slowly spread into one of his cool smiles. "That's too formal for friends."

"We're not friends."

"Not yet."

"Look," she said, blowing out a breath, "if you don't have anything else, I'm going to find my husband." She turned away.

"If I were your husband, I'd be looking for you."

Spinning back around, she asked, "Why are you flirting with me?"

He grinned and held up his hands like he was innocent.

This time, she was the one who stepped closer, but he didn't back away. With just a breath between them, he smiled, but she didn't.

"I don't like the way you talk to me."

One of his eyebrows shot up slightly. "I don't know what you're talking about."

"I think you do, and I'm not having it anymore. The next time you say something inappropriate, I'm going to tell my husband." She paused, thought about Enid, said, "Or maybe I'll just tell your wife."

That made him step back. He laughed, but Jasmine could tell that the shot she'd taken had landed.

"Look," he touched her arm lightly as he directed her away from the ears of the nurses standing at their station. "I'm not trying to make trouble. I wanted to talk to you about your husband and his quest to be pastor. Why does he want it so bad?"

Jasmine frowned. "Because that's what his father wants."

"That letter was a mistake," he said, his voice rising, a little. "The church is my territory."

Now it was his tone that made Jasmine step back a bit. "I wasn't aware the church was anyone's territory. I thought it all belonged to God."

"To God and to me." Her widened eyes made him soften his tone. "I'm just sayin' that City of Lights means a lot to me. I moved to New York with the expectation that I'd be taking over one day."

"I don't know what to tell you."

After a moment, he said, "You know, being a pastor's wife isn't easy. No matter how clean you are, there's always something that could come out."

She frowned. "What does that mean?"

He shrugged. "It's not an easy life, but it's what my wife and I have been called to do."

Jasmine searched his face, trying to see his true thoughts. Then, "I'm going to find my husband."

"And when you find him, talk to him," he said. Even though she was walking away, he added, "Hosea may not realize it yet, but sitting in his father's chair is a big job, too big for him." Before the elevator doors closed the last thing she heard was, "I wouldn't want you to have any regrets."

It took her almost fifteen minutes to find him, but when she saw Hosea, sitting at the cafeteria table, with his eyes staring into a cup of coffee, she knew something was wrong.

She slid onto the bench next to him. "Hey, babe."

He looked up with glassy eyes.

She had to remind herself that she'd just seen Reverend Bush—and he was alive. But the way Hosea looked still made her heart strike hard against her chest. "What's wrong?"

"They've got to operate," he said softly.

"For what?"

"Doctor Lewis said that Pops has been intubated for two weeks, and they don't like to keep people with a tube down their throat for that long, so"—he took a deep breath—"now they have to put in a tracheostomy tube."

"What's that?"

She could see his thoughts as his face contorted. "They're going to cut a hole in his throat and then put a tube in to go to the trachea."

The image of that made her want to run to the restroom. But she pushed the picture in her mind aside and lifted Hosea's hand to her mouth. She kissed his fingers before she said, "That doesn't sound too bad."

For the first time, he looked directly at her. Shook his head and smiled a little. "You're not a good liar."

"What I should have said was, I'm sure the doctors know what they're doing. Some of the best in the country are here."

He nodded and glanced at his watch. "Doctor Lewis said that she'd have the papers for me to sign. They should be ready."

He stood. "But I want to go to Pops's room and pray first." Taking Jasmine's hand, he pulled her up.

All right, she thought as they walked shoulder to shoulder through the halls. This was not what she'd expected today, but she had no doubt that Reverend Bush would make it through fine. They just had to do what they always did—they had to get back to that room and pray.

TWELVE

THE TALL WHITE FELT HAT was trimmed with lace and pearls and felt a bit heavy, but since it perfectly matched the two-piece form-fitting suit with bell sleeves, Jasmine wasn't about to take it off. Hats had never been her thing. Neither were calf-length skirts. But she was a first lady now.

Holding on to Brother Hill's arm as she stepped through the door from the back offices, she glided into the sanctuary as if she were royalty. She tugged a bit at the waist of the skirt, deciding it needed to be a tad shorter to better display two of her best assets.

The suit was dazzling—a bright white silk that almost glowed in the sunlight. It was a bit thin for the thirty-something February temperature, but Jasmine didn't care. She'd ignored the personal shopper at Saks who told her, "This is a fabulous summer suit."

Fabulous was her focus. This was a spectacular outfit for her debut.

Jasmine pretended that she didn't notice Brother Hill's scowl as he led her to her seat. She wanted to tell him to straighten up and get right, but she only smiled. No one would know that she couldn't stand him as much as he couldn't stand her. Her parishioners would see only class and grace and elegance when they looked at her.

It had been Hosea's idea that his godfather escort her into the sanctuary. She'd wanted to walk out with her husband, but he'd told her that was inappropriate. At first, she wasn't happy. If she came out too early, would there be enough people to see her entrance?

But it had worked out fine; the sanctuary was already full, and she could feel the heat of the stares as she stood in her place—the first pew, the first seat, the seat of honor.

The praise team was rocking "Glory, Hallelujah!" when Hosea ambled in slowly, with Pastor Wyatt following. It was Pastor Wyatt who looked at her and smiled, as if he hadn't threatened her yesterday.

But Jasmine's thoughts were not on that man. Instead, she was staring at Hosea—wearing the long burgundy robe that she'd seen his father wear only on special occasions, like funerals.

While the singing continued, Hosea knelt in front of the chair where his father always sat.

A lump crawled up her throat as she watched her husband pray.

I should have spent more time with him this morning.

But the hours before church had been hectic—it took a lot to prepare for her debut. And it wasn't just about her—there was Jacqueline, too. She'd had to oversee every detail of her daughter's dressing—from her white patent-leather Mary Janes to the white faux-fur hat. There had been little time for Hosea.

Through the recognition of visitors and announcements, Jasmine kept her focus on her husband. But his eyes stayed lowered, as if he was still in prayer. So from where she sat, she joined him—and prayed to God to give her husband strength and wisdom, the two things he always asked for whenever they prayed together.

Then the moment came. Hosea stood; Jasmine inhaled a deep breath and didn't let it go.

"It is with an incredible mixture of joy and pain that I stand here today." His voice was low, but strong. "The joy is that I get to speak about the love I have for my heavenly Father; the pain is that my earthly father still sleeps in a coma, in a battle for his life. And I have to admit, church family, there is more than a bit of fear inside my heart."

When he paused, someone yelled out, "Take your time, baby."

Jasmine recognized Sister Pearline's voice.

"But fear doesn't come from God, so I'm able to walk through it and do what He asks, no matter what."

"That's right," many shouted.

"I am able to be obedient," Hosea said, "and that is what I want to talk about today, saints. Obedience. I want to talk about the audacity to obey."

Strong "Amens" rang through the church, and Jasmine finally exhaled.

He continued, "I am here today because I have the audacity to obey. But I am not the first, nor am I alone. This book," he held up his Bible, "is chock-full of people who dared to believe God and obey. Take a look at Noah. He had the audacity to build a boat on dry land. It made no sense; the earth had never seen rain. But he had audacity."

"Preach!" a voice called out.

"And then there was Abraham," Hosea said, his volume rising.

He dabbed at his forehead with his handkerchief, and Jasmine shifted in her seat. He was heating up, and the thought took her back to their home, to their bed. She loved to see him sweat.

"Now you know Abraham had audacity." Hosea waved his handkerchief in the air. "God told him to take his son up for a sacrifice. And do you know what he did?"

In unison, many shouted, "He obeyed."

"That's right." Hosea stomped one foot. "He took Isaac straight up the mountaintop. He didn't have a Plan B. All he had was Plan G—God's plan. And do you know what else he had?"

"Audacity," the parishioners shouted.

It was hard for Jasmine to hear any more of Hosea's words. All she could do was take deep breaths as his skin began to shine. All she could think about was last Wednesday when his skin had glistened that way—as they lay together in the Arlington Hotel.

She crossed her legs, tried to hold back the stirring she felt inside. Tried to focus on his words and not think about what his lips could do.

He said, "And dare I talk about the prophet after whom I am named. Let's talk about Hosea. Y'all know what God told him."

Jasmine's between-the-sheets thoughts stopped right there. If there was any part of the Bible she knew, it was the Book of Hosea.

He said, "God told the prophet Hosea to go marry that ho. Go marry Gomer."

The congregation roared with laughter.

From across the aisle, Mrs. Whittingham took a quick glance at Jasmine before she yelled out, "That's right!"

Jasmine sat straight up and frowned.

He said, "Now you know everybody in Hosea's town was dissin' him. Asking what kind of fool was he?"

More laughter rolled through the church, but not a bit of it came from Jasmine.

Hosea kept it up. "You know they were tellin' him to get rid of that no-good woman."

"That's right!" Brother Hill yelled out.

Jasmine sat stiff, arms folded, lips pressed together.

"I'm telling you, they probably came up with new names for dumb just for my man Hosea."

People were buckled over with laughter.

Okay, Hosea. We get it! She shot a look at her husband that was meant to burn.

"Now, y'all know that story has nothing to do with me." For the first time, he glanced at Jasmine and sent her a smile. But she didn't smile back.

As the laughter simmered to chuckles, he continued, "My point is, even when people were telling him not to do it, Hosea had the audacity to obey God. And that is why I'm here. It was my father's wish that I stand in his place if anything were ever to happen."

The sanctuary was quiet now.

He said, "I have no doubt that my father's desires were not personal."

This time, it was Pastor Wyatt who twisted.

"If my father wanted me here, it was because he had a directive from God. My father obeyed. And like my father, I am here because I, too, have the audacity to do what doesn't make sense.

"So saints, this word today is to assure you that City of Lights will continue. My prayer and my expectation is that my father will recover soon."

"Amen," some shouted.

"Hallelujah," came from many others.

The congregation stood, waving their hands and their Bibles. Saying their own prayers for Reverend Bush. Sending up their own praises to God.

Long minutes passed before the church settled so that Hosea could continue.

"In closing, you should know that I am committed to anything that God, my heavenly father, and Samuel Bush, my earthly father wants. I will stay here until my father comes back, and trust me, he will be back. I have the audacity to believe and the audacity to obey."

They were standing again as Hosea moved back to his chair. He wiped his forehead with the handkerchief and nodded, silently thanking the still-standing, still-praying, still-praising congregation. Finally, he glanced at Jasmine.

She stood, too. Clapping like the others. When their eyes met, with two fingers he tapped the spot on his chest that covered his heart, then blew her a kiss. And in that instant, Jasmine melted. She tossed aside the plans she had to tell him that she wasn't pleased with his sermon.

Because in that instant, all was forgiven, and all she felt was his love.

THIRTEEN

THIS WAS IT. ANOTHER MOMENT. Jasmine pressed her shoulders back, held her head as high as she could underneath the weight of her hat, and then tried not to shift too much from one leg to the other. She had to go to the bathroom bad, but she wasn't about to miss one minute of standing by her husband's side.

She took hold of Hosea's hand, but not a second passed before he let her loose to greet the first parishioner.

"Hosea! Oh, excuse me, I mean 'Pastor.'" Sister Pearline wobbled toward them, balancing her eighty-year-old legs on a cane that looked to be as old as she was. "I've watched you since you were a little boy, but I'm telling you, that sermon was almost as good as any your father ever gave; God bless that man."

"Thank you, Sister Pearline, but I have a long way to go before I'm anywhere near my dad."

The woman turned to Jasmine. "How're you, baby?"

She smiled, but as Jasmine leaned in for a hug, she heard a voice that made her stand straight up.

"I think you're pretty close to your dad right now." Those words came from another woman, a much younger woman, somewhere in her thirties, around Hosea's age.

Jasmine's smile turned upside down as her eyes rolled down,

then back up the woman's slender frame. She'd seen her before, with her fiery red hair weave that was twisted in long curls down her back. Jasmine had never cared for the way the woman always waltzed down the center aisle a half hour after church started, pushing her way to the front, in too-short, bright-colored skirts and too-tight, cleavage-raising tops, as if she was the center of the world. She even suspected that this woman had her eyes on Reverend Bush—as if he would ever be interested in a hoochie like her.

But if Jasmine wasn't feeling her before, she definitely didn't like her now. Especially not the way she stuck the deep V of her purple skin-tight sweater underneath Hosea's nose.

"I think you're just like your dad," the red-haired girl said, taking Hosea's hand. "Only you're younger. And better."

Jasmine's frown deepened. Why did this woman's chest shimmy with every word she spoke?

Hosea smiled. "How are you, Nikki?"

"Ah, you remembered."

"How could I forget?"

Forget what? Jasmine pushed her hand in between her husband's and Nikki's. "I'm *Mrs.* Bush," she said.

This time it was the woman who looked Jasmine up and down and when, after her perusal, she grinned, Jasmine wanted to ask her what was so funny.

"I know who you are," Nikki said, and then looked back to Hosea. "That was a great sermon. Especially the part about the prophet, Hosea, and his whore."

Oh, no she didn't.

But before Jasmine could move to take off her hat and her earrings, the next woman stepped up.

After another, then another, and yet another woman pressed her hands against his hands and her lips against his face, Jasmine turned to get a look of when all of this would end. But the reception line—filled with women—stretched long. Women of all sizes, every shape. Some standing next to a man. Most standing alone. Twenty-somethings, thirty-somethings, forty-, fifty-, even sixty- and seventy-somethings. Every one of them waiting to spend personal moments with her husband.

Jasmine had never paid any kind of attention to the women in the church. Sure, she noticed their demure smiles and cutesy waves as she and Hosea walked across the parking lot on Sundays. But not one woman had ever stepped to him the way they were doing today. As if wearing that burgundy robe had turned him into a lure for all of these female leeches.

"I wanted to pay my respects, Pastor." The next woman in line leaned in and pretended to aim for Hosea's cheek. "Oops," the woman giggled when her lips made contact with his.

Flashback!

Jasmine's fingers curled into a fist. But before she could take a swing, another female was in his face.

"You have certainly grown up." This time it was a gray-haired woman smiling and stroking his hand.

When the woman, who had to be almost twice his age, stood as if she planned on having a long conversation, Jasmine said, "Uh, honey. There're other people waiting."

The woman's blue-shadowed eyes rolled, and she stayed as if she didn't plan to move. But this time, Jasmine didn't have to do a thing. The next woman in line pushed the older woman out of the way.

"Oh, Pastor!"

And Jasmine thought, *What a ridiculous hat!* There were so many feathers on the golden apparatus the woman wore that Jasmine was sure the hat and the woman would take flight at any moment.

The feather-wearing woman said, "I was hoping, Pastor, that you could take some time . . . and pray with me." She lowered her eyes and jiggled her cleavage as if it was her chest that needed prayer. "I could come by your office tomorrow—"

"Why don't you call Sister Whittingham," Hosea said. "We'll have the Intercessory Prayer team lift you up every day this week."

"Well, actually, what I need is personal—"

Before she could finish, Jasmine said, "Next," and, with her hip, shoved the woman out of the way.

It seemed as if an hour passed before all of the kissing and stroking and jiggling was over. And when there was no one left standing, Jasmine waited until Brother Hill escorted Hosea to his office before she dashed into the restroom.

Inside the stall, she breathed with relief and rested on the seat for a moment before she heard the door swing open.

"Did you see that stupid hat?"

The response, "I couldn't believe it. Country! That woman ain't nothin' but country."

"Not just country, girl, a country-bama for real."

When they laughed, Jasmine wanted to join them. She knew who they were talking about: that woman in that ridiculous feathered contraption.

"And wearing white in *February.* How country is that?"

More laughter, and Jasmine slowly rose from the seat.

The chatter continued. "She ain't never had no class. Was nothing but a Jezebel when Pastor met her."

"And not a thing has changed."

"I will never understand why he married her, but why did he stay married after he found out about the baby?"

"It don't make no sense. Especially when he has so many women to choose from right here in the church. Including me!"

"Girl, I saw you pushing up on Pastor. But you better recognize—he's married."

"And how long do you think that's going to last?"

"I'd say forever," Jasmine spoke through the closed door, and imagined their shocked looks. She waited a couple of beats, letting them stew, before she showed her face.

Their eyes were opened as wide as their mouths as she moved toward the women—her eyes on the one in the yellow-feathered device. The one who had asked for special prayer and was about to need it for real.

The two stood frozen until Jasmine was right in front of them. And then, they parted like the Red Sea, giving Jasmine a clear path to the sink.

Not a word was spoken as Jasmine turned on the water, and while she washed, she stared down the women through the mirror. Still they stood, still as stone.

When Jasmine reached for a hand towel, the woman in the yellow hat found enough nerve to stutter, "Ah . . . M-mrs. Bush . . ."

Drying her hands, Jasmine said, "You don't have to apologize."

The one no taller than a third-grader smiled as if she'd been forgiven. "We didn't mean nothin', Mrs. Bush. We were playin'. Just girls talkin'. You know?"

"Oh, I know that." Jasmine dried her hands. "You had to be playin', 'cause I know there's no one crazy enough in this church to mess with me."

Only Jasmine laughed.

"You're right, Mrs. Bush," the short one said.

Jasmine held up her hand. "Don't call me that. My *husband* is the senior pastor; you should be addressing me as 'First Lady.' "

The women looked at each other before they said, "Okay."

Jasmine took two steps toward the door, then turned back. "Change that. Forget about First Lady. Call me Lady . . . Lady Jasmine."

She didn't think it was possible for their mouths to open wider than before—but she was wrong. Jasmine spun around and left them standing in the bathroom.

In the hallway, she lifted the hat from her head. She sighed with a bit of embarrassment, but more with relief—that thing was giving her a headache. It was clear—hats weren't going to be her thing.

Tucking the almost ten-pound apparatus underneath her arm, she marched proudly to her husband's office.

Jasmine held Jacqueline's hand as they walked down the long hallway of the left wing of City of Lights, which housed the children's church. As Jacqueline tottered beside her, Jasmine couldn't stop thinking about the women in the bathroom. She'd never been one to care much about what others thought, but somehow those words hurt. Because it wasn't just about her anymore. Everything she said, wore, or did reflected on Hosea. She couldn't make any mistakes.

White in February?

Those women had laughed, as if someone wearing white in February was the dumbest thing they'd ever seen. What was wrong with that? In L.A., everyone wore white any time they wanted. But this was New York, and maybe she needed help. Maybe she needed a fashion coordinator who could turn her into a true fashionista. She'd get working on that tomorrow.

She looked down at Jacqueline moving merrily beside her, still wearing her fur hat. When she found her fashion consultant, Jacqueline would be her client, too.

The moment she and Jacqueline stepped from the building, her daughter tore away from her and broke into a toddler run.

"Daddy!" she exclaimed, already spotting her father.

Jasmine wanted to tell her daughter to be careful, but all of her attention was on their SUV. And the long, lean frame of the woman perched on the hood like she was posing for an ad. It took only seconds for Jasmine to measure her—the expensive knit suit, the smartly spiked hair, the flawlessly applied makeup. The woman slid off their car when Hosea lifted Jacqueline into his arms.

He kissed Jacqueline's cheek and then did the same to Jasmine. "Darlin', I want you to meet an old friend."

Jasmine sighed. *Another one?* All of her husband's too many old female friends were making her sick. And she planned to tell him that the moment they were alone.

The woman extended her hand and her smile. "I'm Roxie Willis." Jasmine still wasn't feeling her until she added, "It's so nice to meet you, First Lady."

Now Jasmine returned her smile.

When Roxie said, "You must be Jacquie," and then squeezed her daughter's hand, Jacqueline giggled.

Jasmine relaxed, a little. Her daughter was the best barometer, and if she liked Roxie, then the woman had to be okay.

"Reverend Bush has told me so much about the two of you . . . well, the three of you," she said to Jasmine. "I haven't seen Hosea in years, but I wanted to drop by this morning to support both of you. I'm so sorry to hear about your father-in-law."

It was the first time someone offered condolences straight to her, and Jasmine warmed to this woman more. Roxie understood her place as Hosea's wife.

"Thank you," Jasmine said, putting as much grief into her voice as she could. "We're all still prayerful."

Roxie nodded.

Jasmine said, "You're not a member here?"

"No, I'm at First Faith Chapel. But who knows, I might start coming here now."

It was the way she looked at Hosea that tore away every single one of those good feelings Jasmine had for her.

"Listen," Roxie began as she searched through her purse, "I'm going to let you guys get going, but First Lady, let me give you my card."

Jasmine took a quick glance at the simple linen card embossed with Roxie's name and number.

Roxie said, "I don't have much to do these days, and I know you're going to need some help. I might make a good armor bearer."

"Roxie," Hosea began with cheer in his voice, "I can't believe you'd offer to do that. That would be great."

"Yeah," Jasmine added, even though she had no idea what an armor bearer was.

"So give me a call," Roxie said to Jasmine. "We can do lunch and talk about it." Then, before she stepped away, she rested her hand on Hosea's arm and winked. "I'll catch up with you later."

If Hosea hadn't been standing there, she would have torn Roxie's card into a dozen pieces right in front of her face.

What was with these women? They had all but ruined her debut.

Roxie strutted away, and even Jasmine had to take notice how the knit of her dress hugged her ample behind. She turned to Hosea, and when she saw that his eyes were where hers had been, she snatched Jacqueline from his arms.

"Hey," he said, coming out of his trance, "I was gonna strap her in."

"I'll do it. You seem busy."

"Nah, nah, I wasn't busy," he said, before he took a final glance Roxie's way. He held the door open for Jasmine to slip into the car and ignored her when she rolled her eyes.

Turning on the ignition, he asked, "Wasn't that nice of Roxie?"

"Who is she, Hosea?"

A small sigh and a slight nod, as if he understood her jealousy. As if he felt responsible for it. "She's an old friend, Jasmine," he said, his voice filled with patience.

"Seems like you have a lot of those."

"I do, but," he reached for her hand, "I have only one wife. There's only one woman I love."

She wanted to slap him away, but how could she after that? So she squeezed his hand, letting him know that it was all forgiven—for now.

"Anyway," he said as he backed the SUV out of the parking space, "Roxie is one woman you'd never have to worry about. She's not hardly interested in me. She has quite a life."

"What life? She said she didn't have much to do."

"Well, she may not have a nine-to-five, but believe me, her hands are full. Her husband passed away while we were in L.A.—Reverend Willis, remember him? He was one of Pops's mentors."

"Oh, yeah. She was married to *him*?"

Hosea nodded. "She was his third wife and thirty years younger. But Roxie seems to be doing all right. I guess it helps that Reverend Willis left her quite a wealthy woman."

Jasmine's eyebrows rose at the mention of money. "How wealthy?"

He shrugged. "I don't know. The rumors say several million."

"Wow!"

"But it hasn't been all good. His grown children have been fighting her for the money. So I guess she's looking for something to do to get away from the church, his seven children, and the two ex-wives for a little while. I think it would be great if you worked with her."

"She wants to be an armor bearer," Jasmine said, still not having a clue.

"Like your right-hand person. An assistant. Like Brother Hill is for Pops. She'd help you out, teach you a couple of things about the church, look out for you as you wade through all of this stuff."

She nodded, but didn't say a word. Her husband may have thought it was a good idea, but she knew it wasn't. There was something about that woman—her smile was too wide, her hands were too warm, she was too gracious. And she was definitely too attractive to be trusted.

"Make sure you call her," he said.

"I will," she lied.

A million years would pass before she did that. She didn't want the woman as her friend or her armor bearer. All she wanted was for Roxie to have the good sense to stay far, far away from her husband.

Because she didn't feel like having any more flashbacks.

FOURTEEN

In her lifetime, Jasmine had intercepted plenty of telephone calls. But today was an accident—good fortune, really. She'd been passing by Mrs. Whittingham's desk when the telephone rang. She picked it up. And now she was talking to Bishop Henry Bailey, the most renowned pastor in the city.

Jasmine leaned back in the overstuffed chair on wheels that Mrs. Whittingham thought was her throne.

"So what do you think, Bishop Bailey? I would love to stand in for my husband."

In the pause that followed, Jasmine recalled how this conversation started. How she introduced herself to the bishop as Hosea's wife. How the bishop had been thrilled to meet her. How he'd asked about Reverend Bush and then went on to explain the reason for his call—to invite Hosea to attend the annual Mayors and Ministers luncheon, which was limited to neither mayors nor ministers, but included the rich and powerful in the tristate area. Jasmine had a been-there-done-that attitude about the rich, but she rarely had the chance to mingle with the powerful. So after she told Bishop Bailey that she doubted if Hosea would want to leave his father's side on Saturday, she'd offered herself instead.

"Well, you know what, Mrs. Bush," Bishop Bailey began after his long pause, "that might not be such a bad idea. I know there will be many who will be glad to see you . . ."

Jasmine's grin widened.

He finished, "Because they'll want to know what's going on with Reverend Bush."

Okay, so this wasn't really about her.

"Maybe I'll have you get up and say a few words. Yeah!" The bishop warmed to the idea. "I'll make sure you're on the program."

Jasmine jotted down the details and ended the call with more pleasantries, more thank-yous, more promises to keep the bishop posted on any change in the reverend's condition between now and the luncheon on Saturday.

With a smile, Jasmine hung up, leaned back in the chair, and imagined herself in front of the five hundred or so attendees of the two-hundred-dollar-a-plate mixer. But as she settled into the thought of standing on that stage, she heard the cackle, "What are you doing?"

Startled, Jasmine toppled, her feet left the floor, and the chair rolled back, banging into the wall. "Ouch!" she yelled as she hit her head.

But the pain on Jasmine's face did nothing for Mrs. Whittingham. She stood with her hands on her wide hips and flames in her eyes. "What are you doing at *my* desk?" she asked, her voice sounding like there was a man rising up inside of her.

Still rubbing her head, Jasmine stood. "The phone was ringing and—"

"Stay away from my area," she growled, as she pushed Jasmine aside to inspect the chair for damage.

Jasmine rolled her eyes. The woman didn't even care that she might have a concussion. She spun around and marched toward her office, not giving another thought to Mrs. Whittingham. And even though her head still throbbed, Jasmine was past her pain. Her focus was entirely on the luncheon. And who she would meet. And what she would say. And how she would dress.

Yesterday had been her debut at church, but Saturday would be her unveiling to the most important people in New York, New Jersey, and Connecticut.

Being the first lady was paying off already.

FIFTEEN

No one from the media had the courtesy to call her back!

Not the *New York Post,* not the *Daily News,* not the *New York Times.* She'd placed a call to the *Wall Street Journal* and the local TV and radio stations, and even sent a press package to *Oprah*! But after two weeks and a dozen messages, not one journalist (or Oprah) seemed interested in meeting the fabulous new first lady.

That's why Jasmine decided to take destiny into her own hands—and go to the people who would listen. She prepared a press package and article for *Gospel Today* and *Christian News.* Surely, sophisticated church folks would want to read about the influence first ladies had on American culture.

She was so into writing her article that she didn't hear the first knock on her door. Nor the second. It wasn't until she heard the raspy cough that she looked up.

Mrs. Whittingham stood in the doorway, her face masked in a deep scowl adding dozens of creases to her already-wrinkled forehead.

Every time they'd passed each other since yesterday, Mrs. Whittingham had glared at her. As if that was Jasmine's punishment for being at the woman's desk. As if she even cared.

Mrs. Whittingham's lips hardly moved when she spoke. "Hosea's finishing up that conference call with the doctors, and he wants you to join him."

"On the call?"

Mrs. Whittingham shook her head, and her face bunched into an even deeper frown as if the next words pained her. "He wants you to join him for a meeting with Jerome Viceroy."

The woman turned away, but Jasmine called her back. "I have something for you." She grabbed the papers she'd typed earlier. "Here's the church bulletin for Sunday."

Now there were hundreds of lines in Mrs. Whittingham's forehead. "What are you talking about? I do the bulletin."

"I wanted to bring the bulletin into the twenty-first century. So I'll be working on it from now on."

Mrs. Whittingham poked out her lips as she read through the pages. And when her eyes stopped moving and her eyebrows rose, Jasmine knew exactly what part she was reading.

She said, "You want *this* to go inside the bulletin?"

Jasmine crossed her arms. "Yeah!" she said with a what-about-it attitude.

Mrs. Whittingham read the words out loud: "Mrs. Jasmine Larson Bush, the first lady of City of Lights at Riverside Church, will now be referred to as Lady Jasmine." She shook her head, as if she thought those words had been written by a fool. "You want this to go into the church bulletin?" she repeated.

Saying nothing, Jasmine stared her down until Mrs. Whittingham walked away.

Alone, Jasmine sighed, the weight of working with that woman was becoming too much. It was always so difficult to find good people. But there was not a thing she could do about Mrs. Whittingham. She was a fixture in this church—like the old pipe organ that still sat in the sanctuary, even though it hadn't been played in a year's worth of Sundays.

Jasmine straightened the silver frame of the picture of

Hosea, Jacqueline, and her taken last Christmas. She'd brought the photo in to put atop her desk this morning, hoping to make Mae Frances's office feel a bit more like her own. She didn't plan to move too many things around, though, because her friend had reminded her that this space was hers.

"Remember," Mae Frances had begun brusquely when Jasmine told her this morning that she was moving in, "that office belongs to me, and when the good reverend and I get back there, we have a lot of work to do."

Stepping away from the desk, she took a quick glance around. This space was much smaller than the one she had at Rio. And the cherrywood furniture was far from the modern glass-and-chrome pieces that she was used to.

But this room—with its one shelved wall stuffed with Bibles and Christian commentaries, with its tiny, single window that faced the parking lot, with its industrial gray carpet—felt so much like home. Maybe it was because here, she was closer to Hosea. Or maybe it was because here, she was closer to God. Whatever . . . being here made her happy.

She grabbed a pad before she marched down the hall. Hosea was still on the phone, but he motioned for her to come in; it wasn't until she stepped inside that she noticed Jerome Viceroy already sitting on the sofa.

He stood up, dressed, as always, in one of his trademark suits. Today it was brown with gold stripes. He licked his lips. "How are you, First Lady?"

She smiled when he called her that. Jerome Viceroy had never been a man whom she liked much—he seemed too smooth (in a throwback-to-the-eighties kind of way). But if he started calling her Lady Jasmine, then the two would become great friends.

A moment later, Hosea joined them.

"Sorry to keep you waiting." He shook Jerome's hand, then motioned for Jasmine to sit next to him.

They'd barely sat when Jerome said, "I wanted to tell you, Pastor, that was some sermon you gave Sunday."

"Thank you."

"Hallelujah, thank you, Jesus," Jerome said. "After listening to you, I knew I'd done the right thing. It's a new day at City of Lights."

On one accord, Hosea and Jasmine frowned.

Jerome continued, "Yes, Jesus. Giving my approval in the board meeting so that you could become the senior pastor, that was the right thing to do, Amen!"

Jasmine wondered why her husband didn't remind the good councilman that his approval had not been needed.

But Hosea just sat. And smiled. And waited.

"Honestly"—Jerome leaned forward and lowered his voice—"I was glad to hear about your father's letter." He held his hand in the air as if he was about to testify. "Because, frankly, Wyatt . . ." He bowed his head like he was about to pray. "I don't know about that man and his wife. You know, I heard their marriage is one of convenience and—"

Jasmine moved to the edge of her seat, but before Jerome could add another word, Hosea stopped him. "Now, Brother Viceroy, we don't need that kind of talk."

With eyes wide with innocence, he said, "Pastor, this isn't gossip—glory to God. But sometimes it's important to know what's being said in the streets."

"If my father listened to the streets, you wouldn't be here."

Jasmine moved to give Hosea a high five, but then she remembered where she was and sat back in her chair.

The smile that had been on the edge of Jerome's lips faded. "*Everything* that's *ever* been said about me . . . it's lies, all lies, in the name of Jesus."

Jasmine wanted to move her chair several feet away before lightning struck them all. Even she never told a lie in the name of Jesus!

And anyway, Jerome Viceroy needed to quit. The eight-term city councilman moved from one political scandal to another. Extortion. Tax evasion. Money laundering. He'd been charged with all of that and more.

The thing was, Jerome Viceroy had earned his nickname as the Teflon Man. Not one charge had ever held. And after every dismissal, Jerome had been able to stand on the court steps, in front of television cameras, and declare that, "Once again, the government's vast conspiracy to bring down another God-fearing black man has failed! Hallelujah!"

But game recognized game, and even though Jasmine and Jerome played different sports, Jasmine knew this man was a liar and a cheat. She suspected the people of his district knew what Jerome was, too. But that didn't stop them from voting for him one election after another.

Jerome would tell anyone who would listen, "I got Harlem on lock!" And those words were true, because many of his constituents understood that sometimes it took someone who was smooth, someone with game, someone who could make moves to bring changes they needed in their neighborhoods.

"Every single thing that has ever been said about me is a lie," Jerome repeated, as if saying it twice would make it true.

"Well, that's why my father never removed you from the board, Jerome. Nothing's ever been proven. And in this country and this church, you're innocent until someone can prove otherwise."

"No one will *ever* be able to prove otherwise, Pastor. I'm a man of God, thank you, Jesus. I walk the straight and narrow. I—"

"Jerome," Hosea looked at his watch, "I'd like to get to the hospital before dark."

Jasmine giggled—it wasn't even noon.

"So . . ." Hosea motioned for the councilman to get on with his business.

"Oh, yes, well." Jerome pulled a folder from the Louis Vuitton messenger bag he carried. "I'm sure you've heard all about this." He handed Hosea a thick binder. Jasmine scooted her chair closer to her husband's.

Hosea read the cover, "The Harlem Redevelopment Project. Yes, everyone knows what's going on up here."

Jerome frowned a little. "So your father talked to you about this?"

"Not extensively."

"Thank you, Jesus!" Jerome's smile was back, as if he was relieved.

Thank you, Jesus? Jasmine frowned.

Hosea continued, "The only thing my father told me was that he wasn't interested."

Jerome shook his head so hard that Jasmine was sure his 1980s jheri curls were going to fall straight out of his hair. "No, that's not true. We were supposed to get together today to discuss this some more. Your father would have never said no to me, because a no to me is a no to Harlem. And your father would never say no to Harlem. Look at the plans," he said, motioning toward the book Hosea held.

As Hosea flipped through the pages, Jerome kept talking. "Let me get to the bottom line—the developers want this church. City of Lights is right in the middle of the developers' plans. So here's the thing." He grinned. "What they're willing to pay for City of Lights," he raised one hand with his forefinger and pinky in the air like he was throwing a gang sign, "it's stupid."

Jasmine raised her eyebrows. "How much are they talking?"

This time he looked at her. Licked his lips. Said, "They're not talking to *you* about anything." With his chin, he motioned to Hosea. "This is business between men, praise the Lord."

"You know what—" she began.

"Jerome," Hosea stopped Jasmine's words as he pulled her

back down into her seat, "my wife is going to be involved in every aspect of this church's business. You need to recognize that."

Jerome leaned back on the sofa, crossed his legs. "I didn't mean any disrespect. It's just that, you know, your father and I always handled our business."

"Like you said, it's a new day." Hosea paused. "But, it doesn't really matter how much they're offering, because I'm not interested."

"What if I told you they'd pay," Jerome paused, as if he were waiting for a drum roll, "eight million dollars!" He sat back and spread his lips into a grin so wide, every single one of his thirty-two teeth shined.

"That's a lot of money." Jasmine shifted in her seat. What would a check like that mean? Would it all go to the church, or would Hosea get a million or two or three of it as the pastor?"

"And I'm still not interested," Hosea said.

Jerome moved to the edge of the sofa. "Okay, okay, that's what they were talking. But I told them that they were going to have to come correct. So I know that they will go as high as"—he held up his hands—"and this is the final offer . . . twelve point two million!"

Jasmine's mouth was open wide, but Hosea said, "And it's still a no."

"How can you say that?" It was Jerome who asked the question, but that was exactly what Jasmine was thinking.

"Look, let me get to *my* bottom line," Hosea said. "I'm not going to make this kind of decision for my father."

Jerome sat back, stared for a moment. "Can I be honest here?" He paused, licked his lips, glanced from Hosea to Jasmine, then back to Hosea. "We realize this church is important to your family. And we realize that it's a difficult decision for you to make without your father. So what we're, I mean, they—the developers—are willing to do is make it easier for you."

Jasmine grinned. She knew what Jerome was talking about. Game *always* recognized game.

Jerome said, "Cash . . . lots of it . . . can somehow . . . find its way . . . to you. All off the record, of course."

Hosea and Jasmine spoke together.

"How much cash?" she asked.

"My answer is still no," he said.

Jerome heard Jasmine. "What do you need? Whatever, we can make this happen."

Before Jasmine could open her mouth, Hosea said, "Not a thing will be happening here." He stood up, but Jasmine stayed in place. As if she wanted to hear more from Jerome. It wasn't until Hosea stared her down that she jumped up.

But Jerome still sat, refusing to be dismissed. "Seems like we're at a bit of an impasse."

"No, we're not," Hosea said matter-of-factly. "Whatever has to happen in Harlem is fine with me. But City of Lights will not be part of this. At least not while my father is . . . in the hospital."

Jerome's teeth were still shining, but his tone was tight. "We don't have time to wait. We need to make this happen now."

Shaking his head, Hosea said, "Not going to happen on my watch."

"Then maybe your watch needs to come to an end."

Silence. The men stared. Neither flinched. Until Jerome said, "You need to remember that I backed you at the board meeting."

"I appreciate that, but it was my father's decision."

"Things could change if, let's say, there was another board meeting. If we forced a vote, and with your father down, who knows if that letter will hold up."

"It's time to end this conversation." Now Hosea's voice was as tense as Jerome's.

More silence before Jerome stood. "This is not over." He

paused, as if those words were supposed to make a difference. When Hosea shrugged, Jerome grabbed his messenger bag and stomped toward the door. But before he stepped outside, he added, "I've done too much work, made too many promises for this to blow up."

Hosea just shook his head.

Jerome grasped the doorknob, glanced back over his shoulder, and stared at Jasmine—a look that made her shiver.

"You're going to regret this." His words were for Hosea, but his eyes were still on Jasmine. "I'm going to do what I have to do."

And then he was gone.

Hosea's chuckle was without humor. "Can you believe that guy?"

Jasmine shook her head but didn't say a word. Even when Hosea wrapped his arms around her, all Jasmine could do was remember the way Jerome had looked at her.

And she shivered again. Because true game always recognized true game.

SIXTEEN

Even though the duvet covered every part of her body, Jasmine shivered. Jerome's words had stayed with her for the rest of the day, followed her home, and were still with her now as Hosea slept in peace next to her.

You're going to regret this. I'm going to do what I have to do.

Jerome's threat was meant for Hosea, but he'd been looking straight at her—as if she was his real target.

With wide eyes, she glanced at the clock. It was because of Jerome that she lay awake now at three in the morning. But it was because of the flashes of her past that she trembled in the dark.

Since this afternoon, she felt as if Jerome's threat and her past were connected. But they couldn't be. He couldn't possibly know anything about those days. That time was so long ago . . .

Her life as a stripper.

It all began with a phone call back in '83.

From her father.

"Jas, honey, I'm so sorry, but there's nothing I can do."

She had sat on the stool inside her studio apartment with the telephone pinned to her ear. "But, Daddy," she cried, "how am I going to pay the rent? How am I going to pay for my tuition and my books?"

She imagined her father sitting at the small, round kitchen table in their Inglewood home, still in his robe, even though in better days he would have been at work by now. She could see him shaking his head, with tears in his eyes, so sorry for the fact that the savings he'd once had were now gone.

But his sorrow wasn't enough to get her through.

"I don't have it anymore," he said.

Was "it" the money that she needed to finish her senior year at UCLA? Or was "it" some kind of drive—because her father never seemed to have had that. She loved her father to pieces, but he'd always disappointed her as a dad. He wasn't anything like the fathers of her friends who attended the private school that she went to. Those men were doctors and lawyers and teachers. Her father, as hardworking as he was, was a longshoreman, and she was in the second grade when she learned she was supposed to be embarrassed by that. When the kids had laughed at him *and* her on Daddy Day. When they'd made fun of the man who'd shown up in his work clothes—including his plaid shirt and hard hat. Her seven-year-old classmates made it known then that she—and her family—weren't good enough. And that had been confirmed a year later, when she'd overheard a teacher calling her "one of the scholarship students." At the time, Jasmine wasn't sure what a scholarship student was, but the teacher's tone alone made her feel ashamed.

Her father spoke through those bad memories, "I'm going back to work in a few weeks, but with me working one job now, I don't know how I can do it all."

"Daddy . . ."

"I know I've let you down, sweetheart, but . . ."

He paused, so that she could say something like, "That's all right." But she'd been saying "That's all right" her whole life.

She'd told him it was okay when she was in the sixth grade

and she couldn't take the class trip to San Diego. She'd told him she was fine when he didn't have the money for her middle-school yearbook. And forget about the senior prom, or the senior trip, or her class ring.

"We just have enough for the basics and school," she'd grown up hearing. "Because your mother and I want to give you girls the best education possible—and that includes college. We want to make sure you have the kind of future we never had."

Well, the future was here. She had one more year, but her father was letting her down—once again.

Breaking through her lamentation, he said, "When I go back to work, I'll be putting in as many extra hours as I can. We'll get you through school—maybe not in one year, but you'll be able to finish. Your mother would—" He stopped.

Just saying "your mother," made them both sob. But as she cried for her mother, she thought about her father's words.

Maybe not in one year, but you'll be able to finish. How long did he expect her to wait?

"Daddy," she said through her tears, "maybe we can get a loan."

"Sweetheart, you know how I feel about that. And anyway, no one is going to give me any money. Even this house is tapped out because of . . ."

He didn't have to finish; she sobbed even more.

"You know what this means, Jas," her father began through his own cries.

What?

"I can't afford that apartment anymore."

What!

He said, "But I'll take the bus every day so that you can take my car." When she didn't say anything, he added, "Really, honey, this is going to be a good thing. Your sister and I need you. Serena's trying to be brave, but she's only fifteen and"—another sob—"it's going to be so hard without your mother."

Now he cried for real. And she did, too.

It took about a minute before he gathered himself enough to talk and she collected herself enough to listen.

"So you pick a time, and Serena and I will be right there to help you pack."

"Daddy, I'll call you later."

"Jasmine . . ."

She was still sniffing when she'd hung up. Her heart was aching for her mother; her head was hurting from her father. After all she'd been through, did he really want her to move back home? What would her friends say?

And what was worse, how was she supposed to leave Kenny alone, free to wander the whole campus without her? Kenny Larson was no longer the star running back of the UCLA football team, but the hussies still chased her boyfriend like he was about to sign a seven-figure contract in the NFL. Even though he'd been injured, Jasmine was sure Kenny was still going to be a star, and the witches who roamed the campus knew that, too. That's why the women were always hovering, waiting for the opening so that they could step to Kenny. That's why she had to stay close—to protect the investment that she'd had in Kenny since the eleventh grade. As far as she knew, Kenny had always been faithful. But her trust went only so far—her faith definitely didn't go ten miles south on the freeway. If she moved back home, Jasmine knew the temptation all around campus would be too much for Kenny to bear.

Her eyes wandered around her six-hundred-square-foot efficiency apartment. This was all that her parents had been able to afford when she'd moved in at the beginning of her sophomore year. Maybe if they hadn't stretched to pay this rent, she'd have the money to finish school. But she had to have this place—from the moment Kenny had pledged Omega Psi Phi and moved into an apartment with some of his frat brothers, she'd moved close to keep the hoochies away.

It had taken weeks of begging to convince her parents to spend some of the money they'd saved on this three-hundred-dollar-a-month studio. Her argument had nothing to do with Kenny. Instead, she played the danger card—telling them that by having her own place, she wouldn't have to drive all the way from Westwood to Inglewood, risking her life late at night to some carjacker. That image—along with the real ones her mother had seen on TV every night—had been enough. The Coxes had been willing to ante up whatever they had to in order to keep their daughter safe. And she'd convinced them that she'd be better off without roommates to distract her.

Jasmine did help out with work-study during the year and then her summer gigs. But even though she now had one of the coveted rising-senior internships at Sony, the two hundred and fifty dollars a week, which had seemed like so much yesterday, was nothing more than a pittance today. Without her father's help, her biweekly check (after taxes) would barely keep her housed and fed. The money from that eight-week internship (which was part of her financial aid package) would do nothing for the five thousand dollars she needed for tuition, rent, books, and looking cute for her senior year.

If only her mother hadn't gotten sick with Lou Gehrig's disease. If only their medical insurance had paid for all of the expenses. If only grief hadn't stricken her father and kept him out of work for months now. If only her father didn't owe five thousand dollars—exactly what she needed—in medical expenses.

Five thousand dollars. That was a lot of money to pay when the doctors were the ones who were responsible for her mother not being here anymore.

Jasmine closed her eyes, hardly able to stand the thought of living the rest of her life without the only person who truly understood her. With her mother gone, all she had was school . . . and Kenny. The doctors should be paying her for what they'd taken away.

Jasmine's eyes widened. *That's it!*

The hospital should pay them. And they would, if her father sued. He should. After all, the doctors hadn't saved her mother's life. It was probably because of them that she died. Her father could have this tied up in court for years. She could graduate—Serena could graduate—by the time this got settled.

Jasmine looked at the clock—she was supposed to be at Sony at ten, but handling this was much more important.

She coughed. Took a deep breath and then coughed again. Smiled. Yeah, she could pull it off. She'd call in sick from her parents' house.

As Jasmine locked the door to her apartment, her heart was filled with hope. Once she convinced her father to sue, he could take the money he planned to pay the hospital and he could pay her tuition. And who knew what was going to happen—they could actually win the lawsuit. The hospital could pay them a million dollars. Or maybe even ten million or one hundred million!

With her hands stuffed inside the pockets of her jeans, and her Walkman plugged into her ears, she walked as fast as she could to the bus stop. She couldn't wait to get home to talk to her father and let him know that everything was going to be all right . . .

Jasmine rolled over and glanced at the clock; it was almost four now, and she wasn't any closer to sleep. She couldn't stop remembering how it began, so innocently, all those years ago.

She was just a girl, trying to stay in school.

The thing was, she *had* graduated from UCLA. On time. Mother's Day weekend in 1984. She'd marched right into the coliseum with Kenny and the thousands of others Bruin graduates. Because she had done what she had to do.

She closed her eyes, knowing she had to find a way to press away those memories. Jerome Viceroy knew nothing about her past. His threat was just a threat—a tactic to scare Hosea, not her. She wasn't going to expend any more energy thinking about days that had nothing to do with who she was now.

She would have no more thoughts about the past—she would keep her eyes and her mind on what her life was all about. And that was her future.

But an hour later, when her eyes were still wide open, Jasmine knew that she hadn't told herself the truth.

SEVENTEEN

THIS TIME, JASMINE LISTENED TO the saleswoman at Saks. When she strolled into the grand ballroom in the Trump International Hotel Towers, she wanted to call the woman right then and hire her away from the department store.

Heads turned when she sauntered inside wearing the form-fitting twelve-hundred-dollar scarlet-collared money-green two-piece. She paused just inside the door, sucked in her stomach, raised her chin, and posed as if she were waiting for photographers.

It was the smiles on the men's faces that let her know she'd nailed it. Some gawked as if she were mesmerizing. Others stared—she was scintillating. Many gaped—she was simply gorgeous.

And the way the women tossed daggers at her told her that the men were right—she was all of the above.

"Jasmine?"

A petite, bright-blond woman, dressed in a buttoned-up-to-the-collar designer suit that was probably more expensive than her own outfit, held out her hand. "I'm Charlotte," the porcelain-looking woman said, as if Jasmine should know who she was. When Jasmine frowned, the woman added, with a lilt that attested to her good home training, "Charlotte Hollingsworth. You met my husband, Lowell, and me at the Metropolitan Museum of Art a couple of years ago—before you and Hosea were married."

"Oh, yes," Jasmine said, remembering. That was back in 2004: the night Hosea had taken her out for her birthday—first, with a stop at the museum, before he wooed her with a tour of the city, by helicopter. That was the night she knew for sure she'd fallen in love. She said, "It's nice to see you again, Mrs. Hollingsworth."

"Please call me Charlotte." With a squeeze of her hand, the woman led Jasmine a few steps away from the incoming crowd. "Dear, how is your father-in-law?"

"He's doing as well as we can expect. He had surgery last week."

"Yes," Charlotte said. "Lowell spoke with Hosea."

Jasmine nodded. "Even though he's not awake yet, we're still hopeful."

"We all are, dear. Lowell and I visited Samuel when it first happened, but it was so hard to see him that way. We're praying, though." She paused before she asked, "Did you come alone?"

Jasmine nodded. Of course she had. She had no intentions of sharing this light with anyone besides her husband. "Hosea's at the hospital; I'm standing in for him."

"How wonderful." She took Jasmine's hand again. "Let me take you around, dear." As if Jasmine were her protégé, Charlotte guided her through the maze of white-clothed tables, accentuated with gold vases overflowing with springtime blooms. Every few steps, Charlotte stopped and introduced Jasmine to one power broker after another. Government officials, Fortune 500 executives, religious leaders—the people who really moved and shook New York. All greeted her as if she were already a friend.

"It's so nice to meet you," they said, as they held her hand.

Many left it there, but sometimes, when Charlotte turned away, handshakes lingered and glances wandered to the deep cut of her neckline, as the men asked questions about Reverend Bush.

The ones who wore collars and crosses around their necks flirted the most. And Jasmine flirted right back, eagerly taking their business cards.

"Call me if you need anything . . . anything," so many offered. Then they'd step back and, in a voice that wasn't filled with so much lust, they'd add, "And know that I'm praying for him."

If these were the kinds of people praying, Jasmine hoped none of them ever talked to God about her. But she played along, just so she could collect their contact information. Her plan was to send out before the end of this week her press kit—complete with her bio and speaking topics—because by the end of this luncheon, she was sure she'd be in great demand on the speakers circuit.

When the hosts started guiding the guests to their tables, Bishop Bailey escorted Jasmine to the dais.

"We want you sitting up here." He led her to the long table.

"Lady Jasmine!"

This was supposed to be an event filled with top-of-the-line people, in both class and stature. So what was Jerome Viceroy—dressed in a plum-colored pinstripe suit—doing here? And why would someone like him be on the stage? Next to her?

"You two know each other?" Bishop Bailey asked.

"Yes." Jerome held out the chair for Jasmine, but she didn't sit down. He said to the bishop, "I'll take care of Mrs. Bush for you."

The bishop nodded and walked away before Jasmine could tell him that she needed to find another seat. Her eyes searched the table for a setting without a nameplate.

"You're going to have to sit next to me," Jerome said with a grin, "if you want to be up here."

Jasmine rolled her eyes, took a final glance around, but then she sat. She could bear this obnoxious man for an hour or so.

"So have you and your husband thought any more about my offer?"

She leaned back and looked at him as if he'd suddenly grown two heads. "That's the first thing you say to me?"

"Well," he licked his lips and leaned in closer, "I could say that you are wearing that dress."

She wondered, where were all of his "Thank you, Jesus" and "Praise the Lords" now?

"Let me school you—everyone else asked how my father-in-law is doing. But it's always about you, isn't it?"

"Lady Jasmine," he began, as he raised his eyebrows, "this is all about you. You're the one whose father-in-law is in the hospital barely alive, but you're here." She opened her mouth, but before she could speak, he added, "So don't call me out, because the truth is you're just like me."

His words made her stiffen. "I'm nothing like you, Mr. Viceroy."

He chuckled as he flipped his napkin from his water glass and unfolded it onto his lap. "Since it takes one to know one, let's stop this dance." Now he lowered his voice. "How much is it going to cost me to convince you to sell the church?"

"It's not up to me."

"Sure it is." He leaned back and rested his arm on the back of Jasmine's chair. "We both know who wears the pants in your family."

"You must have me and Hosea confused with another couple."

He shook his head. "I don't think so." He pushed even closer. "So how much? I'm willing to put hundreds of thousands of dollars on the table. Name your price."

Jasmine smirked; this man thought he knew her. But Jasmine wasn't who she used to be. It was true; a few years ago, she would be scheming right now, and by the time she got home, she would have a full-fledged plan to coerce Hosea into accepting at least a five-hundred-thousand-dollar check from Jerome.

But her life wasn't just about money anymore. She loved Hosea, trusted him. And if he felt it was best not to sell the church, then she was standing by him.

"Ladies and gentleman!" The bishop stood at the podium, saving her from having to continue to conversate with Jerome.

As the bishop continued to greet the guests, Jasmine scanned through the program that lay at her plate setting. She turned the brochure over, then upside down, then back and forth. There had to be some pages missing; where was her name?

Another pastor stood and was now introducing the guest speakers. He passed right over her.

Then when another reverend came to the podium to bless the food, Jasmine wondered if Bishop Bailey had forgotten that she was supposed to speak.

Through lunch, Jasmine chatted with the man on her left, a rugged-looking priest with a Robert Redford–chiseled face who droned on about the challenges in the Catholic Church. Jasmine was drowning in boredom, but she refused to turn to her right, where Jerome Viceroy sat.

She felt as if she had been tossed a life jacket when Bishop Bailey stood and said, "Before we begin our program, I know everyone has been praying for Reverend Samuel Bush."

In reverence, the five hundred guests put down their forks, twisted in their seats, became silent.

"And today, I am proud to say we have among us Reverend Bush's daughter-in-law, the first lady of City of Lights at Riverside Church, Jasmine Bush."

The applause was polite, and Jasmine beamed.

"First Lady," Bishop Bailey began, "would you mind saying a few words. We all want to know how Reverend Bush is doing."

With a nod, Jasmine pushed her chair back, then paused as she pulled the five folded pages from her purse. She never saw the bishop's frown as she sauntered to the podium.

"Thank you, Bishop Bailey," she began. "I am honored to be here today. And I bring you greetings from City of Lights, where my husband, Hosea S. Bush, is the senior pastor." She looked into the expectant eyes of the people—all waiting to hear about Reverend Bush. Charlotte Hollingsworth smiled up at her from her seat at one of the front tables. And Jasmine felt nothing but glory.

With a deep breath, she said, "Today, I'd like to share with you my thoughts on the role of the first lady in American culture."

She ignored the confused stares and murmurs that floated through the crowd. And now, she could feel Bishop Bailey's frown. But this was her opportunity.

None of the gospel magazines had responded to her well-written, well-thought-through article, and now, today, it wouldn't be wasted. In front of the most powerful people in New York, she was going to show that she was more than beautiful. She was an intelligent, thinking-for-herself first lady who was a dynamo speaker.

She said, "The church is not what it used to be."

Bishop Bailey coughed to get her attention, but she pretended not to hear him.

"That means that the role of the first lady has grown, too. And I plan to step up . . ."

From the corner of her eye, she could see the bishop looking at his watch, but she didn't plan to take too much time.

"There have been many first ladies who have forged a path for us to follow. Coretta Scott King is one, although I see myself more like a political first lady. Like Jacqueline Kennedy."

Jasmine couldn't believe Jerome Viceroy had the nerve to laugh out loud.

She kept on anyway. "What we must do—"

Rising from his seat, Bishop Bailey was at her side in two seconds. With his hand over the microphone, he said, "Uh, I apologize, but we didn't plan for you to address our guests."

"Oh," she said, looking first at him, then turning to the audience. "I'm sorry; I thought this would be something that people would want to hear."

He nodded. "I'm sure, but not today." Taking his hand away from the microphone, he spoke so that everyone could hear him. "I was hoping that you could fill us in on Reverend Bush's progress."

Jasmine paused for a moment, wondering how she could get the rest of her speech in. But the bishop stood next to her, like he was ready to haul her away if she got off track this time.

With a breath, Jasmine spoke as if the words were the ones she planned to say, "Well, as you know it's been three weeks, and he is stable."

"Amen!" someone shouted.

"He had a tracheostomy Friday," she said, hoping to drag this out, "which is an operation that—"

"Uh . . . Mrs. Bush," Bishop Bailey interrupted, "what's the prognosis?"

He just wasn't going to let her shine. So she breathed deeply and tried to come up with the best line to show this crowd that she could think on her feet. "The doctors are hopeful, and we're prayerful." She leaned closer to the microphone. "Thank you for your prayers, and God bless each and every one of you."

"Thank you, Mrs. Bush. Please give our best to Hosea and let him know that we're praying for the reverend."

To polite applause, Jasmine pushed her shoulders back, held her head high, and slipped back into her seat.

Jerome was still clapping when she sat down.

"See," he said, "you *are* just like me." He laughed.

She rolled her eyes, but kept her smile as she nodded her appreciation to the luncheon guests. Then she sat through two hours of mind-numbing speeches, wishing the whole time that Bishop Bailey had given her a chance. She would have added pizzazz to this affair. But even though the bishop had cut her off, Jasmine was sure she'd made an impression.

By the time the bishop stood and gave the benediction, Jasmine was more than ready to leave. With the final "Amen," she pushed her chair back, determined to get away before Jerome could make his move. But he was quicker than she was, and he blocked her path before she could take two steps.

"I hope you'll seriously give thought to what I said. Remember, I'm talking big money."

"You know, Mr. Viceroy," Jasmine said in a huff, "not everybody can be bought."

"That's not true, Lady Jasmine. Everybody has a price. And I think I know yours."

In that moment, she wondered again if he knew anything about her past. But she pushed that thought away. He couldn't know a thing.

She had to step on his foot to get past him, but he didn't even budge. As she moved away, her eyes searched for Bishop Bailey. Even though she was still pissed that he'd shut her down, she was smart enough not to make enemies of the powerful.

"Mrs. Bush?"

Jasmine turned to face a woman who reminded her immediately of Popeye's wife, Olive Oyl.

"I wanted to introduce myself." The woman held out her hand. "I'm Lucy Carmichael, first lady at Lakeside in Queens. I was so impressed with your words up there," Lucy gushed.

Jasmine's smile widened.

"I felt everything that you were saying. In fact, I wanted to give you my card."

"Okay," Jasmine said, pleased that she *had* impressed the audience. This woman was probably getting ready to invite her to speak at Lakeside's Women's Day program. Or maybe even have her as the keynote at the pastor's anniversary.

"I was thinking that we could start a first ladies lunch group."

Huh?

"We could get together maybe once a month and talk about the kinds of programs we can bring to the community. Wouldn't that be great?"

"Oh. Yeah."

"So give me a call," Lucy said, handing Jasmine her card.

Jasmine nodded, said good-bye, but the moment she was in the hallway, she tossed the card into the trash. Having lunch with church ladies was not the path she was going to take. She had much bigger plans.

EIGHTEEN

JASMINE WAS JUST GETTING STARTED.

After the Mayors and Ministers luncheon on Saturday, she was sure that she was on her way to being the premiere first lady in the city. But now it felt like everyone was trying to take it away from her.

"I haven't seen anything like this since I became the treasurer," Malik said. "Tithes and offerings were down almost twenty percent the last two Sundays."

Even though her godbrother was giving the bad news, he still sat on their side of the table, next to Jasmine, who was next to Hosea. Across from them: Pastor Wyatt (sans his wife) and Jerome Viceroy. The two sides of the war.

The other board members were there, but at either ends of the table, sitting on the outskirts. As if they realized a battle was coming, and they were afraid of cross fire.

"Well"—Pastor Wyatt laid his hands flat on the table—"you know what this means." He looked at Hosea as if he'd stolen the money. "It's because of you."

"What are you talking about?" Jasmine asked.

Before he could answer, Malik said, "Eugene, don't go there."

"Why not? Should we wait until next week to talk about this? Or maybe the week after that. Maybe we should wait an entire month, and by then the church will be bankrupt and there won't be anything to talk about." Pastor Wyatt glanced slowly around the room.

No one said a word.

Then he added, "This never happened when I was leading the church."

"You've never led the church," Hosea said.

"I'm talking about the times when your father was away. In fact, there were occasions when I brought in more money than your father."

"I'm not surprised that you were keeping score, but I'm sure my father wasn't. Being the leader of this church was never a game that he had to win. The only winning he's ever been concerned about was winning souls to Christ."

Jerome Viceroy spoke next. "I think Pastor Wyatt is correct," he said, staring straight at Hosea. "This is about leadership, praise the Lord! And the people, they're not comfortable with you as their leader."

"That's not what's going on." Hosea shook his head. "There could be a lot of reasons attendance is down. People are still concerned about the shooting. And many may not know that the services are continuing without my father. Whatever, we'll figure it out. We have to, because"—this time, Hosea was the one who glanced around the room—"I'm not going anywhere."

The way Pastor Wyatt and Jerome exchanged glances made Jasmine frown. It was a good thing that Malik was the treasurer, because if not, she would have sworn that those two had siphoned money from the offerings just to make Hosea look bad.

"Well, I'm with you, Hosea," Sister Clinton said. "That was a fine sermon you gave on Sunday—the second good one in a row, and you'll keep getting better."

"I agree," Brother Hill said.

"Your opinion doesn't count, Daniel," Pastor Wyatt snapped. "That boy is your godson. In fact, you need to remove yourself from—"

Hosea stood up. "First of all, Pastor Wyatt, I'm not anybody's boy. You need to get that straight before we take this anyplace else."

Pastor Wyatt looked around the table, his eyes stopping at Jerome. But the councilman lowered his eyes.

Hosea continued, "And secondly, everyone on this board is free to speak. Those are the rules my father and the original board established, and those are the rules that are in place now. Are we clear?"

Pastor Wyatt glared at Hosea with defiant eyes. Said nothing.

"Good." Hosea moved, as if Pastor Wyatt had agreed. "Now, I understand everyone's concern. But we have to make this work. All churches go through their ups and downs."

"But we're not in the summer or holiday season." Pastor Wyatt returned to his fight. "And offerings being down isn't the only problem." He turned away from Hosea, faced the rest of the board members. "It's come to my attention that our *interim* pastor has turned down the opportunity for this church to receive more than twelve million dollars."

"What?" The exclamation came from all of them, in one note, as if they were singing a hymn.

"You've got to be kidding," Mrs. Whittingham's voice rose above the others.

"It's true." Jerome jumped into the battle. "The Harlem Redevelopment Project is willing to pay City of Lights so that they can continue their good work." The councilman stood, and Jasmine had to squint as she took in his bright gold suit with red stripes. He strutted to the front, and then, with his hands flailing and his eyes opened wide, he told the story of a charitable group of developers who, out of the goodness of their hearts, wanted to make the world—and Harlem—a better place. He explained the details of the proposal he'd shared with Hosea and Jasmine—less, of course, the cash money that Jasmine had no doubt he'd now offered to Pastor Wyatt.

Finishing, he said, "Not only is this an incredible financial opportunity for us, Brothers and Sisters, but we would be doing an incredible service to the congregation. Moving into a safer neighborhood would bring peace to all of us who worry about the men and women of this church. Think of our elderly, someone like Sister Pearline"—he pointed to the woman—"who walks through these gang-infested, drug-polluted, mean streets just to hear the Word of God." His voice rose with every sentence he spoke. "We need to take her and everyone else away from this danger, away from the violence that has cut down our *true* leader, Reverend Bush, in the prime of his life!" With his hands raised in the air and his eyes looking toward heaven, he added, "Glory! Hallelujah! Praise your name, Jesus!" His feet moved from side to side in a little hopping, holy dance.

Jasmine shook her head and wondered why no one told this bootleg preacher to sit down.

"We owe it to our people! Brothers and Sisters, we are not only responsible for their souls," he sang, "but their safety as well. Praise the Lord!"

There were moments of silence as Jerome removed a handkerchief from his pocket and dabbed at invisible perspiration on his forehead.

Then, "We're not selling the church," Hosea simply said.

Pastor Wyatt slammed his hands on the table. "That's not your decision."

"It is." Hosea's calmness made Pastor Wyatt look like a madman. "Check the bylaws. That's the one decision that needs the approval of the senior pastor, no matter what the vote."

"But, Hosea," Sister Clinton said, "maybe you need to think

about what Brother Viceroy is saying. This church has been here for almost thirty years. Maybe it's time to move on."

Brother Stevens added, "And do you know what we can do with that kind of money? We could pay cash for another building and still have money left to help so many of our families. We can start that after-school program we've been talking about for so long. Those are the things that are important to your father, not some building."

Hosea nodded. "I understand, but what Brother Viceroy isn't telling you is that my father had no plans of selling; I'm following his wishes."

"Your father didn't say no!" Jerome slammed his fist on the table, but then pulled back his hand quickly, shaking it as if he was in pain.

"There's no need to lie, Jerome," Hosea said, then looked straight at Brother Stevens and Sister Clinton. Then at Brother Hill and Mrs. Whittingham. "You've been with my father for decades. He's never led you wrong, has he?"

The four shook their heads.

Hosea turned back to Jerome, who still stood in the front of the room, as if he was in charge. "This church will not be sold."

Slowly Jerome returned to his seat, but there was no sign of retreat in his steps, no indication of defeat on his face. And when he looked across the table at Jasmine and licked his lips, she squirmed.

"Well, if that's all." Hosea stood. "I do want you to know that I appreciate every thought, every opinion, every discussion we have. Our collective job is to continue to move City of Lights in the right direction, and my role is to lead that process. I need everyone's help to do that, and I pray that we'll be able to continue to work together under the standards that my father has set."

When Hosea turned his back, the others stood. But Jasmine

didn't follow right away. She waited for a moment, to make sure that the daggers Jerome Viceroy and Pastor Wyatt were shooting at her husband weren't accompanied by a couple of real bullets. Because she had no doubt that if they could get away with it, both of those men would have pulled out a gun and shot her husband right in his back.

"Hosea!"

They both turned, and Jasmine rolled her eyes as Mrs. Whittingham marched down the hall toward them, her wide flowered-print skirt swishing around her.

She huffed and puffed when she finally stood in front of them, as if that short walk took all of her breath away. To Hosea she said, "Can I talk to you . . . privately?"

Hosea glanced toward his wife, then shook his head. He didn't have to say any more.

"All right, all right. Bring her in if you have to." Looking back toward the conference room, she whispered, "Let's talk in your dad's, I mean, in your office."

The moment they were behind closed doors, Mrs. Whittingham put her hands on her hips and said, "Hosea, you know I love you like a son, right?" She didn't wait for him to answer. "But I have to tell you, I'm worried."

"About what?"

"About everything." She waved a hand in the air as if there was much to be concerned about. "This fight with Eugene was bad enough, but I understood why you wanted to step into your father's shoes. I can even take tithes and offerings being down. But this thing—the offer for the church." She shook her head, as if Hosea had turned down the impossible dream. "Taking your father's place is obviously too much for you to handle."

"So you're saying . . ." Hosea paused, letting Mrs. Whittingham finish.

"I can't believe I'm saying this, God help me, because you know that I'm not a fan of his, but maybe you should let Eugene take over."

Traitor, Jasmine yelled inside her head. She had to press her lips together and cross her arms to keep that word inside.

Mrs. Whittingham continued, "You have too much on your mind, Hosea. With your father"—she glanced at Jasmine—"and your family. The church needs the kind of attention that you're not able to give it right now."

"How can you say that? I've been here every day, working, ministering, preaching on Sundays. I'm doing my best to keep everything on track."

"But you're not making good decisions."

"Because I don't want to sell this church? Are you telling me that *you* want to sell, even though you know that's not what Pops would want?"

"He may not have wanted it before, but after what happened . . . we don't know what he would want now."

"Exactly. And that's why we're not going to do anything. When Pops wakes up, he'll decide."

"That's what I'm talking about, Hosea. You're not thinking clearly. We don't know when—" She stopped, as if she was finished. Softly she added, "Your father would have never turned down that kind of money."

"That's not true. I have a feeling this is exactly what he would do."

Her voice rose again. "You're not thinking clearly!"

Jasmine's eyebrows rose. "There's no need for you to yell at my husband," she said, her volume matching Mrs. Whittingham's.

The woman's eyes flashed with fury. "Little girl, you need to be quiet."

Jasmine jumped in front of Hosea and pointed her finger in Mrs. Whittingham's face. "Who are you calling—"

Hosea pulled her back. "That's enough," he said to both of them.

For a moment more, she glared at Jasmine, then Mrs. Whittingham's eyes softened when she turned to Hosea. But she didn't say a word. Just spun around and marched away, slamming the door behind her.

Seconds passed, and then with a sigh, Hosea took Jasmine's hand, leading her out. They walked toward the front, where Mrs. Whittingham sat at her desk, her head down, like she had no plans to speak to either of them.

When Hosea said, "See you later, Mrs. Whittingham," the woman mumbled something that neither could understand.

Inside their SUV, as Hosea maneuvered south toward the hospital, Jasmine broke the quiet.

"Are you mad at me?"

He shook his head. "Not mad. Disappointed." With a quick glance at her, he said, "Jasmine, you can't be jumping in everybody's face. You can't turn every disagreement into a fistfight."

"I know."

"I've never seen you so hostile," he said. "Where's this coming from?"

"I don't know," she said, although she knew the source. It came from that place deep inside where her hurt still brewed. Where the memories of Natasia still rose up. It was Natasia who had turned her violent, who taught her not to take crap from anyone.

But all Jasmine said was, "It's hard to sit there and listen to the way they talk about you."

"Doesn't matter what anyone says. We're supposed to be the leaders." He continued the lecture. "I can't be breaking up fights between my wife and every member at City of Lights! Talkin' 'bout ghetto."

"I'm sorry. It won't happen again." *At least not in front of you.*

"But it wasn't all my fault. Mrs. Whittingham is supposed to be on your side."

"She is."

"How can you say that now? I think Pastor Wyatt sent her out to talk to you."

"Nah, he wouldn't be able to shake her. She's been in Pops's corner for a long time. She's just worried, like she said."

"She didn't sound worried. She sounded mad."

"Whatever. None of them are going to stop me from doing what I know Pops would want."

"I don't know, Hosea." Jasmine shook her head. "The way Pastor Wyatt and Jerome were talking today . . ."

"So? What else can they do? They can only talk, and soon that will die down."

Jasmine took a deep breath and then released a long exhale. Reaching over, he patted her hand. "Don't worry. There's not going to be any more trouble."

But Jasmine didn't agree. There'd been enough trouble in her life for her to recognize it when it was right in her face. She could smell trouble in the air, hear it in Pastor's Wyatt's voice, see it in Jerome Viceroy's eyes. Even Mrs. Whittingham walked like she was holding onto trouble's hand.

Trouble was here. And it felt like it was going to stay.

NINETEEN

THE SANCTUARY WAS SILENT.

That was Jasmine's thought as she peeked into the grand room. She slipped through the door and ventured slowly into the vacant space.

It felt so different being inside here on a weekday afternoon—without the Sunday sounds of music and the chatter of the congregants. Inside the quiet, it felt as if God was here.

She lowered herself onto the front pew in the center and raised her eyes to the cross that hung behind the altar. In her mind were thoughts of all the times she'd heard Reverend Bush teach about how anyone could bring their problems to God.

Well, that was why she was here. Her life felt like the definition of trouble—not only was there the drama with Pastor Wyatt and Jerome Viceroy, but then there was the trouble that kept seeping into her consciousness from her past.

She wondered if God's promises were retroactive. Could she bring all of her troubles, all of her mistakes from the past, to Him now? Would He erase the flashes and the dreams she'd been having from her memory?

Could He go further? Could He wipe out the day that her trouble began? The day she'd met Viva Menendez, the woman who had helped change the course of her life . . .

Viva Menendez, a fast-talking, fast-walking, fast-acting, Puerto Rican–born, New York City–raised girl whom Jasmine befriended her first day on UCLA's campus. The two were standing in line to register for freshman classes, and the girl in front of Jasmine chatted, as if her half-English, half-Spanish banter mattered.

I wish she would shut up, was Jasmine's thought as she twisted her body to the side—clearly an indication that she was not interested. But the girl with a chest so huge that Jasmine wondered how she didn't topple over, kept right on. It was only when she said, "Would you look at him? I could eat that chico with a spoon," that Jasmine perked up.

Her glance followed the girl's . . . straight to Kenny.

Jasmine waved him over, and then she said to the girl, "That's *my* boyfriend."

The girl tilted her head, looked Jasmine up and down, and then made a face like now it was Jasmine's words that didn't matter.

"Hey, sweetie," Kenny said before he kissed Jasmine on the cheek.

When Jasmine noticed how Kenny and the girl grinned at each other, she stepped in front of her boyfriend, put her hand out, and said to the girl, "I'm Jasmine Cox, and I think you and I are going to be great friends."

The girl's eyes glazed over with confusion. But then she shrugged and said, "*Chica,* put your hand down and give me a hug. If you're gonna be my homey, we should at least act like it, right?"

And the friendship was born—with nothing more in common than Kenny Larson. From that day forward, Jasmine kept Viva as close to her and as far away from Kenny as she could.

But even though there were times when she wondered if Kenny and Viva had figured out a way to hook up (since Jasmine didn't trust anyone), her fears faded quickly. Before the autumn leaves had completely fallen, Viva had a trail of guys sniffing behind her. More than once, Jasmine had barged into Viva's dorm room with some campus news, only to find a naked man in Viva's bed.

"Dang, girl," Jasmine said after their English teaching assistant staggered out of her friend's room one afternoon. "How many guys are you sleeping with?"

"Don't hate on me, mama. I've got to use what I got to get what I want."

That had always been Jasmine's philosophy, too, but did Viva have to act like a whore? There were ways to use guys . . . and do it with class.

However, it was Viva's free-thinking, free-spirit attitude that helped Jasmine out when she needed help the most.

The day after Jasmine had gone home to talk to her father about suing the hospital, she'd ended up at Viva's place, bawling.

"He's already paid the hospital," Jasmine sobbed. "There goes my money."

"Oh, *chica,* that's heavy. What're you gonna do?" Viva asked in a tone filled with tears and pain that matched her friend's.

"I don't know," Jasmine wailed. "I gotta keep my apartment; I gotta graduate in May with you guys."

"*Chica,* you know I got you, right? You can move in with me."

Jasmine nodded, although they both knew she wouldn't do that. There wasn't enough space in the one bedroom for Viva, Jasmine, and the men who traipsed in and out constantly.

Viva continued, "But here's the thing: you need money. You need a job."

Jasmine sniffed back more tears. "And where do you think I go every morning?"

"I'm not talking about one of those corporate internships. I'm talking about something that will put some real dough in your hands, mama." Viva grabbed her purse from the floor and took out three stacks of bills, each secured with a rubber band. Jasmine's eyes widened. Even if all the bills were singles, there had to be a couple of hundred dollars there.

"Who gave you that?"

"Not who. What. I'm getting paid. This is what I made this week."

Jasmine looked at Viva with doubtful eyes. About two months ago, Viva had told her that she'd found a new gig as a hostess, but Jasmine didn't know of any restaurant that paid this much in tips.

"I didn't feel like hearing your mouth, so I didn't tell you," Viva began, "but what I'm really doing is, I'm dancing. Out by the airport. At a place called Foxtails."

"Dancing?"

Slowly Viva nodded, and in seconds, Jasmine understood—dancing was a code word.

Although it was surprising, it really shouldn't have been. If there had been a category for Girl Most Likely to Be a Stripper in their junior class, Viva Menendez would have won in a landslide.

"And you know what I'm going to do for you?" Viva asked. "I'm going to hook you up 'cause you my girl, and right about now, you need to make this kind of money, too . . .

With a deep breath, Jasmine pushed herself from the pew and knelt in front of the altar. She needed to get all thoughts of that woman and that time out of her head. She needed to take that trouble to God and leave it right on the altar.

So she closed her eyes and prayed, prayed for God's help.

Long minutes passed, and she kept praying. Didn't stop until her knees started to ache.

When she stood and glanced at the cross, it glimmered in the daytime light. And her lips spread into a slow smile. She could feel it—God's peace that everyone talked about.

With a deep sigh, she released her fears. And somehow, she knew—she wouldn't have any more trouble now.

TWENTY

Almost one month.

That's all it had been since the day Jasmine had walked down these hospital halls for the first time. It hadn't been the year that it felt like.

And in that month, Jasmine had learned a lot. She knew the staff by name. Knew their schedules. Even knew whether they were married. Or had children. She knew the daily goings-on at Harlem Hospital, in the third-floor step-down unit.

What she didn't know was how many more days, weeks, months she would be walking down these halls.

She paused outside of the room where Reverend Bush was sleeping.

Sleeping. That's what Mae Frances called it.

"Is he still sleeping?" she asked every morning when she spoke with Jasmine.

Sleeping. A gentle word with a wonderful implication—that with a kiss from God, one day, he would awaken.

Jasmine pushed the room door open, then paused when she heard her husband's voice.

"Pops, I'm following your wishes, but the church . . . You know, last week, Mrs. Whittingham asked me if this was too much and I'm beginning to think . . . I don't know. The offerings, they're still down. I know you don't care about that kind of thing, but I have to be concerned. We have to meet the budget. I mean, things aren't that bad yet, but if they continue . . ."

With one hand, Hosea held the Bible he'd been reading to his father, and with his other, he took his father's hand and squeezed it.

Jasmine blinked and pressed down her grief.

"I'm going to stay the course, though, Pops," Hosea started again, this time with more strength. "I'm going to stay through Wyatt and Viceroy because this is what you want. But I've gotta tell you, this is definitely your calling, not mine." A moment passed before he put down his father's hand and tucked the Bible by his side.

Silently, Jasmine moved toward him. Softly, she rested her hand on his shoulder.

"I didn't hear you come in." He never looked up, didn't have to. He knew his wife's touch. "How's Jacquie?"

"She's asking about her daddy."

Still not looking her way, he said, "One day . . . I may want to bring her here. Maybe hearing her voice will." He stopped, as if that was a complete sentence. "Maybe." Another absolute thought.

He said no more, just left his hope right there. Together they stood, looking down at his father. And then, together, they lowered themselves to their knees and prayed like they always did—that the same grace Reverend Bush had extended to so many would find its way to him now.

The knock on the door broke through their quiet, and their faces stretched with surprise when Sister Pearline hobbled into the room.

Jasmine pushed herself up and moved quickly to assist the elderly woman. Even though Sister Pearline walked as if each step took effort, she still wore her bright smile.

Gently, Jasmine took the woman's hand and led her to the chair. Her heart held a special place for this kind old lady.

"Thank you, Lady Jasmine," Sister Pearline said. "Whew! That was a long walk."

"Walk?" Hosea frowned. "Sister Pearline you couldn't possibly have walked—"

"Yeah, I did. How else was I supposed to get here from the elevator?" She sighed. "That sure was a long walk."

He asked, "But, how did you get *here*? To the hospital?"

It took a moment for her to gather her breath. "I took the train."

"You should've called me," Hosea admonished. "I don't want you out, especially at this time of night."

She waved her hand, as if his words meant nothing. I've been walking up and down these streets all my life, and I'm not about to stop now. You better believe, if somebody were to come up on me the wrong way," she tapped her cane on the floor, "I got something for them."

Jasmine bowed her head to hide her smile. Sister Pearline was serious—as if that little stick was going to stop somebody.

"Anyway, I needed to get here so that I could have a word with you." She took a glance at Reverend Bush, then closed her eyes. Jasmine and Hosea stood shoulder to shoulder and waited for Sister Pearline to finish her prayer. But she stayed like that for so long that Jasmine wondered if she'd fallen asleep.

Then a soft "Amen" before she opened her eyes. Sister Pearline was still looking at Reverend Bush when she said, "You need to turn in your resignation as senior pastor tomorrow."

"What?" Jasmine said. Surely she hadn't heard this woman, their friend, correctly.

With more calm than his wife had, Hosea said, "Sister Pearline, let's talk about this outside."

"No, baby, I'm fine right here," she said, her tone soft, gentle, as if she hadn't just told Hosea to walk away from all that was important to him.

He whispered, "The doctors don't want Pops disturbed with long conversations. And I know you wouldn't want to do anything to hurt him."

That got her moving, although not very fast. But the moment she was outside, she stood in front of their faces as if she was ten feet tall and repeated what she'd said. "You need to let Pastor Wyatt take over."

Jasmine folded her arms, shook her head. *Where did this come from?* But as quickly as her question came, so did her answer. Surely it was Pastor Wyatt! Somehow that fool had said something, done something to move one of Reverend Bush's faithful servants to his side.

"Now, Sister Pearline, why would I walk away from what my father wants me to do?" Hosea asked, his tone carrying no anger.

"Because you cannot lead a church where your wife is not even a member." She banged her cane on the floor to emphasize her point.

"What are you talking about?" Jasmine exclaimed.

Sister Pearline looked straight at Jasmine, and the bright light of Christian love was gone from her eyes. In its place was a cold glare—as if when she looked at Jasmine, she was staring into the soul of a heathen. "I'm talking about you! And how you're not fit to be a first lady."

"Sister Pearline," Hosea said, "I'm not going to let you—"

But she interrupted, "There's nothing to discuss here, young man." She spoke as if the decision was hers. "How can you lead our souls to heaven when the woman in your own house doesn't love the Lord enough to take the time to become a member?"

"First of all," Jasmine began, her finger raised and her neck rolling. All of her affection for this woman was gone. "Who are you to say that I don't love God?" she asked. This was when

Hosea usually grabbed her and pulled her back to reason. But since he hadn't touched her or said a word, Jasmine kept going. "And secondly, you seem to have lost your memory or your mind, because I've been going to City of Lights every Sunday since Hosea and I were married."

Sister Pearline scrunched her face and looked Jasmine up and down. "Sitting in the pews doesn't make you a member any more than it makes you a Christian. Don't you think that when it's time for you to meet your Maker, God's going to ask about your membership? Don't you think He's going to ask if you've confessed Jesus Christ as your Lord and Savior? Or do you think He's gonna say, 'Come on in, Jasmine; you're with him.'" With her cane, she pointed to Hosea. But when she tried to steady herself again, the cane slipped.

"Lord, Jesus!" Sister Pearline shouted.

With a quickness, they both moved, but Jasmine reached her first, grabbed her arms, and lifted her upright two seconds before she hit the ground.

"Whew!" Sister Pearline pushed her cane into the floor, testing its steadiness before she stood up straight. "That was close. Thank you," she said to Jasmine, her smile back for a moment. But then, "Now as I was saying, Hosea, you need to turn in your resignation, because your father didn't build his church to turn it over to you and a woman who isn't even saved."

You old coot! I should've let you fall.

But right when she opened her mouth to speak that thought, Hosea said, "Sister Pearline, Jasmine is as saved as you are."

"How do you know?" Sister Pearline glared at him. "Only God knows her heart."

"And only God knows yours, but if anyone asked me, I'd say that you were saved, too. Even if you are up here talking all this craziness."

His words made her back hunch over a little bit more. She stared at Jasmine for a moment. "Well," she began, softer now,

"I was surprised when they said—" She stopped, as if she'd spoken words she wasn't supposed to say. Standing as erect as she could, she said, "Your wife's not a member of City of Lights," she said, sounding like she was reciting a script. "That means you can't be the pastor."

With his arms crossed but a smile still on his face, Hosea shook his head. "Now you—and everyone else—should know me better than that. I'm not resigning, Sister Pearline. But your point is taken, and Jasmine will become a member."

"What?" Jasmine and Sister Pearline said at the same time.

"Well, it's the obvious solution. Jasmine needs to go through the membership classes and take the right hand of fellowship, like everyone else."

"But—"

He ignored his wife.

"Sister Pearline, we'll take care of this right away."

"Hosea—"

He kept his attention on the elderly woman. "We have daytime classes every Friday, right? Jasmine can begin tomorrow."

"You can't be serious—"

Still pretending that he didn't hear a word Jasmine was saying, Hosea took the old woman's arm and led her toward the elevator. "Now, Sister Pearline, I don't want you out any later than you need to be. I'd take you home myself, but I want to spend a little more time with Pops, so I'm gonna put you in a cab."

"No." Sister Pearline shook her head. Her eyes moved from one corner of the hallway to the other, like she was searching for an escape route. She took two steps, then stopped. "I don't . . . need a cab." She walked and talked as if she were confused. As if she'd come with a plan, but now she didn't know what to do. "I can . . . get home . . . like I got here."

"I'm not going to let you get on any subway," and then the elevator doors closed and Jasmine heard nothing more. But even though they were gone, she still stood in the hallway, her mouth opened wide.

For Sister Pearline to show up like this—it was clear Pastor Wyatt was not playing. His plan was to sit in Reverend Bush's chair no matter what he had to do.

Well, he didn't know who he was messing with. He didn't know that she sang the same song he did—win by any means necessary.

And she was going to win without sitting in on some stupid new-members class. How ridiculous would it be for her to show up there? She was the first lady, and everyone already knew that she was a Christian. She never missed church and hadn't cheated on Hosea since they'd been married. She never killed anyone, never stole anything, and never lied unless it was absolutely necessary. She read her Bible when she had time and prayed when she needed something. What more was there to learn? She was probably better than half of the people walking the earth.

Jasmine marched back into her father-in-law's room. Hosea had lost his mind if he thought she was going to sit in on any new-members class. And as soon as he came back, she was going to tell him that.

TWENTY-ONE

JASMINE HAD NOT CHANGED HER mind.

She was the pastor's wife and already going to heaven. All she had to do was get Hosea to agree.

Her plan started the moment they strapped themselves inside their SUV on their way home. "You know," she began, "Sister Pearline showing up was no accident. I wouldn't be surprised if someone from the board sent her. Probably Pastor Wyatt."

"It was Viceroy," Hosea said. "He was waiting for her when we got downstairs."

Even though she wasn't really surprised, the gall of it still amazed her. "Why didn't you tell me? What did he say?"

Hosea shrugged. "Said he was visiting a friend and acted like he was shocked to see us. He tried to play it off, and then he offered Sister Pearline a ride because he said he was going her way."

"Yeah, right. She lives around the corner from the church and he lives on Fifty-second Street."

Hosea nodded. "I let him play his game. He knew he was caught. She knew they were caught, but the thing is, Jasmine, they're right. You *do* need to take the membership classes. I don't know how that slipped past Pops and me."

It was going to be harder than she thought, so for the rest of the ride, she stayed quiet. Just thinking. And then, when they were in their apartment, standing at the side of Jacqueline's bed, watching their daughter sleep, Jasmine whispered, "I have so much on my plate," as if those words were just coming to her. She tucked the blanket around their toddler. "With Jacquie, and all that I'm trying to do at the church." She sighed again, letting Hosea hear how tiring her schedule was. "There's so much," she repeated. "And Malik called today. He needs my help over the next couple of weeks."

"Really? What does he want you to do?"

"Help with the budget or . . . something." She waved her hand in the air as if that would rid the atmosphere of her lie. "I'm not complaining. You know I'll do whatever Malik needs. And I'll always be here for Jacquie." She cast a loving glance at her daughter. "And there's you." She grabbed his hand. "And everything that I want to do to help you."

He wrapped his arms around her. "You're right. You do have a lot."

She smiled as he held her.

He said, "Good thing the membership classes are only six weeks."

Six weeks?

He turned and left her alone in their daughter's bedroom.

Now it was a definite that she wasn't going—she didn't have six weeks' worth of time to waste.

She waited until the next perfect opportunity—and it came an hour later when they were in bed.

With her head resting on his chest, she said, "Babe, you know, I just thought of something." She lifted up and grazed her lips across his neck. He stirred, and she opened her mouth. Tickled him with her tongue. Made him moan. He was ready.

She leaned back and said, "You're the pastor, and you know I love God." For extra measure, she did what she always did when she wanted her way—kissed him long. And kissed him hard. Then, "I don't think it would be right for me to be sitting in a new-member class with regular people. How would that look? I mean, I *am* the first lady."

He squeezed her but stayed quiet, as if he was contemplating her words. Then he planted a kiss on her forehead. "It's going to be fine. You're going to be a great example for the *regular* people." He rolled over on his side, away from her.

Jasmine opened her mouth, ready to demand that he turn back. That he listen to her and agree. But after a while, she sank into her own pillows, crossed her arms, and stared at the ceiling. Mad!

In the morning she brought it up again. But before she had a chance to say too much, Hosea ended it. "We don't need to talk about this anymore." Picking up his plate from the table, he dumped it in the sink. "After you take this first class, you'll see. You'll be so glad you went, you'll be thanking me."

She poked out her lips so that he would know just how miserable she was. She lifted Jacqueline from her chair and held her in her lap. Then she went right back to her complaining. "How can I walk in there today? Don't you have to start with the first class?"

"No, you'll be fine. I'll call and let them know you're coming." He kissed her cheek, then Jacqueline's. "I'll be in Pops's office when you're finished. Let's have lunch afterward," and then he walked out the door.

There was nothing else to say; it was a fait accompli.

"Mrs. Sloss," Jasmine called out after she helped Jacqueline finish her cereal.

A minute later, she handed her daughter to their nanny. It

didn't make sense to fight this any longer; she had to get ready for the class.

Jasmine didn't even know who was leading the new-members group. She'd been fighting so hard, she'd forgotten to ask. But it didn't matter—Pastor Wyatt, Brother Hill, even if Jerome Viceroy showed up—she'd be able to handle any of them.

Glancing at her watch, she released a quick breath. It was a bit after ten. She pressed her Bible against her chest, pulled open the door, stepped inside, and almost fell over.

"Jasmine!"

She was facing the only person she couldn't handle.

Mrs. Whittingham glided toward Jasmine as if she were glad to see her. "Hosea told me you were coming. Welcome to the *new*-members class." Mrs. Whittingham spread her arms, as if she was really welcoming her.

Jasmine's shocked eyes moved from Mrs. Whittingham to the women sitting on two of the three folding chairs. She nodded her hello to them, then turned her body sideways and whispered, "What are you doing here?"

"I teach the daytime classes," Mrs. Whittingham sang as if that announcement should make Jasmine happy.

Jasmine's glance went straight to the door.

This time, it was Mrs. Whittingham who spoke in a low voice. "Sit down, *Lady* Jasmine." The sound of happiness, gone from her tone. "You're not the first lady in my class. I'm running this show."

Jasmine glanced quickly at the two women.

Witnesses.

Hosea would surely be voted out as senior pastor if she were to do to Mrs. Whittingham what she'd always wanted.

Slowly, Jasmine moved toward the other women. Slowly, she

lowered herself onto the chair, feeling the chill of the metal beneath her skirt.

"We were just getting started," Mrs. Whittingham spoke again in that joyful tone. She introduced Jasmine to the others, "This is our new first lady. Can you believe it? She has to take a new-members class, too."

Mrs. Whittingham was the only one who laughed. "Okay, let's begin. Jasmine, did you bring a Bible?"

She inhaled. "Of course I did." She held up the book that she knew for sure Mrs. Whittingham had seen.

"I didn't know." Mrs. Whittingham shrugged. "I wasn't sure if you even owned one."

Jasmine squeezed her fingers together. Took deep breaths and made herself calm. Remembered her goal—to help Hosea.

"Today's lesson is about Joseph in the book of Genesis." Mrs. Whittingham turned to Jasmine and asked innocently, "First Lady, do you know where Genesis is in the Bible?"

Jasmine ground her teeth. Counted backward from ten. Recited the Lord's Prayer. Then said the Twenty-third Psalm—at least the part she knew.

And none of that was enough to keep her there.

She leapt from her chair with such force that it fell backward, crashing to the floor. Jasmine moved forward; Mrs. Whittingham jumped back.

Jasmine already knew how she would explain it: she would tell Hosea, and the board, and the police, and the judge that she was laying hands on the woman in the name of Jesus and she had no idea how her fingers ended up wrapped around her neck.

Then in her peripheral vision, she saw them. The two women. Eyes wide with fright.

Witnesses.

That was when reason returned. Jasmine stared down her

enemy for a moment more before she stomped straight out of the room.

Jasmine trudged from one end of the office to the other.

"You should have heard her, Hosea." She continued her pacing. "That woman is crazy. I don't care what you say. I'm not going back there."

"You didn't hit her, did you?"

If she'd been strapped to a lie detector, the waves would have been off the chart with the memory of what she'd wanted to do. "Of course I didn't," she said, insulted by the question.

"Just checking, 'cause recently—"

"You don't have to worry." Jasmine waved her hand in the air. "I behaved with all the decorum of a first lady when she asked me if I knew where Genesis was."

Hosea leaned back in his chair, the ends of his lips twitching into a smile. "So you're going to let these people throw me out of the church because my wife isn't a member?"

She stopped moving, stared at him. "You think this is funny?" She shook her head. "I'm not going back, Hosea. Find me another way. Work it out."

He nodded. "By the way, when she asked you about Genesis . . ."

Jasmine crossed her arms, sucked her teeth. "Very funny." She did not laugh along with him.

"Okay," he said, still chuckling. "There's something else you can do, but it's not going to be easy. You'll have to study on your own—"

"I'll do it!"

"And take the test that anyone joining the ministerial staff has to take."

"I'll do it!"

When Hosea's phone rang, she turned from his office and marched toward her own. Her husband may have found this amusing, but she didn't. These people were dancing on nerves she didn't even know she had.

She was moving fast, head down, still grumbling, when she whipped around the corner.

"Excuse me," she said when she bumped into someone. She looked up and into the eyes of Pastor Wyatt. She scooted to the side to move past him, but Pastor Wyatt blocked her path.

"What do you want?" she hissed. There was no first lady decorum left.

"I wanted to know if you talked to your husband about stepping down."

"Why would I do that?"

"Because you're smart enough to think about what I said the other day—this job is too big for Hosea."

"I've got three points for you, Pastor. The job isn't too big for my husband. He *is* the senior pastor. Get over it."

Her words wiped his smile away. "Remember, this was your choice." The way he spoke through clenched teeth made Jasmine back up a bit. "I gave you a way out. Now, I'll have to do what I have to do."

A lump of fear rose from her stomach to her throat. Those were almost the same words Jerome had uttered. But she didn't back down, just responded as if she wasn't afraid. "Is that supposed to be a threat?"

He shook his head, and his lips twitched into something between a smile and a grimace. "I don't make threats, I just keep my promises." He turned around and sauntered away with that bad-boy strut that made him look like he came straight from the streets.

Jasmine rushed into her office, closed the door, and leaned against it. Stayed right there and waited for her heartbeat to return to its normal rhythm.

"I'm not afraid of him!" she said over and over.

She was Jasmine Cox Larson Bush. She'd been through it all—hadn't had a day without drama since the third grade. And she'd always come out on top. Certainly, this two-bit, second-rate pastor couldn't scare her.

But the way her lips quivered, the way her hands shook, the way her legs trembled, told her that she wasn't speaking the truth. The fact was, she was scared. Very, very scared—and she wasn't quite sure why.

TWENTY-TWO

"DADDY, LOOK IT!" JACQUELINE PATTED her father's knee, then pointed to make sure that he saw the opulent palace that glowed on the forty-two-inch flat screen.

"That's right, baby." Jasmine leaned over and kissed her daughter on the top of her head. "You're gonna live large like that one day."

With a smirk, Hosea shook his head at his wife's words, and Jasmine laughed.

This was the way life was supposed to be: the three Bushes—Hosea and Jasmine sitting shoulder to shoulder, with Jacqueline squeezed in between them.

Jasmine had been surprised when, after church, Hosea had told her that he wasn't going to the hospital.

"I want to go home and be with you and Jacquie," he'd said. "I'll check on Pops later."

And so now they sat, watching Jacqueline's favorite movie and singing along with the sound track as Moses led the Hebrew slaves out of Egypt.

"Daddy, look it!" Jacqueline exclaimed again as she grabbed a fat fist of popcorn.

Jasmine reached for her husband's hand, and although thoughts of doctors and hospitals, associate pastors and board members, the past and the present, weren't far away, at least for a few hours the three of them had peace.

When the telephone rang, Jasmine reached for the cordless without taking her eyes off the screen.

"Jasmine, this is Roxie Willis."

She blinked. "Hi," was all she said as she stood up and edged toward the kitchen. She hadn't seen or heard from Roxie since that first Sunday in church.

"I hope I'm not disturbing you."

Yes, you are. But she didn't speak her thought to Hosea's friend. "What can I do for you?"

"Well, we haven't talked in a while, and I heard what's been going on in the church."

Jasmine frowned. She'd heard what?

Roxie said, "I've been through all of those church politics before, and I think I can help."

All Jasmine could think about was the last time she saw Roxie, winking at Hosea.

"Roxie, Hosea said that we don't have the money in the budget for an armor bearer."

"Money? Is that what Hosea said?"

Uh-oh.

Roxie asked, "Why would he think I'd want to be paid?"

Seemed like that lie was a mistake.

Roxie asked, "Would you mind if I talked to Hosea so that I can explain? Is he home?"

"Well, no, Hosea didn't really . . . I mean, I can't imagine anyone working and not being paid."

"Jasmine, this is my reasonable service. And anyway, I'm blessed. My husband left me . . . well, let's just say money is not something I'm concerned about."

It was the thought of those millions Hosea had told her

about that made Jasmine pause. A woman with that much money could be a good friend.

Roxie continued, "I care about what's going on at City of Lights, and I know I can help."

Then in the background, Jasmine heard, "Roxie, you ready, sweetheart?"

Jasmine pressed the phone closer to her ear.

"In a minute, honey," and then to Jasmine, she said, "I'm sorry. Look, why don't we set up a time to talk tomorrow."

Another thought of those millions made Jasmine say, "Make it around ten," before she hung up.

But she still wasn't sure about that woman or the meeting. And now, that man's voice in the background made her more suspicious. A man's voice, when her husband had just died. A man's voice that sounded so familiar.

Back in the living room, Jacqueline was stretched out, her head resting in her dad's lap, her eyes tightly closed.

"You'll never guess who was on the phone," Jasmine said. Before Hosea could respond, she told him, "Roxie. We're meeting in the morning."

"That's great."

Jasmine nodded, but she didn't say anything else. She still wasn't feeling this woman, but maybe she did need to bring Roxie in. What was that cliché about enemies? Jasmine wasn't sure if Roxie was a friend or a foe. But for now, it might be a good idea to keep that woman close.

TWENTY-THREE

CLOSE. THAT'S WHERE JASMINE WANTED to keep Roxie—close to her. And with the way she was looking today—far from Hosea.

As the woman sat in front of her chatting, Jasmine had a hard time listening. This woman was simply too gorgeous—Halle Berry's mother, if her mama had been black. Today, her short hair was slicked back instead of spiked. And the crisp white tailored shirt and blue jeans that she wore would have been simple on anyone else. But on Roxie, casual became couture.

Then there was her makeup—or the fact that she didn't have any on. But still, her skin glowed, her eyes were bright, and her lips shone.

And like before, Jasmine hated her.

"So after I heard what was going on, I made a list." Roxie pulled her PDA from her purse and clicked it on. "You and Hosea need to take this church back to the things that made it great. Get these people involved in so many programs, they won't have time to be in your business. Like the Women's Forum . . . what's going on with that?"

Jasmine rested her arms on her desk. "What's the Women's Forum?"

"Are you kidding, First Lady? The Women's Forum has been a big event for City of Lights. You've never attended?"

Jasmine shook her head.

"It takes place during the summer, and it's simply wonderful: all kinds of speakers come in to lecture about finances, jobs, fitness . . . this list goes on. But I haven't heard anything about it this year. I think Mrs. Whittingham usually handles it." She lowered her voice, and added, "But frankly, First Lady, that should be your project."

That made Jasmine smile. In the week since Mrs. Whittingham had insulted her in the new-members class, the two hadn't exchanged a single glance or a solitary word. But now Jasmine imagined marching up to Mrs. Whittingham and telling her that her services were no longer needed.

"Is there a Men's Forum?"

Roxie shook her head. "Not at this point, but that doesn't mean it can't be done."

Jasmine said, "Maybe we can combine the two."

"See, that's what I'm talking about, First Lady. The more programs the better."

Jasmine nodded, thought some more. And then another idea. "What about something like a First Lady Appreciation Day?"

"Well," Roxie began with a grin, "I don't know. Have you been a first lady long enough?"

"Please! Does length of time matter?" She stood, walked around her desk, paced the length of the room. "An event like this could really help me introduce myself to the women of this church."

Roxie leaned back in the chair, smiled, and nodded. "Well, if it works for you, it'll work for me. I can handle that, because the first lady shouldn't plan her own day."

That was all it took for Jasmine to like her again.

"So," Roxie stood up, "I guess this means we'll be working together."

Jasmine stopped moving. Today, she'd worn her very best St. John pantsuit—the black, slimming one—knowing that she was going to be sharing the same space with Roxie. But as Jasmine looked her up and down, not even St. John had been enough.

Then she thought about the woman's money. And the First Lady's Appreciation Day.

"Yes, definitely," Jasmine said, shaking Roxie's hand. Walking back behind her desk, she added, "I hope you understand why I was so hesitant."

Roxie held up her hand. "Trust me, I understand. In your position, you have to be careful about who you bring in. Okay, what about if I come into the office . . . three days a week to start. And of course, any time you need more, that'll be fine."

The shadow outside her office made Jasmine frown, pause. And a second later, she saw him.

"What are you doing here?" she growled.

Jerome Viceroy's grin spread across his face. "So good to see you, too, Lady Jasmine."

"I said—"

"He's with me." Roxie stood up, and Jerome kissed her cheek.

The voice!

"Are you ready to go?"

"Yeah," Roxie said. "We're finished here, right?"

It felt like it took a million muscles for Jasmine to nod her head.

"Okay, well," Roxie swung her bag over her shoulder, "we'll start tomorrow . . . around ten?"

Again, all Jasmine did was nod.

She watched them walk out the door and before they stepped into the hallway, Jerome looked back over his shoulder, licked his lips. "You have a nice day now, ya hear?"

Once they were gone, Jasmine fell into her chair. That was

who she'd heard in the background the other night: Jerome Viceroy. Roxie was in bed with Jerome—literally. That was how she knew what was going on in the church. And that was why she was pushing to get close to her.

Roxie must've thought she was a fool! Jerome Viceroy was clearly the enemy. And anyone who was sleeping with the enemy couldn't be a friend of hers.

TWENTY-FOUR

SOMETIMES MEN COULD BE SO naïve.

That was Jasmine's thought as she kissed Hosea's cheek, then jumped from the SUV. She watched her husband hook a left turn and then head south toward the hospital.

"Tell Roxie I said hello," was the last thing he'd said.

She was going to say hello to Roxie all right, and then say good-bye as she pointed her toward the door.

Hosea's words remained in her head as she stepped toward the church.

"You should still work with Roxie."

This was after she'd told him about Roxie and Jerome and it being Jerome's voice she'd heard on the call. But Hosea's response was that Roxie's life wasn't their business.

"I don't agree," she'd said. "They're probably . . . sleeping together. And they're not married. How can we have her working for us when she acts like that?"

Hosea had looked at his wife as if he wanted her to really think about what she'd said. "Do I have to remind you that you weren't always saved?"

After Hosea had said that, Jasmine had stopped talking. She wasn't about to argue when there wasn't a word he could say or a deed he could do to convince her to let Roxie stay. She would have banned her from the Sunday services, if she could.

Mrs. Whittingham looked up when Jasmine stepped inside the church. But then the woman did what she always did. She snatched back her smile and lowered her head.

And Jasmine did what *she* always did—rolled her eyes and stomped right past the desk.

Usually her mind was filled with thoughts of ways she could get rid of Mrs. Whittingham, but right now all she could think about was what she was going to say to Roxie when she arrived. She swung open her office door.

"Good morning!" Roxie exclaimed.

Jasmine stood with her mouth opened.

Roxie sat behind her desk, a yellow pad in front of her. "I was making a list of all the things I want to get started on. I was thinking about—"

"I didn't expect you until ten," Jasmine said, moving toward her.

Roxie chuckled as she edged around to the other side so that Jasmine could sit down. "One of the things you'll learn about me, First Lady, is that I'm very serious about whatever I do. After I thought about it, ten seemed too late. We have so much to organize—the Women's Forum, your appreciation day, and—"

"I've decided that we won't be working together."

"What?" Roxie's eyes blinked as if she didn't understand. "Why?"

Because your friend is my enemy. "I really don't feel comfortable not paying you—"

"First Lady—"

Jasmine held up her hand. "I know what you said, but this is about me and how I feel."

Roxie peered at Jasmine for a long moment. "Is this about Jerome?"

Jasmine stared right back. "Do you know what he's been up to with my husband?"

"If you're talking about his trying to pressure Hosea into selling the church, yes, I know. But that doesn't have a thing to do with me."

"So you don't agree with Jerome?"

"Actually, I do. I think it might be time to move City of Lights out of Harlem. But it's Hosea's call, and as your armor bearer, I would support you." She paused, but Jasmine said nothing. Roxie continued, "This shouldn't have a thing to do with you and me."

"You're wrong about that. Because anyone who doesn't support my husband cannot be a friend of mine."

Roxie folded her arms and stood steadfast, as if she planned to stay.

Jasmine continued, "Thank you, but—" And then she stopped. She'd said enough.

At first, Roxie moved without a word. Grabbed her purse, slowly slipped the strap onto her shoulder. "You know, the first thing a pastor's wife needs to know is who's on her side. And you don't have a lot of friends here, *Lady Jasmine.*" Slowly, she switched her hips toward the door, as if she wanted Jasmine to get a good look. Then she stopped suddenly.

Jasmine rolled her eyes, not feeling the fight that was coming.

But when Roxie turned around, all she did was slip an envelope from her shirt pocket. "I forgot. This is for you. It was on the floor when I came in, looked like someone slid it underneath the door."

Jasmine took the envelope from Roxie and glanced at her typewritten name on the front. She frowned, but when she noticed Roxie still standing over her, she tucked the envelope into her purse, said, "Thank you." And then she folded her hands in her lap and stared at Roxie until the woman finally walked out the door.

How was she supposed to work with someone she didn't trust?

That was the point she was going to make to Hosea when she finally told him what she'd done with Roxie. She didn't really care how Hosea reacted. Roxie was out of the way.

Jerome may have sent his girlfriend to do his dirt, but they all needed to recognize the truth—Hosea wasn't going anywhere.

Jasmine dismissed thoughts of her enemies when she stepped into the elevator and pressed the 3 button. As the chamber ascended, she did what she always did when she was about to see her father-in-law—said a quick prayer that today would be the day. She imagined walking into his room and seeing him awake and well. Then taking him home with her and Hosea, where she would take care of him. When the elevator doors opened, Jasmine said, "Amen."

With hope in her heart, she turned the corner and then . . .

Flashback!

At the end of the hall, there was Hosea. With Ivy. And she had her arms around his neck.

The two were too far away for her to hear the words they exchanged, but when Ivy turned toward Jasmine, she jumped out of the girl's sight until she heard her footsteps come closer. Jasmine stepped from her hiding place and blocked Ivy's path.

"Oh, Jasmine!" Ivy giggled. "You scared me."

"Did I?" But she didn't wait for a response. "Let me ask you something, Ivy, why're you always hanging around here?"

The woman's thick eyebrows bunched into a unibrow. "I'm here for Hosea. We've been friends since—"

Jasmine held up her hand, her palm, barely an inch from Ivy's face. "Save that story."

"Well, then," she squeaked, "you know that I'm here supporting him. I brought him a couple of sandwiches and a soda and—"

"Let me break this down for you; Hosea doesn't need your support or your food. He's my husband, and anything he needs I'll get for him."

She almost cracked up when Ivy's eyes widened so much, Jasmine thought she might bust a vessel. But Jasmine saw only surprise, not fear. So she took another step closer.

It was a bit of a shocker when Ivy didn't back away, but that didn't matter. She was tired of playing; when she finished, many months would pass before Ivy stepped to Hosea again.

"So are we clear?" Jasmine hissed. "You won't be coming back."

A pause. Then, "And if I do?"

This time, it was Jasmine who stepped back.

"I'm not walking away from Hosea," Ivy said, the squeaky voice gone. In its place was a deep tone that came from her throat. "We've been friends for a long time, and you need to find a way to deal with it."

Then the pip-squeak of a woman moved as if she was a foot taller. Marched around Jasmine, pressed the elevator button, and got inside the chamber.

She never looked back to see that, this time, she was the one who left Jasmine standing in the middle of the hallway with her mouth opened wide.

TWENTY-FIVE

It had been the longest day.

Roxie and Ivy had left her with a raging headache and a rumbling stomach.

"Go on in and lie down," Hosea said as he opened the door to their apartment.

He knew she wasn't feeling well. The moment she'd entered his father's hospital room earlier, Hosea had taken a single look at her and knew something was up. But when he'd asked her about it, she'd lied and claimed it was headache. Or a stomachache. Anything rather than tell him the truth about Ivy.

But that was the problem with lying—God had turned her lie into her truth. And now her head throbbed and her stomach was doing somersaults.

"I'll check on Jacquie," Hosea said as they stopped in front of their bedroom. "Then I'll be in to check on you." He pressed his lips against her cheek.

"Thanks, babe," she said. "Give her a kiss for me."

Inside their master suite, Jasmine dumped her purse on the

bed. For a moment, she ignored the keys and papers that spilled from her bag, but then her glance went to the envelope that Roxie had given her this morning.

She'd forgotten about that and picked it up now. She frowned again like she'd done the first time she'd looked at her name—Jasmine Larson—on the front. It was weird—clearly her name had been typed, not printed. And she wondered why there was no mention of her married name. Only Mae Frances referred to her that way.

She slid open the top, unfolded the paper.

Get your husband to step down from the pulpit or else everyone will know what you did in the summer of 1983.

The summer of 1983!

Jasmine could hardly stand up with the way her heart sledged through her chest.

"Darlin'?"

With glazed eyes, she looked up. She wanted to tear the paper into a million pieces before he saw it.

"What's wrong?"

She squeezed her legs, sucked in her lips, took a breath. All to stop her trembling. All to no avail.

"No . . . nothing." Gently, she folded the paper she held, praying the move made no sound. What she really wanted to do was dance a jig so that his eyes would stay on her and he wouldn't notice the note. But fear had her fettered.

He frowned. "It has to be something; you're shaking."

"I just . . ." And then she held the back of her hand to her forehead. Closed her eyes. Took shallow breaths. Fell back onto the bed. All with the drama of one of the *Young and the Restless* divas. "I think . . . I think . . . I think I have a fever!" she exclaimed as melodramatically as she could.

At first he chuckled, as if he knew it was a performance. But then his eyes got small with concern—like maybe she was delirious, and it was delirium that had her acting like she was a soap star.

Jasmine held her breath when he started walking toward her. Said a prayer that he wouldn't ask about the paper that was grasped inside her fist. Then, in case God didn't answer her, she began to form her Plan B—a good lie.

When he placed his hand right above her eyes, doing his own check for a fever, she exhaled and remembered. This was her husband; Hosea cared only about her, not some paper. Knowing him, he hadn't even noticed.

"You feel a little warm. Get in bed, and I'll bring you some tea."

"Thanks so much, babe." Carefully, she leaned over, picked up her purse, and tucked the blackmail letter inside.

"What's that?"

She wasn't sure what was hammering harder—her heart or her head. All she hoped was that he couldn't hear the sound of either crashing through her skin. "What's what?" she asked, with the innocence of a woman wearing a halo.

"What you were reading?"

"Oh, nothing." She turned away so that he wouldn't see the truth on her face. She stuffed the note deep into her purse. If he wanted to see what she was reading now, he'd have to fight her for it.

He stood, waiting for her to say more.

She added to her lie. "It's just a note from Malik. He wants me to help him with—" She turned back to Hosea, held one hand to her head again while her other hand grasped her purse strap so tight, she constricted her blood from flowing to her hand. "Do you think I might be coming down with the flu?"

"I don't know," he said, his concern back to where it was supposed to be. "Let me get the tea."

She didn't move a step until he was out of her sight, and then she dashed into her closet. What she really wanted to do was sleep with her purse close by her side. But that would be hard to explain. So she stuffed the bag deep into the darkest corner. And then she piled six shoe boxes on top.

Even when she came out, she couldn't keep her eyes away from the spot where her secret was buried.

Who had found out? Who knew about the only time of her life that filled her with shame? Who, for God's sake, had found out that she used to be a stripper?

TWENTY-SIX

Jasmine's eyes were closed as she leaned back in her office chair. Now she knew why those memories had been haunting her for weeks; those recollections had been a premonition, a warning to beware of the dire days ahead.

Her hand began to tingle and she looked down at the letter gripped tightly between her fingers. Lifting it, she read it again, as if she hoped the twelve-hour time span that had passed since she'd first read it had somehow changed the words. But the note was the same—and her world remained in turmoil.

This was worse than drama; this was straight trauma. Enough to send her to the hospital and put her in a bed right next to her father-in-law.

But it didn't serve any purpose to sit here now and lament. She had to figure out a way to deal. With this letter. With this blackmailer.

And with her husband. Hosea. The senior pastor.

Jasmine shook her head. She couldn't even imagine the scene. Where she would go to Hosea and say, "Babe, I simply forgot to tell you that I was a stripper." She couldn't get the tape in her mind to play beyond that. She couldn't get to the part where he'd wrap his arms around her and tell her that he believed her. That he understood. The part where he would say, "I forgive you" and "I love you anyway."

No, to Hosea, this would be another secret, another lie, another betrayal.

And with everything that he was going through, Jasmine was sure that this time, he'd leave her—for good. Because this time, the secret wasn't just about her. This time, her secrets and her lies put his father's church in jeopardy.

She wasn't going to confess to Hosea, but she wasn't about to cede victory to the blackmailer either. She was Jasmine Cox Larson Bush, and whoever had sent this letter had forgotten that.

She pushed aside the note and centered a yellow pad on her desk. She had to begin at the beginning—she'd start with a list.

Who wanted to bring Hosea down? That was easy; that was obvious. She wrote: Eugene Wyatt, Jerome Viceroy.

But there were others—many who couldn't wait to see her fall. She added Enid, who seemed to be the brains behind her husband. And Ivy, who would be the first in line to console Hosea if he ever tossed Jasmine out.

And then there were the saints—the board members who'd all challenged Hosea. Sister Clinton, who insisted it was time to move. Brother Stevens, who had his own arguments. Even Sister Pearline came to mind—the letter had been typed, after all. Who else but an old-timer like her would have a back-in-the-day typewriter?

Jasmine wondered about others in their circle: Brother Hill and Sister Whittingham. But although they hated her, they would never hurt Hosea.

She thought about Malik, but he was as out of the question as Mae Frances was.

The knock on her door startled her. Made her grab the pad and the letter. Stuff both into the drawer before she said, "Come in."

"Do you have a moment?"

Seeing Roxie made her frown. She thought about the letter hidden in her drawer. The one that Roxie had given to her. She motioned with her hand, invited Roxie in.

After she sat down, Roxie began, "I couldn't sleep last night knowing how much you really could use my support, even if you don't think you do."

Why is this woman so hell-bent on helping me?

Roxie continued, "Look, I was in the middle of one of these church fights when our board turned on my husband. I know what to expect; I know how to handle this. I can help you get the members of City of Lights behind you and Hosea."

Jasmine didn't let a beat pass. "Does that include getting the members to see why we won't sell this church?"

Roxie looked dead at her. "Yes, if that's what you and Hosea want, as your armor bearer, as your support, I would agree." It must've been the way Jasmine looked at her that made Roxie lean forward. "Jasmine, I don't get anything out of this . . ."

Then why?

"Except for helping you," Roxie continued. "God has placed it in my heart . . ."

Why are people always blaming their dirt on God?

"And I've known Hosea and Reverend Bush for a long time. They've both been good to me; this is my chance to give back." She paused. "Whether you admit it or not, Jasmine, you need me."

Jasmine sat still, kept her eyes on Roxie.

Roxie stared back at her. Frozen. As if she knew she was under a microscope.

Finally Jasmine said, "Maybe you're right."

Roxie's lips spread into a slow, sly smile. Made Jasmine want to take back what she'd said. But she didn't. She had to play this through.

Roxie said, "I just want you to know I understand why you

were so hesitant, but this will work out. Okay, when should we get started?"

"What about now?"

Roxie laughed. "I'd love to, but I found out this morning that I have to be in court for the rest of the week. Can we start on Monday?"

Jasmine nodded. "That'll be fine." She waited until Roxie was gone before she slipped the pad from the desk and added another name to the list: Roxie.

Now that she had the suspects in place, she picked up the phone. She needed help, and there was only one master who knew how to handle this kind of disaster—she called Mae Frances.

TWENTY-SEVEN

It felt like the kiss of a prince.

Waking her from a fairy tale, although her dreams were more like nightmares.

Jasmine opened her eyes and stared into Hosea's concerned ones.

"Hey, babe," she whispered. "I didn't hear you come in."

"How could you?" He took their sleeping daughter from her arms. "Mrs. Sloss said you fell asleep in here holding Jacquie, and she didn't want to wake you. She said you looked so peaceful."

As Hosea laid their daughter to rest in her bed, Jasmine massaged her temple with her fingertips. Her sleep had been anything but peaceful. Instead, her unconsciousness had been crammed with images of her past, images from the summer of '83.

After he covered Jacqueline, Hosea pulled Jasmine up from the rocking chair and held her hand until they were in their bedroom.

"I missed you today," he said.

"I'm sorry. I just wanted to come home." *And stay away from you,* she added inside.

Today was the first day in almost six weeks since Reverend Bush had been shot that she hadn't gone to the hospital. How could she? How was she supposed to face Hosea with the blackmail letter so fresh in her mind? One look in her eyes, and he would have known.

Now she hoped that enough hours had passed so that he couldn't see, wouldn't feel the stress she'd been carrying for twenty-four hours.

But then he asked, "What's wrong, Jasmine?"

Inside, she sighed. She would have stayed away from him longer if she could, but she had to come home.

He repeated his question.

Keeping her eyes away from his, she said, "Nothing. Why're you asking me that?" She could feel him staring at her.

"I don't know." His voice full of suspicion. "It looks like . . . feels like—"

"Nothing's wrong," she said as lightly as she possibly could. "I wanted to come home early to spend some time with Jacquie." And then, she added, "I miss her," knowing he'd believe that.

He nodded. "I do, too." But his eyes didn't move away. "Jasmine, with everything that's going on with my father, with everything at the church, I need to know . . ."

Why is he so suspicious?

She had to face him now. Look into his eyes and make this lie look and feel like the truth. With a breath, she turned, made her fake smile real. "Babe, there's nothing wrong. If I'd known you'd be this concerned, I would've met you at the hospital. But like I said—"

He held up his hand, stopping her. "I'm sorry. I guess it's all the pressure. I'm seeing things, looking for stuff that's not even there." He sighed, slumped onto the bed. "It's all . . . getting to be too much."

Even though her heart was still pounding, she said, "That's okay. I understand. How's Dad?"

Shaking his head, he said, "No change. Doctor Lewis wants to meet with me tomorrow morning, and I don't think it's good news." He stopped and took her hand. "Will you go with me?"

She nodded. "Of course."

With a sigh, he said, "I don't know, Jasmine. With Pops, I don't know if I'm doing enough."

"What more can you do? You've been praying, and the rest is up to God."

"I know, but all these weeks have passed, and there's nothing new. Maybe that's because Pops needs more from me. Maybe he needs to hear my voice more. Or feel my presence more. Maybe I need to be there more." He paused. "I'm thinking . . . about stepping down." He took another moment, as if he needed that time to digest what he'd just said. "Maybe Pastor Wyatt should be leading City of Lights."

It was hard for her to keep standing, so she sank down onto the bed next to him. "Really?" was all she could say.

"Yeah. I've got to do all I can, and with everything . . . it's getting to be too much." Then, without another word, he kissed her forehead and ambled toward the bathroom—all that was on his mind weighing heavily on his shoulders.

Jasmine didn't move. Just stayed there and thought about how God truly did answer prayers.

This was her way out! If Hosea stepped down, the blackmailer, the letter, the threat would go away.

Hosea would never know. She'd never have to convince him that stripping had been her only choice. At least, that's what she'd thought back then; that's what Viva had told her . . .

For days, Viva had been trying to persuade Jasmine to go to the club with her. But over and over, Jasmine had told her no. Never in a million years would she get on some stage in front of a bunch of old men. No way. She was too good for that. And that's what she kept telling Viva.

"Okay, so you're too good to make money, mama?" her friend asked. "Then what're you gonna do?"

Jasmine shook her head. "I'm not exactly sure; I'm still checking out getting a second job for the summer."

"Okay, that'll bring you an extra, what, one hundred dollars a week? And by the end of the summer, you'll have an extra, what? It won't even be a thousand dollars."

Jasmine ignored her skepticism. "I have other options. I made some calls to the blood bank—"

She had to stop talking since Viva was buckled over, laughing.

"And then there are other things," Jasmine added, softly this time, her confidence waning. But when Viva kept laughing, Jasmine added, "I don't care what I do. All I know is that you're not going to find me on some stage dancing half naked!"

"Not half naked, *chica,* nine-tenths naked." Viva laughed. "I take it all off—everything but the drawers."

Jasmine shook her head. "That's not for me. And how would being an exotic dancer help anyway? What am I gonna do—pay my tuition with one-dollar bills?"

"That's bogus, *chica.* Money is money. Those people in the admin building won't be turning down anything that's green. I'm telling you, you can make a truckload of cash—more than you can make anywhere else."

Jasmine turned up her nose, as if the thought of dancing with Viva smelled nasty.

Viva said, "Don't be looking down at me. You need to be asking me to hook you up, 'cause you don't have very many choices . . ."

Jasmine sighed deeply, bringing herself from the summer of 1983 to the winter of 2007. If only what she'd told Viva had been true. If only she'd kept her word that she wouldn't take off her clothes for any reason. If only being a stripper hadn't come so easily.

But as she listened to the sound of the shower spray coming from the bathroom, she thanked God for Hosea's words.

Maybe Pastor Wyatt should be leading City of Lights.

Without knowing a thing, her husband had saved her. All she had to do now was encourage him, tell him that he should step aside, convince him that focusing on his father was the right thing. The right thing for both of them.

Jasmine stripped as fast as she could and headed to the shower. There was no better time to begin to persuade her husband than now.

TWENTY-EIGHT

JASMINE DIDN'T KNOW WHY ALL those people talked about food being the way to a man's heart. The real key to any man's soul was in the bed.

She'd known that before, and she was sure of it now as she rolled away from Hosea, leaving her husband gasping.

After a couple of deep breaths, Hosea smiled. *"Good* morning."

She kissed his cheek. "It was good for me."

"As good as it was last night?"

Jasmine chuckled as she rested her head against his chest. "Definitely." Although she was smiling on the outside, her thoughts were on all those images that had kept sleep away again.

But by tonight, sleep should come easy because of the free pass Hosea was giving her. As quickly as this drama began, it was about to end.

She counted to ten and then said, "I've been thinking about what you said last night."

Hosea frowned, as if he didn't know what she was talking about. As if his thoughts were still on this morning.

"Stepping down," Jasmine reminded him. "I think you're

right, babe. You have too much to offer to be staying where people are constantly trying to bring you down. And once you walk away from that drama, you'll be able to spend more time with your dad, like you want to. And, I will, too. And then we'll both be able to spend more time with Jacquie." Without a breath, she kept going. "And then when *Bring It On* returns in the summer, you won't be so stressed. You'll be able to focus on the show. On what's most important to you. It'll be a better quality of life—for you, me, and Jacquie." She nodded with every word she spoke. "Definitely, give Pastor Wyatt the keys, because it's not worth it."

Hoisting himself up on one elbow, Hosea looked at Jasmine through squinted eyes. "Wow. You gave me a couple of reasons that I hadn't even thought about."

"Well, isn't that what a helpmate's supposed to do?"

He nodded, his eyes still on her. "But why the change? I thought you loved being Lady Jasmine."

"Yeah, but I hate what you're going through; you're my priority." She paused, cupped his face with the palm of her hand. "Babe, I thought about this all last night. You're doing the right thing."

"Well, we're on one accord."

Jasmine smiled, thoughts of the blackmail letter almost gone from her mind. It was over.

He said, "I was thinking about this all night, too. Kinda talked to God as I slept. And I think I was just worn down yesterday." He leaned forward and gently pressed his lips against hers. "Don't worry, darlin', you're still the first lady."

Jasmine blinked, taking seconds to understand. "You're . . ."

"Going to stay," he finished. "The best thing I can do for my father is carry on."

"But . . ."

He kissed her again. "I've made up my mind, so pray for me," he said, before he jumped out of the bed.

He left Jasmine sitting, wondering what had happened. Her plan had been that, by the time her feet hit the floor this morning, City of Lights and her blackmailer would be in the past.

But with what Hosea had said, nothing had changed. The threat was still there. Today was just like yesterday—she was still in trouble.

It was more than the chilled air that made her shiver when she traipsed across the floor, her steps leaving soft prints in the plush carpet. But by the time she got to her closet and grabbed her bathrobe, her confidence was back.

She was ready with another plan.

TWENTY-NINE

THEY WERE HOLDING HANDS WHEN they turned the corner and saw the nurses running from the room. Jasmine and Hosea stood, their eyes wide as a doctor shouted orders.

"We're moving him now!"

Finally, the shock released him, and Hosea ran to his father's room. "What—"

Before he could get out another word, two orderlies wheeled his father's bed through the door, pausing for a second to steady the frame.

The sheet was pulled high on Reverend Bush, but only to his face. And that was where Jasmine saw death . . . in the gray pallor of his skin. In the way his forehead was beaded with sweat. He looked like he was on his way to die.

"Pops!" Hosea yelled, as his father was rushed past them.

"Mr. Bush, we were trying to reach you." Jasmine and Hosea spun around to face Dr. Lewis. "We're moving your father back up to ICU." The doctor spoke succinctly, her tone filled with more urgency than Jasmine had ever heard before in her voice.

"What happened?"

Dr. Lewis shook her head as she directed Hosea and Jasmine away from the door. "We're not sure yet, but his temperature has been rising all night. And then this morning, his blood pressure began dropping," she said quickly.

Jasmine inhaled a huge breath of air. And even though she was sure of the answer, she asked, "Is he dy—"

Hosea didn't let her finish. "What are you going to do?"

"We're putting him on pressors. It may be that he has an infection in his blood."

"An infection in his blood?" Jasmine exclaimed. "Isn't that like poison? What are you doctors doing to him!"

Hosea took her hand, her signal to be quiet.

The doctor looked at Jasmine for a moment, then squared her shoulders and spoke to Hosea. "We're not sure of the source—*if* it's even an infection. But if it is, it could be that his catheter has given him a kidney infection. Or it could be that a bacterium from one of his bedsores has gotten into his blood."

This time, Hosea couldn't keep her quiet. "Bedsores!" Jasmine shouted.

"Yes," the doctor said as patiently as she could. "Bedsores are not uncommon for a patient who's been bedridden for so long. The skin breaks down and ulcers form," she said, stating straight facts. "Whatever the source, your father's condition is not good, and I have to go."

"Doctor," Hosea swallowed hard, "is my father going to be . . . is he—"

The doctor didn't wait for him to ask the painful question. "I'll be honest with you, Mr. Bush. This is life-threatening. That's why I have to go." With a quick glance at Jasmine, the doctor rushed away, leaving the two standing, their eyes following her until she was gone.

"Oh, my God," Hosea finally whispered.

Those were her sentiments, but Jasmine couldn't say a word. All she could do was turn around and hold her husband.

They were holding hands, in the ICU waiting room. Their heads bowed and their eyes closed. Even as the TV played a rerun of *The Cosby Show* in the corner overhead, even as other families wandered in and out, Jasmine and Hosea stayed committed to talking to God.

"Hosea!"

Brother Hill rushed into the room and held his godson. Then he leaned over and kissed Jasmine's cheek, leaving her in as much shock as the news they'd received four hours ago about her father-in-law.

"How is he?"

Hosea shook his head. "We haven't heard too much. Doctor Lewis came out a couple of hours ago to tell us that they had him on pressors to keep his blood pressure up. That's the big problem—keeping his pressure up so that his brain gets enough blood and oxygen. They're concerned about brain damage."

"Wow." Brother Hill sank into the chair next to Hosea. "Samuel was doing so well."

"Not well, Daniel," Hosea said. "He's been in this coma, and we've been fooling ourselves that since he wasn't getting worse, he was getting better."

Brother Hill nodded.

Jasmine squeezed her husband's hand. "But we're not giving up," she said to both of them.

Hosea shook his head slowly. "No, I'll never give up on Pops."

"And you know your father. He's not ready to leave us," Brother Hill said, as if that was his hope. He added, "I called Wyatt to let him know what's going on. Did you know he was out of town?"

"Yeah, he had an engagement somewhere in Mississippi this weekend," Hosea said. "But that's fine. I can handle my father and the church."

Jasmine frowned. She hadn't known that Pastor Wyatt was away. If he was gone, then maybe he wasn't the one who'd slid the note under her door.

"He said he'll be back on Monday."

"Whatever," Hosea said, just as Dr. Lewis stepped into the room.

Thoughts of Pastor Wyatt were gone as the three stood. Dr. Lewis glanced at Brother Hill and Hosea nodded.

"Doctor, I think you've met my godfather, Daniel Hill."

"Yes." Her voice was weighed down by exhaustion. "Well, we've gotten your father stable again. His fever is slowly coming down, and now we have him on a broad range of antibiotics—which means we're trying to kill anything and everything before we even get his blood cultures back."

"And his blood pressure?" Hosea asked.

"Well, if this works, by tonight his pressure should be more stable."

"Okay, then," Hosea said with hope, "this is good news."

The three exhaled, exchanged hopeful glances, and nodded together. But then the little bit of relief they found was snatched away when they turned back to the doctor. Her expression said nothing about good news.

"Is there something else?" Hosea asked.

"I want to caution you. Your father's blood pressure was so low, we don't know what kind of damage was done. If we get him stable, we may want to do more tests."

"Sure." Hosea nodded. "Whatever you need to do."

"Now, if there is extensive damage, that could mean . . . he could be brain dead."

The gasp was so loud, Jasmine wasn't sure if the sound had come from just her.

The doctor asked, "Does your father have a living will, any instructions on how he would want this situation handled?"

Hosea shook his head. "No, I don't think so. He's never talked to me about that."

"Well, if he doesn't have one, then you're going to have to make the decision. Depending on the test results, we may want to think about taking your father off the ventilator."

"But if you take him off . . ." Hosea didn't have to finish.

The doctor nodded. "Then nature would take its course."

"No!" Hosea exclaimed.

As if the doctor had been in this place before, she stood, her eyes and voice steady. "All I'm saying is that we should consider everything."

"No!" He shook his head to help convey his point.

"Think about it. It may be better—"

"You're not hearing me, Doctor!"

This time, Jasmine was the one who had to hold her husband back. She grabbed his shoulder, gently. And, with that little bit of pressure, reminded him who he was. Reminded him he had to stay calm.

Hosea took a breath. "I'm sorry, but you need to hear what I'm saying. We're going to do everything we have to do. The life-and-death decision—that's going to stay in God's hands."

"That's what I'm talking about Mr. Bush, letting nature take its course."

"And I'm talking about your using every talent that God gave you. Your work and my prayers are going to keep my father alive."

Dr. Lewis stood, saying nothing for a moment, her eyes a bit brighter. "You're wrong Mr. Bush. It's *my* work and *my* prayers, too." With a slight smile, she nodded and walked away.

THIRTY

As they waited for Dr. Lewis, Jasmine squeezed Hosea's hand. Her eyes scanned the walls, covered with platinum-framed diplomas that declared to the world that Dr. Lewis knew what she was doing.

"You okay?"

She twisted to face her husband when she heard his soft voice. She wasn't fooled by the way his lips upturned. The story was in his eyes—his fear, mixed with his determination to stand, no matter what the doctor said. She held his hand tight, needing to garner some of his faith.

It had been two days since the reverend's crisis, and although the color had returned to his face, Reverend Bush was still the same. Still wasn't breathing on his own. Still needed every bit of medical technology to keep him alive.

The tension of it all had been almost enough to take Jasmine's mind off the blackmail. Almost, but not completely.

During the day, she had Hosea and Jacqueline to focus on. But in the dark of the night, she was alone with her thoughts, traumatized by the knowledge that her past had found its way to her present.

She did have a plan, but there was no way to work it—not

until this crisis passed. She couldn't move ahead knowing what she was about to do to her husband.

"I'm sorry I kept you waiting." Dr. Lewis broke through Jasmine's musings as she swept into the office.

Jasmine searched her face for some clue, but, like always, Dr. Lewis wore her mask, covering up any feelings.

"Okay," she said, opening a folder on her desk. "I have some good news. Your father is doing much better."

Together, they breathed a long sigh of relief.

The doctor glanced down at her notes. "You know his fever broke yesterday, and this morning, his pressure is completely steady. In fact," she looked up, "when I checked on him, he seemed to be breathing over the vent a little bit."

Jasmine and Hosea frowned. He asked, "What does that mean?"

"It means . . . that some of those prayers we're *both* sending up," she smiled, her mask gone for a moment, "are working. Your father is trying to breathe on his own. That's a sign that he's waking up."

"That's great!" Jasmine exclaimed.

The doctor nodded, then a shadow passed and took her smile away. "We're going to try to wean him off the ventilator," she said, her doctor's voice back, "and see how he does."

"He's going to do fine," Hosea said, just as his cell phone vibrated. He grabbed it from his holster, glanced at the doctor, and said, "This looks important. May I take it?"

The doctor nodded. "Make it quick, and I'll look the other way."

Jasmine gave the doctor a courtesy smile, then diverted her eyes, checking out the diplomas once again. Took her thoughts back to her plan. With Reverend Bush doing so much better, she could move forward now.

When Hosea flipped the phone closed, he turned to Jasmine. "That was Mrs. Whittingham. She can't open the church this morning, something about the pipes in her apartment. Can you get over there?"

Jasmine looked from the doctor back to her husband. "I want to be here."

"But Doctor Lewis has already told us everything"—he turned to the doctor—"right?"

She nodded and stood up. "I'll keep you posted if anything changes."

Hosea turned back to Jasmine. "The serviceman is coming to repair the copier; we really need to get that done. And with Wyatt out of town and Brother Hill at another appointment, you're it, 'cause I want to spend some time with Pops."

"Okay." She gathered her bag before she said good-bye to the doctor, and then kissed Hosea. "I'll be back in a couple of hours."

"Take the car," he offered, handing her the keys.

Outside of the hospital, Jasmine glanced over her shoulder at the blue and white building, thought once more about her husband and her father-in-law, then turned around and left all thoughts of them right there on Lenox Avenue.

Unlocking the SUV with the remote, she jumped inside, then made a U-turn heading in the opposite direction of City of Lights. Her plan was to go downtown, south of Twenty-third Street, where she doubted that she would run into anyone she knew. She had no concern about the copier repair. Now that her father-in-law was out of danger, she had to do what she had to do—and that was to get Hosea to step down.

It did sadden her that she had to give up so much. Six weeks. That was her entire reign as the first lady. How pitiful was that?

But in a small (very small) way, Jasmine wanted to thank the blackmailer. Having Hosea resign really was best. The two of them were too good for this church, these people, this drama. And the measly one hundred thousand dollars they'd decided to pay Hosea annually wouldn't be missed. She'd go back to Rio (where she made much more), and they would return to the life where they belonged. They would be with people who were full of style and elegance—and nothing like the folks at City of Lights.

About fifteen minutes later, she rolled to a stop in front of a Duane Reade. She glanced down one end of the street, then the other. Satisfied, she grabbed the scarf and huge glasses from her purse and secured her disguise. A final mirror check before she slipped out of the car and walked into the drugstore.

Her plan was about to begin.

It hadn't taken long at all.

Glancing at her watch, Jasmine stepped into the church, a bit over an hour after she'd left Hosea at the hospital.

She flipped on the lights, locked the door, then walked down the hall, her mind on her plan. Inside her office, her eyes stayed on the bag she held.

It wasn't until she walked around her desk and sat in her chair that her concentration was broken. She frowned when she felt something beneath her. Slowly, she stood. Looked down.

The rush of blood shot through her veins, taking her pressure higher. The bag she held slipped through her fingers, fell to the floor. But she didn't move her eyes from the wrinkled envelope.

Really, there was no need to touch it. She knew what it was—nothing but trouble.

It was the way the envelope was addressed that made her tremble, made her give up any hope that the first letter, the first threat that had come four days ago, was a hoax.

The typewritten name on the envelope this time: *Pepper Pulaski.*

As she stood and stared, Jasmine remembered the day that she first claimed that name . . .

"Come on," Viva had said, tugging her arm so hard, Jasmine felt like her limb might pop right out of the socket.

Viva pulled her along, but it was hard to move forward. Hard to step past the gaudy neon sign that screamed in the entire rainbow of colors: FOXTAILS.

Jasmine couldn't believe the number of times she'd passed by and never noticed the pink and purple stucco building that was set several feet back off Century Boulevard.

A moment later, she was inside, waiting for her eyes to adjust. Slowly, the darkness became light and the first thing Jasmine saw was the stage; it reminded her of the ones she'd decorated when she was part of the drama club's production team in high school.

But it wasn't the cheap stage that made her stare. It was the act on it. The girl gyrating against the pole as if the gleaming silver piece was a man.

"Don't worry," Viva whispered. "It's early. In a couple of hours this place will be jammed."

Only then did Jasmine notice the sprinkle of men—four, maybe five guys—sitting at the small round tables surrounding the stage, their eyes stuck on the girl like superglue.

Jasmine nodded as if Viva had addressed her concern. But it wasn't the quantity of people in the club that made Jasmine shift from one leg to another. It was the girl. Dancing. Totally naked, except for the slither of a G-string.

Jasmine wanted to cut and run. But the fact was, if she wanted to get this money, this was it.

She'd tried—she'd scoured the employment section in the *L.A. Times,* but there wasn't much for an untrained college student who could work only a couple of hours a week. Still, she'd knocked on the doors of every hospital, every hotel, every bank seeking part-time work. There was nothing. She'd even tried to get hired as an airport shuttle driver, but she couldn't read the *Thomas Guide.*

In a final act of desperation, she'd gone to a local grocery store several miles away from her apartment. She was willing to work a cash register, pack groceries—anything to earn what she needed.

At least the manager at Ralph's had told her yes, they were hiring cashiers. But even they wanted full-time hours, right during the time when she'd have to be in class.

"You need to start looking at this logically," Viva had said when Jasmine complained. "How many jobs are going to pay you what you need?" When Jasmine didn't answer, Viva responded for her. "None! But at Foxtails, you tell Buck how many days you want to work, and I'm telling you, *chica,* the money is *muy bien.*" Viva kissed the tips of her fingers.

It was the *muy bien* that had her here now, following behind Viva, moving in step to Irene Cara screaming through the club, "I can have it all, now I'm dancin' for my life!"

"Hey, Buck," Viva waved to the man behind the counter, "I got a new girl for you."

When the man turned around, his thick, shoulder-length blond dreadlocks whipped over his shoulder. His bushy eyebrows furrowed together as he peered at Jasmine through Coke-bottle glasses.

"'Sup?" he asked in a voice that belied his white skin. If she'd been blindfolded, Jasmine would have sworn this guy was straight from the hood.

"Buck, this is my girl, Jasmine. She wants to dance," Viva said.

"Yo, how ya doin'?" Buck squeezed his wide hips from behind the bar. Standing in front of them, he crossed his arms and stared at Jasmine before he took off his glasses.

"You don't have much on top," he grunted. "Take off your shirt."

"What?" Jasmine exclaimed.

Viva whispered, "Take a chill pill, *chica.* This is your audition. He's checking you out; don't blow it."

She had to remember all the reasons: her tuition, her apartment, her boyfriend, keeping up her image. She had to think about what it would be like if people found out that she didn't have enough money to finish school.

She unbuttoned her blouse, shrugged it from her shoulders, and then dropped it on the bar stool. She stood in just her bra and jeans.

Buck rolled his eyes. "So you gonna dance in your underwear? Come on," he said, waving his hands and sounding as if she was getting on his nerves.

She closed her eyes. Remembered. Then she unhooked her bra.

"Itty, bitty," he said, shaking his head. "You might want to get those taken care of one day."

Jasmine's mouth opened wide.

"Look, I'm trying to help you out, baby. You don't have nothing that you can shake. But what you got will do, 'cause some cats like 'em like that. Okay, drop your jeans and turn around." It must've been the look on her face that made him sigh. "Keep your panties on."

She unclasped the buttons on her jeans, then slipped them over her hips.

"Turn around," he repeated.

Slowly, she moved in a circle as Irene Cara still sang. Her eyes were squeezed tight, her heart was beating fast, and her mind reminded her of her reasons.

He nodded. "They'll like what you're hauling behind ya." After a moment, he asked, "Ever done this before?"

"No!" Jasmine said as if she was insulted. She faced him and crossed her arms in front of her chest.

He peered at her some more and then put his glasses back on. "Okay, you're in."

"So how much do you pay an hour?" Jasmine asked.

Buck stared at Jasmine, then looked at Viva, and back to

Jasmine. And then he laughed. Threw his head back and chortled, like that was the funniest line he'd ever heard. "I don't pay nothin' an hour."

"You don't pay . . ." Here she was standing topless, with her pants wrapped around her ankles, in front of a dread-wearin', calorie-lovin' white guy who was telling her that she wasn't going to be paid?

Jasmine glared at Viva. She was about to kill her friend.

Buck said, "This is straight tips, baby. But I don't have a nightly fee. After you hit off the DJ and the bar, you keep everything else, and you make a dollar commission on the drinks. So with the way you look, you can make hundreds, if you stop actin' like some kind of nun."

Make hundreds were the words that made her stay.

"Yeah, girl," Viva added her part. "I know how to work it to get the big tips." She nodded. "I can teach you how to make it rain for real. Especially with the married ones."

Jasmine wasn't exactly sure what her friend was talking about, but she remembered the stack of bills Viva had shown her—and she had a feeling that rain had something to do with money.

"So you in?" Buck asked.

All Jasmine wanted was to be out—but the thought of five thousand dollars made her nod.

"You eighteen?"

Jasmine nodded again.

"Got ID? 'Cause I ain't about to catch a case for no new girl. Don't want Five-O sniffin' 'round here."

"I got ID," she said, reaching for her shirt.

"Get dressed later," Buck said, sounding impatient. He held out his hand. "Just give me your ID so that I can make a copy and get your papers together for your permit."

After she handed him her license, he said to Viva, "Double up with her tonight."

"Why?" Viva whined. "She can dance."

"You're my best girl, and I need you to double up with the new kid," Buck repeated in a tone that said this was his party. "It's Friday, and I ain't about to lose money with some shy newby," he said, as if Jasmine wasn't standing there. "Either you double up, or she's out."

Both Buck and Viva turned to Jasmine. Stared at her with her hands crossed over her chest, as if that was enough to hide her nakedness.

Buck said, "If she works out, she can work the stage after tonight." And then he turned away, without any kind of goodbye. Leaving Jasmine standing topless and confused.

As fast as she could, Jasmine slipped her arms through her blouse, stuffed her bra into her purse, then pulled up her jeans.

"*Chica,* you better be glad I love you," Viva said, her accent thick, the way it always was when she was upset.

"Why?"

"'Cause doubling up means I gotta share my tips with you—on the floor and on the stage. They're not gonna give us twice the money." She paused and grinned. "Unless we—" She stopped. "Nah, you ain't *even* ready for that."

Jasmine could only imagine what Viva was talking about . . . some girl-on-girl kind of dancing. Her friend was right; she was not about to do that. Getting on this stage was going to be bad enough.

With a sigh, Viva said, "Come on, let me show you the dressing room, and then we can go shopping. I gotta get you somethin' fly if we're gonna do this."

Viva had already told her that she needed a pair of platform shoes and some kind of outfit to perform in.

"Oh," Viva said as she led the way. "You're going to have to come up with a name."

"For what?"

"For the DJ to call you. Do you want him saying, 'Now here's Jasmine Cox?' "

Jasmine shook her head. Not only did she not want anyone knowing her name, she would have worn a mask, if she could. "What name do you use?" Jasmine asked.

Viva grinned. "Dominica Divinci, but everyone calls me Double Dee."

That's appropriate. "Well, obviously, I can't have a name like that, so . . ."

With a big sigh, Viva said, "Do I have to figure out everything?" She stopped moving, turned back to Jasmine. "Okay, this is what some of the girls do—did you ever have a pet growing up?"

Jasmine frowned and nodded. "Yeah," she said slowly.

Viva motioned with her hands for Jasmine to continue.

"A dog named Pepper. But what—"

"That's good," Viva said, without letting her finish. "Now, what was the name of the first street you lived on?"

Jasmine squinted, her confusion growing. "Pulaski Street."

"Perfect! That's your name," she said, turning away and leading Jasmine toward the back again.

"Pepper Pulaski—that sounds like a stripper."

Pepper Pulaski. That was as far away from Jasmine Cox as she could get. *Whatever . . .*

That was what Jasmine thought then. But it had been a name that had served her well. The men who frequented the Foxtails Hostess Club came to adore Pepper Pulaski.

But that was in 1983. No one knew her by that name now.

As if it were a snake, Jasmine picked up the letter by its edge, slowly lowered herself into the chair, then tore open the envelope.

You are running out of time. Get your husband to step down now, Pepper, or else.

Long after she read the words, her hands were still shaking. Could this have come from someone in her past?

No, that made no sense. None of those people knew where

she lived now. None of those people would have been able to walk into this church and lay this letter on her chair.

This was definitely an inside job.

Slam!

Jasmine jumped at the sound of the front door—but she'd locked it, she was sure of that.

"Hello," she called out.

No response.

"Roxie?"

Again, nothing.

That was when her fear began to rise. She was glued to her seat, but only for a moment. Grabbing a pair of scissors, she jumped from her chair and tiptoed across the office. If she could get to the door and close it, she'd be ready for anyone who tried to come in.

But then, she saw the shadow against the wall.

She lunged toward the door, but the man was already there.

She screamed.

He frowned.

"What's wrong with you?" Pastor Wyatt hoisted the strap of the garment bag he carried over his shoulder.

"Are you crazy?" she demanded, as she held her hand against her chest, trying to keep her heart inside. "What were you trying to do?"

"What are you talking about?" he asked, his forehead still creased with confusion.

"I asked who was there . . . you didn't answer."

He stared at her a moment longer. "I didn't hear you." And then he turned toward his office.

She slammed her door shut, but minutes passed before she was steady enough to walk. This blackmail thing was driving her straight to crazy. She had to get control of it now.

At her desk, she unwrapped the package she'd purchased earlier; she pulled out the cell phone and checked the signal.

She pressed in Hosea's cell number, and with the text message already in her mind, she typed: *Quit now or else ur family will be n danger.* The moment she pressed Send, she felt guilty.

But what else was she supposed to do? She'd been dragged into this, and her only option was to win.

Now she turned to the second part of her plan—her suspects: Pastor Wyatt and his wife, Jerome Viceroy, Ivy, and Roxie.

The more she stared at the list, the more confident she felt. It had to be one of them—who else could it be?

Now that she was sure, all she needed was dirt on each of these people so that she could turn the tables.

So that she could blackmail the blackmailer.

THIRTY-ONE

THIS WASN'T THE BEST IDEA Jasmine ever had.

After the way Pastor Wyatt had stalked into the church this morning, she definitely didn't want to be alone in this place tonight. But there was no other way to do what had to be done.

Jasmine glanced at her watch. *What time is that woman leaving?* As soon as she had that thought, she heard Mrs. Whittingham's footsteps approaching.

"Don't you have to pick up Hosea?" Mrs. Whittingham asked impatiently.

If this had been any other day, any other time, Jasmine would have told her to mind her business. But she responded quickly, directly. "Yes, I'll be leaving in a little while."

"Well," Mrs. Whittingham began with a deep sigh, "I'm ready to leave."

"Go on. I'll be okay." Faking a smile, she continued, "There's something I need to finish up here, something that Hosea asked me to do." She pointed to the pad on her desk, confident that Mrs. Whittingham was too far away to notice that the page was blank. It was the woman's frown that made Jasmine add, "This won't take me long." She breathed with relief when Mrs. Whittingham turned away. As she heard Mrs. Whittingham shifting around at her desk, Jasmine began packing her own purse and briefcase, wanting to be ready.

"I'm leaving," Mrs. Whittingham called out.

"Have a good night."

There wasn't a single word of reciprocation from Mrs. Whittingham, but Jasmine didn't notice. Her mind was beyond her nemesis, already on her mission.

She sat at her desk, glanced at her watch. She'd wait five minutes. But not even sixty seconds passed before she was up and out in the front, checking first to make sure that the door was locked. Then she stood behind Mrs. Whittingham's desk, in front of the three file cabinets lined up side by side.

It took her a few minutes, but she found what she needed in the fourth drawer. First, there was Pastor Wyatt's file. There wasn't much, but she jotted down the facts she didn't know, information she hoped to use. She did the same with Jerome Viceroy.

Scanning through the rest of the folders, she eyed the ones for Brother Hill, Mrs. Whittingham, Sister Clinton, Brother Stevens. There was even a file for Sister Pearline. But there was nothing on Roxie or Ivy. That made sense, since neither one was really part of the church.

She returned the files, stuffed the pad with all she'd written into her briefcase, then sat down at Mrs. Whittingham's desk. Here, she wasn't sure what she was looking for.

There was nothing but the usual office supplies—a tub filled with pencils and pens, a stapler, a dish with paper clips, rubber bands; she lifted a book of stamps—the Black Heritage ones. Surprise, surprise—the old biddy had some African pride.

She opened the top center drawer—more pens, more staples, more rubber bands. Just as she slammed the drawer, she heard the sound—a key in the door.

Jasmine jumped, tried to roll the chair away from the desk. But a wheel caught on the edge of the plastic runner. She pushed. Pushed. Then stood, a millisecond before Mrs. Whittingham walked inside.

The woman's eyes were fraught with accusations before she even said a word. "What are you doing?" she demanded to know.

"I was . . . looking"—Jasmine's eyes scanned the desk—"here." She lifted the booklet. "I needed a couple of stamps. But if you're going to act like this, never mind!"

Mrs. Whittingham stomped past her. "Didn't I tell you to stay away from my desk?" She opened drawers, peeked under papers, flipped through binders as if she was searching for proof of a crime. "This is my private space," she argued, as she slammed one drawer, then opened another. "My God. Am I going to have to lock up everything because Hosea has you working here?"

"First of all, Hosea doesn't have me—"

"This is ridiculous. All these years and now I'm going to have to put a padlock on my desk!"

"I *just* wanted a stamp," Jasmine said, letting the woman know how silly she sounded.

"Look," Mrs. Whittingham growled, "you stay out of my space, and I'll stay out of yours."

"Fine." She picked up her briefcase and purse. Pretended that she didn't notice the way Mrs. Whittingham stopped and was now eyeing her bag, as if she was sure the thief was escaping with evidence. Jasmine rolled her eyes and marched out the door.

Inside her car, she screeched out of the parking lot, without another thought about Mrs. Whittingham. Her mind was on the briefcase that rested in the passenger seat. What she'd gathered wasn't much, but it was a start. With Pastor Wyatt and Jerome Viceroy.

The two men on her list.

Men.

And men were her specialty. Knowing them, manipulating them was a talent that she had honed.

All she had to do now was put what she'd learned over the years to use.

THIRTY-TWO

JASMINE SQUEEZED HOSEA AS TIGHT as she could.

"Why didn't you call me?"

He shrugged and motioned for her to follow him into the hallway.

Outside of his father's room, he sighed. "There was no reason to call. Not really. Pops didn't make it without the ventilator. They had to put him back on almost immediately."

"But this morning, Doctor Lewis said that he was trying to breathe on his own."

"It looked that way. She said we should give it a couple of days and see where he's at before they try again."

Jasmine rubbed her hand across his back. "I'm so sorry. I know you were hopeful."

He shrugged. "It's not like I'm giving up. Pops is going to make it."

Jasmine didn't say anything else; just wrapped her arms around him again. But as she held him, she knew now for sure: she was doing the right thing. This time, she wasn't lying just to lie. This time, she wasn't thinking about herself. This was all about Hosea—how could she bring the blackmailer into his life?

When he stepped away from her, he said, "I hate to do this, but there's something else." The way he pulled back made her heart turn into a hammer. "I got this today."

She blinked as he scrolled through messages on his cell phone. It took her a moment to remember. Her text.

He said, "Now, I don't want you to be concerned, but . . ." He didn't finish. Just handed her the phone and let her read the text that she'd sent.

Jasmine's eyes scanned the screen as if she'd never read such words. As if she could hardly believe it.

She held her hand to her chest. Widened her eyes. "Hosea!" she gasped. There was as much fear in her voice as she could muster. "You *definitely* have to step down now. You *have* to quit. You have to think about . . ." She didn't have to say their daughter's name to know that he would get the message.

He shook his head. "I only showed you this because I never want to keep anything from you. But I'm not stepping down."

"What?" she asked. That was not the answer she'd worked for.

He said, "I'm not turning over Pops's church to someone who would send this."

"But you wouldn't be turning it over exactly. You'd still be on the board," she said, though she wasn't sure if that was in the blackmailer's plan.

Hosea was already shaking his head. "No."

She crossed her arms. Paced in front of him. "So you're going to ignore this? You can't. This is serious!"

"You're right." He held her shoulders. "I'm not ignoring it; I called Detective Foxx as soon as I got the message."

She swallowed. It took her a moment to get out, "You called the police?"

"Well, yeah. I mean, Foxx is a friend, and I knew he'd help me decide what to do."

Jasmine shook her head, not believing this. It was getting out of her control.

"I had to call him," Hosea said, mistaking the reason why Jasmine was muttering "no" under her breath. "Someone threatened us, and in today's times, I think this is considered a terrorist threat."

She was going to faint—she was sure of it. The way she couldn't breathe, the way her head began to spin. "What . . . what . . . what did Detective Foxx say?"

"He was out on the island today, but he's going to stop by our place tomorrow and talk to us. He wants to see the text, check it out—" Hosea stopped. "You don't have to worry. Nothing's going to happen . . . to you or Jacquie. I'll make sure of that."

It wasn't until he used his thumb to wipe away a tear crawling down her cheek that she realized she was crying.

"I promise," he said before he pulled her into his arms. "You and Jacqueline will always be safe."

She was grateful that Hosea thought her trembling had come from reading the text. But in truth: it was being the author of that message that had her shaking like she was an earthquake registering 9.0 on the Richter scale.

A terrorist threat?

What would the police do if they found out she'd sent the message?

The man in the drugstore had assured her that the phone wasn't traceable. That's what he'd said when she'd asked.

"Prepaid phones aren't traceable in any way, right?"

The man with the dark bushy mustache and turban on his head had looked at her with suspicion shooting from his black eyes.

"No, not traceable." But he'd kept his gaze on her. The entire time—as she paid him with cash, as he gave her change, as he packed the phone—he studied her as if he was sure he'd have to pick her out of a lineup one day.

But he wouldn't have been able to tell the police too much—her face had been well hidden.

She hadn't been worried at all then, but she had plenty of fear now.

Inside her husband's arms, she prayed that what the clerk had told her was true. She prayed that the phone she'd used wasn't traceable at all.

Jasmine's eyes were wide open as Hosea's snores rang in her ear. It had been a bit more than an hour since they'd gone to bed. But now, Jasmine was sure that she could move.

Slowly, she slid her leg from between his, paused, then gently slipped from beneath his arm. Even though she barely breathed as she moved, she sat on the edge of the bed and waited a moment before she grabbed her robe from the recliner, wrapped herself in the silk, then tiptoed across the apartment to the room they used as an office.

Even though the meeting with Detective Foxx was heavy on her mind, she couldn't be sidetracked—especially since Hosea refused to resign. The blackmailer was still looming, and she had to work her plan.

As she waited for the computer to boot up, her mind was already working on the lie she'd tell Hosea if he woke up. Her story would be that she couldn't sleep. That the text message and the meeting with Detective Foxx had her on edge. At least her lie was 90 percent truth.

She clicked onto the Internet and created a new Yahoo! account. She had all the fake information ready. Name: Mariah Carter—hoping that a name similar to the singer's might conjure up good images. Birth date: September 9, 1982—what better age than almost twenty-five? Next, she created a password and then signed on.

She started with Pastor Wyatt, since he was the married one and men with wives were always the easiest to trap.

Pastor Wyatt: I wanted to send you an e-mail to let you know that I admire you so much. I think your sermons are beyond wonderful. I come to City of Lights every Sunday just to see you. You are an amazing man and I hope . . . Jasmine stopped. Changed "hope" to *pray that you'll e-mail me back, not that I want anything. All I want is to know that you got my e-mail and that you know that you're appreciated. Peace and love, Mariah Carter.*

She read the e-mail again before she pressed Send. Then, she typed an e-mail with a few changes to Jerome Viceroy. She wasn't sure what she expected to get from him, since he was single. But men did all kinds of things when it came to sex and women. This was just phase one—tossing it out to see what would come back.

Her plan had been to sign off, go back to bed, and hope that by morning, her fish would have taken a bite. But she knew she wouldn't be able to sleep.

She glanced at the clock. It was after three. Surely neither of these men would be up at this time, lurking through cyberspace.

Still, she sat and sat. And she waited and waited.

Just sat and waited for something to happen.

THIRTY-THREE

"Detective Foxx, I really appreciate your stopping by." Hosea shook the man's hand as he stepped through the door.

"Not a problem." The detective shrugged off his raincoat, then glanced toward Jasmine. He nodded. "Morning, Mrs. Bush."

Jasmine mumbled her greeting behind a yawn. It had been almost six when she finally tiptoed back into her bedroom, minutes before the alarm would awaken Hosea. And even though she had hoped that exhaustion would give her at least an hour's worth of sleep, she'd stayed awake, praying that she'd considered everything with the prepaid phone. But she wasn't sure. Detective Foxx had to know something about tracing these phones—what other reason could he have for coming to their home on a Saturday morning?

Fear rumbled inside of her. She could imagine the detective, taking one look at the text, then jumping up, handcuffing her, and telling her something about the right to remain silent before hauling her off to jail.

"Detective," Hosea said, his voice interrupting her wide-awake nightmare. "I don't want to hold you too long." He handed the detective his cell phone.

Jasmine held her breath as she watched the man focus on the screen, scroll down, then back up. All she could do was pray.

"So you really think this came from someone at church?" Detective Foxx asked, shaking his head as if he couldn't believe that.

"I don't know what to tell you except that it's from someone who wants me out. But I can't imagine anyone I know sending something like this." He paused. "You know, if this was about me, I wouldn't have even called you. But once they threatened my family . . ."

"I'm glad you called. We need to check this out." The detective stared at the phone for a moment longer. "Let's try something." He punched a button. "I don't know if this will work. Can't imagine that someone would be this stupid, but I've met dumber criminals."

Jasmine swallowed before she whispered, "What are you doing?"

"I'm calling the number." It was the way her eyes widened that made him say, "I know, I don't expect anyone to pick up, but you never know."

"I tried that yesterday," Hosea said, "But there was no answer."

Jasmine looked at her husband with fresh eyes. Maybe he was better at these games than she was—she hadn't even thought about his calling that phone.

There was no way she was going to be able to continue breathing. All she did was close her eyes and, inside, pray harder.

Lord, if you get me out of this . . .

She prayed and prayed and tried to remember if she'd turned off the phone. And then she prayed that if she hadn't, they wouldn't hear not even the faintest sound coming from deep in the back of her closet.

When the detective breathed deeply, so did she. "No answer." He clicked off the cell. "I suspect that number is for one of those throw-away phones." He jotted the telephone number down on a pad, then handed the cell back to Hosea. "I'll do a little searching around. Find out where this number was purchased and see if the store personnel can tell me anything." He paused. "But I really doubt this is going to be traceable."

Those were the best words Jasmine had heard in years.

He continued, "I really don't think you have anything to worry about, though. Don't really think this person is trying to harm you. In fact, if I had to guess, I'd say the text came from a woman."

"A woman?" Jasmine and Hosea said together.

"Yup. I've done some profiling in my day, and looking at this message, the words are soft—like someone is trying to scare you, not pose a real threat. Very feminine." He stood. "But the intent doesn't matter. When we find them, they will be arrested."

Lord, if you let me get out of this . . .

"So you think you'll find out who sent this?" Hosea asked.

He nodded. "Blackmailers always mess up. It'll be something small, but they get careless. They make mistakes. And the more they communicate, the greater the chance of catching them—that's a fact." He shrugged his shoulders back into his raincoat. "Let me know every time you get a text."

"You think I'll get more?"

"Definitely. This is an amateur. You'll hear from them again and again." Over his shoulder, he said, "Enjoy the rest of your day, Mrs. Bush." He looked back at her and then stopped, as if he saw something. Turned around. Moved toward her.

Jasmine closed her eyes. Expected that what she would hear next was the detective telling her to remain silent and start thinking about an attorney.

But he only stood in front of her and said softly, "I can see that you're upset, but your family's not in any danger. Now if anything changes, you can bet we'll be right on it. But really, you're fine."

She wanted to kiss him for not wrapping handcuffs around her wrists. "Thank you," she said before he walked toward the door.

Her plan had been to keep sending messages until Hosea stepped down, but now all she wanted to do was get rid of that cell phone. She couldn't wait to take a ride to the West Side and dump her evidence deep into the Hudson River.

But while the detective had made every part of her tremble with fear, at the same time he's given her hope.

Blackmailers always mess up.

That's what he said. If her blackmailer kept sending letters, then eventually he would mess up.

That's what she needed—one big mess-up. And she needed for this mess-up to happen real soon.

THIRTY-FOUR

Jasmine tapped on the keys to her computer, switching from the Word document with the church's newsletter back to the fake e-mail account she'd created.

"I cannot believe this, Mae Frances," she whispered, even though she was alone in her bedroom. Hosea had long ago left for the hospital. But she didn't even want Mrs. Sloss overhearing her. "I haven't heard a thing from anyone in five days." Her eyes scanned through the spam that had filled her new e-mail account.

"I would think that's a good thing."

"How can you say that?" Jasmine switched back to the church's newsletter. "I would've thought Pastor Wyatt or Jerome would have responded by now. I need something on them."

"You think one of them was going to answer that silly little e-mail? Please. That letter you read to me didn't fool nobody. It sounded like a setup."

"Then why did you tell me my plan was good."

"Because it was . . . for an amateur. But I told you that you were playin' with the big boys and that you needed to let one of my connections handle this."

Jasmine sighed. There was no doubt that Mae Frances could

probably help, but her connections always came with a bill. And without her own paycheck, it would be difficult to pay and not leave a trail for Hosea to find.

"I'm going to stick to my plan," Jasmine said. "I'm going to be all right." Although she wasn't quite sure she believed that. She switched back to her e-mail account, and this time the new mail icon was up. She clicked, then sat straight up in her bed.

"Mae Frances, I've gotta go."

"Why? What you gotta do that's more important than talking to me?"

Her eyes were on the new e-mail. "I gotta . . . take . . . Jacquie," she stuttered. "I'll call you back later." She could hear her friend's protests as she hung up.

Tossing the cordless phone aside, she read the e-mail aloud.

"Thank you, Mariah, for such kind words from what I can tell is a beautiful girl. How old are you?"

That was it. There wasn't much to work with, but at least it was a start.

Jasmine hit Respond, but before she typed a word, she clicked back over to read Jerome's e-mail again.

"How old are you?" she whispered Jerome's question out loud. That was not the first question a smart man would ask a woman, even though no one ever said Jerome Viceroy was smart.

After a moment, Jasmine signed off, folded down her laptop, and leaned against the bed's headboard. There was no need to rush this; she needed to think it all the way through.

Finally, progress—contact with Jerome. Obviously, she needed another path to Pastor Wyatt and Enid. And Roxie. And Ivy.

But she was sure she'd find it. Jerome's e-mail had filled her with confidence.

THIRTY-FIVE

THIS DIDN'T FEEL SO MUCH like the seat of honor anymore—this first pew, first seat that she had coveted for so long. It was probably exhaustion that was making her feel this way; the mental erosion from being on edge—waiting for something to happen, trying to make something happen.

Jasmine hadn't heard from the blackmailer in over a week, but she was sure it was a trick. She'd be a fool to believe that the threat was gone when it was probably sitting in the sanctuary with her right now. All she wanted to do was to turn around and search for the culprit. Find the eyes that were watching and waiting for her to break. But she had no intention of giving anyone that satisfaction.

That's why she'd come into the sanctuary early, taken her place as always. The blackmailer needed to know that she would not be intimidated.

As the hum of chatter rose around her, Jasmine kept her eyes fixed to the altar and the golden cross that hung high on the wall.

Lord, if you will just get me out of this . . .

She closed her eyes, inhaled a deep breath, and then her lids parted wide. A sweet fragrance sailed beneath her nostrils.

She frowned and for the first time noticed the potted plant in front of her, blooming white flowers that generously sprayed their scent inside the sanctuary.

Fear swelled within her when she inhaled the familiar bouquet. Her memories were as fresh as the flowers, and it was the fragrance that dragged Jasmine back to 1983 . . .

Foxtails had been empty that afternoon when Viva had first taken Jasmine to meet Buck, but by night the hostess club was jammed like a sports bar on Super Bowl Sunday. The club pulsed with men and music.

Jasmine sat in the middle of the dozens of other girls, all primping and prancing and preparing for their show. She faced the mirror and wondered again what she was doing here, wondered again if she could really pull this off, and tried again to remember all of her reasons.

"Okay, if we're going to share the stage, we're going to have to put on a show," Viva spoke to Jasmine's reflection in the mirror.

For a moment, Jasmine wondered how her friend recognized her. With the stark-black, wavy hair that fell to her waist, the fake eyelashes that hid her eyes, and the fire-red lipstick that smothered her lips, she didn't look like Jasmine Cox. Which didn't bother her at all. Jasmine doubted that anyone she knew would ever stroll into Foxtails, but just in case, this costume was a good thing.

Viva said, "So how flexible are you?"

Jasmine frowned.

"You know . . . what can you do with your legs?"

"I guess . . ."

"*Chica,* we don't have time for guessing." Viva grabbed Jasmine's hand and pulled her up. "Can you do this?" In the middle of the room with girls flittering around her, Viva slowly inched her legs apart until she dropped into a full split.

Jasmine shrugged, hoisted her dress a bit higher on her hips and then did the same.

"Way to go, mama." Viva laughed and pushed herself up. "What about this?" She spread her legs shoulder-width apart, leaned forward, grabbed her ankles, and looked back at Jasmine through her legs.

Jasmine took the same stance and grasped the top of her four-inch Lucite pumps.

Her friend gave her a high five. "That's a money shot. Raise what you got in the air like that, and it'll be raining for sure."

"This is crazy." Jasmine wrung her hands together. "I should've practiced for a couple of days first."

"Practice? This ain't no Broadway show." Viva shook her head. "And anyway, it's not about the dance. It's about getting naked. Just remember. Take off the clothes slowly. Drag it out, and we'll get more money."

Jasmine glanced down at the nurse's outfit she wore. How was she going to take her time with this? There wasn't anything there—just a one-piece dress that was nothing more than a long blouse. The hem rode high up on her hips, allowing the edge of her garter to peek through. And when she glanced over her shoulder and looked in the mirror, half of her butt was already hanging out.

As if Viva heard her thoughts, she added, "Unbutton it slowly. And remember, you do have your bra to play with. You can toss it into the audience, but you'll never get it back. Oh, and remember, you have to always keep your G-string on. That's the law."

A roar from the front seeped to the back and a raven-haired girl (whom Viva had introduced to her earlier as Susan from USC) came traipsing through the curtain with a bunch of bills stuffed in her garter and in her hand.

"It's pouring out there." She waved two fists filled with money and strutted back and forth like she was oblivious to the fact that just a couple of inches of cloth covered her.

"Okay, we're up next." Viva grabbed Jasmine's hand. As they waited for the cue from the DJ, Viva gave her final instructions.

"If this starts to feel hard, pretend you're someone else. Focus on the men wearing wedding bands, and remember they all just want attention."

The voice came from the other side of the black curtain. "Gentlemen, are you ready for our very own Double Dee!" The hoots and whistles made the DJ pause. "And Double Dee has a special treat tonight. She's got a friend—let's hear it for Double Dee and Nurse Pepper Pulaski."

Viva squeezed Jasmine's hand, then shared last words of wisdom. "Let's make it rain, baby!"

Money was on her mind as Jasmine strutted behind Viva. As Rick James belted out the lyrics to "Cold Blooded," Jasmine waved to the DJ just as Viva did, and then she pressed her lips into a tight smile to keep them from trembling.

The DJ said, "Oh, yeah. Nurse Pepper! She's hot! Look at all of that junk in her trunk!"

The cheers—which were really cackles—made her feel a little bit better, but it was still the money that made Jasmine swing around the second pole, like Viva was doing, and then sway her hips from side to side as she unhooked the first button on her dress.

"Freaky, baby!" the DJ sang along with Rick.

Jasmine looked out into the darkened room. Black men. White men. Men in suits. Men in sweats. Old and young. There were even a few women in the place. But male and female—everyone was watching her.

And they were gawking. And whistling. And clapping . . . for her.

That was when the trembling slowly began to twist into a delicious tingling, though Jasmine wasn't quite sure why. But in that instant, it became easier to jam to Rick.

"Because I think you're so sexy, sexy, sexy Cold Blooded!"

Jasmine closed her eyes, swung her hips from side to side, then dropped into a squat.

Men howled.

Then something tickled her ankle.

Her eyes popped open. There were bills at her feet. That made her smile. Until she looked to the other side of the stage—there were so many bills on Viva's side, it really did look like it was raining money.

Yeah, Viva was the veteran, but the always-had-to-be-the-winner in Jasmine kicked in.

She raised her hands high above her head, then brought her arms down, letting the tips of her fingers inch lower along her curves.

Now, her dress was completely open and when she looked down, there was more money at her feet—a twenty-dollar bill! Jasmine searched for the man who'd tossed that her way.

His eyes were like laser beams. That's how she found him—the average white man. That was the only way to describe him.

As he sat, she couldn't tell if he was tall or short. He was Caucasian, but he wasn't very light, nor was he dark. And in his suit, Jasmine couldn't see if he was thin or heavy. Nothing about him stood out.

Except for the twenty-dollar bill he'd just thrown at her feet.

And the flower he wore in his lapel.

Not a boutonniere, a flower. Like something he'd just plucked from a bush right outside.

Jasmine danced her way closer, and when she paused at the edge of the stage, the sweet, flowery scent wafted up and wrapped itself around her like a lover's arms.

The man's thin lips slowly spread into a small smile, and Jasmine, now wearing only the red satin bra and G-string she'd bought that afternoon, kept her eyes on the man. As she gyrated, her glance moved to his hands resting in his lap. And there, on his left hand, she saw the golden loop that Viva said was the key to a stripper's success.

She was eager to test Viva's theory; so she spread her legs and pushed herself lower, lower, until she was in a full split right in front of him.

Others howled, but it was this man, with the flower and the wedding band and the twenty-dollar bills, whom she wanted to impress.

And impress him she did. This time, two twenties landed right between her legs.

She traced her lips with her tongue as she danced away from him, swirled around the pole again, but kept her eyes on him when she could. Then she edged to the front of the stage where other men waited for her.

Following Viva, Jasmine tossed her bra away and was surprised when she felt nothing but exhilaration when the men hooted and hollered. When they tucked bills into her garter. When they tossed money at her feet and cheered, wanting more.

But as she ground her hips in a circle-eight motion, she kept looking back over her shoulder. At him. And he kept his eyes on her.

She spread her legs again, reached down, touched her toes, and, through her legs, glanced back at the man with the money.

Even upside down, she could tell that she took his breath away. Not two seconds passed before he tossed two more bills onto the stage. Jasmine couldn't see how much he'd given her this time, but the way perspiration made the top of his forehead glisten, she imagined that she had danced her way to exactly what she wanted.

"Cold Blooded" was coming to an end, and she wanted a bit more. Holding on to the pole, wearing nothing more than her G-string, she glanced over her shoulder at him and then shook every single thing that her mama had given her. Quaked her behind like she was part of the San Andreas Fault.

She almost laughed . . . when she saw tears in the man's eyes. And then he tossed a couple of more twenties her way.

Jasmine thanked him with a smile. Inhaled a long breath and took in more of the sweetness that came from his flower.

"Let's hear it for Double Dee and Pepper Pulaski!" the DJ sang as Jasmine and Viva gathered their money from the stage.

Viva backed away, still smiling, still waving. But Jasmine was already gone, headed back toward the curtain, her brain a high-speed calculator, adding up the money.

"*Chica,* that was wicked. You were bad, girl!" Viva high-fived her. "How much did you make?"

Jasmine's instincts set in. "I don't know," she lied, and looked down at the bills she held like it was too much to add up. "What about you?"

Viva flipped through the bills in her hand. "The usual—close to one hundred."

"That's great," Jasmine said. "Maybe tomorrow, I'll be as good as you."

"No way, mama." Viva laughed. "You heard Buck; I'm the best." Viva locked her money inside her drawer, then tossed her blond wig over her shoulder. "Okay, let's clean up a little, and then we'll work the floor."

Jasmine was glad Viva hadn't asked her again how much she'd made. Didn't think it was a good idea to tell her friend that there was a new "best girl" in town.

Inside, Jasmine trembled with excitement; she'd almost doubled what Viva had collected—one hundred and eighty-three dollars. For a ten minute dance!

Now Jasmine couldn't wait to get back out there. "Are we going on the stage again?"

"Not sure," Viva said, "but what you really want to do is work the floor. If you think there's money on the stage, there's stupid money one-on-one. Some of these guys will get off of fives and tens when you got your stuff all up in their face."

Fives and tens? Jasmine smirked.

As they stepped into the front of the club, Viva schooled Jasmine, "Now, remember, *chica,* look for the men with the wedding rings 'cause they're willing to give you everything for a sample of somethin' they're not getting at home. It's all about the money, so don't be shy."

Her friend must not have been watching her. Jasmine had given up shy about twenty minutes ago. And Viva was wrong about the money—it wasn't about just that anymore.

All Jasmine could think about was the way the man with the flower had looked at her. She remembered how she had made him gasp. Made him perspire. Made him damn near cry.

And he didn't even know her name.

She'd been able to do all of that with just her body. Yes, she still needed thousands of dollars, but she'd found something better than money here. In the middle of the strip club, she'd found power.

Jasmine followed Viva through the crowd, pausing every few steps as men stopped them. She kept a smile plastered on her face, but her eyes were on her destination. She searched the room for the only man she wanted to see.

But by the time she inched her way to the edge of the stage, her moneyman, the man with the flower was gone . . .

He was gone that day, but Jasmine felt as if that man was here—at City of Lights. It was the scent—of the flower he wore then and the flowers that were in front of her now.

Pushing herself from the pew, Jasmine paused to steady herself before she took the short steps to the plant. She sniffed again. Remembered more, and those memories made her tremble.

She whipped around and faced the multitude—the parishioners who'd come early to get the best seats and chat with their Sunday friends. There were already hundreds of people in the sanctuary. But who'd brought in these flowers?

Breathing deeply, she forced herself to calm down. She had to be alert, aware of everyone, every move.

Her eyes scanned the crowd and she focused first on Jerome Viceroy. He stood, dressed today in a purple suit with pink stripes. His shoulder-length curls shined under the sanctuary lights. And in the middle of the center aisle, he was holding court—with a group of teenagers. He beamed as the girls giggled and chatted, their eyes overflowing with admiration for the man who was always on television.

When Pastor Wyatt and his wife strolled in front of Jerome, Jasmine's glance followed them as the two moved toward Enid's seat of honor—the front pew on the other side of the sanctuary.

The couple moved together like they always did—side by side, but not in a lover's kind of way. Enid was whispering into her husband's ear while Pastor Wyatt just listened.

And then Jasmine saw Roxie and watched as she walked up to Jerome, kissed his cheek, then joined in the chatter with the girls. And then Mrs. Whittingham passed by. And Brother Hill . . . and Sister Clinton . . . and Brother Stevens. And all. The. Others.

She inhaled to gather herself, but the fragrance of the flowers assaulted her again and flooded her with even more memories.

Her eyes darted from one side of the church to the other, in search of the one who was torturing her.

Or maybe this had nothing to do with City of Lights. Maybe it was someone rising from the ashes of her past. There was an entire list of people who would delight in her suffering: Brian Lewis, her daughter's biological father, who hated her as much as she hated him. And Alexis Lewis, his wife, who'd found out only months ago that her husband had fathered Jasmine's child.

Then there were the packs of women whose husbands Jasmine had bedded over the years. Much time had passed since she'd lived that life, but the pain that came with marital betrayal didn't have an expiration date. There were dozens of wives who'd been waiting to exact their revenge.

The list of her enemies was long; trying to count the names made her head pound as hard as her heart.

"Hello, Jasmine."

There was so much pain in her head, she had to squint when her eyes moved to the voice.

Ivy! It had been weeks since the woman had jumped in her face at the hospital. And Ivy was on her enemy list, too.

"Are you all right?" Ivy asked.

Jasmine searched the woman's face for any clues that she was the perpetrator. But she saw nothing but concern.

"I'm . . . fine," she stuttered, feeling hot. "I need to . . ."

Another whiff overwhelmed her. Without finishing her thought, she grabbed her purse from the pew and dashed past the altar. The eyes were on her—she could feel them. The blackmailer was among them, of that she was sure.

But she had to get away from the scent, the sounds, the sanctuary.

She burst through the door that led to the offices. Busted through and bumped right into her husband.

"Darlin'?" His concern was instant. "What's wrong?"

"I don't know," she panted. "I feel . . . hot."

Taking her hand, Hosea led his wife to his office, closed the door, then helped her to the couch. With the back of his hand, he felt her forehead. "You do feel a bit warm." He filled a cup with water from the cooler and then held the cup as she drank.

She leaned back, her breathing steadier now.

He said, "You've been feeling faint a lot lately."

Jasmine heard her husband's question inside words he hadn't even spoken. Shaking her head, she wished that his suspicions were true—she wished that it was pregnancy bringing on this anxiety.

"I'm not," was all she said.

There was disappointment in his eyes, although he tried to hide it. "You should go home. I can have someone drive you."

She shook her head. "I'll be fine. I'll lie here for a little while." Her head was already down on the cushions before she spoke the last word.

As she lay, Hosea slid her pumps from her feet, then he covered her with the jacket he'd worn to church. Her eyes were closed when he kissed her forehead, clicked off the overhead light, and left her alone.

Lord, if you help me get out of this . . .

Resting in the quiet, Jasmine felt the sting of held-back tears pressing hard behind her eyelids. But she wouldn't cry. Tears did nothing to help her figure this out. She needed to put all of her energy into winning. That was the only way to survive.

There were lots of voices inside her head, inside her dreams. But these were new ones—voices from the outside.

Jasmine's eyelids fluttered open. It took a moment to remember where she was. And the memory made her snuggle deeper into the sofa; she was safe in here.

But then she heard the voices again, coming closer.

"Why are we still talking about this?"

Jasmine sighed at the sound of Mrs. Whittingham. Obviously the service was over, too soon for her.

She pushed herself up and staggered across the room, hoping to close the door that Hosea had left partially open before the woman realized she was there.

Jasmine heard Mrs. Whittingham again, her tone sharper this time.

"You need to forget about it!"

It was the way the woman hissed that piqued Jasmine's curiosity. Who was she talking to?

Mrs. Whittingham continued, "It doesn't mean anything."

"But don't you think it's weird? Why would it say that Mama was eighteen on my birth certificate?"

Ivy.

Jasmine pressed her ear closer to the door.

"Ivy, I don't know. People make all kinds of mistakes. It was a human error."

"Well, I'm worried because of my passport," Ivy said. "I need to contact somebody and get Mama's age corrected."

"Please, nobody cares how old Mama was when you were born. The only reason . . ."

The murmur of other voices coming closer blocked out the rest of Mrs. Whittingham's words. But Jasmine wanted to hear more. She leaned closer against the door, then suddenly . . . *bang!*

The door swung open, knocking Jasmine back. She stumbled and hit the wall.

"Ouch!" Her hand rose to the spot right above her eyebrow where the edge of the door had assaulted her.

"What the . . ." Hosea clicked on the light. Stared at his wife sprawled against the wall like a rag doll. "Jasmine, what were you doing behind the door?"

"I was . . . getting ready to come out." She shook her head. "This really hurts."

"Let me take a look."

It ached enough to make her sit down, lean back, and let Hosea examine her injury. It ached enough to make her promise inside that she would never eavesdrop on anyone again.

THIRTY-SIX

TRUTH AND TRUST.

That was Hosea's mantra for their marriage. And Jasmine really did want to honor him that way. But it was hard to get this lying-to-her-husband habit under control, under these circumstances.

It was because of the blackmailer that she'd lied to Hosea this morning, told him over breakfast that she wasn't going to the church.

"Instead," she began her lie, "I have to head downtown and work on a project for Malik."

He'd believed her lie, like he always did, and a part of her was saddened by that. She wanted to be deserving of the faith he had in her. And as soon as this blackmailing business was over, she would find a way to be worthy of his trust.

The taxi rolled to a stop on the corner of Fourteenth and First, and Jasmine tossed the bills into the driver's hand. She climbed out, then dodged across the avenue, crisscrossing through the horn-blasting, driver-shouting, snarled morning traffic.

The Starbucks line was long, though most of the tables were empty since, at this hour, coffee addicts were just stopping long enough to grab their morning java.

Even though it was difficult to see through the darkened lenses, Jasmine kept her oversize sunglasses on as she checked out the crowd; there wasn't a familiar face in the shop.

Satisfied, she ordered a Grande Chai, parked at a small table in the corner, then sipped her tea as she waited for her laptop to power up.

Her plan for the next couple of hours was already thought out—she was starting with Jerome.

It had been almost a week since she'd heard from him, but she knew exactly what she was going to say in her return e-mail. She typed:

Mr. Jerome: I was so xcited when u wrote back. Thnk u. I've been so buzy @ school. I hope 1 day I can meet u, but Im kinda shy. I'm 15. Hit me back if u can.

Jasmine sipped her tea, read the words she'd written again, then hit Send.

She was playing a hunch—it started with the question he'd put in his e-mail last week: How old are you? And then her intuition grew with the way he'd held court in the sanctuary yesterday with those young girls.

Jasmine shook her head—this was a long shot, but if she was wrong, nothing was lost. She'd create a new e-mail, start again.

Now she turned to the browser, typed in "Jerome Viceroy." She scanned through the seven screens of articles that chronicled the scandalous life of the councilman. The stories of his life read like a script from a straight gangsta movie. He'd been charged with extortion—holding corporations financially hostage unless they succumbed to his demands. He'd been charged with tax evasion a few times, and even money laundering. Federal charges had been brought against him five times, but he was his name—the Teflon Man.

Jasmine sighed and tried not to hear the question inside her mind: If the government couldn't catch him, what made her think she could? But her hope was in the fact that the ones who'd gone after him before were men. This was her advantage—she was a woman who knew how to trap a man.

Jasmine closed that window, returned to the browser, and typed in "Eugene Wyatt."

There were only three articles on the pastor; and as Jasmine surveyed the stories, there wasn't anything new.

The associate pastor and his wife were from a small town—Hogeye Creek, Georgia, population, twenty-five hundred. Eugene had become the pastor of the oldest church in Hogeye Creek—Church of the Solid Rock—in 1997. During his tenure, he'd grown the church to three hundred members, making it one of the largest churches in the county.

There wasn't much more—a couple of stories about an adopt-a-drug-baby program the church had organized, a protest march in front of the mayor's office to get a second gas station in the town, and numerous bake sales and chicken fries held to raise scholarships for college-bound students.

The last story covered the celebration the town held for Pastor Wyatt and his wife, Enid, as they prepared for their move to New York City.

By the time Jasmine read the second paragraph, she was on the edge of her seat:

> Returning to the pulpit for the first time since the accident and what would be his last time as the pastor, Wyatt addressed the standing-room-only crowd. Still wearing bandages and his right arm in a sling, Pastor Wyatt thanked his well-wishers not only for their good wishes as he and his wife prepared for New York, but also for their prayers during this difficult time. "When my brother, Earvin, and I lost our mother and father all those years ago, so many of you stepped in as surrogate parents to fill the void their

> deaths left behind. I know there were many of you who were disappointed in the way things worked out with Earvin, but I tell you, he was about to turn his life around. He'd served his time and had come back home to make you all proud." The pastor went on to talk about how his brother had died too young, but that he was not one to ever question the Lord. "God spared my life for a reason," the pastor said. "I'm here and Earvin is not. God reached down from heaven and took my brother out of that automobile, but at the same time he left me to go on. I feel like a piece of me is gone . . ." It was then that the pastor buckled over with so much grief that his wife had to help him from the pulpit. As the two crossed the sanctuary weeping together, there was not a dry eye in the church . . .

Jasmine stopped there and leaned back in her seat. Pastor Wyatt had a brother who'd been killed in some kind of accident, obviously an accident that he'd been involved in as well. And he had never mentioned this?

Surely, this was a testimony that an arrogant, self-serving man like Pastor Wyatt would have used over and over. But not once had she heard this story. Maybe it was because his brother had been to prison—the article said he'd served his time.

That's when the tugging began—from that place inside her heart where she stored her knowledge of men.

She grabbed her cell and punched the speed-dial number. She was already talking when Mae Frances answered.

"I think I have something," she said, not holding back her excitement.

"Well, good morning to you, too, Jasmine Larson," Mae Frances mumbled. "I can't believe you call somebody and don't even have the courtesy to say good morning. Don't you have any manners?"

Jasmine rolled her eyes. As if Mae Frances knew anything about manners. "I thought you'd want me to get straight to the gossip."

The change in her tone was instant. "You've got gossip?" She sounded like a child on Christmas morning.

"Yeah, I may have something on Pastor Wyatt. I Googled him and something interesting came up." Jasmine glanced at the article again. "Pastor Wyatt had a brother who died right before he came to New York."

There was a long pause. Like Mae Frances was waiting for Jasmine to say more. And when Jasmine stayed silent, Mae Frances said, "I hate to break to it you, Jasmine Larson, but you can't blackmail a blackmailer with the fact that he has a dead brother."

"I know, but . . ." She bit the corner of her lip. Read over that paragraph again. "I need to find out more." She took a breath. "I'm going to take a trip to Hogeye Creek, Georgia."

"Why?"

Jasmine squinted, trying to understand the question that tugged inside of her. "I'm not sure, but this accident that killed his brother, why hasn't Pastor Wyatt ever mentioned it?"

"How do you know that he hasn't?"

"If he'd talked about it, somebody would've said something. You know our church. I never told a soul that Hosea wasn't Jacqueline's father, and everybody knows anyway. City of Lights passes more gossip along than Page Six."

"Well, that's true."

"According to this article," Jasmine continued her case, "Pastor Wyatt was in a serious car accident that killed his brother and his brother had just gotten out of prison. But he's never once stood up during one of our Testify and Triumph services and said a word about it."

"That's true," Mae Frances repeated, sounding like she was beginning to see Jasmine's point.

"He's the kind of man who wouldn't let something like that go," Jasmine kept on. "You know how he is about the media. Knowing him, he would've tried to get on *Oprah*, or at least *Montel*."

"Maybe he doesn't like to talk about it. Maybe it's too painful. Maybe he's embarrassed by a brother who'd been in jail."

Jasmine thought about her friend's words and tried to reconcile them with the Pastor Wyatt she knew. The man with the bad-boy swagger who didn't seem to fear anything. She shook her head, then stated what she'd been thinking. "Maybe he never mentioned it because *he* had something to do with his brother's death."

Now there was a longer pause. "Jasmine Larson," Mae Frances began softly and slowly, "this sounds like a job for my people."

"No, I want to handle this."

"But there could be trouble. If he's a murderer—"

"I'm not going to confront him." She took a breath. "I'm just going down to Hogeye Creek to see what I can find."

"I'm going with you."

In the seconds that passed, Jasmine wondered if that was a good idea. Would it be possible to sneak into the small country town with a loud, gruff, five-foot-eleven, take-no-prisoners-if-you-pissed-her-off, mink-coat-wearing (because since it was March, Mae Frances would definitely be sporting her thirty-five-year-old mink coat) woman who had just found Jesus? No, there was no chance for discretion if Mae Frances was with her.

She shook her head. "I would love for you to come, but I need you to do something else while I'm away. Do you think one of your connections can look into getting something on with Roxie and Ivy?" she asked, knowing that would satisfy her friend a little.

"Yeah," she said, sounding a bit more chipper. "But I still think you'd be safer if—"

"I'll be fine; I promise."

When they hung up, Jasmine perused the article once again, her fascination building.

And she had a feeling that even more captivating news waited for her in Hogeye Creek.

THIRTY-SEVEN

THE MOMENT SHE HEARD THE footsteps, Jasmine lowered the computer screen on her laptop, hiding the travel Web site she'd been viewing. She was already looking up when Roxie stood at her door.

"Mrs. Whittingham gave me this for you."

"Thanks," Jasmine said, reaching for the FedEx envelope.

"I'm getting ready to get out of here, unless you have anything else."

Shaking her head, Jasmine said, "Nope." Roxie tried to peek at her computer, and Jasmine lowered her laptop lid even more.

"What're you working on?" Roxie asked.

"Nothing."

Roxie sighed, but Jasmine didn't care. Being here was her idea—and with her friendship with Jerome, Jasmine was never going to let her get close. Plus, it wasn't like she was sure that Roxie wasn't the blackmailer—even though she was beginning to doubt it.

Roxie said, "I was thinking about stopping by the hospital. Is Hosea there?"

Jasmine nodded.

When Jasmine didn't add anymore, Roxie said, "Okay . . . well, then . . . I'll see you."

The moment Roxie was out of sight, Jasmine opened her laptop again. She hadn't decided when she would go to Georgia, though she was leaning toward this weekend. That way, she could attend the Sunday service at Church of the Solid Rock. If that church was anything like City of Lights, it would be the best place to find a loose-lipped lady who'd want to talk about her former pastor.

With her eyes on the computer screen, Jasmine picked up the FedEx package, ripped it open, then pulled out the single page. She held it for a moment, before she turned her eyes to it and then dropped the paper as if it was a snake on fire.

The letter fell onto her desk, faceup, the words right in her face, taunting her:

Get your husband to give up his position or else at the next board meeting, Mr. Smith will be there to tell everyone about '83.

Jasmine's hands shook as she stuffed the letter back into the envelope. She checked the FedEx slip—the package had been addressed to her, and in the return address was her name and home address!

Her heart pounded even more as she pushed herself from her chair and rushed to the front of the church.

"Where's Roxie?" she demanded to know.

Mrs. Whittingham turned away from her computer and glared at Jasmine over the rim of her glasses. "She's *your* assistant."

"Where is she?" Jasmine growled.

Mrs. Whittingham frowned, but this time she answered, "She just left."

"Did you give this to her?" Jasmine waved the FedEx packet in her face. "Where did you get it?" She was trying not to sound frantic, but the look on Mrs. Whittingham's face told her she wasn't succeeding.

The woman sat back, eyes wide, as if she wondered if Jasmine's hysteria was dangerous. She gripped her desk and kept her eyes fixed on Jasmine, ready to make a move if the madwoman in front of her did something crazy. "The man," she began, "from *FedEx* gave me the *FedEx* package."

"This came as a delivery?"

"Yes, that's what FedEx men do. They deliver packages," she said slowly, as if that would help Jasmine understand and maybe calm down. "That one came for you and this," she held up another package, "came for Hosea."

Now, it was Jasmine's eyes that widened. The envelope Mrs. Whittingham held was identical to the one in her hand. It was the blackmailer—exposing her!

She snatched the packet from Mrs. Whittingham and rushed away before the woman could yell "Hey!"

Inside her office, she slammed the door shut and took a closer look at the envelope she'd just hijacked. It was addressed to Pastor Hosea Bush, with a return address from First Presbyterian Church.

But that was only a trick, she was sure. She ripped the package open and quickly read the letter inside. Twice. Just to make sure.

It was an invitation from the anniversary committee at First Presbyterian Church for Hosea to attend the celebration of Reverend Godfrey's fifty years in ministry.

Jasmine let the envelope and letter slip from her hand to the floor; then she slumped into her chair.

She'd been so scared that the blackmailer was contacting Hosea. Telling her husband all about her secret life, all about her secrets with the man she came to know as Mr. Smith . . .

The man with the money and the flower came to the club every day for the first seven days Jasmine worked at Foxtails. But after each of her sets on the stage, he'd vanish.

Then after her first week, he was gone altogether.

It was hard working and not seeing the twenty dollar bills falling at her feet, but still Jasmine danced every night that Buck let her—usually four times a week. And the money that rolled in was more than she'd been making at her internship position at Sony.

But although she averaged about five hundred dollars a week at Foxtails, it wasn't going to be enough to totally pay what she needed with the four weeks that were left in the summer. Still she danced—it was her only option.

It didn't take many days for Pepper Pulaski to become the club favorite. It was her hips that brought her infamy.

But Jasmine knew that she would need more than her body to make the kind of money she needed. So she worked to perfect her craft.

She found an adult video store ten blocks away from Sony, and each day during her lunch breaks, she walked to the shop, and paid three dollars to sit in a booth and watch videos. The porn stars became her teachers; she measured it all, studying their gestures, their facial expressions—all the things they did to make men happy.

Then at night, she took her lunchtime lessons to the stage. And she slowed down her music. While the rest of the girls loved all that up-tempo, new-style hip-hop music, she stayed with the R&B hits of the day—especially the slow ones—like Marvin Gaye's "Sexual Healing." She became the sensual stripper.

On her one-month anniversary, Jasmine had almost clapped with glee when she sashayed onto the stage to the rhythm of Prince's new release, "Do Me Baby" and swung around the pole. That's when she got her first whiff of the flower. Her eyes rapidly searched the chairs at the edge of the stage and there he was—her man, with the money and the flower.

She turned it up once she saw him. Rocked and rolled her hips, dipped into splits, swirled upside down and around on the pole. By now, she was used to the cackles and the hoots from the crowd, but it was this man's sweat and gasps and tears that she wanted.

This time, she took no chances, and when Prince belted out his final, "Do me, baby!" she jumped off the platform, leaving the clothes she'd stripped off right there on the stage.

It was against the rules, and Buck would have a screeching fit—but she'd apologize, promise never to do it again, and Buck would leave her alone. He had to. She was his top moneymaker—the men drank and drank, in anticipation and appreciation of getting to stare at Pepper's ample apple-shaped behind.

"Hey, there," she said in a voice that came from her throat. She'd learned that from her porn teachers, too.

She leaned against the stage, pushed her long hair back so that it fell behind her, and kept her hands at her side. She wanted to make sure that he could appreciate every inch of her full glory. "I've been looking for you," she said.

His small round eyes wandered over her nakedness. Finding his voice, he spoke softly, "Have you?"

"Uh-huh. I've missed you."

"Could you . . . would you . . . have a drink with me?" New perspiration popped onto his bald head.

She smiled, hearing the shyness inside his gentle tone. It had probably taken great effort for him to ask that. "Of course," she purred. "But you know, I can't sit down." She leaned closer to him, inhaled the fragrance of his flower, and smiled at the way his head glistened. "Why don't we do this?" She watched his chest rise and fall, more rapidly with every word she spoke. "*You* drink, and *I'll* dance," she said, knowing that he could feel the heat of her breath. "I'll dance just for you. Will that work?"

He twisted in his seat, adjusted his pants. "Oh, yes!" His head jerked in a nod so many times, she worried that he might break his neck.

Jasmine motioned to one of the bartenders, and then she

danced. She used her hands more than she did on the stage—touching herself, touching him, knowing that Buck would look the other way like he always did.

More than once, she grabbed his tie and allowed the expensive silk to slip through her fingers. She pulled him close enough for a kiss, but their lips never met. And even though she had her hands all over him, he never touched her.

Forty minutes later, he gave her two hundred dollars. And she wanted to kiss him for real.

He said, "I want . . . I want . . . you to dance for me."

"Okay." She frowned a bit and wondered what he thought she'd been doing. Turning her back to him, she rolled her hips in a wide circle motion.

For the first time, he touched her with the tips of his coarse fingers. She was surprised; his hands felt like he worked in construction. But that was totally contradictory to the rest of him. Although he was a slight, shy man, he was dressed well in a top-shelf suit. Jasmine didn't know the names of many designers, but she'd learned quality from the men who visited the club. And his suit had to cost hundreds.

She faced him when he touched her.

"Not here," he whispered.

Jasmine's eyes moved toward the back of the room, to the red door that led to the VIP Lounge. In the month that she had worked the club, she had managed to stay out of there, where, for a price, anything could happen. To Jasmine, the girls who took clients in the back were nothing more than whores. But she didn't get down like that—she wasn't about to give her body to anyone. Not for any price. After all, she had a boyfriend, and she really did love Kenny.

As if he knew what she was thinking, he said, "Not back there. You're too good for that."

She exhaled a long breath of relief.

"I want you to go with me."

"I can't leave," she said, shaking her head. She already had her excuse—it was the same one she'd given the others who over the weeks had tried to coerce her into giving them an extra-special VIP treat. "They penalize us for leaving early, and I can't afford those fees."

"I'll take care of that for you."

She paused for a moment. No one had ever offered that. But still, he wanted her to go with him. Outside of this place. She knew what that meant. And she was not a whore.

He said, "I'll pay you five hundred dollars."

"Five hundred?" she asked, thoughts of whoredom fading. He'd already given her two hundred, and with her other tips, this could be her first one-thousand-dollar night.

He nodded. "Plus your fees," he said softly. And then he added, "At a hotel. You'll be safe; I know I have to leave my card with Buck," he said, as if he'd done this before and knew all the rules. When he saw the hesitation still in her eyes, he reassured, "Just to dance. That's all."

There's a big difference between dancing and whoring, she thought as she agreed.

She'd rushed to the back to change while the man took care of the business with Buck.

And that was the first night she left with the man she later came to know as Mr. Smith . . .

Jasmine looked, once again, at the letter that threatened to expose her. Threatened to introduce Hosea to Mr. Smith.

Detective Foxx said the blackmailer would leave a clue. Her eyes searched the note—there was nothing to reveal the face behind the words.

But Jasmine began to put her own features on the blackmailer. It was inside her gut—she was sure this had come from either Jerome Viceroy or Pastor Wyatt, although it seemed unlikely that one of them could have found out so much about her past.

She had to get to Hogeye Creek and get what she could on Pastor Wyatt. And she had to up her game with Jerome. Then, pray that Mae Frances found something on Roxie and Ivy and . . . in the next instant Jasmine's thoughts came to a screeching halt. It could all be such a waste if none of her suspects was the blackmailer.

But then she took a deep breath, inhaled fortitude, and shook those doubts away. What other choice did she have?

Her hands were still trembling when she clicked back onto the travel Web site. This time, she didn't review all her choices—the decision had been made: she had to get to Hogeye Creek now.

She selected her Saturday and then Sunday flights. Once those plans were taken care of, there was only one more thing to do.

She picked up the phone and called Mae Frances.

Tonight, they were once again on their knees at the edge of Reverend Bush's bed, and Jasmine felt as if she could stay here for hours. She was praying for her father-in-law, but even though she talked to God about Reverend Bush, she could feel that God heard more than her words—He heard her heart, too. He knew all the trouble she was in, and through soft whispers, she was sure she heard Him saying that it was going to be all right.

Her eyes were still closed when she felt Hosea move next to her and help her stand. She'd just rested her head on his shoulder when they heard the gentle knock on the door.

"Pastor Bush?"

Both Hosea and Jasmine frowned at the young guy in the leather bomber jacket and jeans.

"I have a delivery for you."

Jasmine gasped. This was just like earlier; the blackmailer

had come to the church, and now he had followed her to the hospital.

"I need your signature," the man said.

Jasmine wanted to rip the package away from her husband. Tell him that he could never read it. But the envelope was securely tucked under his arm as he signed.

It's over! her mind screamed as she paced back and forth. She needed to confess—tell Hosea right now that she had been a stripper before he read those ugly words. Then she could drop to her knees and beg for his forgiveness.

"I wonder what this is." Hosea slowly peeled back the lip of the packet. "And why would anyone send a messenger here?"

Before he pulled the letter out, Jasmine breathed, "Babe . . ."

He stopped. Looked at her. "What's wrong?"

Her heartbeat accelerated. She wanted to tell him, needed to do it. "I just . . . I just . . . I love you."

He squinted, as if he was confused. "Okay. I love you, too."

Jasmine closed her eyes. Waited for him to start screaming.

Lord, if you will just get me out of this . . .

He shouted, "I cannot believe this!"

Her eyes were already filling with tears.

With a glance at his father, he motioned for Jasmine to follow him as he stomped into the hall.

"Look at this!" he said, the moment they were outside. He shoved the letter into her hand.

She trembled, swallowed, then took a breath. Looked down and faced her fate.

This is to inform you of an emergency board meeting to be held in ten days for City of Lights at Riverside Church. The purpose of the meeting is to hold a special vote for the chair of senior pastor. . . .

There was more, but the water falling from her eyes blinded her vision.

"Oh, darlin'," he said, taking her into his arms. "I didn't mean to upset you."

"I'm not upset," she sniffed. "I get emotional about everything these days."

He nodded, understanding. "Can you believe this?" he asked, taking the letter from her.

No, she couldn't. She couldn't believe that God had answered her prayer.

"They want to vote you out," she said. "Can they do that? What about your father's letter?"

"I don't know." With a sigh, Hosea lowered himself onto a bench. "Wyatt wouldn't have called this meeting unless he had talked to everyone he needed to on the board. Obviously, he left out Brother Hill, Sister Whittingham, and Malik, of course. But everyone else was fair game." Hosea shook his head. "He must have the votes to move me out."

And if Pastor Wyatt did, what would that mean for her? If he had enough votes to make Hosea step down, would the blackmailing stop? Would the threats of exposing her and Mr. Smith end now?

"What are you going to do?"

He looked down at his hands, went into deep thought before he turned back to his wife. "I'm going to fight—that's what Pops would want."

Jasmine exhaled—it was not over. That meant that she had to fight, too.

"Come on," he said, taking her hand. "Let's go say good night to Pops and then get out of here."

The March night was cold as Jasmine and Hosea walked out of the hospital. Still, they strolled to their car, both lost inside their own thoughts. In her mind, Jasmine focused on the unwritten script that she'd prepared, practicing in her head the words she was about to say.

And as Hosea helped her into the SUV and closed the passenger door, she set her plan in motion.

She waited until he slipped inside, and then she pressed her turned-off cell phone to her ear.

"Oh, hi, Mae Frances," she said. She paused, listening to nothing. "Yes, we're leaving the hospital now." Another pause.

Hosea tapped her leg. "Tell her I said hello."

She nodded. "Hosea sends his love." She paused again. "Oh, no!" And from the corner of her eye, she watched her husband's expression metamorphose to new concern. She spoke quickly, "Mae Frances, you know I would do anything for you, but I can't leave New York right now."

Hosea whispered, "What's going on?"

"Hold on, Mae Frances." As Hosea edged the car away from the curb, Jasmine told him the story that she and Mae Frances had concocted that afternoon. "Her mother has to go in for more tests this weekend, and she's afraid to do it alone."

"Mae Frances, afraid?" Hosea frowned.

Jasmine covered the mouthpiece as if someone was really on the other end. "Babe, you know it's hard on her. She tries to be strong, but this is her mother."

Slowly, Hosea nodded. "Yeah, I understand that." When he paused, Jasmine knew thoughts of his father were going through his mind. "She wants you to go down there?"

"Uh-huh, but I told her no."

"Go on. It's just for a day or two, right?"

Jasmine nodded. "But I don't want to leave you."

"It's okay. Here," he reached for Jasmine's cell phone, "let me talk to her."

Jasmine froze.

"Give me the phone."

And then, her angels came—New York's finest. A patrol car rolled up next to them and rescued her. "Babe, you can't talk to her right now." She motioned with her chin toward the police. "You don't have your earpiece."

He nodded. "Thanks! That's the last thing I need—a ticket tonight."

Quickly, she held the phone back to her ear. "Ah, Mae Frances, sorry 'bout that. Hosea said I should come." She stopped. "Okay, I'll fly in on Saturday, and come back home on Sunday. Okay. Love you."

She couldn't click off the phone that was already turned off fast enough.

"Her mother's having tests over the weekend?"

"Ah . . . yeah . . . I guess. Mae Frances said they were special tests."

Hosea nodded. "I'm glad you're going. She needs you."

Tears burned in Jasmine's eyes when she looked at the man who had given her more love, more grace, more forgiveness than anyone ever had in her life. "I love you."

"Ah," he said. "Spoken like a wife."

She was glad that he had lightened the moment. Glad that he hadn't tried to dig deeper into the reasons for her sadness.

She said, "I'm a wife who's so in love."

When he smiled, she prayed that he would remember this moment and the many others they'd shared in their years together. She prayed that it would all be enough to make up for the great despair that was coming—for both of them—if she couldn't pull this off.

Under the cover of darkness, Jasmine once again sat in their home office. Her lie was ready if Hosea found her—she was looking for her ticket for Texas.

But her real objective was to get online and send Jerome

another e-mail, even though she'd sent him one this morning. She was desperate for results.

She signed onto the e-mail account, and her mouth opened wide. Jerome Viceroy had beaten her to the computer.

Dear, dear Mariah, so you're fifteen and shy. You sound so sweet and I want to meet you, too. Don't worry about being shy. Where do you live?

That was all there was, but for Jasmine, that was enough. Why would a grown man tell a fifteen-year-old that he wanted to meet her? Why would he ask where she lived?

It wasn't a lot, but it was enough to let her know that this eight-term councilman was a fool! He was either a pedophile or a man heading that way.

This was bigger than anything she'd expected. But trapping Jerome didn't make her happy; it made her sick, thinking about what this man may have done before. Still, she had to move forward. This e-mail alone was not enough.

Her stomach twisted when she pressed her fingers against the keys:

I stay on Morningside.

Then she stopped. Isn't that what teenagers did? Just answered the question?

She pressed Send, hoping that he would respond again, ask Mariah more questions. Establish a dialogue. Send lots of e-mails that would prove that he was headed for a permanent address deep in the bowels of hell—and at the same time give her the ammunition she needed to keep all of her secrets safe.

THIRTY-EIGHT

"Jasmine."

She jumped and slapped closed the cover of her laptop.

"I'm sorry, I didn't mean to scare you." Roxie sauntered into Jasmine's office. "I wanted to check your calendar—just found out there's a first ladies conference coming up that would be great for you to attend."

"When is it?" Jasmine asked, though her eyes were still on her computer. She couldn't wait to get back to what she'd been reading.

"Not until August." Roxie tilted her head. "Maybe we could go together."

"That would be great!"

It was the way she'd responded, so excitedly, that made Roxie frown. "Are you all right?"

She grinned as wide as she could, hoping Roxie would get the hint and leave. "Fine. Are you on your way out?"

Roxie paused. "I guess I am now."

"Great!" Jasmine's grin was growing wider and faker by the second. "Has Mrs. Whittingham left?"

Roxie shook her head. "No, but Pastor Wyatt and Enid are gone."

Now she was interested. "I didn't even know they were here."

"They were in and out in two minutes. They said they were taking a trip."

Jasmine almost wanted to invite Roxie to sit down now. Have her tell everything. "I didn't know they were going away. Did they say where?"

Roxie shook her head. "Nope. Just heard them tell Mrs. Whittingham that they'd be gone until next Friday."

"Oh." She wasn't surprised. Of course the Wyatts would leave town; they'd sent that letter, and now were getting the heck out of Dodge. Cowards!

"Okay," Jasmine said. "Well, I guess I'll see you on Monday. Can you close my door on your way out?"

The way Roxie looked at her, Jasmine was sure the woman was ready to give up, tell her to find another armor bearer. But after a moment, the shadow faded from her face and Roxie smiled. "See you on Monday," was all she said before she strutted out the door.

Jasmine waited a couple of beats before she slowly reopened her computer. And read Jerome's e-mail again.

Hi Mariah. You live on Morningside. That's close. We should get together. Want me to take you to lunch?

This man really was a fool! And she was going to take him down—whether he was the blackmailer or not.

Typing quickly, she responded: *whn do u wnt 2 get 2gether? ths s xcitng. cnt w8!*

Now that Jerome was taken care of, she could focus on Pastor Wyatt. Jerome was a pedophile. Could Pastor Wyatt be a murderer?

She'd had a strong feeling the truth was waiting for her in Hogeye Creek, Georgia.

THIRTY-NINE

THE TIRES KICKED UP EVEN more dirt when Jasmine eased the Jaguar into a right turn onto Owl's Head. She edged the car along the side of the half-paved, half-dirt road, then slowed to a stop. Glancing once again at the map the man at the one-pump gas station gave her, she sighed. Had he told her to make a right on Owl's Head, then go down to where the old oak tree was across from Finley's candy store, or was she supposed to make a left?

She couldn't remember. And she couldn't tell a thing from this map. She tossed the flimsy paper onto the floor. Not even the GPS system could help—the satellite signal had long ago deserted her, about 150 miles outside of Atlanta, right when she sped past the sign that said, WELCOME TO HOGEYE CREEK, GEORGIA, HOME OF HICKORY HOGS.

Jasmine peered through the windshield at the gray wooden shack in front of her and wondered if it made any sense to knock on that door. She wasn't sure what to do as her eyes scanned the rest of the street.

The man at the gas station had told her that Owl's Head was the main street in this town, but she hadn't seen a soul. Twenty-five hundred people lived here—where were they?

She revved up the engine and eased the car forward, passing Greenlee's Thrift Shop with a CLOSED sign in the window. The next building looked sturdier than most she'd seen—it was brick, though it was still as small as the others. She searched for a sign, then saw WILSON'S DEPARTMENT STORE on a card tucked in the lower corner of the front window.

Still inching forward, she slowed the car in front of the next shack. She wasn't sure if there was anyone inside, but the $2.00 FRIED EGGS & GRITS sign in the window and the few pickup trucks parked in the dirt lot on the side led her to believe there were folks here who'd be able to help.

Pulling up beside a pickup with lumber stacked high in its bed, she slipped out of her car, then struggled to keep the heels of her three-inch Gucci pumps from sinking into the dirt path. She peeked through the glass pane but couldn't see too much through the shaded window; as she got closer, though, she could hear chatter and clatter. Relieved, she pulled open the door and stepped inside to the smell of all kinds of food frying.

The bell above the door jingled, but that was the last sound she heard. Every eye inside the café turned to her, and that was when the world stopped. Mouths stopped moving, heads stopped bobbing, hands stopped feeding—Jasmine was sure that, in the seconds of that quiet, not even an eye blinked.

Only the jukebox continued to play some country ditty as if it was the only thing in the place that didn't realize the world had been invaded by an alien.

Then, movement—from a pale-skinned, thin-lipped, candy-stripe-apron-wearing woman, who ambled toward her. Her gray hair was twisted into two pigtails that sat high on the sides and bounced in rhythm to her steps.

"Can I help ya, gal?"

Jasmine's eyebrows shot up, she crossed her arms, snaked her neck; but before she said a word, her mind told her to take another quick scan of the place.

As she looked into the eyes of the plaid-flannel-shirt-wearing men with wrinkled red necks and bushy eyebrows, and women who were as thick and as mean-looking as the men, she would have bet all her designer clothes that every single person in this place had voted for George W. Bush—twice. And if she wanted to get out of Hogeye Creek alive, she'd better keep her northern attitude to herself.

"I'm looking for Church of the Solid Rock," she said in the most polite voice that she could find.

"That's on the colored side of town," the woman drawled.

Colored?

The woman grabbed a pencil from behind her ear and used it as a pointer. "Go on down to where the old oak tree is across from Finley's store," she said in her southern twang, "then turn there, and about a half mile down you'll run right into it. You'll see all the colored people."

Jasmine wanted to ask her who she was calling gal and who she was calling colored and which way should she turn if she ever found that old oak tree.

But all she did was smile her thank-you, swivel, and walk as fast as she could out the door and down the wobbly steps. Then she tried to maneuver her spiked heels through the dirt once again.

She could feel the eyes on her, staring from the window. No doubt half of the restaurant had gotten up to watch the colored city gal. So she gave them a show, let the wheels of her Jaguar skid through the dirt and kick up a trail of dust.

But once she hit the road, she sighed deeply. How was she supposed to find an old oak tree? She had no idea what an old oak looked like. And what was she doing down here, deep in the South with people who still used 1920s vernacular to refer to her? What did she expect to find anyway?

"This was a silly trip," she whispered, but she still kept moving. Still kept looking for the oak tree. And still kept hoping that there would be something in Hogeye Creek, Georgia, that she could take back with her to New York City.

She couldn't believe she found it. Finally, after maneuvering through the maze of all of those no-name roads, Jasmine had found the tree and Finley's, and now, rising in front of her, atop a small hill, was the Church of the Solid Rock. It was a tiny timber structure with a huge cross on the roof that looked too heavy for the wooden planks to hold.

Jasmine eased into the graveled lot, filled with ten-year-old sedans and beat-up pickup trucks. She slipped her car next to an old green Cadillac.

It wasn't until she flipped down the visor to check her makeup in the mirror that she saw them—a band of kids behind her. Not that many, but too many to count. Boys and girls. Tweens and teens. All staring at her through the rear window. She kept her eyes on them as she freshened her lipstick, then tucked her compact back in her purse.

The children had not moved; they stood, staring with wide eyes. Until she stepped out of the car. Then together they sang a chorus of "oohs," and "aahhs," as she secured the lock with the remote.

"Hello," she said to all of them.

Not one responded, but their eyes stayed on her—same as the people in the diner—looking at her like she didn't belong in Hogeye Creek, Georgia.

But the moment she stepped away, their chatter began.

One boy said, "She must be a movie star!"

A girl responded, "Nah, I ain't never seen her on TV; she's just rich."

With a smile, Jasmine tossed her hair over her shoulder and continued to move as if she really was somebody.

But then she heard, "I wonder how much we can get for those tires."

Jasmine whipped around, her eyes searching the small crowd. It wasn't hard to find the big-headed, afro-wearing teen who'd said that. Everyone else was looking straight at him while his eyes were focused on the ground.

Moving back, Jasmine grabbed the boy by his arm.

"Ouch!" he squealed as the others watched, their mouths now open as wide as their eyes.

Jasmine dragged him several feet away so that no one would hear the threat she was about to make on his life. But then she had another thought. With a final pinch, she released the boy and whispered, "Do you want to stay alive and make twenty dollars?"

He stopped rubbing his arm where she'd assaulted him and grinned. "Twenty dollars. What I gotta do?"

Grabbing a twenty-dollar bill from her wallet, she said, "Keep your grubby hands off my car and make sure your friends"—she motioned toward the group, still watching them—"stay away from it, too."

He nodded and then snatched the money from her.

With a final glare at the boy and then an even more ominous glance at his friends, Jasmine made her way to the church.

The harmony and the heat hit her the moment she opened the door. Someone was rocking that old organ as the pastor pranced across the altar.

Jasmine waved the gold-toothed, white-gloved usher away as she stood against the wall, searching. Her eyes scanned what appeared to be the only room in the whole building for the perfect person to sit next to. Jasmine already knew who she wanted—a woman, not a man. One older, not younger. Someone who looked like she'd put in her time and her tithes at Church of the Solid Rock.

The back of her sleeveless silk sheath was already sticking to her skin when she finally squeezed in between two gray-haired women. The moment her butt hit the bench, it began to ache.

And not only that, she was burning up. Drowning in black people body heat. There was nothing like it.

There were about sixty worshippers in the pews, but their heat, mixed with the outdoor eighty-degree temperature, topped off with the four opened windows as the only form of ventilation in the church, made Jasmine feel as if she was sitting at the steps of hell.

But she sat and sighed and wiggled in between the two women, who were making it worse by recirculating the scorching air. They were waving their cardboard fans from the Hogeye Creek Memorial Funeral Home right in her face.

And then there was the preacher, making his own contribution to her misery. Jasmine didn't even know his name, but the man was whooping and hollering and hopping behind that pulpit, seemingly oblivious to people who were falling out (probably from heatstroke) and being carried from the sanctuary by those white-gloved ushers.

I should've waited outside, Jasmine thought. She inhaled a deep breath and choked on the hot air. She coughed. And coughed. And coughed.

"You all right, sugah?" the woman on her left asked.

It took her a moment to nod and breathe again. Lesson learned—she wouldn't take another deep breath inside this brick oven that was masquerading as a sanctuary.

"Here, drink some of this." The lady pulled a plastic bottle of water from her purse.

Jasmine frowned at first. She didn't know this woman. Didn't know what was really in the bottle. But still, she grabbed it. And took a swig of the water that was the same temperature as the room. But at least it was wet.

"Thank you," she breathed, feeling a bit of relief.

"You're welcome, sugah." The woman tucked the bottle back into her bag and said, "You ain't from 'round these parts, are you?"

"No, ma'am," Jasmine whispered.

"I knew it. I know everything that goes on in this town." She glanced at Jasmine sideways. "Who's your people?"

Jasmine shook her head slightly. "I don't want to talk through the service." She pointed to the preacher, as if she didn't want to be rude. She hadn't come all this way to do any talking. All she wanted to do was listen.

"Oh, okay." The woman nodded. But that didn't stop her.

"Hmph. Hmph. Hmph. Would you take a look at that one there?" the woman said.

Jasmine's glance followed the woman's pointed finger to a lady leaning back into two ushers' arms. Another two stood at her side as they struggled to carry the heavy burden outside.

The woman said, "That's Willie Mae. She pass out like that every week. Just trying to get attention. I guess she think one day one of them mens is going to marry her." Then, as if she hadn't missed a word the preacher said, the woman waved her handkerchief in the air and yelled out, "You better preach, Pastor!"

A few minutes later, she was back. "Um-hmm. Now that one," Jasmine's pew partner pointed to another woman being carried away, "she ain't fakin'. She's pregnant, though she ain't told nobody yet, 'cause she don't know which one of them mens is the real daddy."

Jasmine leaned back and looked at the slender woman next to her who, with her cinnamon skin and hazel eyes, was surely dangerous back in her day. Even now, Jasmine was certain that the sixty-something-year-old could still turn the heads of males ten years younger—if the men were blind—and couldn't see that beehive hairdo (same as Enid's) that sat atop her head looking like some kind of bird refuge.

"Now that one there," the woman offered again, "she's a fast one. Only fifteen . . ."

The 4ll kept on coming. Every time the preacher gave a

scripture, Jasmine's new friend gave up some more information. And Jasmine smiled and nodded and listened. She found out who was sleeping with whom, who was about to get a divorce, and her friend even pointed out the three biggest gossips in town.

"Yup," she said. "You can't tell any of them a thing. Unless you want your business all over Hogeye Creek by morning!" She shook her head. "Ain't nothin' but a sin and a shame the way people talk about other people." The woman folded her hands in her lap and began to rock to the rhythm of the preacher's singsong sermon.

Then the woman said, "You see those girls over there?"

Jasmine nodded as she glanced at the twins sitting across the aisle. They couldn't have been more than seven or eight, but they were stiffly still as if they'd been trained well.

"They think Pastor is just their pastor." She paused. Gave Jasmine a small, sly smile. "But they need to be calling him 'Daddy.'"

Jasmine nodded as if she was telling the woman that she understood. But what she understood even more was the gift she'd received by sitting next to the town crier!

With her hand, Jasmine began to fan herself. But it wasn't just the heat. She was ready to go and take this woman somewhere so they could talk. Well . . . so that the woman could talk. All Jasmine planned to do was listen to every word her new best friend had to say.

Even though she'd left the church almost an hour ago, the heat was just as stifling in this four-room house. Now it was an electric fan that recycled the hot air, offering not a bit of relief. But her new friend came to her aid, and Jasmine almost fainted with gratitude when Mrs. Evans handed her a frosted mug filled to the brim with cool lemonade.

"Thank you so much." Jasmine grabbed the glass and took a gulp. She moaned with delight as the drink took a bit of the edge off the heat. "This is wonderful."

The woman beamed as she lowered herself into the rocking chair across from the sofa where Jasmine sat. "You sure you don't want nothin' to eat? I can whip us up somethin' in a couple of hours. I bet you ain't never had roasted pig. Nah, you're from the city. You need to have a good meal, southern-style," the woman said. "You sure you don't want nothin'?"

"I'm sure, thank you." Jasmine kept the smile on her face and the horror from her voice. Her plan was to talk to this woman, see if she suspected Pastor Wyatt of anything, and then get the heck out of Hogeye Creek. She had no plans to wait a couple of hours for anything—let alone a roasted pig.

Mrs. Evans continued as if she hadn't heard Jasmine. "If I'd known I had company coming, I would've had it all prepared."

Jasmine rested her glass on the table and glanced at her watch. It was already nearing three, and her plane was scheduled to take off from Atlanta at seven. It was doubtful that she'd be able to make that flight, but there were two departing later. She had to get started now.

"Mrs. Evans, I wish I could stay for dinner," Jasmine began, shifting her legs on the sofa so that her skin wouldn't stick permanently to the plastic slipcover. "But I really have to leave tonight."

"That's too bad, sugah. How you gonna write an article for that *Essence* magazine about Hogeye Creek and our church with this little visit?"

That was the lie she'd told the woman the moment they stepped out of church. That was when Mrs. Evans invited her to her home to come and "rest a spell."

Mrs. Evans continued, "Now, Kyla . . . that's what you said your name was, right?"

"Yes, ma'am."

"Where's your camera, Kyla?" When Jasmine frowned, Mrs. Evans said, "How you gonna take pictures for the magazine if you don't have a camera?"

"Oh, we'll be back for that," Jasmine said. "All I'm supposed to do today is make sure there's a good story here."

"We got plenty of stories for you." The chair creaked as Mrs. Evans settled back and rocked to her own rhythm. "Uh-huh, you came to the right place." She nodded. "But when're you gonna talk to Pastor Hubbard?"

"Well, we didn't want to bother him until—"

"Sugah, you're not bothering him." She pushed herself up. "Let me give him a call. He'll be over here quicker than—"

The telephone was already in the woman's hand when Jasmine yelled, "No!"

Mrs. Evans eyebrow's rose.

"I mean . . . we're not even sure that we're going to do the story yet. And if we bring the pastor in . . . let's just keep it here. I'll let you know when I need to speak to Pastor Hubbard."

Mrs. Evans lowered herself back into the rocking chair. "Okay," she said slowly. But now her eyes were small, as if she wasn't so sure about the woman she'd invited into her home.

Jasmine said, "We'll be back next week, but the thing is, we want to center the article on someone really important, someone real, someone who everyone in town looks up to." Jasmine took a sip of her lemonade. "And remember, this is *Essence,* so we want to feature a woman . . . a very important woman."

Mrs. Evans cleared her throat. "That would be me." Her smile was back.

Jasmine pulled a small pad from her purse, trying to make this look legit. "Now, even though this is going to be about you, I'd like to find out a few things about Church of the Solid Rock. Let's see, Pastor Hubbard . . ."

Mrs. Evans leaned forward. "His full name is Billy Ray," she spoke slowly, making sure Jasmine wrote his name correctly. "Billy . . . Ray . . . Hubbard."

Jasmine scribbled his name. "So Pastor Hubbard has been the pastor for a bit over a year, is that right?"

"Yes!" Mrs. Evans nodded. "You sure are a good reporter."

"Remember, I work for *Essence.*" Jasmine held her pen in the air, and Mrs. Evans beamed. Jasmine continued, "And the previous pastor was Eugene—"

"Wyatt," Mrs. Evans said, before Jasmine could finish. Now that she was sure Jasmine was for real, the town crier was back. "Yes, Pastor Wyatt led Church of the Solid Rock for ten years. But he's up in New York now, bless that man."

"So Pastor Wyatt decided to leave?"

"Well, now see," Mrs. Evans leaned forward and lowered her voice even though the two were alone, "the story is that Pastor Wyatt left to become a big-time pastor in New York, but I think that wife of his pushed him." She leaned back, shook her head. "Enid. Even as a little girl, she was the uppity one, thinking she was better than all the other kids and too good for Hogeye Creek." Mrs. Evans folded her arms. Sniffed and made a face like she smelled something bad. "Yup, it was that woman. All of us knew that Pastor Wyatt never wanted to leave. Hogeye Creek was where he was born. This is where his mama and daddy are buried." Then she bowed her head like she was about to say a prayer. "And his brother, too."

That made Jasmine scoot to the edge of the sofa; the plastic ridges scraped against the back of her leg, but she ignored the pricking. Keeping her reporter's face on, she said, "Yes, Pastor Wyatt's brother. He was killed in an accident, right?"

"Uh-huh. Poor thing, that Earvin. He had such a hard life. Got all caught up in those drugs. He was sellin' them and some say he was usin' them, too." She sucked her teeth and shook her head. "I think God took him away so he would stop all that stuff. Everybody was talking about how he'd paid his dues and he was coming to God, but I know the truth. That boy was still caught up, and God reached right down in that car and took him away so that he would leave that stuff alone. 'Cause you know, there ain't no drugs in heaven!"

"So it was a car accident?" Jasmine asked, even though she already knew. But with the revelation that Earvin had been involved with drugs, now Jasmine had the motivation for murder.

"Yes, a couple of weeks before Pastor and the first lady were supposed to be moving up to New York." Mrs. Evans shook her head. "It really is something the way the Lord works. A few years ago, those boys lost their parents in a car accident over on Highway Eighty. And then, Eugene lost his only sibling the same way." In her voice, Jasmine could tell that Mrs. Evans still had a hard time believing that truth.

"Are you sure Pastor Wyatt was in the car with his brother?"

Mrs. Evans frowned as if she didn't understand the question. "Yeah, they were in there together. The police found both of them."

Jasmine's theory fizzled like a pricked balloon. Pastor Wyatt couldn't have rigged the car.

Mrs. Evans continued, "Both of the boys were unconscious when the ambulance got there. Those emergency workers were telling everybody that they didn't think either one of them was going to live." Mrs. Evans shuddered at the memory. "When we got to the hospital, we found out that one had lived and the other died."

Jasmine frowned. "*One* lived? You didn't know which one?"

Mrs. Evans shook her head. "We were all in the waiting room, but we didn't know." Her eyes were glassy as she remembered. "But we just knew . . . we knew that God wouldn't take our pastor . . . and He didn't." She sighed. "I'll never forget when Enid arrived and went back in the ER. We were holding our breath until she came back and told us our pastor was alive.

God forgive us, but we all cheered and laughed and hugged each other. Not that we wanted anything to happen to Earvin . . ." She waved her hand in the air. "But . . . you know."

"Did Enid have to . . . identify her brother-in-law, too?" Just the thought of that made Jasmine feel sorry for the woman, but only for a moment. She didn't like her enough to expend more than a few seconds of sympathy.

Mrs. Evans nodded. "The doctors weren't sure because the car was a mangled mess, and, although one wallet was found, it was thrown from the car. So neither one of them were identified until Enid got there."

Mrs. Evans continued, "The doctors waited for Enid, but I could have done it," she boasted.

Jasmine smiled. Of course. Was there anything Mrs. Evans wasn't capable of?

"Yes," the woman continued, "I learned a long time ago when I used to babysit those boys how to tell them apart."

"Tell them apart?" Jasmine frowned.

Mrs. Evans nodded. "Yup, you know, not everyone can tell twins apart. But I could."

Twins!

The woman continued, "Earvin had the cutest dimple—just one, right here." The woman pointed to her cheek.

Jasmine's mind was spinning with this revelation.

Mrs. Evans said, "They were the dearest little boys, but there was something about that Earvin. Always in trouble, but he knew how to squirm out of it. It was that face; he'd use his dimple to melt everyone." Her smile started to fade. "He was my favorite. Eugene was a little too serious for me. I could've told you he was going to grow up to be a preacher."

That was something that Jasmine couldn't imagine. She could hardly see Pastor Wyatt as a pastor now . . . with his bad-boy swagger and his smile that melted . . . her thoughts stopped.

She was trembling when she said, "Mrs. Evans, you said Earvin had a dimple. What about Eugene?"

She shook her head. "Nope the only one with a dimple was Earvin. That's how I was able to tell them apart. Now, don't get me wrong." Mrs. Evans held up her hand. "Eugene is a handsome man. But there was always something about his brother."

A tornado of images swirled through her mind. Memories of Pastor Wyatt smiling at her, with that deep dimple in his left cheek. Then, images of the newspaper article and the picture of Pastor Wyatt when he was addressing the congregation for the final time—wearing bandages on his face.

To hide the dimple.

Jasmine got it—what she'd come for and so much more. Her hands were still shaking when she reached for her glass and drank the last bit of the lemonade. "Mrs. Evans, may I trouble you for more?"

The woman rocked herself forward. "Of course, sugah."

The moment Mrs. Evans stepped out of Jasmine's sight, she grabbed her purse and dashed to the front, banging the screen door behind her. She was already in her car when she heard Mrs. Evans scream out from her porch.

But she didn't give a word of explanation. Didn't turn around. All she left Mrs. Evans with was a trail of dust from the speeding wheels of her Jaguar.

FORTY

THERE WAS NOTHING BUT EXHAUSTION in Jasmine's sigh when she closed the front door behind her. She'd forgotten how awful it was to fly on Sundays, but the blessing was that she'd gotten the last seat on the last flight. And now, she was home, albeit way past midnight.

But although fatigue made her bones ache, joy made her heart sing. What she'd discovered was far better than anything she could have hoped. Even though she'd had hours to ponder her discovery, it was still hard to believe—Earvin Wyatt had taken over the life of his twin brother. The drug dealer had become the pastor. And not a soul knew, except Enid, of course. Of that, Jasmine was sure. If Mrs. Evans could tell the brothers apart, surely the wife could. And there had been others who'd been able to tell Eugene from Earvin. That's why Earvin had worn the bandage covering the left side of his face for so long.

Now all I have to do is figure out how to use this, Jasmine thought as she dragged into the interior of her darkened apartment.

First, she tiptoed in to check on Jacqueline. After tucking her blanket over her, she treaded just as softly into her own bedroom. But the moment she stepped inside, the room became bright with light.

It took a second for her eyes to adjust, and then she smiled at her husband, resting in their bed on his back, his hands now hooked behind his head.

"Hey, babe," she said before she kissed him softly on his lips. "I was trying not to wake you."

His eyes followed her as she bounced from the bed and walked into her closet. "Jasmine?"

"Yeah."

"Where were you?"

It was a simple question that took her breath away. Why would he ask her that? What did he know? "What?" she asked, staying inside, stalling for time.

"Can you come out here, please?"

He wanted to look into her eyes—she knew that. He wanted to see if she was telling the truth.

"Okay," she said, as chipper as she could. "Let me change."

Her mind raced as fast as her heart. What or who had given her away?

It was only when she couldn't hide any longer that she inhaled deeply, found her game face, and strolled back into their bedroom. The confusion that was etched on her face was real when he asked again where she'd been.

"I was with Mae Frances."

He had not budged from the way he was when she'd first walked in—only now, his eyes moved rapidly, searching her face for clues.

"Then why did Mae Frances leave a message on our phone for you?"

"What?" She shook her head, truly puzzled.

He sat up, swung his legs over the side of the bed. But his eyes didn't leave her face. "She left a message—something about she couldn't wait to hear about your trip because she had some good news for you." His eyes didn't move from her. "She said for you to call as soon as you got in."

"Really?" Her mind was already swirling with lies.

He said, "So if you were with Mae Frances, why did she leave that message?" She opened her mouth, but before she could get a word out, he said, "Please don't lie to me, Jasmine."

Again, she formed her lips to deny, deny, deny, but then she paused. She was at an emotional intersection—the corner of truth or dare.

Should she tell the truth? And relieve herself of the burden she'd been carrying? It would be such a release to share the secret she'd been saddled with for these weeks and end all the lies now.

But did she dare? The way Hosea had reacted the last two times he'd found out her secrets—when he'd found out about their daughter's paternity and when he'd found out that she'd been married before—had left an indelible mark on her memory. He'd walked away from her—both times, leaving her for weeks with great doubts that he would ever return.

He had come home, but what she knew for sure was that if he ever left again, he would never come back. And she loved him too much to lose him.

In seconds, her decision was made, and truth lost.

"Hosea, you know how Mae Frances . . . she just talks and talks. She probably just meant that she hoped my flight home was good. And maybe she got some of those test results from her mother."

His eyes were filled with doubt. "That's not the way she sounded."

"And because of the way she *sounded,* you're accusing me of something?" She exhaled a deep sigh and grabbed the phone. "If you want to know why she called, ask her."

"I already called her."

Jasmine's heart quickened; he knew something, and he was

trying to trick her. Had he somehow trapped Mae Frances into telling the truth? No, she couldn't imagine that. Her friend was better at ducking and lying and dodging than she was. Mae Frances would never give her up.

Jasmine slammed down the phone. "So if you already spoke to Mae Frances—"

"I didn't speak to her," he responded, much calmer than she was. "I called to see what was up, but I got *her* voice mail."

"You really think I wasn't with her?" She shook her head. "I am so tired of this, Hosea."

"Tired of what, Jasmine?"

"Tired of your not believing me. Every time something happens, you think I'm lying."

"Can you blame me?"

If she had been telling the truth, she would have been stone mad at his words. But her proficiency at this helped her to stay calm. Calculate every word she spoke, every emotion she showed, every move she made.

She said, "This is ridiculous. You're the one who's always talking about truth and trust. Well, I've told you the truth; when are you going to start trusting me?" She crossed her arms and stood there, indignation plastered all over her face.

He stared back, and with the way his eyes pierced into her, she wondered if God was telling on her—telling Hosea the real truth.

Lord, if you let me get out of this . . .

It was Hosea who broke first. "I'm sorry," he said, pinching the bridge of his nose like he was trying to squeeze exhaustion out of him. "Maybe it's everything that's going on with Pops and now the upcoming board meeting—I guess I'm suspicious of everything."

Inside, she sighed with relief, but on the outside, she didn't let go of her righteous anger. "Hosea," she began stiffly, "I know I've made a lot of mistakes, and I'm really trying to change."

The sincerity of that truth came through in her tone. "But that doesn't seem to matter to you."

"It does matter, but you can't fault me for having doubts."

"Well, if you're going to doubt everything I say, everything I do, maybe I just need to go back to who I used to be." She stomped toward the door.

"Where are you going?"

She whipped toward him. "I don't know," she said, her anger building. "All I know is that I came home from a long trip, exhausted, and all I wanted was to see you. But then you come at me with this crap and I—" She stopped when the heat of tears came to her eyes. This wasn't part of her act. She really did want to cry. Cry at the way lies rolled so easily off her tongue. Cry at the way she was blaming her husband so skillfully when he had no guilt in this. Cry at the fact that although she wanted to change, there was always something dragging her back.

Slowly, Hosea walked toward her, and when he laid her head on his shoulder, she let the tears fall. Then he leaned back and, with his thumbs, wiped away the emotional water that dampened her cheeks.

"It's taking me longer than I thought to completely trust you again."

The honesty of his words stung, and she responded with her own truth, "I understand."

"But if we keep working on this, I promise, we'll end up where we're supposed to be."

She nodded and looked into his eyes. "I really want to do everything right for you."

He shook his head. "You're human; it won't always be right. But what you've got to know is that when something goes wrong, you can come to me. I don't want any kind of wall between us."

Here she was at that intersection again. And like before, she knew her faith was too small to tell the truth.

He took her hand and led her to the bed. Laid her on her back and rested on top of her. Kissed her gently. Then with more urgency.

Proved to her, right then and there that, though she didn't have his total trust, there was no doubt that she had long ago earned his absolute love.

FORTY-ONE

Jasmine lied again.

She'd lain awake almost the entire night and, at dawn, finally eased from the bed. Minutes later, when she came from her closet dressed in a jogging suit, Hosea had rolled over and asked where she was going.

"For a jog."

"Really?" He peered at her with sleep-filled eyes. "You haven't done that in months."

"I know. But I need to do something about all of this stress."

He propped himself up a bit. "Is it because of last night?"

She shook her head and with a smile pretended that she'd forgotten about his accusations. "No, it's the stuff that's going on with Dad and at the church." She shrugged. "And it's not a bad idea to start exercising again," she said, patting her stomach to show him where she carried the few extra pounds she'd gained.

The way he smiled and fell back against his pillow, Jasmine could tell that Hosea thought her lie was a good idea.

"Okay, maybe I'll join you tomorrow," he said, before he rolled back over.

Jasmine dashed from the apartment and out onto the just-arousing New York City street. Early joggers met her as soon as she stepped outside, their focus on getting to the running paths in Central Park. But Jasmine walked in the opposite direction—heading east and turning right on Sixth Avenue.

Only then did she pull her cell phone from her pocket and do what she'd been thinking about all night. She pressed the Speed Dial button.

Mae Frances's groggy voice greeted her, but Jasmine didn't have a single regret that she'd awakened her friend at five thirty in the morning, Texas time.

Mae Frances had barely said hello before Jasmine charged into her, "What're you trying to do to me?"

"Jasmine Larson, is that you?"

Jasmine walked up Sixth Avenue, her anger propelling her to move so fast she *was* almost jogging. "You know it's me, Mae Frances. Don't play." She stopped in the middle of the street. Turned around and went back the other way. "I am so mad right now I don't know what to do."

"Why're you mad? It's too early for me to have gotten on your nerves."

"Not true! I've been pissed at you for hours. I couldn't even sleep! Why did you leave a message on my phone? Now Hosea thinks I lied to him about being in Houston."

"You did lie to him!"

That truth made her mad enough to want to reach through the phone and choke her friend. "That has nothing to do with it, Mae Frances! Are you *trying* to break up my marriage?"

"What kind of stupid question is that?" Mae Frances pushed back. "Preacher Man's never going to leave you. And anyway, I've left you a million messages on your cell phone before and it was never a problem."

"But you didn't call my cell, you called me at home!"

"I did?" She sounded confused. "Well, I thought I was calling your cell. You know I don't know how to work this thing; you gave me this phone," she said, as if this was Jasmine's fault. "All I did was press your name like I always do. I guess the darn thing dialed your home."

But Jasmine was too mad to settle down. She turned around, stomped back down Sixth Avenue.

"Well, you need to be more careful. You shouldn't have called me at all. You should've just waited until I called you!"

And on the streets of New York, not one person turned to look at the woman who was screaming, with hands flailing like she wanted to kill somebody.

"Well, I couldn't wait," Mae Frances shouted, now as indignant as Jasmine.

"Why not?"

"Because I got the information you wanted."

Her anger made her deaf. "Don't you know that if Hosea catches me in one more lie—" Then, she stopped—stopped moving, stopped talking. Her voice was lower, calmer when she asked, "What information?"

"Hmph, that's what I thought." Now it was Mae Frances who huffed. "I guess you're gonna slow your roll."

"Mae Frances, what did you find out?"

"I shouldn't tell you a thing," her friend grumbled. "I love you as if I gave birth to you myself, but how do you think I feel with you calling me up in the middle of the night—"

Jasmine rolled her eyes. "It's not the middle of the night—"

"Yelling at me," Mae Frances continued, "like you don't have a penny's worth of sense."

"I'm sorry, Mae Frances. But if you knew what Hosea said to me last night . . ." She paused, knowing she'd have to say it again. "I'm sorry." Jasmine tried to be silent so that her apology could sink in, but it was hard to wait. "Did you find something on Ivy?" the question rushed out of her.

"No."

"Oh. On Roxie."

"No."

Jasmine frowned. Had she apologized for nothing?

"But," Mae Frances began, with a bit of taunting in her tone, "I do have something on that Whittingham lady."

Jasmine pressed her lips together so that she wouldn't start screaming all over again. What was Mae Frances trying to do to her? She hadn't asked Mae Frances to find anything on Mrs. Whittingham!

"I couldn't find anything on those Ivy or Roxie girls," Mae Frances explained, "but I wanted to get something for my money. So I told my connection to keep digging."

What a waste!

"Now, that Daniel Hill, he's got a couple of traffic tickets that he's never bothered to pay . . ."

She's driving me crazy!

"But our good Mrs. Whittingham . . . seems that she's not so good after all."

Jasmine rolled her eyes, her anger rising.

Mae Frances asked, "Did you know that she had a child?"

Jasmine shook her head, then took a breath so that she wouldn't yell. "Mrs. Whittingham doesn't have any children."

"Well, I don't know what she did with the one she had, but you can trust what I'm telling you. You know Johnnie Cochran?"

"Yeah?" Jasmine's response sounded like a question. What did Johnnie Cochran have to do with this?

"Well, he and I were good, good friends, God bless him."

Jasmine's eyes rose to the heavens. "Mae Frances—"

"Let me finish!" she snapped. "Well, at a New Year's Eve party back in eighty-seven, Johnnie introduced me to Sonny Santana."

"Is this going to be a long story?"

"Santana is one of my connections," Mae Frances continued, as if she hadn't heard Jasmine, "who has a lot of connections, and he's never wrong. It seems that back in seventy-one, our little miss holier-than-thou Whittingham went off to college, and by the second semester of her freshman year, she was with child."

Jasmine's head was filled with confusion.

Mae Frances continued, "She had a baby girl born at the end of seventy-two, when she was only eighteen."

"That's imposs . . . ible . . ."

And then Jasmine remembered. The conversation she'd overheard a couple of Sundays ago while she'd been resting in Hosea's office. Before he'd come in and knocked her upside her head with the door.

Why would it say that Mama was eighteen on my birth certificate?

That had been Ivy's question, and it hadn't really interested Jasmine at the time. But what was interesting was the way Mrs. Whittingham had responded, with such venom. Not a bit of it had made sense then.

All of it made sense now.

"Her daughter is Ivy," Jasmine whispered.

"What?" Mae Frances shouted so loud, Jasmine had to pull her phone away from her ear.

Jasmine stood still, said, "Her sister is her daughter," more to herself than to Mae Frances. "Mae Frances, I gotta go." But before she hung up, she said, "And I'm really sorry that I yelled at you. Thanks for always having my back."

She clicked off the phone and continued down Sixth Avenue to Fifty-seventh Street. She didn't stop, not even to browse in the windows of the unopened designer shops that she loved. Instead, she marched to Seventh Avenue and made a right, thinking the whole time about Mrs. Whittingham—Ivy's mother.

This is amazing! Jasmine thought. All this time, that woman had judged her about Jacqueline. How hypocritical was this?

It was too bad that Mrs. Whittingham wasn't the blackmailer. Jasmine would have loved to drag that woman down from that high-uppity horse she rode on.

This information was useful, though—if Ivy was the one blackmailing her, Jasmine was going to blow up her world with this news.

But if Ivy wasn't the one, she would keep the old woman's secret. She wasn't going to throw her indiscretion in her face the way Mrs. Whittingham had done to her. She was going to be the better Christian.

Jasmine shook her head as she stepped back into her apartment building. Jerome, Pastor Wyatt, and now Sister Whittingham—all saints at City of Lights.

But it was becoming harder and harder to tell the saints from the sinners.

FORTY-TWO

ALTHOUGH HER MIND WAS PACKED with other thoughts, Jasmine smiled as Jacqueline jumped up, her ponytails bouncing as she raced around the slide once again.

"Look it, Mama!" she exclaimed and climbed the steps. At the top of the five stairs, Jacqueline sat down, held her hands high above her head, and pushed forward. "Whee!" She screamed and giggled as if she were sliding down a hundred-foot apparatus. At the bottom, she jumped up again, clapping her hands as she ran around Jasmine so that she could do the routine all over again.

Pure joy radiated from Jacqueline's face, and Jasmine sighed, wanting that joy, that peace. Her hope was that peace would soon return to her life—especially with all the dirt she'd gathered.

Jasmine wasn't sure who was more scandalous—Jerome, who with the two e-mails he'd sent last night had proven he was a straight fool. She couldn't believe the man actually propositioned the girl for sex over the Internet. Hadn't he ever watched any of those investigative shows?

Then there were the Wyatts. Earvin hadn't killed his brother . . . he just wouldn't let his brother rest in peace.

And finally, she had Ivy, through Mrs. Whittingham. She'd get the old woman to control her daughter if Ivy turned out to be the blackmailer.

Only Roxie appeared to be clean personally, though she was sleeping with a pedophile. Jasmine could turn Jerome's issue into Roxie's problem if she had to.

Her plan now was to confront each of them and make a deal—a secret for a secret. In truth, she wished that she could expose them all—their secrets were far more immoral than hers. But for now, all she planned to do was go to them one at a time, tell each what she knew and pray that one would fall to their knees and confess.

Then this nightmare would be over.

She smiled to herself and tried to ignore the other side of her where fear still stirred. Fear that told her she was wrong. That even after all of this, her secret would still be looming out there because none of her suspects was the blackmailer.

"Wheeeee!"

As Jacqueline's glee rang in her ears, Jasmine pressed back her fear and turned her thoughts to her plan. She had three days to confront her suspects. She would go to Jerome first, since the Wyatts were out of town. She would save Ivy for last, since she was sure it was one of the men.

No matter how hard she tried though, she couldn't keep uncertainty away. Suppose, after all of this, she walked into that board meeting on Friday and Mr. Smith was there, like the blackmailer had promised? That thought sent ice through her veins.

It couldn't go down that way. The ending couldn't be such a disaster, not when the beginning had begun so differently . . .

It started the night she'd left Foxtails to go with the man.

After he'd paid her fees and got clearance from Buck, Jasmine had walked past the other girls who stared at her with knowing eyes. But she stepped without looking their way. It was a gift that Viva wasn't working that night—she didn't want her friend thinking that she was like her. Yes, she was leaving with a customer, but her reasons were far loftier than those of any of the other girls. And she was not going to sleep with him.

As she followed the short, slight man into the parking lot, Jasmine moved to a chorus that played inside her head, but it wasn't a tune from the club. This was a song she'd been singing for the weeks that she worked at Foxtails; *Money for school. Money for school.*

"Would you mind . . . sitting in the back?" he asked, when they stopped at his black Mercedes sedan.

It was a polite demand, in the form of a question. She slid inside and wondered if he'd changed his mind. Was he asking her to get in the back because he wanted to have sex in the car? *It's not going to happen,* she thought. Even if this was a Mercedes.

Her frown deepened when he went around, got into the driver's seat, and then pulled off as if he was her chauffeur.

The car was filled with the scent of his flower, and she inhaled the sweetness. But as they moved, anxiety washed over her, and she kept her eyes on the familiar streets, taking note in case she had to make a quick escape.

When they entered the 405 Freeway, she needed to talk, to make this anomalous moment feel normal.

"So . . . are you from Los Angeles?" she asked, not caring, but not knowing what else to say.

"No."

"But you live here now, right?"

"Yes."

She bit her lip and searched her mind for the right question, one to which he couldn't give a monosyllabic response.

"What kind of work do you do?"

This time, he didn't respond at all.

She tried to catch his glance in the rearview mirror, but his eyes were focused on the road.

And even when she repeated the question, he said nothing.

So she shut up. And pressed her hands and legs together so that it didn't look like she was scared, even though she was beginning to tremble. This was starting to feel too weird.

But what was she afraid of? Surely, she was safe. Girls left the club with men all the time—and they always came back. And this man—who was barely five feet five inches tall and who probably didn't weigh 150 pounds—couldn't possibly be dangerous. He was a regular at the club; dozens of people could identify him. He'd talked to Buck and had left his information. And how many men had watched them walk out together? No serial killer left a trail that hot.

Jasmine sat back and made more mental notes as the car edged onto the 110 Freeway and sped toward downtown. Within minutes, the Los Angeles skyline came into view, and not long after that, the man stopped the car in front of the Bonaventure Hotel. When he handed the keys to the valet, Jasmine wondered how it would look when they checked into this fancy hotel without bags.

But once inside the lobby, the man led Jasmine straight to the elevator bank, where an empty glass chamber waited that whisked the two up the side of the building.

The first thing that hit her when she followed him into the thirtieth-floor room was the aroma—of the dozen plants that bore the same scent that the man wore in his lapel. The plants were everywhere—on the nightstands, the dresser, the desk. Several were lined up at the foot of the bed.

She stood in the center of the magnificent room with its king-size bed, thick comforter, and more pillows than she'd ever seen. And the panoramic view that felt as if she was overlooking half of the city was spectacular.

When she turned away from the window, the man was sitting at the bed's edge, his jacket off, his tie loosened. As she had taken in her surroundings, she'd forgotten for a moment why she was in this place—and the mental cocktail of anxiety and apprehension came rushing back.

"So," she began, but then stopped. Looked around the room as if she might find more words somewhere. "What kind of flowers are these?" She leaned over and took a whiff of one of the sweet petals.

"Jasmines."

That made her stand up straight. She looked at him with wide eyes, but he only smiled back.

It's a coincidence. But still, the fear she'd pressed down began to slowly rise again.

"You don't have to worry," he said, as if he knew she was afraid. "All I want you to do is dance."

Jasmine nodded, although she was having a hard time believing that. She didn't have any idea what the hotel room cost, but surely it was too much to pay when she could've danced at the club.

"Just dance," he repeated.

"Okay?" she said, turning that affirmation into a question.

The man scooted back, rested against the pillows, crossed his hands and legs and motioned for Jasmine to come toward the side of the bed.

She glanced quickly around the space for a boom box or something; she certainly couldn't dance without music.

When she looked back at him, he whispered, "Please, just dance."

So she closed her eyes and began to imagine that she was on the stage.

It was bizarre, at first, swaying and swinging and grinding without a pole or the pulse of a beat. But when she felt the familiar tickle on her ankle and she glanced down at the bills that he had tossed at her feet, this oddity began to feel comfortably familiar.

It took longer for her to disrobe in the street clothes that she wore; nothing ripped away easily. But finally she was down to the costume that he was paying for.

She swung and swayed some more, still conscious of the missing music. But she squatted and did splits, and finally, she rose from the floor, stood with her hands on her hips, and waited for the man to tell her what he wanted next.

His smile was wider than usual when he asked, "Would you mind taking that off?" He pointed to the royal-blue heart-shaped G-string.

She hesitated, but only for a moment. This still wasn't sex, and it was all about the money.

When she honored his request, he inhaled a deep breath and asked, "Would you mind getting on the bed?"

"I'm not—"

But before she could finish, he said, "I want you to dance. Do you think you can do that standing on the bed?"

It was getting weirder and weirder. But really, it was no stranger than being in this room in the first place. So she worked it, unsteadily at first, until she found her footing on the firm mattress. She danced, without clothes, without music. A lap dance, on a bed.

Her legs began to tire; moving was much more exhausting standing over him like this. But while she was wearing down, he seemed more exhilarated. So she turned it up, getting closer to him, taking in the scent of his flower up close. Sharing her scent with him.

She danced.

He panted.

She wondered if talking would help move this along faster. She asked him, "Do you like it when I do this?" She was in his face.

His breathing quickened, and he nodded.

She turned around, shook everything she had, and his breathing became so heavy she thought he was going to have a heart attack.

He said, "You . . . can . . . stop now. Sit down, if you want to."

She bounced off the bed, so ready to take her money and go.

As she reached for her clothes, he asked, "Would you mind . . . can you . . . lie down . . . next to me?"

She frowned.

"Nothing more. I want to lie next to you." And then he added, "I'll pay you more."

More than five hundred dollars just to lie down? She agreed.

He clicked off the light. She adjusted her position to his. He, fully clothed. She, totally naked. As her head rested on the softness of his cotton shirt, she wondered, Who was this man who held her as if he knew her?

Light streamed in from surrounding high-rise buildings, adding a soft golden glow to the room. And soon, Jasmine could do nothing more than relax in the stillness.

It was the peace that made her stop thinking, made her ask before she had time to stop herself, "Who are you?"

His arm tightened around her a bit, not in a threatening manner, but in a way that made her think for a moment that he cared.

"My name . . . is Mr. Smith."

When he squeezed her even more, she was surprised when she snuggled closer to him. This man was a stranger, yet he didn't feel like one right now. She wondered how long he would want to lie this way; surely, his wife was expecting him.

For the first time, Jasmine wondered about the woman who

had put the ring on his finger: What did she look like? How old was she? She was certain his wife didn't know what Mr. Smith was doing. But like Viva had said, there had to be something that was missing at home—something that had driven this man into her arms. Something that she was giving him that his wife couldn't.

That made her smile. For the second time since she'd joined Viva at Foxtails, she felt empowered. In this moment, she was far better than his wife—at least that's what Mr. Smith thought or he wouldn't have been here.

"Thank you for coming with me," he whispered in the dark.

She wasn't sure why she shared, "I was afraid to, at first."

"I know." He held her tighter. "But you don't have anything to be afraid of with me."

She believed him; that was why she closed her eyes to rest for a minute. She was sure Mr. Smith would be getting up to leave soon. She couldn't see a clock, but it had to be close to midnight.

Her eyes didn't open again until sunlight splashed through the window. She sat up with a start, her eyes darting around until she remembered. She scoped the room for any sign of Mr. Smith. But all that was left of him were the plants and an envelope on the nightstand. "Jasmine Cox" was scrawled on the front.

She was startled to see her name. They'd been told not to share their identities with the men. But her man—Mr. Smith—knew who she was.

She'd suspected it last night, when he'd told her about the flowers. *Buck must've given him my name.*

Jasmine slipped the ivory note card from the envelope and twelve fifty-dollar bills fell out.

When you are ready, a car will be waiting for you downstairs to take you home. In the meantime, order anything you like from room service. I will see you tonight, Jasmine.

I will see you tonight. Those were the words she focused on. Did he want to do this again? Would he pay her six hundred dollars next time also?

She leaned back against the soft pillows and calculated in her head. With Mr. Smith and Foxtails, she really would earn enough to finish school—and have money left over!

Jasmine bounced from the bed, tossed the bills above her head, and laughed as the money rained on her. She ignored the chill of the air conditioner as she danced around the room, thinking about all that she'd be able to do now. Like move into a better apartment. Maybe a two-bedroom, which would send all of those women who didn't like her into a real tizzy. And she would be able to dress better. And get her hair done every week: get manicures and pedicures whenever she wanted.

But this wouldn't be just about her. She'd give her dad a little bit of money, too. And she'd be able to buy Kenny anything he wanted—she'd start with the new Walkman he'd been talking about.

She laughed. "I wonder how much Mr. Smith would pay to sleep with me?"

Her laughter stopped. She couldn't believe she was thinking that. Mr. Smith just wanted her to dance—and that's all she wanted to do. So why had that thought come to her? She didn't want to do that, did she . . .

"Mama," Jacqueline called as she tapped her mother's hand. "Mama!"

Jasmine snapped from her reverie. "Yes, baby?" But her eyes wandered down to the rhinestone letters that were on the front of her daughter's T-shirt. She had on a matching one that Hosea had brought home for his favorite ladies two weeks ago.

Like mother, like daughter.

Jasmine lifted Jacqueline into her lap and hugged her. "I love you, you know that, right?"

"Yes," Jacqueline sang and giggled. "Sing song, Mama."

With the memories of her sins fresh in her mind, Jasmine sang the song about God's love with her daughter. And as she sang, she prayed that God would always keep Jacqueline in His hands so that her daughter never, ever became like her mother.

FORTY-THREE

GENTLY, HOSEA PASSED THEIR SLEEPING daughter to his wife. "I'm going to get the mail."

Jacqueline was knocked out, and in her sleep she weighed heavy in Jasmine's arms. But even though her limbs were already aching, Jasmine could have held her daughter forever. She sighed, lulled by the calming rhythm of Jacqueline's sleep breathing.

It had been a great time with her daughter, the perfect way to spend the day before the storm. Tomorrow it would begin, starting with Jerome Viceroy.

Jasmine followed Hosea into their apartment.

"Want me to put her down?" he asked.

Jasmine shook her head as she hugged Jacqueline tighter. "I want to hold her a little longer."

Hosea nodded as he sorted through the envelopes he held. "What's this?" He held the packet up higher. "Jasmine Pepper Bush?"

She had to fight to keep standing, to keep holding Jacqueline.

With a deep frown, he asked, "Why would someone call you Pepper?"

"Oh, you know," Jasmine began. She had to rock Jacqueline in her arms to stop herself from snatching the envelope from him. "That was what some of the kids called me back in the day. Back in college."

"Really?" he asked, taking Jacqueline from her arms and handing her the envelope. "I never knew that."

"Yeah." She laughed, hoping that her chuckle hid some of her shaking. "People used to tease me for using so much pepper on my food. My friend, Viva, started it."

"Oh." He was already moving toward Jacqueline's bedroom, thoughts of "Pepper" already gone from his mind. "I'm going to lay my pumpkin down."

She had a gift—Jasmine knew that. The way her lies came so easily. And the way she could integrate just enough fact, right in the middle of her fiction.

Hosea wasn't out of her sight before she spun around and dashed into their office. When she closed the door, she had to wait for her heart to slow down, wait for the shaking to stop.

This was her hell. Suppose she hadn't been home? Suppose he'd opened the letter?

Calm down, she told herself. That nightmare had not happened.

She ripped open the manila envelope and snatched the letter from inside.

You have until Friday or your sins will come to light. You and Hosea will be destroyed—unless he steps down now.

She read the letter again, looking for that clue that Detective Foxx assured her would come. But how could a mistake be made in so few words? Just like with the last letter, there was nothing to be found.

She closed her eyes, leaned against the door, and let the envelope slip from her hand. Her wish was that she could stay locked up in this room through eternity—never having to face Hosea, or the church board, or anyone.

But then her fight came back. She had her plan; she could still win.

Shaking, Jasmine knelt down, grabbed the envelope, then moved to the desk. Her eyes scanned the letter and the envelope again.

Then she looked at the letter.

Back at the envelope.

Again and again.

It'll be something small, but they get careless. They make mistakes.

She saw it!

"Jasmine?"

She jumped a foot into the air, startled by Hosea's voice. With a quickness, she stuffed the letter into the desk drawer. "Huh?" she called out.

Her heart was beating wildly, but it wasn't fear that sent blood pumping fiercely through her veins. It was exhilaration—she'd inhaled the sweet scent of victory.

She peeked into the hallway, looked at Hosea as if their world was normal. "I'm checking my e-mail. Malik said he sent me something to review."

"Dang," Hosea shook his head, "I love your godbrother, but he needs to put you back on the payroll if he's going to work you like this."

"I know, but you don't mind, do you? It won't take long. And I think he's going to hire someone to replace me soon."

"Nah, I was kidding. Go 'head."

"I'll make this quick," she said, before she stepped back into the office.

Sitting in the chair, she slid the letter and envelope from the desk drawer and stared at both. Like Detective Foxx had said, her blackmailer had made a mistake!

All she wanted to do was to rush out right now and confirm it. But she didn't have a good enough lie that would convince

Hosea that she needed to leave their apartment in the middle of the night.

She'd have to wait until morning.

Still, she exhaled a long sigh of relief. After all these weeks. After all those threats. After all her nightmares . . . it was almost over.

Her line of attack was already in her mind.

First, she'd get confirmation.

Next, she'd go to the source.

And then, Jasmine Cox Larson Bush was going to get her sweet revenge.

FORTY-FOUR

Jasmine's day began in the middle of the night.

She rose, moved stealthily through their bedroom, dressed inside her closet, and was sitting in front of the computer before the hands on the clock rolled around to five o'clock. The new day still had not yet begun to dawn when a half hour later, she scribbled a note to Hosea explaining how she'd forgotten to tell him about a very early meeting she'd scheduled with Malik. And it was a bit before six when the rental company delivered the car she'd ordered online—so that she could move around freely—to the front door of her apartment building.

As she climbed into the Lexus, she turned over what she was going to do. There really wasn't much to her plan—just two parts: Confirm. Destroy!

Fifteen minutes later, as the tower of City of Lights at Riverside Church came into view, Jasmine could feel the hard beating of her heart, its pace rising as she got closer. She'd timed her arrival perfectly; the sun had made its debut when the tires of her car rolled over the gravel of the vacant parking lot.

Months had passed since Reverend Bush's shooting, yet she still felt unsettled about being in the church alone. But her eagerness trumped her fear.

After turning off the ignition, she sat for a moment, praying that this was truly the beginning of the end. Then once she said, "Amen," she shot into action. She jumped from the car and dashed to the door.

Her hands were shaking as she aimed the key for the lock—more anxiety. Stepping inside, the rubber soles of her sneakers allowed her to take silent steps across the area that Mrs. Whittingham claimed as her own. But Jasmine wasn't worried about anyone hearing her—no one ever came to the church this early.

By the time she sat behind Mrs. Whittingham's desk, the familiar emotional cocktail stirred inside of her. Her eyes scanned the desktop, but then her excitement waned a bit when she didn't see what she was looking for. She scrambled through the folders that were neatly lined in the middle of the blotter, not caring about the neat stack that Mrs. Whittingham had left.

When she still found nothing, Jasmine opened the center drawer, rummaged through the rubber bands and paper clips and pens and pencils.

Her heart began to beat harder, but this time, it wasn't from anticipation. Now it was fear . . . that she had been wrong.

She opened the top drawer on the left.

And she saw it.

The roll of stamps.

The Black Heritage ones that she'd discovered on Mrs. Whittingham's desk weeks before. The ones that matched the one on the blackmail letter that had been sent to her apartment.

It will be something small. But blackmailers get careless: they make mistakes.

Mrs. Whittingham had made her mistake, Jasmine was sure. To anyone else, this evidence may have seemed flimsy, but Jasmine knew she was right. Mrs. Whittingham was the person who had been tormenting her. Mrs. Whittingham was the blackmailer.

It was on now.

FORTY-FIVE

"JASMINE LARSON, I CAN'T BELIEVE you're calling me this early," Mae Frances raved when she answered her phone without even saying hello. "Did you forget that I'm an hour behind you? Though sometimes I feel like I'm fifteen hours behind you. No, where I am in Texas sometimes I feel like I'm fifteen years behind you . . ."

"Mae Frances!" Jasmine yelled through her friend's rant. She eased up on the accelerator and slowed down as the green signal turned to red. What she really wanted to do was to take every light. Get down to Mrs. Whittingham in record time. "I know who it is!" she screamed.

"Who what is?" Mae Frances asked through her yawn.

"The blackmailer. It's Mrs. Whittingham!"

Jasmine could almost see her friend's frown. "Sarai Whittingham?" She sounded alert now. "She's not one of the suspects."

"I know! Can you believe this? I'm still having a hard time digesting that she would do this to Hosea, but she's the one."

"How do you know?" Mae Frances asked, sounding doubtful.

Jasmine paused, not sure that she wanted to share what she'd found. She could imagine Mae Frances's reaction.

A stamp? her friend would say before she laughed. Mae Frances would think that was ridiculous. *You think she's the blackmailer because you found a stamp? Anyone could have used her stamp.*

And then Mae Frances would talk and talk until she talked Jasmine out of such a preposterous theory.

But this was a mind-heart thing. In her mind, she remembered what Detective Foxx had told her, and in her heart, she knew she was right.

Jasmine said, "I know it's her, and I'm on my way over there now."

"You're sure about this?"

"Yup. You were right; Mrs. Whittingham did have a daughter, and then she let her parents raise her child as their own," Jasmine said, giving Mae Frances the story she'd put together during her sleepless hours last night. "Can you believe how much of a hypocrite she's been? I cannot wait to take her down."

"Maybe you should think about this," Mae Frances said slowly.

Jasmine couldn't hide her shock. "Think about what? This woman has been torturing me for weeks. For years, really. Now, I'm gonna show her that she messed with the wrong one."

There was a pause before Mae Frances said, "Sit back for a minute, Jasmine Larson."

"You're amazing." Jasmine shook her head. "I thought you'd want to be on the first thing smoking out of Texas, wanting to get a piece of her yourself."

"Now, you know Mrs. Whittingham is not my favorite person, but this situation—if you expose it—I have a feeling it could blow up on you."

"But you're the one who gave me the information!"

"Because I wanted you to have what you needed, but I want

you to be smart, too. Before you do anything, think. It might be time for a little compassion."

"She never had any compassion for me."

"Well, those idiots in the Bible didn't have compassion for Jesus either . . ."

Oh, brother! Jasmine closed her ears and rolled her eyes. Why had she ever taken Mae Frances to church? Her friend had been a much more effective ally when she'd been an atheist.

Mae Frances said, "All I'm saying, Jasmine Larson, is to talk to her and make sure she doesn't say anything to Preacher Man about your being a whore—"

"Don't use that word!"

Mae Frances ignored her. "But after that, let it go."

Even though her friend couldn't see her, Jasmine's head whipped from side to side. "I'm not about to let her get away with this."

"Think about all the things you've gotten away with," Mae Frances said. "There're people who look at you and don't think you deserve to be married to Preacher Man."

Jasmine wished her friend was sitting right here so that she could slap her. "How did this become about me? And when did you turn into Mother Teresa?"

Mae Frances continued as if Jasmine hadn't spoken. "Remember, you've gotten away with quite a bit in your life, and as my good friend, Jeremiah Wright, always says, If you're not careful, those chickens will come home to roost!"

What did that have to do with her? Her chickens weren't going anywhere; she hadn't done anything wrong. It was Mrs. Whittingham who needed to pay—big time.

"Jasmine Larson, are you listening to me? I know what bitterness can do. I used to be you, and I don't want you to grow up to be me."

Jasmine twisted her car from 132nd Street into the curved driveway of the high-rise brick building with LENOX TERRACE stenciled on the glass in gold letters. "Mae Frances, I've got to go."

"Don't you hang up on me, Jasmine Larson," Mae Frances barked. "I know you don't want to hear me, but—"

"What? Mae Frances? Can you hear me?" Jasmine pulled the phone away from her ear. "I think I'm losing you."

"You're not fooling me one bit—"

"I can't hear you. I'm losing the signal . . ." Jasmine clicked off her phone and then pressed the Power Off button. She knew for sure Mae Frances was going to call back—mad.

But she didn't have a single word to say to her friend. Mae Frances had gone all the way Christian on her. Not that she wasn't concerned about God, but sometimes there were situations that you had to handle yourself.

"How long are you going to be?" the doorman asked as he pointed to the car she'd parked in the visitor's space. "You can only stay there for thirty minutes."

Jasmine glanced at her watch. It was just barely seven. "I'll be back way before my thirty minutes are up," she said with a nod.

What she had to do wasn't going to take long at all.

"What do you want!" It was an exclamation more than a question. Then Mrs. Whittingham's eyes grew huge. "Did something happen to"—her hand covered her mouth—"Samuel?"

Jasmine pushed past the woman as she stepped inside.

"No, my father-in-law is—" Jasmine stopped. She couldn't bring herself to think about Reverend Bush; whenever she did, her heart softened.

Jasmine knew he'd be saddened by what she was about to do. He would tell her to pray, to let Jesus take the wheel, to forgive all that Mrs. Whittingham had done.

But Jasmine turned away from those thoughts of grace that

she'd learned from him. Instead, she turned her heart over to the dark side and then faced the woman who'd brought such havoc into her life.

"If nothing's wrong with Samuel," Mrs. Whittingham slammed the door, "then why are you here?"

Jasmine had been thinking about the words she would say at this moment, and she had no plans to drag this out. "Because I wanted to look into the hateful eyes of the evil, conniving witch of a woman who had the audacity to blackmail me."

Many images had gone through her mind when Jasmine wondered what this moment would look like, and one picture was that Mrs. Whittingham would stare back at her with blank eyes. Her fear was that the woman would have no idea what she was talking about.

But the glimmer that shined in Mrs. Whittingham's eyes, even for a millisecond, filled Jasmine with relief and rage at the same time.

"You really are a case," Jasmine said. "You pretend to love Reverend Bush, you pretend to love Hosea, you pretend—"

The woman didn't let her finish. "Don't come into my home and preach to me about love!" Mrs. Whittingham tightened the belt of the flannel bathrobe before she pointed her finger in Jasmine's face. "You don't know a thing about loving anyone but yourself."

"You think you know me?" Jasmine sneered. "It's obvious that you don't, because if you did, you would have known that you just made the biggest mistake of your life."

With bold steps, Mrs. Whittingham came closer. "Oh, really?" she scoffed. "It was a mistake to send you those letters?" She chuckled. "And what are you going to do about it?"

Jasmine's eyebrows rose. Audacity surely made people stupid, sometimes.

Mrs. Whittingham mistook Jasmine's silence for defeat. "That's what I thought. There's nothing you can do. In fact"—

she moved away from her—"I'm glad that you found out. And since you have the nerve to come up in my face like this, I think I need to call Hosea. Need to let him know who you really are. Then maybe he'll do what he should have done a long time ago—maybe after he talks to me, he'll finally divorce you."

Jasmine chuckled. "You really think you have that kind of power over my husband?"

Mrs. Whittingham passed her a wicked smile. "When I tell him that he has more than a name in common with the prophet, Hosea. When I tell him that his wife is no different from Gomer—and that he, too, married a whore. . . ."

Jasmine flinched, wanting to smack the woman down for that.

Mrs. Whittingham continued, "We'll see what he says."

Even as she moved toward the telephone, Jasmine stayed silent. She remained that way until Mrs. Whittingham lifted the receiver.

Then she said, "Before you make that call," Jasmine powered up her cell, "can you give me Ivy's number?"

Through the slits that Mrs. Whittingham's eyes had become, Jasmine could see the woman's uncertainty. "What do you want with my sister?" she asked, her bravado a bit less.

Looking straight at her, Jasmine frowned. Then she tilted her head, as if she was baffled by Mrs. Whittingham's words. "Your sister? You mean your daughter, don't you?"

Mrs. Whittingham stood stone still, frozen in the moment and in fear.

With slow steps, Jasmine moved toward the woman who'd been tormenting her. Her eyes flashed with the fiery fury that had been building inside of her for weeks.

"And you have the nerve to call me a whore? At least I claimed my daughter."

"What . . . are . . . you . . . talking . . . about?" Her words were so shaky, it didn't sound as if she was speaking English.

Jasmine laughed. "Oh, come on. You can come up with something better than that."

The phone slipped from Mrs. Whittingham's trembling hand, but neither one of them watched it fall to the floor. Their eyes were locked on each other.

Jasmine said, "For all the years I've known you . . . the way you looked at me, talked to me, like I was so beneath you. But we really are the same person, aren't we, Sarai? So if I'm a whore who kept her daughter, what kind of whore are you?"

The water was already welling in the older woman's eyes. "What," she began, her voice still trembling, "are you going to do?"

Jasmine glared at her for an extra instant before she shrugged. She lowered herself onto the yellow-flowered Chesterfield. Leaned back and crossed her legs like this visit was a pleasant one. "I'm not sure yet."

It took some time, but Mrs. Whittingham found her voice. Lifted her chin as if she found some courage, too. "Looks like we're at a standstill," she said.

"Oh, really? And how do you see that?"

"Because now . . . both of us have a secret and something to lose."

Jasmine twisted her lips as if she was in deep thought. "I don't quite see it that way. I'm thinking that maybe I should tell Hosea about . . . that little summer I had when I was so young, and then you'll be the only one with a secret and something to lose."

Mrs. Whittingham's eyes got wide with the thought of what that would mean for her. "You're bluffing," she said.

"You think so?"

Mrs. Whittingham nodded. "Hosea will leave you."

Jasmine cocked her head. "I know that's what you're hoping, but think about it, Sarai. Hosea has been upset with me before. But no matter what, we always work it out. Because here's the thing—he loves me. And he always comes back, because whether you want to believe it or not," she leaned forward, "I am the woman God chose for him," she said, repeating what Hosea always told her. "So my husband and I will get through this.

"But you and Ivy," Jasmine shook her head, "I don't know. You've been lying for over thirty years. And what will Ivy think? What will she do when she finds out that her sister is really her mother?"

Mrs. Whittingham's beach-sand-colored skin paled more and for a moment, Jasmine thought the woman was going to drop to the floor right then.

Still, Jasmine pressed. "It's so tabloid, so soap-opery. *Your sister is your mother.*" She paused, letting those words settle. "My bet is that Ivy will never speak to you again, never forgive you, probably wish that you were dead. She might even send up a couple of prayers to God asking that He help with that."

Mrs. Whittingham gasped, and every bit of resolve she had melted with the tears that sprang from her eyes. "Please, if there is anything good inside of you—"

"Inside of me?" Jasmine shot up from the sofa. "You didn't have any compassion for me when you sent me those letters. And what about Hosea? Why would you want to humiliate him? Why would you want him to step down from what his father wanted him to do?"

"Because . . . because. . . ." Mrs. Whittingham choked on her sobs. "It was getting to be too much for him. He wasn't making the right decisions. The pressure . . . it was all too much, and it was best that he focus on his father. He didn't need to be worried about the church. But he wouldn't listen to me."

"So you thought the best way to get him to listen was to blackmail his wife? To disgrace his family?"

"You're the one who brought disgrace to him!" Mrs. Whittingham shouted through her tears. "You're the only one who could have brought Hosea down. You're the whore!"

Jasmine had never been punched with a swing to her gut, but she imagined that this was how it would feel. Without a word, she turned away and marched toward the door.

"Jasmine!" Mrs. Whittingham's voice was filled with panic. "What are you going to do!"

Jasmine's eyes were as hard as her heart when she turned back.

The woman begged again. "Please! I know you hate me, but don't destroy Ivy's life."

All Jasmine said was, "I'll be in touch."

"What does that mean?" Mrs. Whittingham cried.

Jasmine closed the door on her words. She stood in the hallway for a moment and then . . . a thump! As if Mrs. Whittingham had fallen to her knees. It startled Jasmine, at first. Until she heard the muffled cries that filtered through the closed door. The whimpering followed her as she strode toward the elevator. Even when she pressed the Down button, Jasmine was sure she could still hear Mrs. Whittingham weeping.

But there was no compassion in her heart, especially not after the way Mrs. Whittingham still spoke to her.

You're the one who brought disgrace to him!

Those words sliced her.

As she rode down in the elevator, Jasmine heard Mrs. Whittingham's voice again and again. Like the woman was standing right there, spewing them over and over.

You're the only one who could have brought Hosea down. You're the whore!

That was the truth. And that was why, even though she'd told Mrs. Whittingham that she might tell Hosea about that summer, it *was* just a bluff. Jasmine would never, ever say a word to her husband about what had happened in '83. She had good reasons for taking that job at Foxtails, but would she ever be able to explain to Hosea what had come next . . . ?

For the last four weeks, Jasmine had been making it rain for real!

The fall semester had begun, and she'd become an expert at juggling her time—a student by day, a stripper by night.

She split her evenings between Foxtails and Mr. Smith, leaving weekends for Kenny, who'd been thrilled that his girlfriend suddenly had enough money for both of them. It had been easy to explain her newfound wealth: she told her boyfriend that her money was the final gift from her dead mother, a monthly allowance that was paid from an insurance policy.

That was a good lie.

She was able to explain away her missing evenings, too—telling Kenny that her internship with Sony didn't stop when the summer ended.

"I'm a production assistant on one of the shows they're setting up for a pilot, so I'll be putting in a lot of hours after classes."

That was a better lie.

Kenny had been impressed, and so he asked few questions when she wasn't available on Monday, Tuesday, Wednesday, or Thursday evenings.

The truth was, on Mondays and Tuesdays, Jasmine helped pack the house at Foxtails. Men came from all over the city to lose their minds when Pepper Pulaski hung on to the pole, turned her back to them, and, with her long dark hair draped down to her butt, honored them with her signature earthquake move—something that not one of the other girls had learned to do.

As the club favorite, Jasmine now brought home almost five hundred dollars for those two nights of work.

Then she spent Wednesdays and Thursdays in one of the five-star hotels in Los Angeles with Mr. Smith. Inside the privacy of some of the best rooms in the city, Mr. Smith paid her double what she made at Foxtails.

And she never had to do anything more than get naked.

Her mind was filled with that proud thought now, as she closed her eyes and gyrated to beats that only she heard in her head. Mr. Smith liked to watch her move without music; he said there was nothing to distract him from the pure beauty of her dancing.

Tonight, she danced atop the bed in the Beverly Hills Hotel. This was her favorite place to come with Mr. Smith. With its golden walls and cream-and-taupe bedding, Jasmine felt like a queen in this castle. Especially surrounded by the many antique Louis XVI pieces—the armchair, writing desk, and armoire.

Before Jasmine had met Mr. Smith, she hadn't known an armoire from an aardvark. And she definitely hadn't known anything about neoclassical designs. But her benefactor had become her teacher, exposing her to the best of many things.

She glanced down on the bed where Mr. Smith lay beneath her. Weeks ago, when she'd done this for the first time, Mr. Smith had been fully clothed. But as time passed, his clothes began to shed, as if being naked was contagious.

Now he lay beneath her, as he had for the past two weeks, wearing nothing more than his wedding ring. But it didn't bother Jasmine. If it turned him on, then it worked for her.

For a moment, she wondered if she'd been turned over to a reprobate mind—she'd once heard her best friend Kyla's pastor talk about how some people fall so far into sin, there was no turning back.

Be careful, she remembered Pastor Ford's words. *Once you open doors leading to sins, it's hard to close them.*

Well, she wasn't sinning. She was just dancing and giving the customer what he wanted.

"Are you tired?" Mr. Smith broke through all the thoughts

she had as she danced. His concern for her was always the same; she heard it in his caring, gentle tone.

She nodded and, like she always did, dropped to her knees, then fell into his arms. They rested together, skin to skin, as if they were a couple.

It still felt strange; every night after she danced, they would lie together, and Mr. Smith would hold her as if he loved her. Invariably, she'd fall asleep, then hours later, she'd awaken—always alone.

It was his absence and the envelope that he always left filled with fifty dollar bills that reminded her that this didn't have a single thing to do with love. But make-believe wasn't just for kids, and often she daydreamed about what life would be like with Mr. Smith.

Not that she thought that truly possible. First of all, he was white—and there was no way she was taking home a white man. Next, he was old. She didn't know his age, but the wisps of white hair that covered his scalp and the wrinkled skin that covered his bones let her know that he had a good three decades over her. And she never forgot about the fact that he was married.

But his money kept her dreaming. Kept her pretending about all the what-ifs.

Minutes passed and then Mr. Smith said, "I have a gift for you."

Jasmine leapt from the bed, parts of her bouncing as she moved. For several seconds she jumped up and down in front of him, pretending that it was only delight that made her do so. But in truth, it was part of the show. Part of what he loved. It was the reason that he often came with gifts.

Watching her jiggle may have been his favorite part, but rushing to the closet where he always hid the presents was hers.

In the weeks since he'd started bearing gifts, he'd given her diamond stud earrings, plus a slew of other items—a sterling silver bracelet, a pearl necklace. He'd even given her a two-hundred-dollar gift certificate to Chanel, and she'd bought her first designer purse from the store on Rodeo Drive.

She couldn't imagine what he'd bought her today when she pulled out the oblong-shaped brown box. But the moment she pulled off the top, she gasped. A pair of shoes. Gucci.

"Oh, my God!" she exclaimed.

"Would you model them for me?" Mr. Smith asked as he pushed himself up in the bed to get a better view.

She slipped on the pumps and strutted back and forth across the soft mauve carpet, twisting and turning and satisfying Mr. Smith with every move.

She was posing with her hands on her hips, when Mr. Smith blurted out, "Would you sleep with me, please?"

Time and her heart stopped. She stood so still, Mr. Smith repeated his question as if she hadn't heard him.

"Will you sleep with me, please?"

He was such a polite man. Always gentle, his concern always apparent. But no matter how respectful he was, she wasn't about to do what he asked.

"Please," he said again. She noticed the way he leered at her. Not that his eyes hadn't always been filled with lust when she danced, but Jasmine always knew how those times were going to end.

She didn't know what it was, but never before had she truly felt naked in front of him, yet now all she wanted to do was yank the blanket from the bed and hide herself.

"Please," he said, his voice still soft. "Just this once. And then you will never see me again."

She couldn't speak the word, but her head was shaking, her body was still saying no.

"I will pay you five thousand dollars."

Her head stopped moving. She slowed her breathing. *Five thousand dollars?*

But then she shook herself out of the short stupor that the mention of that much money had thrown her into. She'd already made five thousand dollars and more just dancing all these weeks. Why should she do anything else?

He answered her silent question. "I'm leaving Los Angeles," he said simply. And in the air were more words, unspoken, but impossible to ignore . . . *There will be no more money.*

"When?" she finally asked.

"The day after tomorrow. My job, the network—I'm taking over as bureau chief in Washington. We'll never see each other after tonight."

Jasmine felt her future slipping away. She wanted to demand that he stay. And watch her dance. And keep paying her.

Still, it didn't matter that he was leaving. She'd still make money at Foxtails, and as popular as she was, Buck would let her work every night if she wanted to.

"Five thousand dollars," he repeated, as if he wanted to remind her what was most important to her.

Jasmine had never seen that amount of money all at once.

Mr. Smith said, "And I'll pay the rest of your tuition. Whatever you owe."

She'd told him once that she danced only for school. Did he think school was enough to turn her into a whore?

He continued to plead his case, "Or whatever you need, I'll pay it. Plus, five thousand dollars."

Most of her school bills were paid, but there was her rent.

No! The moral part of her screamed. *I'm better than that.*

Five thousand dollars!

That money would buy her new clothes, plenty of new shoes, the kinds of things that Mr. Smith had helped her to appreciate.

"Five thousand dollars?" She wasn't sure if that was a question for Mr. Smith or a statement to herself.

He nodded and reached for her, as if he was sure.

And why shouldn't he be? Money had gotten him whatever he wanted from her. All he ever had to do was raise the stakes, and she was his.

"Five thousand dollars?" she asked again.

Now he shook his head and did what he always did. "Six thousand!"

For the first time, she noticed how small, how beady his eyes were. And how wrinkly his skin was.

She cringed and made up her mind.

She slipped off the pumps and slipped into his bed. When he pressed his thin lips against hers, Jasmine closed her eyes, ready to sell her body and her soul.

It would be just this once. And one time certainly didn't make you a whore . . .

The knock on the car window startled Jasmine. Made her open her eyes and sit up straight.

"Miss, you've got to move," the man said.

Jasmine looked up. She was still sitting in front of Mrs. Whittingham's building. She didn't even remember getting into the car, her thoughts had been so far away.

She revved up the engine, trying to push Mr. Smith from her mind. But ever since Mrs. Whittingham had forced her to remember, the memory of that last night with Mr. Smith had been hard to forget. The memory that she had sold herself for sixty one-hundred-dollar bills, plus the three-thousand-dollar check he'd written to her landlord.

That was the part she never wanted Hosea to find out. Shame kept her lying. Shame and the way she was sure her husband would look at her once he found out that she and Gomer shared much more than a husband with the name Hosea.

And as bad as that night had been, the worst part was that it was just the beginning.

Just like Pastor Ford had said, she'd opened sin's door, and it became impossible to close it. Once Mr. Smith had walked in, countless men had followed. Married men, single men. Black and white. And her greatest shame . . . there'd been nights when she'd taken two at a time. All kinds of men who paid big money to share a few hours with the freak who could do the same things in bed that she did on the stage.

She had turned herself over to a reprobate mind.

And therein lay her biggest problem: If she told Hosea about Foxtails and Mr. Smith . . . if he asked whether that man was the only one . . . what would she say?

With a sigh, Jasmine swerved the car to the right and headed downtown. Why was she spending so much time and thought in the past? She was so far from being that woman. She had God in her heart now. And Hosea. She was better because of both of them. And Reverend Bush had taught her that she truly wasn't who she used to be.

She shook her head. No, she didn't need to think about the past. All she needed to think about was her victory.

She could now blackmail her blackmailer.

One down.

FORTY-SIX

JASMINE STRUTTED DOWN THE LONG hall, walked straight to her husband, and kissed him on his cheek. Then she turned to Mrs. Whittingham and tapped her on her shoulder.

"Would you mind coming into my office?"

Without a single glance toward her, Mrs. Whittingham shot right up and walked back down the hall, retracing the steps that Jasmine had just taken.

Hosea whispered, "What's that about?"

"I want to talk to her." Jasmine leaned back and looked at him innocently. "I want her advice about a new design I'm looking at for the bulletin."

"Oh, okay." He grinned. "I'm glad you guys have found a way to get along."

"You have so much on your mind, babe, that Mrs. Whittingham and I made a pact. There's no need for us to keep acting like we're in high school."

She kissed him again, and Jasmine's smile was wide as she moved toward her office. She could feel Hosea's eyes, and she added a bit more sway to her swagger—a promise of things to come when they got home.

She turned back and winked at him before she stepped into

her office. But then all of her good feelings faded fast when she saw Mrs. Whittingham, standing at the edge of her desk, staring out the window.

"Thanks for coming in," Jasmine said, her power making her civil.

The woman turned to her, eyes weary, shoulders slumped, a stance of defeat. Jasmine had to work hard to push aside the sympathy she felt rising. She sank into her seat. "I need you to do something for me."

Mrs. Whittingham said nothing, just waited for her orders.

"I need you to postpone the board meeting for tomorrow."

Mrs. Whittingham blinked, taking a moment to register the request and then more time for her brain to figure out if Jasmine's words made any sense.

"How am I supposed to do that?" But the edge that was usually on every word that Mrs. Whittingham spoke to Jasmine was gone, and for a millisecond, Jasmine wished for that fight to be back. It was no fun to spar with a beaten partner.

"I don't care how you do it," Jasmine said. "I want the meeting postponed."

Mrs. Whittingham shook her head. "It's not going to change anything. Pastor Wyatt still has enough votes to have Hosea removed. It's only—"

Jasmine held up her hand, stopped the woman from talking. "I don't need much time. Just postpone it until Monday. And don't let anyone know that I had anything to do with this." Then she wiggled her fingers in a dismissive wave.

With a sigh, Mrs. Whittingham turned around, but before she got to the door, Jasmine called out, "Wait." Then she asked the question that had given her another sleepless night. "How did you find out about . . ."

Jasmine stopped right there. No more was needed; Mrs. Whittingham knew what she was talking about.

Mrs. Whittingham's lips curved a little, and she spoke as if her next words were her greatest joy. "From Samuel."

Mrs. Whittingham's joy was Jasmine's pain. A pain that shot right through her center. "Reverend Bush?" Jasmine whispered, as if she needed clarification. As if she hoped that there was another Samuel in Mrs. Whittingham's life.

Mrs. Whittingham's weak smile strengthened when she nodded.

Jasmine asked, "He told you that I . . ."

Mrs. Whittingham stood taller, raised her head higher. "Not directly." Triumph was in her voice when she said, "He was having you investigated."

"What?"

Mrs. Whittingham nodded. "I read the private investigator's report."

Jasmine had to remember to breathe in, breathe out. And not show any signs of weakness to the enemy.

All kinds of reasons, all kinds of possibilities drifted through her mind, and she couldn't come up with one that made sense. Why would her father-in-law have her investigated? Their animosity was years behind them. Reverend Bush had accepted her (and Jacqueline) into his heart even before Hosea had been convinced to do the same. Reverend Bush had forgiven her—for everything. At least that's what he'd said.

Seemed like what he'd said had been a lie.

Except Jasmine had been lying for a long time; she knew a liar, and her father-in-law was not one. No, Reverend Bush was on the opposite end of the spectrum, the kind of man who would look you dead in your face and tell you nothing but the truth.

So he was having her investigated? That couldn't be.

Jasmine stared at Mrs. Whittingham, searching for clues that *she* was lying.

"Where's the report?" Jasmine demanded to know.

For a moment, Mrs. Whittingham stood, lips pressed together, defiant. But when Jasmine began a slow rise from her seat, Mrs. Whittingham remembered which one of them was in charge.

She said, "It's at home," as she glared at Jasmine.

"I want it." Her look was as fierce.

A pause before, "I'll bring it tomorrow."

Not even a second passed before, "I want it now."

"You want me to just leave the office?" she asked, as if Jasmine's request was ridiculous.

Jasmine sat, her answer in her stare.

Mrs. Whittingham broke away first, lowered her eyes, and trudged out of the office.

Jasmine turned to her computer, but her hands wouldn't move across the keys. She couldn't work. She wouldn't be able to concentrate until she saw that report. And could figure out why her father-in-law had had her investigated.

FORTY-SEVEN

THERE WAS NEVER ANY REST for the tormented.

Jasmine's eyes were once again wide open while Hosea rested next to her, deep in a peaceful sleep.

Tonight, she was tortured by thoughts of the report Mrs. Whittingham had given her this afternoon. The FedEx packet that was now hidden deep in the secret corner, in the back of her closet.

When Mrs. Whittingham had given her the package earlier, Jasmine had frowned. She recognized the packet—she'd held it in her hands the morning after Reverend Bush had been shot. The hospital administrator had given it to her, along with his other personal affects.

Jasmine remembered being curious when she saw the return address for L.A. Investigative Services. But then the hospital administrator had walked in and had taken her attention away. Right then, Jasmine had handed Mrs. Whittingham all the ammunition she needed to blackmail her.

But with Mrs. Whittingham's blackmail behind her, those were not the thoughts she had as she surrendered to her sleeplessness and sat up in the bed. What made her restless now was the question she could not get out of her mind: What did her father-in-law know? And why had he commissioned the investigation in the first place?

"Are you okay?" Hosea's groggy voice eased its way into her thoughts.

"Yeah, I'm going to the bathroom."

That was a good excuse because, by the time she stood, Hosea's head was back on his pillow and the rhythm of his breathing let her know that he'd returned to his peace.

With heavy steps and an even heavier heart, Jasmine made her way into the living room. Like so many nights before, her plan was to pace until she tired. But tonight, a storm raged inside of her—thunder and lightning collided in her mind.

Jasmine couldn't remember if the package had been opened when the hospital administrator handed it to her. She'd asked Mrs. Whittingham this afternoon, but when the woman told her that the packet had been opened, Jasmine wasn't sure if she believed her.

Her hope was that Mrs. Whittingham was lying. But if she wasn't, then her father-in-law knew everything . . . like Mrs. Whittingham did. But this information was much more lethal in Reverend Bush's hands.

After long minutes, Jasmine slumped onto the sofa, but her mind was still fully charged. Once again, she reviewed the report she'd read. She didn't need the pages in front of her; she'd memorized almost every word.

Whoever Leonard Hobbs was, the investigator had earned his money. The report had been complete—from the club she'd worked at to Buck's name and current information to the clients who had become her regulars, including Mr. Smith. The only thing that was missing was exactly how much she'd been paid. And although the report didn't quite say that she had slept with Mr. Smith or any of the other men for money, the inference was there. It was there in the fact that she'd moved to a luxury apartment. It was in the fact that bank records showed how her balance had grown from zero to thousands.

Her father-in-law knew everything.

For a fleeting moment, she wondered if maybe she should tell Hosea the truth and end all the drama. That was her true desire, but what would she say?

I used to be a stripper.

And how would she answer the questions that followed.

Then I became a whore.

He would never look at her the same way. No, Hosea could never find out—not from Mrs. Whittingham. And definitely not from his father.

She would do whatever she had to do to keep this from her husband.

FORTY-EIGHT

JASMINE YAWNED AS HOSEA PASSED her the single paper.

"Here's the financial report from Malik. He e-mailed it to me for the board meeting tonight." Hosea paused before he added, "Maybe you need to see the doctor."

"For what?" she frowned.

"You haven't been able to sleep in weeks; you haven't been feeling well. Maybe you're—"

He stopped short of saying it, but that didn't make Jasmine feel any better. What could she do to take her husband's mind off of their having a baby? It broke her heart every time she had to tell him that wasn't going to happen.

She shook her head, denying his hope without words. "There's a lot on us right now, and this is how my body handles stress."

The knock on the door made them both look up. Mrs. Whittingham stood, facing them, her lips pressed firmly together.

"Hosea," she began, her eyes only on him. "I wanted to let you know that the board meeting has been postponed until Monday."

Hosea's eyes widened. "What's going on?"

Standing stiffly, Mrs. Whittingham said, "There were some scheduling problems with Pastor Wyatt, I think . . ."

Hosea waited for more, but Mrs. Whittingham turned and left them alone.

Hosea was frowning when he faced Jasmine. "That was weird."

"What do you mean?"

"Why would Wyatt postpone the meeting? I would've thought he would want to walk into the sanctuary on Sunday as the new pastor."

Jasmine shrugged. "Mrs. Whittingham said scheduling—"

Hosea shook his head. "Wyatt's too eager to move ahead with this." He paused. "What's he up to?" He sat thoughtful for a moment and then reached for the phone.

"What are you doing?" she asked.

"Calling him."

"Don't." Jasmine held up her hand. "Leave it alone," she said slowly. Then, softly added, "Let this play out the way God wants this to play out."

Like he always did, Hosea paused whenever his wife mentioned the Lord. In the next moment, he put the telephone down.

Jasmine glanced down at the budget report that Hosea had handed her, wanting to change the subject. Her eyes widened a little. "Babe, this looks good. Tithes and offerings are almost back to where they were with your dad."

He nodded. "But you know, that's not what's most important to me."

"I know . . ." Her voice trailed off, but her smile stayed. Mrs. Whittingham had come through; the postponement gave her the time she needed.

"Babe," Jasmine began. "I need to run a few errands for an hour or so."

"Go on. We'll go by the hospital when you get back."

She kissed his cheek and marched out of his office, her mind already on her tasks. It wasn't exactly errands that she had to run—there were a few anonymous calls and deliveries that had to be made. And she needed to be out of the church to do that.

FORTY-NINE

Hosea's hands were perched under his chin. His eyes, closed. Praying, Jasmine was sure.

She took soft steps toward him, but he sat still on the edge of their living room sofa, even though she was sure he knew she was there. Lowering herself in front of him, she kissed his forehead.

The moment he looked at her, she could see the bad news behind his eyes, and her heart ached.

Slowly, she asked, "Was that the hospital?" The phone had rung a few minutes before, but she had been in Jacqueline's bedroom. It didn't occur to her that all was not well—not until she walked in and saw her husband.

"Yes."

Jasmine swallowed. "Is it your father?"

He nodded.

She inhaled deeply.

"She had to put him back on the vent this morning. She keeps trying to take Pops off, but . . ."

She exhaled; her thoughts had been much worse. "He just needs to get stronger." She spoke in a tone that was meant to convince them both.

"Yeah," he said, though it didn't sound like he agreed. "And there's something else."

Jasmine waited for him to speak.

"Doctor Lewis asked about his DNR status."

She frowned.

"Do not resuscitate," he clarified. "She said she needs to know what we want to do if his heart stops beating."

Her glower deepened. "Why would she ask you about that?"

"Because Pops *doesn't* have a living will, and I have to make the decision on whether to have Pops shocked back to life or . . ."

Jasmine swallowed to get the nerve to ask, "What did you tell her?"

Looking straight into her eyes, he said, "I told her to do whatever she had to do to keep him alive." She breathed with relief until he said, "But I just don't know anymore."

"Hosea, you *can't* give up."

"I'm not; it's just that I never thought I'd be making these kinds of decisions for Pops."

"You've made all the right ones. He came out of that infection fine. And I believe that the only reason he's still asleep is because that's the best way for his body to heal. He's going to wake up, Hosea," she said, as if God Himself had told her that.

It was the strength of her conviction that made his eyes brighten a bit. Leaning forward, he kissed the tip of her nose, right when his cell phone hummed and vibrated on the table. He frowned as he glanced at the screen, then flipped the phone open. "Hello."

Jasmine tilted her head as her husband's glower deepened.

"What allegations?" she heard him say.

Her heartbeat quickened, and she bunched her eyebrows together into a frown to fake her concern.

Hosea's forehead wrinkled more with each passing second.

He said, "No, I don't have any comment." He flipped his cell closed. "Wow."

"What?" she asked, hoping her voice was filled with enough sincerity.

"That was Shirley Gant from the *Post.* Jerome was detained overnight by the police." His head was shaking, his frown still deep.

"Jerome Viceroy?" she asked, as if she didn't know.

He nodded. "Apparently, they pulled him in last night for questioning. For soliciting sex with a minor over the Internet."

Jasmine's mouth opened into as wide an O as she could push her lips. "Jerome?" She held her hand to her chest in mock surprise. "That's impossible. No way. I don't believe it."

Now Hosea frowned at her, and Jasmine hoped she hadn't overdone it. When she said nothing more, he nodded. "Shirley's confirmed it with sources at the station. She wanted my comment."

"Well . . ." Jasmine began slowly, "you know, he's been in trouble before."

"But not this kind of trouble. This sounds serious."

As if extortion and tax evasion and money laundering aren't serious.

He flipped open the phone. "I've got to get in touch with Brother Hill, see what he knows."

"Okay, I'm going to check on Jacquie before we run up to the hospital."

He nodded, but his thoughts were already beyond her words. The way he paced, Jasmine knew her husband was concerned—about his father, and now about Jerome Viceroy.

She hated putting more on his shoulders, but this had to be done. As soon as her back was turned to him, her lips spread into a slow smile.

Two down!

FIFTY

As QUICKLY AS SHE COULD, Jasmine tucked Jacqueline into her bed, then rushed back into the living room.

"Is Jacquie asleep?"

Jasmine shook her head. "Not yet, Mrs. Sloss is with her." But their daughter was not what she wanted to talk about. "So . . . the letter."

Hosea handed her the envelope that Mrs. Sloss had given them the moment they'd walked in a half hour ago.

"It came by messenger," their nanny had told them.

Now, looking down at the paper, Jasmine read out loud:

> *"To Whom It May Concern:*
>
> *"Please accept this letter as my official resignation from the Board of Directors of City of Lights at Riverside Church. I am leaving to pursue other opportunities."*

Jerome's signature was scrawled at the bottom.

Jasmine shook her head. *Other opportunities? Yeah, right,* she thought. She guessed that was a good way to look at it; surely prison would be a new experience.

But her eyes were filled with as much concern as she could

muster when she slipped the letter back inside and looked up at her husband.

"I still cannot believe this. So . . . do you think . . . what Shirley told you this morning"—Jasmine lowered her voice for effect—"could it be true?"

Hosea slumped back onto the couch, shook his head. "I don't know. But his resignation and Shirley's phone call have to be connected. He wouldn't be resigning—not with the upcoming vote—if he didn't have to."

"You're right."

More shaking of his head. "I don't understand why Jerome hasn't called me or Brother Hill back . . . this is all so weird."

"Weird?"

"Yeah. First the board meeting was canceled . . ."

"That's no big thing," Jasmine said, not wanting Hosea to put too much thought into this.

But he kept on. "And now, this thing with Jerome. If I didn't know better . . ." He stopped. Looked up. Stared at her.

Jasmine stood, her stance soft, but her eyes daring him to accuse her of something. Then, as if he was shaking away bad thoughts about her, he shuddered before he said, "I don't know . . . it's just weird."

"That's how you might explain it, but I've learned enough from you to know that this might be God's favor."

"No one else's misfortune is God's blessing to me."

"I'm just saying that maybe God is revealing things about people—information that's important, that you need to know."

"Maybe . . ."

"You're so focused on your father that you don't know what's going on in the church."

He looked at her through squinted eyes. "Do you know something?"

"No! I'm just trying to give an explanation for what's going on. I truly believe that God's making sure everything is okay with City of Lights."

After a moment, he sighed. "Yeah, maybe. But the board meeting is still on Monday, and even without Jerome, Wyatt may still be able to pull this off."

"You never know what Monday will bring." Before the words were all the way out of her mouth, she wished she could take them back. With the way Hosea was frowning, she knew she'd said too much. She opened her arms and beckoned him to come to her. Said, "Can we not talk about this anymore? It's too much with everything we have going on."

He said, "Definitely," just as glad as she was to change the subject.

She embraced her husband, but Jasmine's smile didn't come easy. After all Jerome had taken them through, after the way he'd taken Pastor Wyatt's side against Hosea, after he'd sent those nasty e-mails to Mariah, she should have been clicking her heels in the air.

But there was a part of her heart that held no pleasure at the thought of this man's fall from grace. She'd done the right thing, for lots of reasons, but she didn't have the fullness of joy that she'd expected.

But there was no room or time for sorrow. She still had more work to do. Mrs. Whittingham had told her that Pastor Wyatt was returning tomorrow—a day before the meeting. And so tomorrow, she'd make her final move.

The Wyatts were the ones she wanted to bring down the most.

FIFTY-ONE

SHE HAD BEEN WAITING FOR this, waiting to see him ever since she'd returned from Hogeye Creek last Sunday.

Jasmine's eyes tracked Pastor Wyatt as he sauntered through the church door in front of his wife. He strutted through the hall with the surety of a man who had all the winning numbers. And when he paused at Mrs. Whittingham's desk and shot Jasmine a quick grin, she noticed his dimple first—still deep, still inviting.

Only now, Jasmine knew who he was.

She didn't take her eyes off of him or his wife.

Stopping in Hosea's doorway, Pastor Wyatt straightened his jacket lapel before he boomed, "Good morning, Pastor."

Jasmine had never heard Pastor Wyatt address Hosea that way. But she guessed his generosity came from his certainty that by the time next Sunday rolled around, he'd be the man sitting in the big chair behind the altar.

From inside his office, Hosea came to the door and shook the associate pastor's hand. "Pastor Wyatt," he began. "Welcome back."

The two men stood, hands and eyes locked. And in that moment, Jasmine admired her husband even more—for looking into enemy eyes and still maintaining decorum. Because if it had been her, this moment would be going down in a totally different way.

"Well," Pastor Wyatt said as he broke away from Hosea, "I'll be in my office. You know, I like to spend a few minutes with the Lord before we begin the service."

Jasmine didn't care if he saw the way she rolled her eyes. He was lucky that she didn't yell out, "Earvin, you need to quit."

Pastor Wyatt motioned to Enid, who stood behind him with her hair exactly the way it had been last time Jasmine had seen her. But her eyebrows rose as she studied Enid's suit. She couldn't hate on the lavender two-piece St. John.

That witch is thinking she's going to be the new first lady.

Enid scurried behind her husband as if he was the big man in charge. But Jasmine was sure that behind their closed doors, Enid Wyatt was the one in control. She had to be—Enid was the one who'd convinced everyone in Hogeye Creek that Earvin was Eugene; she'd given her brother-in-law a new life, a new hustle.

Jasmine's head was shaking as she moved toward her husband. "I can't stand that man," she said to Hosea.

"Be careful, babe. It's Sunday," he joked.

She followed him into his office. "I don't know how you can be so civil when you know what he's trying to do to you."

Hosea settled behind his desk. "What can I do? There's no need for me to get mad or to say anything I'll regret. Like you keep saying: it's going to play out the way God wants it to."

She nodded, though she knew the truth—this was going to play out the way *she* wanted it to.

She pressed her lips against her husband's. "I'm going to check on Jacquie before I go into the sanctuary. I'll see you out there."

Inside the hallway, she paused in front of Pastor Wyatt's office. She wanted to walk in there right now and tell the bogus pastor that the gig was up. Then Hosea wouldn't even have to share the altar today with that man.

But this wasn't the time, wasn't the place. She already had her plan, and she could certainly wait a couple of hours.

Smiling, she stepped from the church into the sunlight. Inhaling, she took in the smells of spring—the flowers were already blooming, even in Harlem.

What a beautiful Sunday, the perfect day for Pastor Wyatt to meet the woman who was truly his match.

Sometimes Jasmine wondered if she needed a journal. It was getting difficult to keep track of all of the lies. Especially the ones she told about Malik.

Like the one she'd told Hosea when the second service ended an hour ago.

"Babe, can you take Jacquie home?" she had asked. "Malik sent me a text. He's stuck in a meeting and he asked if I could stop by his office to clarify something."

"On a Sunday?"

Jasmine had shrugged. "You know Malik is a workaholic. That's why he goes to first service, so he can work after church." And then, she did what she always did when she needed to take his attention away from what she was actually saying. She kissed him. Long and hard. "Don't worry," she said, when she finally pulled back, both of them breathless. "I'll be home in an hour."

That was her plan, she thought, as she handed the cab fare to the taxi driver. She would be home in an hour, maybe less.

And after today, she wouldn't tell another lie. That was a promise she was making to herself and to God.

She slammed the cab door and then she tried to peek through the restaurant's tinted window. But she couldn't see much.

It was because of Mrs. Whittingham that she was here.

When she'd asked if she knew where the Wyatts would be this afternoon, Mrs. Whittingham hadn't even looked at her with any curiosity. She just told Jasmine what she needed to know.

"They usually go to B. Smith's after church. I heard Enid making the reservations right before the second service," Mrs. Whittingham had told her, as if she was an employee, reporting information to her boss.

The sounds of the Sunday brunch accosted her the moment Jasmine pulled open the restaurant's heavy glass door. She pressed inside, squeezing behind the cluster of awaiting couples in the small space near the hostess's desk.

Jasmine's eyes slowly scanned the long, narrow restaurant until she spotted the Wyatts—in the back, in the corner. How appropriate.

"Excuse me," she whispered as she pushed her way through the crowd. Her heart hammered heavier with each step she took.

At first, Jasmine hadn't been sure if she'd wanted to talk to the Wyatts together. There were plenty of reasons why she'd thought about talking to Enid alone. First, Jasmine was convinced that Enid was the brains behind this hoax. And second, there was the fact that Earvin was not a good guy. There had to be some residue left over from his drug-dealing days. She didn't know what the man was capable of.

That's why she'd come up with this plan—confront them in public. There would be little Earvin or Enid could do.

"Hey," Jasmine said. Moving quickly and smoothly, she slid into the booth side of their table next to Enid. "Imagine bumping into you two."

She was already sitting down by the time Pastor Wyatt and Enid looked up.

"What . . ." That was all Enid could say as her fork, filled with a mouthful of rice pilaf, still hung in the air.

But while Enid was shocked, her husband kept on as if someone hadn't just invaded their space.

He's a cool one, Jasmine thought. She wasn't surprised when he sliced his steak and a bit of red juice oozed from the blood-colored center.

"Hello, *Lady* Jasmine," he said with a smirk, right before he slipped a small cube of medium-rare meat between his lips. Looking at Enid, he took a few chews before, "You know why she's here, right?" As if Jasmine wasn't sitting beside his wife, he continued, "She wants to beg for her husband's position."

He chuckled and Jasmine did, too. Enid was the only one who didn't find any humor in this situation. But still, Enid nodded. Took the example set by her husband and kept on eating.

Jasmine sat back and smiled. For a moment, she wondered what kind of man Earvin Wyatt could have been if he'd had the right woman beside him.

"Now, I know we haven't known each other very long," Jasmine began, "but Pastor Wyatt, do you think I'd beg you for anything?"

He looked at her, his mouth stuffed with food, and chuckled again. "Oh, I can think of a few ways I could get you to beg."

She couldn't believe he'd said that. And in front of his wife. But the way Enid sat there, saying nothing, Jasmine had a new thought—these two probably weren't even married.

"So you want to test it out, Jasmine?" He leaned closer to her. "You wanna test out this begging thing?"

"I'd rather have a root canal."

His chuckle was louder this time.

"Plus," she continued. "I don't have to beg for a thing. Hosea's position is pretty secure."

"Well then," Pastor Wyatt said, "obviously you haven't heard about the vote we're taking at the board meeting tomorrow." He pointed his fork at her. "It was interesting the way you had the meeting postponed . . ."

Jasmine kept her face still, didn't reveal a thing. She wasn't surprised, though, that he'd figured out she was behind the change. Game always recognized game.

He continued, "Yeah, I know it was you. Can't figure out how you did it, but it doesn't matter. You can't stop what's inevitable. Tomorrow, Hosea will be out." He paused and leaned closer. "And guess what that means?"

"It doesn't mean anything because you're going to withdraw your request for a vote," she said calmly. "You're going to tell everyone that you want Hosea to remain the senior pastor."

Pastor Wyatt leaned back and laughed, his guffaw blending with the chatter and clatter and laughter around them. He said, "Now, why would I do that?"

Jasmine leaned forward and rested her arms on the pristine tablecloth. "Because you wouldn't want to be arrested."

Even though she was inches away from Enid, Jasmine felt her stiffen. But not Pastor Wyatt. Not breaking his stride, he raised his fork again, this time the utensil was smothered with mashed potatoes. Slipping the fork into his mouth, he used his tongue to clean the gravy residue that lingered on his lips.

With naked desire, Jasmine watched the tip of his tongue outline the curve of his mouth. And like she always did when he was that bold, she sighed. But this time, she didn't get mad at herself. She allowed the few moments to pass so that she could wallow and wonder in the pleasure of what might have been. Because in minutes, the Wyatts would have some decisions to make. And Jasmine didn't know if she'd see this man, or his smoldering eyes, or his kissable lips, or his dimple, especially his deep dimple, ever again.

"Jasmine, from the things I've heard about you, I know that you don't have much class," he said.

She inhaled and swallowed her anger. There was no need to lose control.

"But, please, sweetheart," Pastor Wyatt continued, "I'm sure you've had enough home training to know not to interrupt anyone's dinner."

She had planned to drag it out a bit more because she was enjoying this verbal sparring. But he'd made her mad. It was time to take him down.

"And what kind of home training have you had, Pastor Wyatt? Oops." She raised her hand and covered her mouth. "Why did I call you 'Pastor'? Have you even taken a seminary class . . . *Earvin*?"

Enid gasped, and now even Pastor Wyatt paused.

Jasmine said, "Yes, you heard me right." She repeated the name, *"Earvin."* Then she leaned back in the booth.

Four eyes drilled through her. Both of the Wyatts wanted to know what she knew. But both of them were smart enough not to ask.

So she told them. "I know that you're not Eugene," she said in a reporter's tone. "I know that you're his twin brother. I know that Eugene actually died in that car accident, but that you," she said, turning to Enid, "told everyone that it was Earvin who was killed."

The sounds of Sunday continued around them. But the three were frozen, as if they were in their own time capsule. Each waited for the one who would make the next move.

Enid broke first. "What are you—"

The way Earvin held up his hand and the way Enid stopped speaking, Jasmine wondered now who really was in charge in this bogus relationship.

"I don't know who told you those lies," Pastor Wyatt spat. His voice was strong, as if he had the truth behind him.

But no one knew this game better than Jasmine, and she could see, smell, and call a bluff.

"You know what?" Jasmine glanced at her watch. "I don't have time to go back and forth with you, so let's get to the point.

"No one lied to me. I know everything about Hogeye Creek.

Down to"—she glanced at Enid—"everyone wearing their hair two feet high on their head."

Enid sucked in more air.

Then Jasmine's eyes moved to the man who'd been calling himself Pastor Eugene Wyatt. "And the fact that Earvin and not Eugene had a dimple in his left cheek."

He moved without thinking, his hand automatically raised to his face.

"Look," Enid said before Earvin could speak. "We don't want any trouble."

Jasmine shrugged. "It's too late for that. The two of you have caused my husband plenty of trouble."

"We can be out of New York in twenty-four hours," Enid negotiated.

Jasmine's eyes moved to Earvin. He sat quietly, transmitting his hate through his eyes.

Enid was back in charge. "There's no need for any of this to come out. We"—and then Enid glanced at Earvin—"he can resign, and we can leave . . . quietly."

Jasmine shook her head. "That's not what I want." She paused, said slowly, "I want you and Earvin to stay."

"What?" the two said together.

She spoke to Enid. "Look, I don't like what you did, and I certainly don't like what you and your husband, or your brother-in-law, or whatever"—she waved her hand in the air—"I don't like what you tried to do to my husband. But you," she looked at Earvin, "have been a decent *associate* pastor. So you should stay."

Earvin's eyes got even smaller than they already were. "We should stay . . . so you can hold this over us. So you can blackmail us?"

Jasmine cocked her head. "Blackmail is such an ugly word. And this certainly isn't blackmail. I'm telling you to stay, keep your job."

"Why?" he asked. His lips hardly moved. "It doesn't make sense."

"Because," Jasmine leaned closer to Earvin, "even though I don't like you, my husband needs you. He's going through a lot and he needs someone at the church to have his back."

"He could always hire a new pastor," Earvin grumbled.

Jasmine nodded. "He could." Her eyes stayed on the pastor. "Let's just say I understand wanting to change your life."

And in that moment, Jasmine recognized the reason for their chemistry. They were bookends, each with chapters of their lives that they wished could be rewritten. They each understood the other one.

Jasmine said, "So if you want a new beginning, you should have it."

Pulling the strap of her purse onto her shoulder, she said. "You have my word. This will remain between the three of us. All you have to do is drop the vote." She stood, looked down at both of them, but neither one looked back at her. "So I'll see you in the board meeting tomorrow?"

Their eyes were still on each other, and they still said nothing to her.

Jasmine shrugged. "Enjoy the rest of your day."

And then she walked away and back out into the sunlight of the wonderful Sunday afternoon.

Three down.

It was done.

FIFTY-TWO

JASMINE PACED IN FRONT OF her desk as Mae Frances read the article from the *Le Marque Daily.*

"And the last paragraph says, 'Although no formal charges have yet been made, sources say that Viceroy's arrest is imminent.'" Then, the sound of paper crinkling as Mae Frances pushed the newspaper aside.

"Wow," Jasmine said, still moving. "Who would've thought that would have made it all the way down there?"

"I'm not surprised. Jerome Viceroy was always trying to make it onto the national scene. He was an aspiring Al Sharpton."

"Who aspires to be Al Sharpton?" Jasmine smirked.

"You better show some respect, Jasmine Larson," Mae Frances huffed. "The good reverend is a friend of mine."

Jasmine rolled her eyes. Was there anyone who wasn't a friend or a connection?

Her friend said, "So now that you have Jerome Viceroy and Mrs. Whittingham out of the way, what do you think Pastor Wyatt will do?"

"What can he do?" Jasmine whispered. Even though her door was closed, she wasn't taking any chances of being overheard. "Pastor Wyatt is going to show up, give a resounding speech about Hosea being the best man for the job, then sit his butt down until I tell him what to do next."

A pause and then, "Jasmine Larson, does that sound like the Pastor Wyatt you know?"

"The Pastor Wyatt that I know doesn't exist anymore. I'm in charge now."

This time, Mae Frances's pause was longer. "You know what rats do when they're cornered?"

"Oh, please. Do you think I'm scared of him? Knowing that Eugene is really Earvin is all the rat poison I need."

The knock on the door stopped the conversation.

Hosea peeked inside. "You ready?"

She nodded. "Mae Frances, I'll call you after the board meeting." She clicked off her BlackBerry and took her husband's hand.

"How's Nama?"

He'd asked that question, but Jasmine could tell by his tone that, if she answered, he wouldn't hear her. His eyes were focused ahead, on the path of this long hallway that led to the conference room.

His burden was on her heart, too. She knew his fear—that he was about to lose his father and his father's church at the same time. She wanted to throw her arms around him and let him know that the church part was under control. She wanted him to know that she had his back when no one else did, now and always. And that in an hour or so, they'd walk out of the church exactly the way they'd come in—with Hosea Bush, still the senior pastor.

But Jasmine had to stay silent. And pretend that this situation was playing out by itself.

Right outside the conference room, she squeezed Hosea's hand. And then she stepped inside, wearing enough confidence for both of them.

The chatter stopped when the two walked in. But Jasmine pretended that she didn't notice.

"Hey," she said to Malik, as he stood to hug her.

In a hushed tone that was normally reserved for a funeral, Malik asked Hosea, "How you holding up?"

Hosea nodded as the two bumped knuckles.

Jasmine glanced at the members surrounding the table, but only Sister Pearline had the guts to look at her. Even though the old woman smiled, Jasmine's lips stayed flatlined, her anger at Sister Pearline apparent.

No one else at the table looked their way, which let Jasmine know that, even with all of the lies she'd had to tell, all the tricks she'd had to play, she'd done the right thing, because if there had been a vote, she had no idea who would've been on their side.

Her eyes stopped when she looked at Mrs. Whittingham. She was sitting at the opposite end, staring down at the blank notepad and rocking a little.

She was going to have to speak to her about looking so disconsolate. People were soon going to start asking questions, and she didn't want Mrs. Whittingham buckling under the scrutiny.

"We're waiting for Pastor Wyatt," Brother Hill began, "And then we'll get started." He glanced at his watch. "Did anyone see him today?"

A chorus of nos rose through the room.

Brother Hill shook his head. "I don't know what's keeping him." And then under his breath, he grumbled, "He's the one who wanted this darn meeting."

Sister Pearline said, "Well, I don't want to be here all night. Somebody needs to call him so that we can get started." Jasmine wanted to growl at the old woman for being such a traitor. "Y'all know that I don't like Monday meetings. Don't make no sense that I have to miss my *CSI.*" Jasmine rolled her eyes, but the woman continued, "And anyway, I've been thinking about this. It don't really make no sense to vote in a new pastor when we already got a perfectly good one." She passed Hosea a girlish grin. "I don't know what I was thinking, baby. These people," she pointed to Brother Stevens, "they had me confused."

Brother Stevens's eyes widened. "Sister Pearline . . . huh, I don't think we need to talk about this yet—"

"That's right," Brother Hill agreed. "We need to wait until everyone is here for the full discussion."

"Then somebody needs to call that pastor!" Sister Pearline pounded her walking stick against the floor. "I'm not going to sit here all night."

Hosea said, "Brother Hill, would you mind giving Pastor Wyatt a call? Make sure he's on his way."

Brother Hill nodded before he stepped out of the room.

The murmurs began, one-on-one conversations around the table.

Malik whispered to Jasmine, "I would've thought Wyatt would have been the first one here."

Jasmine nodded. "Maybe he came to his senses."

"You're working under the assumption that the man has some sense to come to." He chuckled. "And speaking of losing your mind"—he twisted his body so that he faced her and lowered his voice even more—"looks like they're really pressing charges against Viceroy. Can you believe it?"

Jasmine shrugged. "I haven't been following the story."

"I don't know how you can stay away from it. I turn the volume up every time a report comes on New York One about him. I can't stop—I got that watching-a-train-wreck thing going on." Malik shook his head. "Soliciting sex from a minor. I would've never thought it."

Before she could say anything else, Brother Hill returned, stopping all the talk. "I can't find Pastor Wyatt. He's not answering his cell, and neither is Enid. And there's no answer at their home."

Hosea's frown deepened. "What could have happened?"

This time when the confused mutters began, only Jasmine sat quietly. There was no need for her to speculate—she knew exactly what had happened—those fools had left New York City! Cowards!

That was not what she wanted. Her hope had been to keep Earvin and Enid around. Work them like she was working Mrs. Whittingham.

She glanced, once again, down to the other end of the table. Mrs. Whittingham still sat silently, staring. And rocking, even more now, looking like Sofia—Oprah's character in *The Color Purple*—after she'd been released from prison.

Jasmine sighed; that woman was all she had.

Hosea said, "We can't do this without the person who called for the vote. So . . ."

"We should adjourn." Brother Hill made that statement as if it made him happy. "I'll catch up with Pastor Wyatt, and we'll reschedule."

"Make sure it's not next Monday," Sister Pearline demanded.

Brother Hill ignored her. "If there are no other issues—"

Malik piped in, "This wasn't on the agenda"—he opened the folder resting in front of him—"but I had planned to share these today—the financials for the last month." He passed the pages around the table. "We don't have to discuss this now, but I wanted everyone to see tithes and offerings are almost back to where they were two months ago before Reverend Bush—" He stopped, just like everyone else did when they mentioned the reverend.

After their eyes scanned the financial page, Jasmine watched Brother Stevens and Sister Clinton exchange a long glance. She wondered if they were willing to vote against Hosea now.

Not that it mattered—there would never be a vote.

Brother Hill said, "If there's nothing else, we'll reschedule and Sister Whittingham will be in touch."

Hosea pushed his chair back and leaned toward Jasmine. "Let's get out of here," he kept his voice low, "I want to stop by the hospital for a minute."

She smiled, knowing what he wanted to do—he was going to tell his father. "Let me get my purse."

"Good night." Hosea raised his voice and his hand in a farewell wave to the others.

Jasmine departed without saying a single word to anyone except for Malik. Why should she talk to them after the way they'd turned on her husband? Soon enough all of them would be in line the way they were supposed to be—the Bushes were back in control, and that meant she would keep her crown.

It had been a hard fight, but she'd won! She deserved to be wearing a tiara. A tiara—that was a good idea. Maybe she would go out and buy one so that she could wear it to church on Sunday.

And then she'd be Lady Jasmine for real.

FIFTY-THREE

JASMINE PRESSED 4 TO LISTEN to the message again.

"Ah, this is Roxie." The woman sounded flustered. "Ah, I need a little time. Away. I'll call you when I'm ready to come back. I'm sorry."

"Yeah, right," Jasmine whispered as she hit 7 for delete. She knew what this was about—Roxie had probably gone far away so that no one would look at or talk about the woman who'd been dating a pedophile. She would have said good riddance, if she didn't feel so sorry for Roxie. But she wasn't too worried—that women had millions to help her find happiness.

Tossing her phone onto her desk, she strolled to the front of the church for what had to be the fiftieth time in the last two hours. She tried to tiptoe past Hosea's office, but each time she walked by, he looked up.

"What's going down?" he called out to her.

Dang! She walked backward until she stood at his door. And with a childlike, totally guiltless gaze, she said, "Nothing. I'm working on that Women's Day event and I've been trying to find some of the old programs in the files."

"Oh, okay."

Jasmine hated the way he looked at her sometimes, as if he

still doubted every word that came out of her mouth. That was no way to treat his wife.

She stood in the center of the hallway, away from Hosea's view, and waved until Mrs. Whittingham looked up. Then she motioned with her finger toward the woman.

It seemed to take minutes for the woman to waddle behind her, but once the two were alone, Jasmine whispered, "I need you to do something for me."

Mrs. Whittingham gasped, and Jasmine wondered if she was going to be sick.

"What's wrong?"

Mrs. Whittingham shook her head. "I can't do this."

"I haven't asked you to do anything yet."

"I can't jump at your every demand!" the woman exclaimed as her hands flailed through the air. Her voice rose, "I can't be your slave."

"Would you calm down?" Jasmine said, closing her door. She lowered her voice and hoped the woman would follow her example. She didn't have a lie ready if Hosea came down here and found Mrs. Whittingham hysterical. "I'm not asking you to be my slave."

"Yes, you are!" she shot back with tears in her eyes and her voice. "I can't . . ." And then the sobs came.

Jasmine moved toward her, but that was where her compassion ended. "I was going to ask you to let me know when Brother Hill comes in. Or if he calls Hosea."

The woman sniffed. "But what about next time? What are you going to want me to do in the next minute, or an hour from now, or tomorrow?"

"Look," Jasmine began, her voice stiffer now. "I'm not the one who started this."

The woman stared at Jasmine with pleading eyes. "Ivy can never know," she whispered.

Jasmine felt a pinch in the corner of her heart. But she ignored it when she said, "I'm just asking you to do me a few favors. It's nothing like what you did to me."

Mrs. Whittingham looked at her for a few moments longer, then nodded. As if she accepted her punishment.

With a sigh, Jasmine said, "Just let me know when Brother Hill comes in."

Without a word, Mrs. Whittingham turned. Opened the door and then dragged away toward the front, as if her desk were located on death row.

Jasmine slumped into her chair and blew out a long breath of air. It wasn't easy being a blackmailer.

Only twenty minutes passed before Mrs. Whittingham buzzed her.

"Daniel just came in," she whispered. "He's in Hosea's office." Then she slammed down the phone.

Jasmine pulled the receiver away from her ear. She couldn't believe Mrs. Whittingham had dissed her that way, but her thoughts quickly moved beyond that.

She rushed into the hall, then tiptoed down the carpeted passageway until she was outside Hosea's office. She ignored Mrs. Whittingham's disapproving stare and leaned against the wall, trying to hear what Brother Hill and Hosea were saying.

Their voices were low, muffled—she heard words, but nothing she could understand. Jasmine rushed back to her desk, grabbed a folder, then marched into the hallway. Right outside of Hosea's office, she took a breath.

"Babe," she said as she stepped inside, "I can't figure—" She stopped. "Oh, Brother Hill, I didn't know you were here."

She smiled at him, and Brother Hill gave her a fake smile back.

Hosea said, "Jasmine, the Wyatts are gone."

"Gone?" she asked, as if the word was foreign to her.

The two men nodded.

Brother Hill said, "I was able to convince the super to go into their apartment. He'd seen me with Eugene a few times, and I explained that the Wyatts had been missing for a couple of days and that I thought something may have happened. He still didn't want to let me in, said that he would check himself, but when he opened the door, I followed him inside."

Jasmine's eyes were wide with amazement. "And they weren't there?"

"No." Brother Hill shook his head. "All of the furniture was there, but no clothes in the closet, no luggage anywhere. They're gone, that's for sure."

"What do you think happened?"

As if it was choreographed, the men shrugged. Then together, they shook their heads.

Standing still, as if she was in total shock, she finally said, "Okay, I'll be in my office, Hosea." She had what she needed.

She left the men sitting silently, pensively, as if the right amount of quiet thought would give them answers.

She marched back toward her office with her head high. By herself, she'd taken down all those saints and saved her husband, his position, and his father's church.

Someone needed to give her a medal. She deserved the Olympic gold for Wife of the Year.

Jasmine rolled over and, as her eyes adjusted to the dark, she could see her husband, lying on his back, his hands folded behind his head, his eyes wide open. Exactly the way he'd been when she'd turned off the lights about three hours before.

"Babe," she whispered, "are you okay?"

"Yeah," was all he said.

Jasmine clicked on the lamp and glanced at the clock. It was almost two in the morning. She pushed back against the pillows and pulled the sheet to cover her bare chest. "I wish you would talk to me."

He shook his head, glanced askance at her. "I'm trying to figure this out."

"What? The Wyatts?"

He twisted and leaned on one arm, facing her now. "Yeah, the Wyatts, and so much more. I mean, look at what's gone down in the last few days. First, the board meeting gets postponed; then, Jerome gets hit. And now, the Wyatts disappear without a word, without a trace. *Something's* going on."

Jasmine shrugged. "Maybe this is the favor of God that you're always talking about."

He shook his head. "I keep telling you, no one else's misfortune is God's blessing to me."

Jasmine could hear the slow seconds ticking on the clock as she sat in the quiet, waiting for Hosea to say something. But he just stared, and she shifted under the heat of his scrutiny.

Finally, "Do you know anything about all of this?"

By the time the last word came out of his mouth, Jasmine's heart was pounding. "I don't understand what you're asking me." She had no idea how she kept her voice calm.

He peered at her, even longer this time. And now she squirmed inside and out. "I'll just come out and ask: Did you have anything to do with everything that's going on? With Jerome's arrest? With the Wyatts?"

Jasmine jumped from the bed, mostly to hide her trembling. "I can't believe you're asking me that," she yelled, totally unaffected by the cool air that rushed her naked body.

Hosea sat up. Motioned with his hands for her to lower her voice. "I'm just—"

She didn't let him finish. "So I'm the reason that Jerome's in jail? What do you think I did? Do you think I held him at gunpoint while he sat at some computer and tried to solicit girls over the Internet?"

He shook his head but still didn't get a chance to speak.

"And what did I do with the Wyatts?" Her hands thrashed through the air. "You think I have them chained in a basement somewhere?"

"Jasmine, calm down."

But she didn't. "And why stop there? You probably think that I'm responsible for global warming. Or the war in Iraq. Or the Red Sox beating the Yankees. Blame all the problems of the world on me!"

He paused, contemplating her words. "Okay, what I asked . . . maybe it was wrong."

"Maybe?" She crossed her arms.

"Can you blame me?"

"Yeah, I can. Because Hosea, I'm tired. I'm so tired of answering your questions."

"You're right."

"You always say that. And I haven't done anything to make you doubt me like this since we returned from L.A."

"I told you before, I'm trying."

"It's not enough. I need you to promise that no matter what, you'll believe in me." She paused. "I'm your wife, Hosea," she said with a shaky voice. And this time, she wasn't acting. "I need that. I need to see something else in your eyes when you look at me. Something besides doubt and disbelief."

"You forgot love."

"What?" she snapped.

"In my eyes, you've got to see how much I love you."

But even though she was wrong, she refused to give in. He didn't know she was lying; and because of that, he shouldn't have questioned her. He was supposed to just trust her.

She stood there, her arms crossed, her toe tapping an impatient beat. She stood, silent. Glaring.

Until the phone rang.

Then they both stood like stone. They stared at each

other before both pairs of eyes shifted slowly toward the telephone.

The thought in their minds was the same—no one called in the middle of the night unless it was bad news.

Even when Hosea grabbed the phone, Jasmine didn't move. She just closed her eyes and went straight to God. Begged him to make it all right, whatever it was.

"Yes. Yes. Yes." The words were sharp. And then, "We'll be right there."

He was halfway to his closet before he hung up the telephone. "It's Pops," he exclaimed. "We have to get to the hospital!"

As Jasmine and Hosea raced down the hall from one end, Dr. Lewis approached from the other.

"Doctor!" Hosea called out to her. "What happened?" he asked, when they stood in front of the ICU room where Reverend Bush had been moved.

"We've been watching this for a few hours," she said. "I've been on the phone with the other doctors. Your father's temperature started going up earlier."

"When?" Then he added, "I was here this morning," as if that should've made a difference.

"It was a gradual rise that we were trying to manage. That's why we didn't call you," the doctor said. "But a couple of hours ago, his blood pressure started dropping. We've started the pressors again. Let me get in there."

Holding hands, Jasmine and Hosea rushed behind the doctor, who was dressed as they were—in a sweatsuit, the appropriate outfit for a middle-of-the-night emergency. But the moment Dr. Lewis realized the couple was behind her, she stopped them.

"Please. Wait outside. I'll be out as soon as I can."

"Doctor!" one of the nurses called her.

"Please," she said, this time with more urgency.

Slowly, Jasmine and Hosea backed away, but Jasmine's eyes were plastered on the place where her father-in-law lay. She needed to get a good look at him even as she prayed that this wouldn't be the last time she saw him alive.

Jasmine took in all that she could. The gray of his skin—like before. The stillness of his form—like he'd been from the first day.

It wasn't until they were in the hallway and the door had closed on them that Jasmine breathed.

Hosea leaned against the wall, his forehead against the white plaster, his eyes closed. Jasmine stood next to him, staying quiet, sure that the mental photo of her father-in-law that she'd taken was the same image in Hosea's mind.

They stood together, in that space, listening to the muffled commands that seeped through the door. They stood together until Jasmine took Hosea's hand and led him a few feet away to the plastic chairs lined up against the opposite wall.

"I should have come back tonight," Hosea whispered.

"That wouldn't have made a difference," she tried to assure him.

Hosea leaned back and closed his eyes. Jasmine knew he was praying and she needed to join him, but she was tired.

For more than two months, they'd lived half of their life in this building, their hope secured inside a roller coaster not in their control. How many times was God going to take them to the brink of death?

As they sat, time passed. Another doctor went in. Then another nurse. And no one came out.

More time went by. Then the door swung open, and Dr. Lewis ambled out. And this time, the mask that she usually wore was gone, all of her emotions apparent. She was shaking her head, gloom etched on her face.

The last sliver of Jasmine's hope vanished.

Hosea stood and used the arms of the chair to steady himself. "Doctor . . ."

"He's alive," she said, and then she allowed a beat to pass, as if she wanted them to appreciate those words. "But it's not good."

"What's wrong?"

She shook her head. "We're still not sure; we're waiting for the blood cultures, and I suspect it's another infection. We have him back on the antibiotics."

"So then he's going to be all right," Hosea stated. "Like last time."

In a tone that was softer and without the strength that she always carried, Dr. Lewis said, "That's my prayer," as she gently touched Hosea's shoulder.

The doctor's words, her gesture brought tears to Jasmine's eyes.

Dr. Lewis said, "Why don't you two go into the waiting room? I'm going to check on your father again."

Once alone, Jasmine put her arm around Hosea's waist and led him into the waiting area. She helped him first sit in a chair, and then she sat next to him. She rested her head on his shoulder, so that he wouldn't see all the fear in her eyes.

"Is there anyone we should call?" she whispered.

He shook his head. "It's the middle of the night. If we call . . . I don't want to scare anyone."

She wondered why not. She had enough fear to share.

He said, "Let's see what happens."

In her head, Jasmine tried to count back the hours: How long ago had it been when she sat in the boardroom? How much time had passed since she'd been filled with such victorious joy?

It seemed like ages ago.

Victory was gone. But she refused to allow defeat to rise up in its place.

So she closed her eyes. And even though she was tired, she prayed.

Twelve hours passed.

Jasmine paced the length of the hospital hall, not wanting to return to Reverend Bush's room.

She couldn't sit in there anymore. Couldn't stare into the ashen face of her father-in-law any longer. This time, there were more machines and more tubes and more doctors stopping by, as if Reverend Bush was a case study in imminent death.

Imminent death. Those weren't the words that Dr. Lewis had used, but they described what she had told them.

"He's not responding," she'd told Hosea and her two hours ago. "His blood pressure is still too low. And his fever . . . we may need to pack him in ice."

"Like ice from the freezer?" Jasmine had asked as if she'd never heard of anything more ridiculous.

"Yes," the doctor had responded. And then, with a breath, she told them all the other problems. "We drew some labs, and he has multisystem organ failure."

Jasmine remembered how her eyes had clouded as the doctor rambled on and on about Reverend Bush's kidneys shutting down. And enzymes showing damage to his liver. And how his heartbeat was erratic.

But as bad as all of that was, it didn't compare to the words the doctor had spoken next.

"Your father's body may be letting us know that it's not healthy enough to sustain life, and we should really listen to it."

With a voice packed with emotion, Hosea asked, "What are you saying?"

The doctor had looked him straight in his eyes. "Even if your father pulls through this time . . ."

"He will," Hosea said as if *he* were the doctor.

The doctor nodded. "If he does, this could happen again. And each time, there's more damage to his brain." She paused. "Would your father want to live this way?"

"Yes." Hosea's chin rose a bit higher and his shoulders squared a bit more when he added, "The point is, my father would want to live."

But Dr. Lewis was as determined to make her point. "I don't think he'd want to live if he weren't functional. What we're doing right now, Mr. Bush, is keeping someone alive who seems to be dead. Would your father *really* want to live like this?" she had asked again before she walked away, leaving her words behind.

With a huff that Jasmine had not seen in her husband this whole time, he'd stomped back into the room to be with his father.

And she'd been with him, too. Sitting next to Hosea at the edge of the bed. Praying with him and not moving even when Brother Hill came in. Hosea's godfather had stood at the other side with his head bowed. Then Malik had come with Sister Pearline. And the two had taken their posts at the bottom of the bed before they began to pray.

When Mrs. Whittingham and Brother Stevens had shown up, Jasmine felt like they were holding a vigil—some kind of watch service, waiting for Reverend Bush to die.

The thought had overcome her with nausea, and she'd rushed to the bathroom.

Now she stood outside, wanting never to go back in.

But even outside, the images of Reverend Bush stayed in her mind. She squeezed her eyes, trying to rid herself of the sickly image of the man she'd loved for just a few years—although in her heart the love she had for him was big enough for a lifetime.

"Jasmine?"

She looked down and into Ivy's eyes.

"How are you?" she squeaked, her forehead etched with lines of concern.

Jasmine shook her head, slightly.

Ivy asked, "Has something happened to—"

"No, he's still . . ." Jasmine couldn't bring herself to say alive. He wasn't alive to her.

Ivy looked toward the door. "Who's in there?"

"Your . . ." Jasmine caught herself before she spoke. "Your sister and Brother Hill. Malik and a couple of other people. And Hosea."

Ivy frowned. "I thought they only let two people in at a time."

"They're breaking the rules for us."

Ivy gave Jasmine a long stare, knowing what those words meant. Then she tugged at the bottom of her suit jacket and scurried into the room.

Not a minute passed before the door opened again and Hosea joined her. Without saying a word, he leaned against the wall, taking the same stance as her.

They faced the nurses' station, but the women behind the desk ignored them, probably used to families in their grief finding refuge in the halls.

Finally, Hosea whispered, "What're you doing out here?"

"I don't know." She shrugged. "Just thinking."

He nodded, gave her a look that told her he understood. "I've been thinking, too." He paused. "I want to go home. I want to get Jacquie."

Her eyes widened a bit.

"Remember we talked about bringing her here? I want to do that now," he continued. "So that she can see Pops."

Slowly, Jasmine nodded; the golf-size lump in her throat didn't provide enough air for her to breathe, let alone speak. She knew what this was—Hosea's first step toward his final good-bye.

She fought, but she lost the battle to keep the tears away. And when he wrapped his arms around her, she sobbed even more.

Hosea was making plans to let his father go, but Jasmine wasn't ready to do that. She'd done this too many times—more than twenty years ago with her mother, and much too recently with her father. How would she do this again?

Minutes passed before she was able to sniff back the rest of her tears. Looked up into her husband's eyes and said, "Let's go home. Let's get our daughter."

FIFTY-FOUR

"CAN YOU HAVE JACQUIE READY?" Jasmine asked. "We're on our way now." She clicked off her phone when the nanny agreed.

Hosea's eyes were on the road, as if he couldn't face his wife when he asked, "You don't think this is a good idea?"

Jasmine turned so that he could see her. "Yes, I'm fine with it."

He exhaled a long breath. "I want Jacquie to see . . . I want her to have a chance . . ."

She rubbed her hand on Hosea's shoulder, silently letting him know that she understood and truly agreed.

As the SUV rumbled down Central Park West, he said, "I hope it'll be okay for her. She's so young."

"But we'll be there."

"I don't want her to be scared."

"She won't be," Jasmine said in a tone that was a lot surer than what she felt. That was her fear, too—that Jacqueline would take one look at her grandfather and cry. This wasn't how she wanted her daughter to remember him. But she also knew that Hosea needed this moment—with their daughter, with his father.

Not even an hour later, they were back in the car, Jacqueline secured in her car seat. As they sped north, her toddler's voice rang out, "He got the whole world," as she clapped her hands.

Today, she sang alone.

Glee came from the back, but didn't make its way to the front. When Jasmine glanced at Hosea, even in the dusk of the evening, she could see the water in his eyes. And her heart ached. For her husband. For her daughter, who would never remember her grandfather.

Jacqueline kept singing as Hosea drove. Her song continued, even as they parked and her father carried her through the halls of Harlem Hospital.

It was the privilege of pending death that allowed Jacqueline to be taken past the security guard and into the elevators.

"Pumpkin, I want to tell you where we're going," Hosea whispered in Jacqueline's ear as he held her in his arms.

With a toddler's curiosity, Jacqueline's glance wandered around the elevator.

"We're going to see Papa," Hosea told her.

Her eyes brightened. "Papa!" She giggled, her excitement coming through.

Jasmine wondered if there were words she should say to prepare her daughter. But what was she supposed to tell her two-year-old? How could she make her understand that they were going to say their final good-bye to her grandfather when that was something Jasmine couldn't even accept yet?

The elevator doors parted and they took slow steps down the hall. Outside the room, Malik stood next to Mrs. Whittingham, but no one could gather a smile—not even for Jacqueline.

Hosea paused. Looked at Jasmine as if he wanted her permission. She nodded, then pushed the door open.

Brother Hill and a nurse who had been by Reverend Bush's side tiptoed away, but Jasmine kept her eyes on her daughter, searching for any signs of fear.

Jacqueline's eyes widened as she looked first at the machines surrounding Reverend Bush. The beeping and the lines, capturing her attention.

"TV!" Jacqueline pointed a pudgy finger.

Jasmine's chuckle was not from a place of humor. "No, baby."

Hosea tightened his arms around her as they moved closer to the bed. It took Jacqueline a few moments to look down.

Then she saw him. She squealed, "Papa!" and tried to wiggle from her father's arms, her legs aimed for the bed as if she wanted to lie next to her grandfather.

It amazed Jasmine—the bandages, the tubes—none of that mattered to Jacqueline. All she saw was the man she loved.

"No, pumpkin." Hosea had to shift to keep Jacqueline in his arms. "Papa's sleeping."

"Sleeping?" She stopped twisting. Looked down at her grandfather. Her eyebrows bunched together as she studied Reverend Bush. Then shaking her finger at him, she demanded, "Wake up, Papa!"

"He's not going to wake up right now, baby," Jasmine said. "Papa has to sleep. He's tired."

"Tired?" Her eyes were still on her grandfather. "Wake up, Papa!" And then, she began to sing, "He got the whole world . . ."

That was not what Jasmine had expected. And then she remembered—Jacqueline's favorite song . . . her grandfather had taught her!

Singing with my granddaughter is one of my life's greatest pleasures.

It was the same for Jacqueline.

And so as Jacqueline sang, Jasmine joined in, "In His hands. He's got the whole wide world . . ."

Hosea made them a trio, "In His hands . . ."

The three Bushes softly sang together over and over. They serenaded Reverend Bush while the machines beeped, as if those sounds of life were part of the melody. They sang until Jacqueline was ready to stop, until she rested her head against Hosea's chest and yawned.

A few seconds of silence passed and then Hosea whispered, "Okay." He looked across the bed at Jasmine. "It's time to go."

The peace of these last minutes was why Jasmine didn't want to leave. And then there was the knot that was growing inside, telling her that this was going to be the last time.

She said, "Do you want to stay? I can take Jacquie home."

He stared down at his father for a long moment, giving thought to Jasmine's words. Then, looking back at her, he said, "I'm going home. With you." To Jacqueline, Hosea asked, "Do you want to kiss Papa bye-bye?"

The girl nodded, and when her father lowered her closer to the bed, she pressed her lips against her grandfather's. "Bye-bye, Papa!" she exclaimed. And then she waved her finger once again and made her final demand, "Come home."

Those words made Jasmine want to sit down right there and cry. Jacqueline had said to Reverend Bush what they'd all wanted to say, but what each of them was beginning to suspect would never happen.

Hosea stood over his father for a moment longer before he turned away. Jasmine followed her husband and daughter, until they got to the door. There she looked over her shoulder, wanting to take her final glance at Reverend Bush.

"Good-bye," she whispered before she stepped out of the room.

FIFTY-FIVE

THERE WAS TOO MUCH SADNESS in the quiet.

But Jasmine didn't know what to do. She certainly didn't have anything to say because her mind was flooded with more images than words. Pictures of the years that she'd spent with Reverend Bush—the man who'd loved her and taught her so much about the Lord.

The silence stayed as Hosea maneuvered their car toward home. And as the miles spread between them and the hospital, their sorrow thickened.

Jasmine almost wanted to wake up her child—tell her to "Sing song!" But Jacqueline dozed in the backseat, the only one in the car who had peace.

Inside their apartment, they put their daughter down and watched her sleep until Jasmine couldn't stand up anymore. Then in their bedroom, they lay together, atop the comforter, still fully clothed.

But even though exhaustion made her ache, Jasmine stayed awake. Even as the clock ticked past midnight, her eyes would not close. And inside her husband's arms, she knew that he could not sleep either.

Although they hadn't shared a single word in hours, Jasmine knew they shared the same thoughts. They were waiting—for that call to come. They were waiting—for that final one.

But then, time dipped into the early hours of the next day and the phone never rang. When the sun began to reveal its first light, Hosea rolled over.

He asked, "Do you think it's too early?"

Jasmine looked at the clock. It wasn't even six. "It's not early at all."

Together, they jumped from the bed. And for the first time that Jasmine could ever remember, they left their apartment without either of them bothering to shower or change.

Their steps were eager as they walked down the hallway. Jasmine kept thinking, *The phone never rang,* and that gave her a triple dose of hope.

But as they approached Reverend Bush's room, Jasmine's feet and heart stopped when she saw the doctor stepping through the door.

"Doctor Lewis," Hosea and Jasmine called her name at the same time. Their mouths wouldn't move anymore, but their eyes questioned why the doctor was there so early.

"Your father is fine," she rushed to tell them. "In fact, he's really fine. I came in early when the nurse called to tell me that his fever had broken. And he's just beginning to respond to the pressors; his blood pressure is slowly rising." She shook her head as if she was talking about a miracle. "He's doing even a little bit better than he was before."

Jasmine's eyes widened when, a moment later, Hosea lifted Dr. Lewis in the air and spun her around in a full circle.

"Whoa!" the doctor squealed.

"I'm sorry," Hosea said, putting the doctor back on solid ground. "I don't know . . . it's just that—"

Dr. Lewis held up a hand. "I understand. This is something to be excited about. But let me caution you—"

"I know, I know. He's not well *yet.*"

She shook her head. "He's not. He hasn't awakened in two months," she said, as if they needed to be reminded. "That's serious. But he's a fighter, and he has that going for him."

"Oh, Doctor, he has that and a whole lot more," Hosea said, before he raised his eyes toward the ceiling.

"I hear that!" Dr. Lewis grinned. "Go on in there with your father."

Jasmine hugged the doctor. "Thank you," she said, before she followed her husband into the room.

" 'You are the God who performs miracles,' " Hosea softly read the psalm, " 'you display your power among the peoples.' "

Jasmine stood at the foot of the bed, with her eyes closed, as she listened to her husband reading the Bible.

This did feel a little bit like a miracle.

Even though Jasmine was exhausted by another day of the long hours in the hospital, today she didn't mind. Each hour that passed brought a bit more improvement.

"It's not much," Dr. Lewis told them every time she came in to check on Reverend Bush. "He's taking baby steps. And I want to caution you . . ."

Jasmine smiled now, like she did then, as she thought of the doctor's words. Yes, they all knew they had to be cautious. But at least they could wrap their caution, now, inside a supersize order of hope.

Hosea stood, raised his arms above his head, and stretched.

"You've been sitting down for a long time," Jasmine said.

He nodded. "I'll read the whole Bible to him if that's going to help." He released a deep breath and tucked the Bible at his father's side. "I'm gonna grab a soda. You want anything?"

She shook her head.

"We'll stay a little longer and then get out of here." He kissed Jasmine lightly. "I want to go home and give Jacquie a hug."

After a moment alone with Reverend Bush, Jasmine walked to the window and looked out at the view that she'd taken in for so many days. But as she stood in the quiet, her thoughts were far from Harlem.

Staying in place, she turned and glanced again at her father-in-law. He was as still as the day he'd been shot, but inside of him, her secret lived.

A secret that never left her mind. A secret that made her ask herself over and over: Why had her father-in-law had her investigated, and what did he know?

She sighed as she remembered the words of the investigator's report that told her dirty history.

"Why, Dad?" she asked aloud, still facing the window. "Why? What were you looking for?"

And then a thud!

Startled, Jasmine turned wide-eyed to the place where the noise had come from. She half expected to see Reverend Bush on the floor, but all that had fallen was the Bible Hosea had left at his father's side.

With a frown, she inched toward the bed, all the time wondering how the book had fallen. She lifted the Bible and placed it on the bedside table.

Standing over her father-in-law, she looked for signs of life. But only his chest moved, the single indication that breath was still within him.

"What do you know?" she whispered.

There was nothing but silence.

"Why were you having me investigated," she said into his ear.

Still nothing, except for the beep . . . beep . . . beep of the life-support machines.

Sighing, she returned to the window. She wasn't sure why she was worried about this now. Even though Reverend Bush had improved since yesterday, he was still much closer to death than to life. It might never matter.

She closed her eyes and imagined Reverend Bush reading the report. What had been his thoughts? What had been his plans?

"Jasmine."

Startled once again, she turned around. Looked at Hosea. "What?"

"How'd that get there?"

Her glance followed where he pointed. The thin blanket that had covered half of Reverend Bush's body had been tossed to the floor.

She shook her head. "I don't know. It wasn't there a minute ago when I—" She stopped, stared at the blanket for a moment, before her glance slowly crawled back up to her father-in-law.

"Hosea," she called to her husband slowly and softly, not taking her eyes off of Reverend Bush. "We need to get Doctor Lewis in here right now!"

Jasmine could hardly breathe as she watched the doctor.

"Reverend Bush!" Dr. Lewis called as if he was deaf. "Samuel, can you hear me?"

The doctor stood over him with a penlight in her hands.

"If you can hear me," she continued to talk as if Reverend Bush was in another room, "squeeze my hand."

They waited.

Nothing.

As she watched the activity moving around her, Jasmine tried to imagine all the ways the Bible could have fallen to the floor. Or the way the blanket could have found its way to the same place. But no scenario fit—nothing could have made those items move—except for Reverend Bush.

The doctor stepped away and turned to Hosea. "Sometimes patients in a coma do have involuntary movements . . ." She glanced at the reverend. "It was probably nothing."

"Let me try." Hosea quickly stepped around the doctor. He leaned over his father. Mimicked everything that the doctor had done—her words, her tone.

More nothing.

"Pops," Hosea kept on calling.

Singing with my granddaughter is one of my life's greatest pleasures.

Slowly, Jasmine moved to the opposite side of the bed. She stood across from Hosea and lowered her mouth close to the reverend's ear.

Softly, she began, "He's got the whole world . . ."

She kept her eyes down, knowing that the doctors and nurses who stood around probably thought she was a fool.

But she wasn't—the Bible and the blanket were the first signs of life from Reverend Bush, coming hours after Jacqueline had visited. Her presence was the only thing that had been different, and she was his delight.

So Jasmine sang. "He's got the whole world . . ." She kept her head down, her voice low. And she just kept singing.

And then, Hosea yelled, "He did it! He squeezed my hand."

The doctor pushed Hosea aside and continued her own calls to Reverend Bush.

The warm sensation of water gathered behind Jasmine's eyes, but she kept right on singing. Even when the first tear crawled from the corner and crept down her cheek, she didn't stop.

"Reverend Bush, can you hear me?" the doctor called again.

Jasmine inhaled a deep breath and sang, "He's got you and me and Jacquie, in His hands . . ."

And slowly, Reverend Bush's eyes fluttered open.

FIFTY-SIX

It was hard to stop laughing! And crying.

Reverend Bush was alive—for real.

Even now, as Jasmine leaned back in her chair inside her office, she couldn't stop thinking about those first moments after her father-in-law opened his eyes.

"Okay," Dr. Lewis had said. "Reverend Bush, take it easy."

He had squirmed against the doctor's hold, like he was agitated. And his mouth kept opening, but not a sound came out.

"Reverend Bush," the doctor had called his name over and over, trying to settle him.

Then Hosea had moved to the side of the bed. "Pops!"

The sound of his son's voice made Reverend Bush's eyes move rapidly, searching to find his son's face.

And when he found him, he settled down.

His mouth opened, but there was no sound.

"He can't talk?" Jasmine had asked.

"It's the tracheostomy," Dr. Lewis responded. "Don't worry; we'll get that fixed right away."

It had taken the doctor only a few minutes to complete her assessment. "Welcome back," she said to the reverend before she pulled Jasmine and Hosea aside.

"Now, he's going to be disoriented." Her voice was low. "He's lost two months of his life, and it's not going to make sense to him, so you're going to have to be patient."

They'd both nodded eagerly.

"He's not going to remember a lot of things, and there're some parts of his memory that may never come back. We just have to see."

"When can he go home?" Hosea had asked.

The doctor chuckled. "Let's give it a few days, okay? And then ask me that question again. I just want you to remain—"

"Cautious!" Jasmine and Hosea had said together, "We know . . . we know."

Last night, Jasmine hadn't wanted to leave the hospital, but Hosea had insisted.

"Go home with Jacquie. Pops and I will be here in the morning waiting for you."

When she had kissed her father-in-law good-bye, he'd spread his lips into what she knew was a smile. And Jasmine realized then that Reverend Bush didn't know . . . or he didn't remember anything about her.

Her secret was the only thing that took a bit of the shine off this miracle. His healing could bring hell right to her front door, if she didn't do something about it.

She strolled to the front of the church, stopping in front of Mrs. Whittingham. Jasmine waited for the woman to look up; she didn't. Jasmine coughed. Slowly, Mrs. Whittingham raised her gaze.

Smiling, Jasmine said, "I'm going to be on an important call, so I don't want to be disturbed."

With eyes heavy with her burden, all Mrs. Whittingham did was nod.

"Buzz me if Hosea comes in." Not that she expected him; Hosea didn't plan to leave his father's side. But she didn't want to take any chances—she couldn't have anyone walking into her office and overhearing the call she had to make.

When Mrs. Whittingham only nodded again, Jasmine sighed and walked away. She hated the way Mrs. Whittingham was making her feel. Blackmailing wasn't easy.

Inside her office, Jasmine turned her attention to the report. This was one time when she didn't have a definite plan. All she knew was that she at least had to start here.

"May I speak with Leonard Hobbs," she asked the moment the man answered and announced that she had called L.A. Investigative Services.

"Mr. Hobbs no longer works here," the man said. "Can someone else help you?"

Jasmine's assessment was quick—it was a younger voice, probably in his twenties, with the deep intonation of an African American male.

"Oh, no," she whined in her best damsel-in-distress voice. She added a bit of a southern twang when she said, "I really needed to speak to Mr. Hobbs."

"Maybe I can help you?" he asked.

"Well, you see, Mr. Hobbs did some work for . . ." She paused and decided to keep her lies close to the truth. "For my father. And he's in the hospital right now, but he wanted to speak with him."

"Sorry to hear about your father, but did he want another investigation? Because I can connect you with someone else."

"No." Jasmine paused, still not sure what she was looking for. "My father wanted to talk to Mr. Hobbs about the work he already did."

"Well, it's going to be hard to get in touch with him. Mr. Hobbs retired almost three years ago."

Jasmine frowned. "But that can't be, because he just sent us the report . . ."

"Oh, that," the man said. "Well, we did have to clear out his files. He asked us to mail any of the reports that were never sent to his clients."

"Oh." Her brain was turning fast. If Leonard Hobbs had retired that long ago, that meant Reverend Bush had hired the investigator before she and Hosea were married.

"So why didn't Mr. Hobbs mail us this before?"

"Well, I couldn't really tell you, but reports are usually only kept if someone cancels an investigation, if someone changes their mind. Maybe that's what happened with your father."

Maybe.

The man continued, "But by law, we can't destroy the report for a couple of years. When did your dad file for the investigation?"

"Uh . . . I . . ."

"Do you have the report with you?"

"Yeah," Jasmine said, flipping through the pages.

"Maybe I can help you figure this out. There's a date of origin—usually on the last page."

Jasmine flipped to the back. Saw one number that didn't make sense. "There's nothing here except two, zero, zero, four slash zero, two."

"That report was originated in February 2004. If your father is just getting it in the mail, he probably canceled the investigation and we just sent him the part that Mr. Hobbs had already done."

It was with great relief that she said, "Okay, it makes sense now. Thank you so much for your help."

"Anytime. Let us know if your father . . . or you . . . need any more work."

Slowly, she dropped the phone into the cradle. A cacophony of thoughts spun through her mind, but at least it was all good.

Reverend Bush had hired an investigator in Los Angeles when he first met her. When he didn't trust her. But once he came to love her, he'd canceled the report, probably believing that whatever was in her past needed to stay there.

The only thing was, now he *did* know. He hadn't requested the report, but it was in his hands, nonetheless.

Jasmine nodded, her brain already working. She had no plans to tell Hosea, if Reverend Bush never said a word, never remembered. And that was her prayer—that the report would be lost forever in his mind.

Only time would tell if that prayer would be answered.

But even if Reverend Bush remembered, it would be weeks, months, before anything would happen. Dr. Lewis said he'd be confused for a while, so she had plenty of time to come up with another plan.

This was nothing but God's grace.

Jasmine shook her head with that thought. How the years had changed her. She never used to think about God, but now she couldn't get away from Him. Not that she wanted to. It was as if He was always trying to show Himself to her. As if He wanted her to know that He was always there.

She was beginning to get it—seeing grace from the inside. Maybe it was time to pass a bit of that grace on.

She pushed herself from her chair and walked to the door. She called out to Mrs. Whittingham; there was no answer.

Jasmine strolled to the front, but the chair behind the woman's desk was empty. Mrs. Whittingham and her purse were gone.

Oh, well. She'd found that compassionate place in her heart, and she wanted to share. But she'd see Mrs. Whittingham later today, or tomorrow. And then she *would* share the grace that had been passed on to her.

Jasmine wasn't sure if it was relief or seeing grace from the inside, but when she returned to her office, she dropped down on her knees and thanked God for all that He'd done.

He had never forgotten her, and her prayer was that she always remembered that.

FIFTY-SEVEN

It was ridiculous the way good works kept evading her.

Jasmine was trying to do this wonderful deed, but no matter what, she couldn't get to Mrs. Whittingham.

Last night at the hospital, the woman had walked out of the room as soon as Jasmine had come in. After she'd sat with Hosea and her father-in-law for a couple of minutes, she'd searched the hospital halls for Mrs. Whittingham, but she was gone again. Then this morning, she'd waited for Mrs. Whittingham to show up at the hospital, but she never came.

Jasmine knew that the woman was doing everything to avoid her, and at first she thought about waiting until tomorrow. Surely, Mrs. Whittingham wouldn't miss church. But the thought of the call she'd made to the private investigator yesterday stayed on her mind, and she knew she had to do this now.

Jasmine twisted the SUV into the visitor's space of Lenox Terrace, in exactly the same spot where she'd parked more than a week ago. She really couldn't believe she was even here. After all that Mrs. Whittingham had taken her through, it was ridiculous that she couldn't even last a week as a blackmailer.

"I'm not going to be thirty minutes," Jasmine told the doorman before he asked. She marched to the elevator, pressed the button, and went over the plan in her mind.

This was going to be short, much sweeter than the last visit. It should take five, ten minutes tops to ring the woman's doorbell, walk inside, and then say what she'd come to say.

"You don't have to worry anymore," she would tell Mrs. Whittingham. "I'm not going to say a word to Ivy about your being her mother. I'm not going to tell Ivy or anyone."

Jasmine was sure that Mrs. Whittingham would stare at her with fire burning from her eyes, a look that was a cross between disdain and disbelief. And then she would scream in her wicked witch's voice, "Why should I believe you? Why should I trust you?"

But she would reply with calm and class, "Because of God. I'm only here because God wants me to be."

In Jasmine's mind, the fairy tale played out. Mrs. Whittingham's fangs would burst through her gums when she said something like, "God! Do you know God, you heathen!"

But she would ignore the woman's hatefulness and sweetly say, "Yes, I know God." And then she would add the part that she really wanted Mrs. Whittingham to understand, "I know you never thought I was good enough for Hosea, but what you don't get is that he's always been good enough for me. It's because of him—and God—that I always want to do better. I might not make the mark all the time. In fact, most of the time, I miss it. But that's never going to stop me from trying."

More fire would come out of the woman's eyes, but Jasmine would go on.

"So," she would say, "you can go back to hating me, but I will never again treat you as if I hate you."

Then she would walk out the door. And even if Mrs. Whittingham didn't live happily ever after, she would.

The story ended right before Jasmine stopped in front of

Mrs. Whittingham's door. She took a breath. Rang the doorbell. Waited. There was no answer. She rang again. Nothing.

With a sigh, she turned away. Here she was, trying to do the right thing, and she couldn't make the right thing happen. Maybe this was a test—to see if she would do it, even if doing it was hard.

I'm gonna pass this test, God!

If she didn't see Mrs. Whittingham today, then she would see her tomorrow in church, or the next day. No matter how long it took, she was going to make this right.

FIFTY-EIGHT

JASMINE STRODE SLOWLY TO THE front of the church with the strut of a survivor. As she made her way down the center aisle, she was giddy with all of her plans. She was going to start with the Women's Day event; it was going to be the biggest, baddest affair the church had ever seen. And after that, she'd move right into planning the First Lady's Appreciation Day program. Only now, she wasn't thinking about a single day—it was going to be a weekend gala. And of course, once Reverend Bush was released from the hospital, there would have to be a welcome-home affair for him.

Stopping in front of her seat of honor, Jasmine smoothed out the lines of her suit—a lavender St. John, similar to the outfit Enid had worn last week.

That thought made her pause. This was the first time she'd spent more than a second thinking about the Wyatts. After the board meeting on Monday, she knew what no one else did—that those two hustlers were far gone and had probably already set up house in another state far away. Maybe they were even at another church. Or maybe Earvin had found a new gig.

Jasmine couldn't stop grinning when Hosea entered the sanctuary. It was the way he walked, taller than he had in months.

He sat down in his father's chair, for the first time looking as if he now knew that the chair had been made for him.

She settled into the pew when he moved to the podium, laid his Bible atop the stand, and then smiled, just a little, at the congregation.

His voice was low when he first spoke. "Today." He stopped. Then, a little louder, "I want to give all glory and honor to God."

"Hallelujah," rang through the sanctuary.

"I don't think," Hosea continued, "there is one person in here who doesn't know my good news."

Heads nodded. The murmurs began.

His voice rose a little more. "When the doctors told me to give up," he sang.

The chatter was louder now.

"I told them that my father's life wasn't their decision!"

"Amen!" the shouts started.

"I told them that this was all in the hands of the Lord."

Now came the cheering.

"And do you know what the Lord did?"

Hosea didn't get a chance to answer that question. Every one of the parishioners was on their feet, answering Hosea's question for themselves. Jasmine rose with them, water filling her eyes as she clapped her hands with the thousands.

It was a harmonic blend of "Hallelujah," and "Thank you, Jesus," and "Amen," that sounded through the church like a song. Hands were clapping and feet were stomping and the keyboard player hit single chords, turning the sanctuary into a Sunday morning praise party.

Hosea stood on the altar and did his own dance, raised his own hands, let tears fall from his own eyes. And from her seat, Jasmine joined her husband.

She had no idea how long the celebration continued. But exhaustion made her drop back into the pew, although the revelry kept on around her.

Hosea let the parishioners rejoice for long minutes. And then he held up his hands.

The music stopped. The congregation settled. And Hosea was able to once again speak.

"All I can say," he puffed, out of breath, "is that God is good."

"Amen!"

Hosea continued, "But while we're raising praises to God for my father, at the same time, we have to send up prayers for Pastor Wyatt and his wife."

The mumbles were softer now.

"As most of you know, it appears that Pastor Wyatt and Enid have moved away."

More murmurs.

"And while we may never know what was on their hearts, what caused them to leave without a word . . ."

Jasmine squirmed.

"God knows," Hosea finished. "Even though the Wyatts had secrets, God knows the inner parts of their hearts. He knows those dark places where we don't want to let anyone in.

"Saints, if you don't let anyone else into your heart, let God in. Get on your knees and talk to Him. Because there's one thing I know." He paused. "There is no taller man than one who's on his knees."

"Hallelujah!"

"Never keep anything on your heart, so hidden that you have to run," Hosea pleaded. "So shameful that you have to hide." Hosea paused. Looked down at his Bible and tilted his head, as if he was listening to something that only he could hear.

Then he stepped away from the pulpit and took one step down the altar. He held out his hands to the congregants. "There is someone here who needed to hear that. Someone who is holding on to a secret . . ."

Jasmine's eyes and mouth opened wide at the same time.

Her gut told her to look down, turn away from him before he glanced her way. Before he could see in her eyes that she was the one he was talking about.

But she was frozen in her shock, unable to move at all.

How does he know?

Her heart hammered a hard beat to every word he spoke.

"Don't hold on to the secret anymore," he admonished. "Bring it to the altar, and you'll be able to leave it—with all of the heartache and the pain and the shame—right here."

No! Jasmine yelled inside.

She pressed her legs against the pew, making sure that her heart didn't move her to do something she didn't want to do.

"Come now." Hosea held his arms open, an invitation to the sinner. "Come now to the Lord."

No! She wanted to jump up and beg him to stop. Tell him to change the subject, to go back to talking about the Wyatts or his father. Even Jerome. She wanted to tell him to stop talking about her.

"It's time for the secret to come out," he said.

No!

And then, a wail.

It startled her. Made her jump. Ripped her straight from the trance that she was in.

Jasmine's head whipped to the side. Her eyes searched for the place from which the cries came.

It was Mrs. Whittingham who wept. Who stood. Who trembled. Who staggered to the altar and then fell into Hosea's arms.

"Oh, Lord, forgive me!" the woman howled.

Brother Hill rose, flipped a handkerchief from his pocket, and handed it to his friend.

Mrs. Whittingham buried her face in the cloth, but it did nothing to stop her tears. Her body heaved and jerked, like she was receiving electrical shocks.

Now others stood, gathered around her, offering comfort. Many had their hands stretched toward her, praying for her release, praying for her peace.

And in her seat, Jasmine prayed, too. Prayed that this nightmare would end.

Hosea reached for Mrs. Whittingham again and tried to rest her head against his chest, but she pushed him away.

"I have to tell you," she said, shaking her head from side to side. "I have something to tell all of you."

No! Mrs. Whittingham couldn't tell her secret. She couldn't say a word about Ivy. Or the blackmail. Because if she did, it would lead to Jasmine. And her secret.

"Go ahead, Sister Whittingham," Hosea gently coaxed.

Her face was hidden by the cloth Brother Hill had given her, but she moved the handkerchief away. Turned and faced the congregation.

"I have to confess," she sobbed. And then, she glanced at Jasmine.

And in her eyes, in that moment, Jasmine saw the future.

"I . . ." Mrs. Whittingham began.

The word that had been lodged in her throat burst through Jasmine's lips as she sprang from her seat.

"Nooooooo." Jasmine screamed so loud she didn't recognize her own voice. "No," she yelled again, just to make sure that Mrs. Whittingham heard her. "No," shrieked to shut the whole service down.

Mrs. Whittingham turned to her, shocked into silence just like everyone else in the sanctuary.

"Jasmine?"

She heard her husband's voice rushing toward her, but she couldn't look at him. She didn't dare take her eyes away from Mrs. Whittingham.

"Jasmine?"

She heard him again, this time next to her. But by that time, the shaking started in her soles. And it inched up, bringing heat with it. Now her head pounded harder than her heart.

"Jasmine?"

Her hands rose to her head. To stop the pounding. But it wouldn't go away. And then her head exploded. She screamed.

Hosea reached for his wife, a split second before she collapsed inside his arms.

Jasmine had been here before—in this dark place. Where she could hear the voices—Hosea's, Brother Hill's, and then others that she didn't recognize. But they were all so far away.

She fought to open her eyes, but the effort made her head pound harder than before. She wanted to scream out at the pain, but her lips wouldn't move.

She had to find relief.

Help! That came from inside, but she couldn't get her cries out.

She tried again, but still nothing. And it hurt to do anything more. It hurt even to think.

It was her head. Just pounding. Pounding.

She wanted to get away. Go back to that dark place. Where she couldn't see. Where she couldn't hear. Where she couldn't think.

Where there would be no pounding.

She closed her mind's eye and dropped back into the abyss, falling deeper this time. And inside that darkness, she rested in that peace.

FIFTY-NINE

IT FELT LIKE A DEEP, long sleep. No dreams, no sounds. Just sweet peace.

Jasmine's eyelids fluttered until she was fully alert. But the glare of the light made her quickly close her eyes.

"Darlin'?"

It was his soft voice that made her want to see. Slowly, she forced her lids apart. And through a murky veil, she saw her husband's face.

She tried to lift herself, pushing her shoulders from the bed. And her head spun.

With a moan, she fell back onto the mattress.

"No, Jasmine. Stay there," Hosea said, gently pressing his hands against her.

Jasmine frowned, and from her prostrate position her eyes scanned the room. This was not the ceiling of her Central Park South apartment. She tried to figure it out, but her thoughts were gray.

She spoke, though her mouth felt as if it was stuffed with cotton balls. She took a breath. "What?" She pushed out the question. "Where?"

"You're in the hospital," Hosea answered softly. With gentle fingers, he stroked her hair. "But you're okay."

Hospital? She frowned, closed her eyes again, and pressed hard to remember. But the few memories she had were jumbled together—Reverend Bush waking up, her feeding Jacqueline breakfast. She did remember this morning and getting ready for church. But that was where her life ended.

"What . . ." It was difficult to speak through the web in her mouth. She licked parched lips. "Water."

It didn't take Hosea long to move from her side and fill a paper cup from the pitcher on the table. He held the cup to her lips.

She still felt dizzy when she sat up, but she was grateful for the few sips she was able to take. She asked again, "What happened?"

Hosea smiled and held her hand. "You got a little sick in church."

"In church?" she asked, confused.

"Yeah." He chuckled a little. "I was preaching and . . ."

Her world snapped back into clarity: Mrs. Whittingham's confession. Mrs. Whittingham's secret. And then her own.

Jasmine's eyes widened as the events of the day flooded her. She remembered now—the way Mrs. Whittingham had started to confess. She remembered the way her eyes closed and how she had fallen. And then there was nothing.

"Oh, my God!" Jasmine searched her husband's eyes for the answers that she needed. What had Mrs. Whittingham told him?

"Jasmine?"

She couldn't tell anything through the fog. She couldn't see him clearly. He smiled at her, but she didn't trust his smile. She didn't trust him.

"Jasmine?"

"Oh, my God!" She could tell by the way he called her name

over and over that he knew. He knew everything. And he was just waiting to see if she was going to tell him the truth. He had tried to trick her that way before.

"Darlin', you're all right." He comforted her. "It was just your blood pressure. That happens to you . . . look, I have something to tell you."

She shook her head. She couldn't let him tell her what he knew. She had to do it first. Then he wouldn't be able to accuse her of keeping another secret. He wouldn't be able to say that she was telling more lies.

And then he wouldn't be able to walk out on her.

Pushing herself up, she said, "I have to tell you—"

"No." He chuckled. "This is one time where you're going to let me go first."

His laugh sounded like a growl to her. His grin looked like a sneer. Through the fog she couldn't see his joy.

So together, they spoke.

She said, "I used to be a stripper!"

He said, "You're pregnant!"

A FEW MONTHS LATER

Jasmine huffed as she forced her weight against the glass door of Lenox Hill Hospital.

"Here, let me get that." The security guard grabbed the door for her.

"Thanks!" She paused and breathed as if she'd been walking for miles. Trying to get that door open had left her totally spent—it was much heavier than it had been last month. She should've used the revolving one, but she needed every bit of exercise.

But by the time she made it to Dr. McKnight's fourth-floor office, she was ready to give up exercise until well after this baby was born.

"I can take you back right now," the nurse said, once she'd greeted Jasmine. Looking over her shoulder, she asked, "Are you by yourself?"

Jasmine nodded.

The nurse's smile faded as she looked at Jasmine with eyes that said she felt so sorry for pregnant women who were alone.

"Well," she began, her tone now conciliatory, "you do look very nice today," as if her compliment was the consolation prize.

Jasmine smiled her thank-you, even though she wanted to slap the nurse upside her head for lying like that. Sure, she looked nice—if you liked elephants in tutus. The black dress she wore had looked fashionable—last month. But now, with carrying a baby who felt like it was ready to make its debut well before the eleven weeks from now when it was due, the dress was busting at the seams. But this was the only black outfit she had to wear to the funeral.

Inside the examination room, the nurse helped Jasmine slide onto the padded table. "Doctor McKnight will be right with you," and then she was alone again.

She sighed and massaged the swell of her belly. She hated having to come here so often, but her blood pressure had to be monitored regularly so that there wouldn't be any more fainting spells.

Jasmine sighed whenever she thought about that. Low blood pressure and fainting spells. Something that happened to her during pregnancy. That was why she'd passed out in church that Sunday. That's how she'd found out she was three months pregnant.

And that's how Hosea had found out about her secret.

Thinking about that day was the perfect antidote to her medical problem because she could feel her pressure rising whenever she thought about what happened.

She had to have been delirious when she'd shouted out, "I used to be a stripper!"

For the rest of her days, Jasmine would never forget that moment. She had shocked Hosea, and he had done the same to her . . .

"What?" they spoke together again.

"I'm pregnant?"

"You used to be a stripper?" Hosea held up his hands.

"Wait, we've got to do this one at a time. What are *you* talking about?"

That was exactly what she wanted to know: She was pregnant? She pushed herself up on the gurney.

"Jasmine," he called her name in a tone that said he was waiting for an answer.

There was nothing but deep confusion in the crevices of his face, but she kept her lips pressed together. She didn't want to take the chance of blurting out anything else.

"Jasmine." This time he whispered her name. "What do you mean you used to be a stripper?"

Her drive to survive set in—a million thoughts spun inside her mind. First, she was pregnant . . . with Hosea's baby! Her hands moved to her center. Covered herself so that she could protect the child she carried.

Their baby!

She didn't have any choice now; she had to lie. She had to protect this child. And Jacqueline. And herself. Because if Hosea found out this truth, he would leave her for sure.

It came to her instantly—the lie she would tell. She would say that she was delirious. That she didn't know what she was saying. She could faint again—only this time, she'd fake it. And when she woke up, she wouldn't remember saying a thing.

Jasmine opened her mouth, ready to tell her story. But his look stopped her. Inside the windows to his soul, she could see his love, his faith, his trust.

All that was missing was the truth. And when she parted her lips, it was the truth that came out.

"I was a stripper."

His shoulders sagged, the weight of that truth too heavy for him to stand straight.

Her heart was beyond pounding when she continued, "In college, the year that my mother passed away, I became . . . an exotic dancer . . . so that I could pay for my last year in school."

She prayed that he wouldn't ask her for any more, but the way his eyes got small, then widened, then small again, let her know that his brain was calculating—and more questions were coming.

"Okay," he finally breathed, although there was nothing in his expression that said that any of this was okay. "But you've kept this from me for so long, why're you telling me now?"

"I didn't want to tell you," she said honestly, "but you were going to find out. And this time, I wanted you to hear everything from me."

His head moved from side to side as if he needed to shake her words away. "A stripper?" He looked at her, then quickly turned like she was no longer worthy of his glance. Now it was his hands that he studied when he said, "But . . . you told me . . . that there were no more secrets . . . no more lies."

The pain inside his tone made its way to her heart. With her eyes, Jasmine tried to will her husband to look back at her.

But he wouldn't.

She said, "I don't know what to say . . ."

Now, he looked up. "Try. The. Truth."

His tone sliced right through her, and she wanted to tell him anything but the truth. But now that she started, she was going to play it through. Count on the fact that with truth, she'd win.

So she said, "When we talked about those secrets and my lies, Hosea, I swear," she shook her head, "I wasn't even thinking about that long ago. I was so focused on your finding out about my being married before and my age, I just . . . I just . . . I just forgot."

"No one forgets that she was a stripper."

"I know. And I don't blame you for not believing me, but truly, Hosea, that's what happened. Back then, those days, they were so bad for me. I'd lost my mother, my dad didn't have the money, I'd searched for other jobs—"

He closed his eyes and held up his hands, like he wanted her to stop.

She continued anyway, "I was so ashamed of the dancing; it's something that I wanted to forget." She reached for his hand, but he stepped back, away from her grasp. Tears sprang right to her eyes. "I'm telling you the God's honest truth. I didn't even think about that time of my life, or else I would've told you. But when it came up, a few weeks ago, I couldn't tell you."

He looked at her with the exact stare that she'd expected . . . and feared. Now she was the one who looked away from the disgust in his eyes.

Still, she kept on. "I couldn't tell you because you were going through too much with your father and the church."

His stare continued, like he was trying to see inside of her. Like he couldn't trust the words from her mouth, so he would search for the truth in her heart.

"I knew it all along, Jasmine."

Looking up, she frowned.

He said, "I knew that something was going on, but you made me believe that it was me and my suspicions. You made me feel guilty for not trusting you." Moments passed, and then his eyes wandered down to her lap. Slowly, his arm moved toward her, and Jasmine gasped with a bit of relief—he was thinking of their baby; he would never—could never—leave now.

But then his hand froze in midair before he pulled back and swiveled toward the door. "I need to think," his voice quivered. "I need some air."

He was gone before she could beg him.

It was a déjà vu moment; he was walking out on her again . . .

Jasmine shut her eyes now, trying to close the door on those memories. Why was she doing this? Why was she taking herself back to that day, that place where there was so much pain?

"Jasmine."

Slowly, she opened her eyes and smiled, then she turned and saw him standing in the doorway.

"Hey, babe," she said. As Hosea moved forward, her smile turned into a grin when she eyed the bunch of flowers he held. They looked just like the ones he'd brought her that day when he had come back to the emergency room to tell her that he did forgive her.

The words he had said to her then as she'd lain back on the gurney, crying a river of tears, never left her mind.

I don't care who you were or even who you are now. I'm here because when God chose you as my wife, it was all about who you were becoming, who He wants you to be.

On that day, Jasmine suspected that he was also there because of their baby, but it didn't matter why he was back—only that he had returned.

Now, as she took the flowers from his hands, Jasmine's eyes flooded with those memories.

"What's wrong?" Hosea searched her face, concerned.

Wiping away her tears, she sniffed. "You know how it is. I cry at everything these days."

He kissed her cheek, where tears still dampened her skin. Then he leaned back and smiled.

Jasmine had hope. Her greatest fear when she told Hosea the truth was that he wouldn't look at her the same way. And she'd been right.

The memory of her past was always in his eyes. But with each day and every new glance, her past dimmed. And her prayer was that by the time their child was born, there would be no sordid memories at all—for either of them.

"So, Doctor McKnight hasn't come in yet?" he asked, as he took the flowers from her and placed them on the counter.

She shook her head. "I told her that I'd be in a hurry today; maybe I should have canceled because of the funeral."

His eyes darkened a bit with his sadness, but he shook his head. "We've got to keep your blood pressure under control; don't worry, we'll get to the church on time."

"I just hate for you to be distracted."

He said, "This is our baby," as if that was explanation enough. Gently, he placed his hand on her stomach. "I'm glad that I'm here, glad to have this reminder that as life ends, a new one begins."

She nodded, then covered his hand with hers. And they held each other and waited in silence and in peace until Dr. McKnight came to assure them that everything with Baby Bush was absolutely fine.

The people were already beginning to gather when Hosea rolled their car past the black hearse parked in front of the church. He pulled into the parking lot and edged into the space reserved for the senior pastor.

Hosea helped Jasmine ease from the car, then held her hand as she stepped cautiously across the gravel. By the time they opened the door, Jasmine was winded, but her smile was instant as soon as the two entered the back offices.

"Hey, Pops!" Hosea stepped to Reverend Bush first and hugged his father.

Reverend Bush beamed at Jasmine. "What did the doctor say?" His words, even months after waking up were still a bit garbled.

"I'm fine."

Jasmine bent toward him, but he held up his hands, trying to stop her. "Don't hurt yourself."

She leaned against the arm of his wheelchair anyway. "You'd better let me give you a kiss."

"Would you stop smothering that man!"

"Nama," Jasmine looked up and shook her head at her friend, "I'm not about to hurt my children's grandfather."

Mae Frances twisted her lips. "All I'm sayin' is give him room to breathe," she grumbled, as she straightened the blanket that rested across Reverend Bush's lap.

Rolling her eyes, Jasmine resisted asking her friend when she had become a nurse. At least, that's the way Mae Frances had been acting since she'd returned home the day after she found out that Jasmine was pregnant.

"What took you guys so long to get here?" Mae Frances barked. "I thought I was gonna have to roll the good reverend out to the altar so he could begin without you."

"And I would've done it, too," Reverend Bush chuckled, before spinning his wheelchair around and following Hosea into his office.

He'd turned over the leadership of the church to his son, but Reverend Bush was as involved in City of Lights as his daily physical and speech therapy allowed. And Hosea welcomed every bit of input from his father, just waiting for the day when they would stand together behind the pulpit as copastors.

"Hosea."

Jasmine turned to see Mrs. Whittingham walking in from the sanctuary.

"They're ready." She wore a slight smile, until she pivoted and faced Jasmine. "Hello," she said coolly. Her tone lacked the warmth of a friend, but it was without the contempt that had always accompanied her words over the years.

As the two women shared an embrace of strangers, Jasmine recalled the conversation she'd finally had with Mrs. Whittingham. And as she'd expected, the woman didn't believe her. But she'd kept her promise—she'd never told Ivy.

The problem was, neither had Mrs. Whittingham. Jasmine's fainting spell in church that Sunday had scared Mrs. Whittingham straight. Made her rethink, restrategize. Made her decide to take the secret that she shared only with Jasmine to her grave.

Since she'd made that decision, Mrs. Whittingham had aged years in just months. And Jasmine truly felt sorry for her, knowing the burden of secrets.

Hosea trudged from his office, donned in that special-occasions burgundy robe. Jasmine kissed his cheek, then she and Mae Frances followed Reverend Bush down the hallway.

"Now you be careful, Reverend Bush," the words dripped from Mae Frances's mouth like syrup.

Jasmine wanted to laugh. Could her friend be any more obvious? She didn't care how many times Mae Frances denied it, she was sweet on Reverend Bush. Maybe now that the wheelchair had slowed him down a bit, she'd be able to catch him.

But all thoughts of teasing her friend went away when Mrs. Whittingham opened the door to the sanctuary and the sorrow that hung heavy in the air wrapped around them.

The City of Lights choir was rocking "Going up Yonder," and as they sang, some in the congregation cried. Many were standing and swaying. And a few still sat, as if grief had them fastened to their seats.

Slowly, Jasmine followed Reverend Bush and Mae Frances. As her father-in-law and friend stopped to give condolences to the family, Jasmine paused in front of the coffin and looked down at Sister Pearline.

In the months since the board meeting, when Sister Pearline had told them all that they didn't need a new pastor, she had stepped back into Jasmine and Hosea's lives as if she had always been on their side. And no one had been more thrilled when she and Hosea announced that they going to be parents again.

"Isn't that great?" Sister Pearline had beamed as she greeted Jasmine and Hosea in the reception line. Then she'd grabbed Jasmine's elbow and hauled her aside. Lowering her head and her voice she asked, "It's his baby for real this time, right?"

Jasmine smiled now, as she had then. How could she get mad at that? Sister Pearline was only asking to her face what most were whispering behind her back. She'd assured the woman that the father of this child was the man she loved.

After a final glance, Jasmine took her seat. The music faded, and Hosea stepped to the podium.

"While our hearts are heavy and we must face our grief, it is important to understand that there are two ways to grieve. We can do it society's way, which brings despair. Or we can do it God's way, which will bring peace. So I'm going to talk to you about God's way, because the truth is, our Sister Pearline has made an exciting transition—I can assure you today that she is home!"

The mourners rose to their feet, shouted and applauded. Even Sister Pearline's family stood, sending up praises.

Jasmine clapped from her front pew seat, but then, she whispered a quiet, "Oh," and placed her hand on her stomach. Their baby was kicking, as if it wanted to be part of the home-going celebration.

Reverend Bush leaned over. "Are you all right?"

She nodded and took his hand. Rested it on the place where her child was doing its own little holy dance. Watched as Reverend Bush experienced for the first time the next generation.

In the middle of this sadness, joy illuminated Reverend Bush's face. As people around them celebrated the end of one life, Jasmine and her father-in-law rejoiced in a life to come.

The look of awe in his eyes made Jasmine turn away or she would start crying for sure. She sat back and watched her husband as he raised his Bible in the air.

"I'm telling you, saints. There is nothing but goodness in God. In the middle of this tragedy, He will show you the wonder of His love."

Jasmine nodded hard at her husband's words, because if there was nothing else she understood, she got it now when it came to

God's love. "Thank you, Jesus," she whispered. She closed her eyes, and as her husband preached, she made promises to God, pledged that from now on she would be different; she would get it right, no matter what the situation.

Her hand moved again to the place where her new joy still jumped around. She couldn't wait for this baby to get here so that she could love him as much as she loved her daughter.

Yes, she would love *him.*

She knew her baby's sex, but Hosea didn't. He'd changed his mind after the ultrasound, and Dr. McKnight insisted that it was never a good idea for one parent to know, so Jasmine had agreed to wait until the baby was born.

Not! There was no way she was going to be able to do that. After that appointment, she'd gone home and, while Hosea was in the bathroom, called Mae Frances. Within forty-eight hours, one of her connections had delivered the news.

Jasmine was carrying Hosea's son.

As Jasmine watched her husband stand at the podium and minister God's love, she thought about how excited he would be to have a namesake. She had no doubt that he'd always love Jacqueline—she was his heart. But a son would be his pride.

Hers, too, of course.

Now she had two children whom she could raise in her own image. And as she sat in the middle of this sadness, all she could do was smile. Her life was one big happy ending.

She couldn't wait for Hosea S. Bush II to be born.

ACKNOWLEDGMENTS

HERE WE ARE AGAIN AT that awful place—the part of the book where I have to talk about real people. My characters always know my heart—they know that I try to do the right thing when it comes to writing about them. But I can't say the same thing about the real people and my acknowledgments. My friends and family (especially family) have said some things to me that I will never forget and would never repeat (because I don't use profanity) after they've read previous acknowledgments. So to increase my chances of having a wonderful Thanksgiving and Christmas, all I will say to my friends and family is that I love you and thank you.

Whew! Now that I've made sure that I will have a great holiday season, I can move on.

First to my Lord and Savior, Jesus Christ, who always knows my heart. Thank you, Lord, for continuously keeping me and loving me even during those times when I don't feel very lovable. I pray that every word that I write and every story I tell honors you.

To the team who helps me to keep these books coming: my editor, Trish Grader. Thank you for always demanding the best, because that's what I want to be. I continue to learn so much from you. To Elaine Koster, my agent, you're simply the best. To Shida Carr, the world's preeminent publicist. Okay, that may be what I call you, but just wait a few years—everyone will be saying the same thing.

I would have never been able to do all the "medical stuff" without Dr. Sherri Lewis, who is an extraordinary Christian fiction writer in her own right. Check her out, y'all! Thank you, Sherri, for making it look like I knew what I was talking about.

To my pastor, Dr. Beverly "BAM" Crawford. One of the things I hate about taking my characters out of Los Angeles is not writing about you! Pastor Ford has quickly become a fan favorite, and I am always so proud to say that she is based upon my real pastor. Thank you for keeping me covered, for always praying for and loving me! I truly would not be able to write these books without you.

Finally, to you, the reader. Whenever I write and ask you to buy a book or cast a vote or spread the word, you always respond. My career continues to grow only because of you and I am so appreciative. There are not very many ways I can tell you how grateful I am, but let me try . . . *merci, gracias, danke, grazie, spasibo, arigato, abrigado*...in other words, THANK YOU! For everything! And as long as you keep reading, I'll keep writing.

TOUCHSTONE READING GROUP GUIDE

Lady Jasmine

For Discussion

1. The novel centers around Jasmine Larson Bush's deep secret—one that she is willing to do anything to keep concealed in order to save herself, her marriage, and her family. The reader is let in on the secret very early in the book, however. How does this immediate revelation affect your reading of the story? What assumptions did you make about Jasmine within the first few pages?

2. If you've read other books that feature Jasmine—*Temptation, A Sin and a Shame,* or *Too Little, Too Late*—what is it about this character that makes for such compelling reading? Do you find Jasmine likable? Do you identify with her in any way?

3. Though Reverend Samuel Bush is in a coma for most of the book, he remains an important and influential figure. How does his absence or presence affect the lives of Hosea, Jasmine, Pastor Wyatt, and the other church members?

4. Is Mae Frances being a good friend to Jasmine by doing whatever it takes to help her out when she's in trouble, or is she simply enabling Jasmine's scheming and devious ways? What's your definition of a good friend?

5. Is Jasmine capable of being a responsible first lady of City of Lights at Riverside Church, or is she interested only in glamour and prestige?

6. What motivates Jasmine? Is she driven by pure motives such as love for her husband and child, righteousness in the eyes of God, a quest for truth, or a desire to change? Or is she driven by temptations like lust, money, fame, and revenge?

7. How would you characterize Jasmine and Hosea's relationship? What is it built upon? Do you think they will have a lasting marriage? Why or why not?

8. The novel pulls back the curtain on the messiness and divisiveness of church politics. Have you ever been part of a church, workplace, or other organization that was nearly undone by disputes over leadership or direction? Describe that experience.

9. In Hosea's debut sermon in chapter 12, he speaks of "the audacity to obey." What does this phrase mean in the context of his story? What does the phrase mean when you apply it to your own life? Provide examples if you can.

10. In her search for her blackmailer, Jasmine seeks to bring down all her potential enemies—Jerome Viceroy, Pastor Wyatt, and Mrs. Whittingham. With a bit of digging, Jasmine discovers that all of them harbor secrets that would shock the church congregation. Do each of these characters get what they deserve? What does Hosea mean when he says, "No one else's misfortune is God's blessing to me"?

11. In the end, does Jasmine do anything that surprises you? She has the power to reveal some very dark secrets and destroy

people's lives, but she refrains from wielding that power. Why do you think she holds back?

12. Hosea faces a very difficult decision when he must choose whether or not to keep his father on life support. What would you do if faced with a similar situation?

A Conversation with Victoria Christopher Murray

This is your fourth novel featuring the beloved and despised Jasmine Larson Bush. When you wrote *Temptation*, did you envision her as a recurring character?

Never, never, never! When I first brought Jasmine to life, I never expected to write about her again. Look at her—she's not very likable. Who would want to revisit her? Those were my thoughts, but those thoughts did not belong to the readers. Jasmine Bush has become my Erica Kane—she's the woman that most love to hate!

Jasmine's juicy secrets and schemes seem simply endless. Will there be additional books featuring this intriguing woman?

I can't tell you that! But truly, how many more secrets can one woman have? Oops, we are talking about Jasmine, aren't we? Well, the truth—I'm not sure if Jasmine has any more secrets, but there's something that I have been thinking about: Doesn't there come a time when one has to pay for their past sins? Hmmmm . . .

How do you relate to Jasmine personally? Is she inspired by anyone you've known, or is she a purely fictional creation?

Are you kidding me? I don't know anyone like her. Jasmine is truly a figment of my imagination.

You've had such an interesting and inspiring life, spending many years in the corporate world and as an entrepreneur before giving it all up to write fiction. How do you share your story of faith and courage to other people who may feel a similar calling?

When I left corporate America to venture into this writing life, I never saw it as a big step of faith. That's because I really believed that I was supposed to be doing this. Plus, I do have a lot of faith and one thing I know is that you don't need faith when you're inside the box. You don't need faith to keep doing what you're doing. Faith is only necessary outside of the box. So stepping out gave me a chance to exercise my faith. I tell people that if you have faith, use it!

There's certainly a religious theme to your novels, but it doesn't seem to be heavy-handed or overly judgmental. What role do faith and religion play in your life, and how have they helped to shape the stories that you tell?
I tell people this anytime they ask this question. I am a Christian and I love the Lord. Period. For me, my Christianity is not an adjective—it's a verb. It's far more than a way to describe me; it's what I do. I always say that if I were a bus driver, people would have said, "There goes that Christian bus driver." Or if I were a teacher, people would have said, "Have you met the new Christian teacher?" My Christianity goes with me wherever I go.

You seem to love the characters that make the greatest mistakes, always treating them with a sense of humor, often giving them second chances or hope for forgiveness. Where do you get such compassion for "the sinners" in your stories?
I've got lots of compassion for sinners—since I'm one of them. I haven't committed the same sins as my characters, but I sin nonetheless. And I thank God for His compassion and His grace, and His mercy every day. So it's easy for me to have that kind of compassion for my characters and pass on to them the same forgiveness that God gives to me every moment of my life.

What do you hope readers will take away from a story like *Lady Jasmine*?

I'm not sure there's a specific message—I don't write my books that way. What I try to get across in all of my stories is that no matter what you do, no matter what you're going through, no matter who you are, God is there for you.

Aside from the story of Hosea and Gomer, do any other parts of *Lady Jasmine* have subtle biblical parallels?

Hmmmm . . . I don't know. I didn't put any other biblical parallels in the story, but you never know what a reader may find.

Do you have a favorite Bible verse? What's the significance for you?

I have so many favorite scriptures, but there is one that does stand out for me. Jeremiah 29:11. Although I've read the Bible completely several times, this scripture didn't stand out to me until 2001—just days after my husband passed away. I was in a Christian bookstore with my best friend, Tracy, and as she was shopping, I noticed Christmas cards. I was overwhelmed with the thought that for the upcoming Christmas, I was going to sign cards with only my name on them. Grief rolled over me and I told Tracy that I didn't feel like I had any hope; I didn't feel like I had a future. Tracy tried to comfort me, but still she decided that we needed to leave. As we stood at the cash register, both of us noticed a poster behind the counter. *For I know the plans I have for you, says the Lord. Plans to prosper you and not to harm you. Plans to give you hope and a future.* Tracy and I were both shocked—I had just said those words! From that point, I've stood on that scripture. And God has fulfilled His promise. He's given me mounds of hope. And He's given me quite a future.

Enhance Your Book Club

1. For a laugh, use Viva's method of coming up with your "dancer" name. Like "Pepper Pulaski," take the name of a childhood pet for the first name, and the street you grew up on for your last name. Share the humorous results with the group!

2. Detective Foxx says, "Blackmailers always mess up." Check out some other criminals who aren't so good at covering their tracks at www.dumbcriminals.com.

3. For more information on the novels of Victoria Christopher Murray, visit the author's website, www.victoriachristophermurray.com. If you'd like a chance to meet the author, be sure to check the tour dates. Murray tours extensively and could be reading and signing at a bookstore near you!